I0593611

The Bonehead Resistance

Narelle King

BLACK COCKIE PRESS

The Bonehead Resistance

Published by Black Cockie Press

Copyright © Narelle King 2022

The moral right of the author has been asserted

Cover design © Natalie Muller 2022

Distributed by IngramSpark

Printed by IngramSpark

ISBN: 978-0-6454896-0-6

About The Author

Narelle King has a background in environmental science, which has led to her stalking giant pandas through bamboo thickets in China, wandering around the Australian bush at night with an unreliable spotlight and living for six months in the middle of a zoo. On one occasion, she caused the evacuation of a university chemistry lab, which is why she now works with words rather than dangerous chemicals.

Whenever possible, Narelle escapes the real world by reading, writing or daydreaming about magic and monsters.

Narelle lives on Gundungurra land in the Blue Mountains, Australia, with her son and ninja cat.

You can connect with her at instagram.com/narellekingauthor.

Dedication

For Dylan

One

'I don't think you should take Ollie to the protest.'

Adam's words were lost in the revving of car engines outside. Amber pushed the window down. It caught, as always.

'You'd think,' she gritted her teeth, 'That a million dollars would buy you an apartment with windows that fricken close.' She tossed the phone onto her bed and pushed with both hands. The window slammed shut.

She grabbed the phone. 'Sorry, what?'

'I don't think you should take Ollie to the protest.'

Amber squinted at the cracked screen, though she didn't need to see Adam to picture the pained look he'd be wearing.

'I haven't got anyone to leave him with.'

'Can't you leave it a week? I'll be back by Friday.'

She parroted what Bec had said to her, hoping Adam wouldn't realise. 'If ordinary people don't fight, Walker will get away with cancelling the election. It'll be the end of democracy in Australia.'

She leaned the phone against the pillows and laid the baby carrier on the bed, placing Oliver on top. Oliver blew spit bubbles, adding new stains to the white quilt cover.

Adam tried again. 'What if the protest's violent?'

'Bec assured me it'll be peaceful. She should know - she's one of the organisers.'

'Of course she is,' Adam muttered, 'Is there a protest she wouldn't attend? Rights for cane toads, maybe?'

Amber pulled a face at him, confident that he wouldn't see through the broken screen. 'She stands up for what she believes in. I wish I did that more often.' She wrapped the baby carrier

5

straps around her waist and struggled to clip them together.

'Far be it from me to argue with Bec, but it might be out of her control. Walker seems to be willing to do whatever it takes to stay in power. There's some weird rumours coming out of Canberra.'

'Weird is right. Did you hear the one about the monsters?' The clasps snapped together. She pulled the carrier over her arms and settled Oliver so they were both comfortable.

Adam snorted. 'Walker has a secret army of monsters? No doubt believed by the same people who think vaccines are used for mind control, coronavirus was spread by 5G mobile phone signals and there's a secret cabal of Satan-worshipping paedophiles.'

Amber grinned. 'Don't forget the fake moon landing.' She changed the subject. 'How's Dubbo?'

'The same. Stinking unbearable dry heat. And the project's a mess - the CEO keeps changing his mind about what he wants. I keep telling Steve that we need to pin him down or we'll never deliver, but you know what he's like - all talk, no action.'

Adam made similar complaints about most projects he worked on, always interlaced with criticisms of his boss, Stephen West. Amber made sympathetic noises and checked herself in the ensuite mirror. She grimaced at her new look - black hair falling in a short, layered bob around her face, and just a touch of mascara on her eyelashes. It was a far cry from the flawless look she'd worn to work. Before Oliver arrived - cute, adorable wrecking ball that he was.

Adam was still talking. 'I'm counting down the days until I can get the hell out of here.'

'Me too,' she said, clenching her teeth to stop the truth slipping out. It was her mother's help she was missing, not Adam's half-hearted efforts.

She glanced at the clock. 'I've gotta go - I promised Bec I'd meet her a couple of hours before so we can get coffee and find a good spot.'

'Give me a call later so I know you're okay.' He sounded resigned.

'Will do. Love you.'

'You too.'

The street was hazy with smoke, blown from several small grassfires that were burning in western Sydney, and some larger bushfires in the Blue Mountains. She pulled the hood of the carrier over Oliver's head and settled a mask over her face - light blue, to match her blue tank top. Light grey clouds blocked the worst of the sun's heat, but the air was thick and humid. Sweat dripped down her chest to where Oliver was nestled.

Out front, the line of Saturday traffic lurched its way towards the bridge across the Epping train line. The odd driver tooted a horn. Amber outpaced the cars as she strode down the footpath, but took her own turn waiting for the slow change of traffic lights at Carlingford Road, a western artery from Epping to Carlingford. She passed a succession of Asian restaurants hugging the footpath, dodged bus passengers spread across the footpath and glanced inside the pub, which was dead apart from two early morning pokie players.

Leaping the station stairs two at a time, she took silent pleasure in beating the people who had squashed themselves into the small lift. She was less pleased that she'd just missed a train. On the escalator, she ran her hands through her hair. The back, where it touched her neck, was damp with sweat. The platform was dominated by large billboards advertising tutoring services and real estate agencies. Rocking from side to side to keep Oliver relaxed, she inspected the other passengers. None met her gaze - most of them staring at their phones with glazed eyes.

The train arrived with a screech. It was forty minutes to the city.

Amber tried to relax, but found herself squirming in her seat, almost upsetting Oliver. A year ago, Adrian Walker, a minor minister in the Australian government, had orchestrated a leadership spill and wrestled the Prime Ministership from its previous incumbent. In the following months, he'd brought in a succession of new security and anti-terrorism laws, claiming they were needed to fight unspecified terrorism threats. The new laws centralised control over the military and federal police in the Prime Minister's office and sidelined the other ministers and the judiciary.

The sad thing was that most Australians didn't notice. Amber had been aware of the issue, because Bec had attended weeks of protests opposing the new laws and filled her social media feed with links to articles and petitions about them. But Amber had scrolled past, focused on the excitement and discomfort of pregnancy, and then overwhelmed by the constant demands of looking after Oliver.

That had changed a week ago, when Prime Minister Walker cancelled the Australian election, due to be held by the end of the month. Several members of the government and minor parties, and all of the opposition, had opposed the move. They'd been arrested and were being held without charge, or access to lawyers, under one of the new security laws. The Governor-General, who people expected to have an opinion on the matter, had disappeared under mysterious circumstances.

Amber squirmed again. It was unprecedented. People should be rioting in the streets. But - it was a normal Saturday morning in Epping. Were she and Bec the only ones in the world who cared?

The train pulled into Wynyard station. Amber jumped over the gap and wiggled her shoulders to move the carrier into a comfortable position. A smooth, wooden balustrade guided the way down into the depths of the station - a reminder of the more optimistic time in Sydney's life when the underground station had been built. A modern metal balustrade had been installed in front of it - no doubt safer, but not as attractive. Amber found most of the station too utilitarian to be beautiful, with its square white pillars, low silver and white ceilings and grey tiles and electronic ticket gates, but she loved the art installation that hung above the escalators at one of the exits. Created from the old wooden escalators, it twisted and turned above commuters' heads, the antithesis of the monotonous commute suffered by most of the people who walked under it.

A dozen men overtook her on the stairs, some coming up behind her, and others ignoring the signs and painted arrows directing them to keep to the left side of the stairs. They wore grey or black bandana-style face masks that covered their necks up to their noses. She wondered how they could stand the thick jackets they were wearing in the heavy humidity. One tripped on the stairs next to her. She gripped his arm to help him regain his balance.

'Are you okay?' Her words trailed off as she glimpsed something black and thin poking out the bottom of his jacket.

'Fine, thanks.' He tugged the jacket down and fled down the stairs.

Amber froze on the step as the men disappeared into the crowd.

'Come on.' A girl pushed past, her thick blonde hair escaping from under a blue denim cap. Amber followed her down the stairs. She was holding a large piece of cardboard with I Want My Democracy Sausage printed in coloured marker, above a rough outline of a sausage. Amber smiled at the reference to the fundraising sausages sold at many polling booths on election days.

She hesitated at the gate, searching for Bec. The station was busier than usual for a Saturday.

'Amber!' Bec barrelled through the people heading away from the gates, a force of nature - all wild chestnut hair and flowing skirts. Her face mask was black with the word freedom printed on it. 'You brought the baby?' Her intense blue eyes zeroed in on Oliver. 'Shit, you cut your hair!' She tugged at one of Amber's short strands and gave her a hug.

Amber jerked out of her embrace. 'I just saw someone with a gun.'

Bec returned her gaze to Oliver. 'I didn't know you were bringing him.'

'Of course I did - I told you Adam was away.'

'Yeah, but I thought your mum would be falling over herself for a chance to babysit.'

'She's in China with Dad, visiting my grandparents. Did you hear what I said about the gun?'

'Sorry, a gun?' Her eyes swept the station.

'I can't see him now. It was under his jacket. There were a bunch of them - all wearing jackets. Maybe they're all hiding guns!'

'Maybe it was something else,' Bec suggested, 'You're not familiar with guns, are you?'

Amber frowned. 'I might not have fired one, but I know what they look like.'

Bec was distracted by a man with pasty skin and long, curly grey hair flowing out from a red, rolled bandana, lugging a painted wooden placard that said Australia Votes 1 for Democracy.

'It's a good sign that some oldies are coming,' she said. The man glared at her.

'They won't if you insult them.'

Bec dismissed this with a shrug. She ran critical eyes over Amber and froze. 'First your hair, and now this.'

'What?' Amber said, patting her hair.

'I've been telling you for years that make-up is a tool the

patriarchy uses to control women. You finally listened to me!'

Amber pulled a face. 'I just don't have time to put it on anymore.'

Bec beamed. 'Exactly! Do you know that women who wear make-up spend an average of nine days a year applying it?'

Amber rolled her eyes. 'Where do you get these figures?'

Bec ignored the question, scanning the stream of people coming out of the station. Half a head shorter than Amber, the difference in their height was accentuated by the weight Bec had put on in the past couple of years. All the nights Bec spent debating politics over gourmet pizza and organic red wine were catching up with her. Amber grimaced, feeling a pang of guilt for the uncharitable thought.

She opened her mouth to repeat her concerns about the man with the gun. Bec didn't give her a chance. 'Let's go,' she said, whirling away.

Amber hurried after her to the station exit. As soon as she caught up, Bec pulled her into a throng of protesters ambling towards Martin Place on either side of the light rail line, spilling out onto the tracks. Amber wrinkled her nose at the smoke haze, which was much thicker in the city than in Epping. The cloud had cleared, and the sun drifted above the station: a squat, baleful red blob in the sky.

A train came up behind the protesters, ringing its bell. The protesters on the tracks pushed back onto the footpath, forcing Bec to slow down. Amber caught her breath and eyed the crowd. Bec had dragged her to a few rallies over the years. Most of the protesters had been young and, apart from some protests about Aboriginal rights, white. This crowd was different. It was a mix of younger people, families and older people of a variety of ethnicities. The mood was different, too. The protesters looked grim and resolute, prepared for a tough battle. About two thirds of the crowd wore face masks. It was unclear if they were concerned about the smoke in the air, coronavirus, or the latest conspiracy making the rounds on social media - that the Government was arresting dissidents by using real time facial recognition through CCTV cameras.

She saw a group of Asian students wearing the all-black T-shirts, jeans and face masks worn by democracy protesters in Hong Kong. For a few minutes she and Bec were engulfed by a group of middle eastern families - children with their hands clutched by women in headscarves, or riding on the shoulders of men; teenagers laughing and elbowing each other, their voices loud and noticeable in the grim crowd; older people fanning themselves in the heat. Bec kept moving and they left the families behind, following two middle aged women in activewear, their hands clutching cardboard signs that read Walk Away, Walker and Free What's-His-Name, the latter with a cut-out picture of the opposition leader. Amber screwed up her face, trying to remember what his name was. He had been having trouble getting cut through with the Australian people even before he was arrested.

A line of relaxed state police officers watched the protesters entering Martin Place Mall. Bec's eyes were drawn above them to the General Post Office Building, awash with pillars and arched windows, a majestic clock tower rising above it. She turned 180 degrees until she faced the GIO building, which had a more utilitarian look, its many levels of plain windows drawing the eye to its limited columns and the tower that capped it. Amber watched a preschool child approach the police officers, trailed by his father. An officer knelt to chat with the child, showing him a portable radio and taser.

Bec spoke into her ear to be heard over the noise of the crowd. 'Let's find somewhere out of the way, since you've got Ollie.'

Amber pulled her attention back to Bec. 'You don't have to do anything?'

'Nah, I've done my bit - helping set up and get the word out.'

Bec pushed through protesters and deeper into Martin Place, stopping every so often to glance at one of the heritage buildings. No matter how many times she came to Martin Place, Bec always enjoyed the architecture. Amber kept her eyes on Bec's back, afraid of losing her in the crowd.

A large group of year 11 and 12 students of various ethnicities perched on and around the Cenotaph, a large square block of stone flanked by a bronze soldier and sailor that commemorated Defence personnel killed in World War I. In defiance of sensible health precautions, the students passed a cigarette around, each taking a drag. The smoke merged with the smoke haze from the bushfires.

Bec wove her way to a coffee shop about a third of the way along the mall. She pushed the door open and they entered, a blast of air conditioning hitting them. There were a few people in a line ahead of them. Amber luxuriated in the cooled air hitting the sweat on her body. Inside, the smell of smoke was muted. A harassed young man in a plain black T-shirt was on his own behind the counter. His nametag read Josh Zadravec. He made their coffees and slid a Portuguese tart and croissant into separate paper bags for them.

The heat when they left the shop took Amber's breath away. She looked for a shady spot, but all the available shade had a swarm of people huddling under it.

'Where to?'

Bec shrugged. 'Here will do.' They took up position next to the door of the shop.

More people flooded into the mall. Despite the large crowd, there was little pushing. People were courteous. Amber unhooked her mask from one ear to sip her coffee. She tried to relax, but kept thinking about the man with the gun. Adam's words came back to her. Walker seems to be willing to do whatever it takes to stay in power. She shivered.

'This is fantastic,' Bec said, her eyes sparkling as they followed a group of Aboriginal people carrying the Aboriginal flag. A middle-aged Vietnamese woman squeezing the hand of an older woman followed behind. 'This is an even better turnout than we'd hoped for. I overheard that family saying they came down from Katoomba.' She nodded at a family standing next to them, wearing long pants and sneakers. One child whined about the heat.

A group of young people marched past with a green banner that read young nationals. Amber suspected this was the first time that Bec's interests had aligned with those of the conservative National Party.

She finished her coffee and checked that Oliver wasn't overheating in the carrier. His hair was wet with sweat. Concerned he might get dehydrated, she sat down on the ground to breastfeed him, throwing a wrap over her breasts and his head for modesty. There was an uncomfortable tug in her breast as he started to suck and a hot flush spread across her body, warming her even more. Her mouth went dry. She sipped water from her water bottle.

Without detaching, Oliver reached out with a hand and tore the wrap off his head.

'Well, I tried.' Amber screwed the wrap up and shoved it into the pocket of the carrier. She broke a piece off her croissant and shoved it in her mouth, dropping crumbs into Oliver's hair.

Bec took snaps of the crowd on her phone and posted them on her social media account. She squatted down next to Amber.

'Look what just came up on my feed.'

Amber took the phone and shaded it with her hand. It was the entry to the Australian Parliament House, in Canberra. Two blurred figures stood in the shadows. She squinted at them. They appeared to be a man wearing a lumpy red hat, standing next to a child. 'What am I looking at?'

'Apparently the small figure is Walker, and the tall one is one of the monsters that are supposed to be working with him.'

Amber snorted and passed the phone back. 'I only believe in human monsters.' She switched Oliver to the other breast, finished her croissant and replaced her mask.

Bec bit into her Portuguese tart, frowning at the phone. A woman their age stumbled past with a takeaway coffee and a placard with several penises painted on it. Bec read the placard out loud with a grin. 'Only politicians with small penises are afraid to face an election.'

Oliver's mouth slipped off Amber's nipple. His eyes closed and his lips curled up in a drunken smile. The mall filled up. A sea of feet and legs surrounded Amber. She adjusted her clothes, slid Oliver back into the carrier and stood up. Bec stood, too, and snapped photos of herself within the crowd. People continued to arrive. State police directed recent arrivals away from the mall. They filled the side streets leading into Martin Place and snaked down George Street.

A microphone crackled into life. Amber squinted through the crowd. A stage had been set up roughly halfway along the mall. The MC stepped up to the microphone. His curated look - well-cut suit, designer blonde hair falling into his eyes - was marred by the sweat staining his shirt. She strained to hear what he was saying but couldn't make it out, despite the large speakers dotted around the square. A group of teenage girls to her left didn't seem to mind - they had started cheering before he even spoke. 'We love you Mitch!' one shrieked.

Amber nudged Bec. 'Is he famous?'

'You don't recognise him? Mitch Keady? He won one of those singing competition shows last year.'

'Oh, right, reality TV.' Amber rolled her eyes.

Bec shrugged. 'Always helps to get celebrity endorsement of the cause.'

The state Premier stepped up to the microphone. Amber caught some of her words - her voice loud and full of passion. 'A betrayal of the trust Australians place in the office of Prime Minister... A betrayal of our Australian values... A betrayal of what it means to be an Australian! We stand before you, Prime Minister, all of us, representing twenty-six million Australians, to say you are no longer worthy of this office!'

The crowd cheered as she stepped away, to be replaced by the state Opposition leader, the two speaking in unison for once. Other speakers followed - the leaders of the state Nationals and Greens parties and the Mayor of the City of Sydney. The MC returned and led the crowd in chants.

The crowd lost its grim feel and developed a party atmosphere. Amber couldn't help enjoying herself. 'Shout it out - one, two, three - Australia is a democracy,' she called in unison with the crowd.

She trailed off as the people closest to the stage stopped chanting and thrust backwards. They were blocked by the people behind them. The chanting was replaced by shrieks.

'What's going on?' Bec clutched Amber's arm and stood on her toes, lifting her chin to see past the people in front of them.

Amber strained to see the stage. 'I don't know.'

Loud bangs rang out across the square. People screamed and pushed.

'Gunfire.' Bec's voice quivered. Her fingernails bit into Amber's arm.

'Ow!' Amber tried to pull her arm free. Bec didn't seem to notice.

The crowd was moving like a crazed beast. Amber watched the woman with the small penises placard fall. Other people were forced over the top of her.

She wrapped her free arm around Oliver. Adam had been right.

She shouldn't have brought him.

Someone wrenched her arm away. 'This way.' She met the eyes of Josh, the young man who had made their coffees. He tugged her towards the shop. Bec hung on to her other arm so they wouldn't be separated. People nearby followed, jostling one another, until there was a mob in the small shop. Bec, Amber and Josh were crushed against a display cabinet filled with cupcakes with smiling animal faces. Amber blinked at a panda cupcake, disconcerted by its beaming face.

'Thank you,' she said to Josh. He was staring out the shop window, his eyebrows pulled in tight towards his eyes, and didn't seem to hear.

'Oh fuck,' Bec breathed, 'There really are monsters.'

She had pulled herself up onto the bench to see past the people between them and the shop window. Amber followed her gaze. The woman with the small penises placard lay unmoving on the ground. Three people ran past, including a child. Shots rang out, and they fell to the ground. Amber clapped her hand over her mouth, and turned to see who had shot them.

Despite Bec's words, she expected to see people. But the three figures firing automatic weapons into the remains of the crowd - though humanoid - weren't people. Over three metres tall, they towered over the panicked humans. They wore identical black combat pants, jackets, gloves and boots, but no body armour or protective vests. And no helmets. A hysterical laugh bubbled up in Amber's chest as she looked at their heads. They had no need for helmets. Their foreheads were covered by a deep mahogany, bony plate that swept back from their nose and ended in a half circle over the back of their heads. The bone tapered to six horns, evenly spaced around the half circle. The horns were sharpened to lethal points, but set so far back on their heads that she thought they could only be decorative, not weapons. They each wore a very long and thin sword scabbard made from black leather. A long sword hilt protruded from each scabbard, wrapped in matching black leather. It struck her as incongruous that they were equipped with automatic weapons and swords.

She swallowed the hysterical laugh before it burst out, and swung around. Josh's eyes bulged at the monsters. She had to swallow a couple of times before she could speak. 'Do you have a back exit?'

'Uh, yeah. Follow me.'

Their words broke through the protesters' shock. The ones within earshot started moving, and those further behind scrambled after them. Amber stuck by Josh's side, shielding Oliver with her arms. Her eyes sought Bec.

Bec stayed on the bench, her eyes glued to the action outside the window. She ignored the people jostling her legs to follow Josh.

Amber pushed her way back through the frenzied protesters and grabbed Bec's arm, glancing back out the window.

'That's the man I saw!' Her voice squeaked.

The men who had overtaken her on the stairs at Wynyard station slipped through the last of the fleeing protesters, keeping low and sliding between buildings until they surrounded the monsters. They'd discarded their bulky jackets. Each of them held a sleek black rifle. At some invisible signal they fired at the monsters. A rain of bullets hit the monsters, stopped short, and tumbled to the ground at the monsters' feet, the kinetic energy drained out of them. The monsters turned to opposite sides, their backs together, and fired. Two of the men fell. They fired again, and another two fell. The remaining men became frantic. A volley of bullets hit the monsters, but every bullet fell to the ground. The monsters continued to pick the men off. The last two men tried to flee. They were hit from behind. An unnatural silence enveloped the mall.

'Bullets don't kill them,' Bec said.

'Let's get out of here.' Amber tugged her off the bench. 'Before they kill us.'

One of the monsters turned towards the shop. The skin on its face was wrinkled and grey - elephant skin. Its eyes were completely black, as though it had no iris or sclera, just a giant pupil. Somehow this was more menacing than the conspicuous bony plate and horns. Amber shuddered.

Bec looked around, blinking, and seemed to realise for the first time that they were alone in the shop. She allowed Amber to drag her out the back. The last of the protesters were retreating through a second door into an alley. Amber and Bec followed. Amber looked for Josh, but he'd disappeared. The remaining protesters fled, avoiding eye contact with each other.

Two

Amber led the way down small side streets between high-rise buildings. Bec trailed behind, looking at her phone.

'The monsters arrested the Premier and state opposition leader. And some of our other speakers. They even took Mitch away.' She rubbed the back of her neck. 'They knew it was risky speaking today, after what happened to the federal politicians. But they all thought it was worth the risk.'

The unmistakable green domes and sandstone walls of the Queen Victoria Building came into sight. She nudged Amber. 'Let's go into the QVB.'

The cool, clean air inside the QVB was a relief, but the dazzling interior made Amber cringe. The whole building screamed opulence - gold swirls through the black carpets on the top levels, and intricate tiles lining the lower levels. Half-circle stained glass windows sat above each of the boutique shops, selling luxury and designer goods. Two magnificent clocks hung from the domed ceiling. The news about what had happened at Martin Place hadn't spread yet. People were shopping in a relaxed manner.

Amber clutched Oliver's carrier with shaking hands.

A group of polished women in their early twenties walked past, laughing. Amber launched herself at a tall brunette, grabbing her arm. 'Get out of here! There's monsters coming!' The sudden movement woke Oliver. He started crying. The brunette yanked her arm free and backed away, her sculpted eyebrows rising up her forehead. Two of her friends followed, giggling, but the third stopped and cast a concerned look at Oliver, glossy copper curls framing her well made-up face.

Bec seized Amber's arm. 'Get a grip,' she said through gritted teeth, 'We need to get out of here without attracting attention.'

The girl's face cleared when she saw Bec take Amber's arm. She jogged after her friends.

Bec's eyes darted around the centre. None of the other patrons were paying attention to them.

Amber took several deep breaths. 'I'm okay,' she said to Bec, trying to draw her arm back. Bec searched her face before releasing her. Amber wrapped her arms around Oliver and rocked from side to side. 'You're okay, you're okay,' she soothed him.

'Let's get the hell out of here,' Bec said, 'Don't talk to anyone, okay?'

Spooked by Amber's behaviour, Bec sped through the QVB, taking the underground route to Town Hall station. She wove her way through the other patrons, almost bowling over an elderly man.

'I thought you didn't want to attract attention,' Amber muttered under her breath, smiling an apology to the man. He glared at her.

At the station they saw the first sign that people had heard about what had happened at Martin Place. Three teenage girls had stopped in front of the gates. They gaped at a phone, oblivious to the people trying to push past them.

A middle-aged woman with neat grey hair and a floral facemask waved her phone in the faces of two young men in business suits. Mouths falling open, they pulled out their own phones. After a few minutes, they joined her in showing passersby their phones. It was an unusual sign of community for the Sydney CBD. A harried woman leaving the station with two young boys read the information and hurried her children back to the platform.

'But I want to go to Luna Park,' the eldest boy whined as she dragged him away.

A man in a tailored suit thrust the phone back to them and stormed through the gates, muttering 'fake news'.

Bec avoided the woman and young men by slipping through the end gate. She hurried Amber down the stairs and along the narrow platform until they stood apart from any other passengers.

Amber stared at a screen looming over the train tracks. A weather forecast was replaced with an ad for an upcoming action movie. There was a close-up shot of the lead actor firing a semi-automatic gun. Amber shuddered and turned away.

'You told me it would be a peaceful protest.' Her tone was accusing.

Bec had also been staring at the ad. She looked confused. 'I didn't know there were going to be monsters.'

'I'm not talking about the monsters; I'm talking about the men with guns.' Amber heard her voice rising to a squeak.

'We took precautions. To protect everyone if something happened. But we thought it would be soldiers, police - not monsters that can't be shot.'

'You talked me into coming today, and putting Oliver in danger!'

Bec bristled. 'You didn't tell me you were going to bring him. I can't read minds.'

Amber's head was screaming. She wanted to smash Bec's complacency. 'You could have told me to take him home when we arrived at the station.'

Bec stared at her. 'Fine,' she spat the word out, 'I won't ask you to join me again.'

The train arrived, its squealing brakes echoing around the platform. Bec nodded at the carriage. 'Your train's here.' She didn't move to give Amber a hug.

Amber strode over the gap between the platform and the train, already regretting her words. She considered saying something conciliatory before the train left, but Bec was engrossed in her phone and didn't look up. Amber's face flushed and she gritted her teeth, her regret evaporating. The doors closed and the train lurched away from the platform.

Amber sunk into a blue and yellow splattered seat and loosened the baby carrier to breastfeed Oliver. While he sucked, she leant her face against the window, the glass cooling her hot cheek. She felt petty and small for fighting with Bec after what she'd seen at Martin Place.

Monsters. Real ones. She'd been naive. She'd assumed the other politicians, police and army would sort Walker out. But what could they do about monsters? Not just monsters - monsters that can't be shot.

She slid her phone out of her pocket and gazed at it, trying to decide what to tell Adam. It was tempting to tell him everything had been fine, but the news was already spreading through social media. She pulled a face and tapped on his name.

'Hey, this is Adam, leave a message.'

Amber breathed a sigh at the reprieve. 'Hey hon, just letting you know Ollie and I are safe and on our way home. Talk to you later.'

She hung up and closed her eyes, napping while Oliver fed, the train carrying them away from the city.

A handful of people left the train at Epping and padded through an empty station. Even the station staff were gone - the gates at the top of the escalators open.

Beecroft road was quiet too. Restaurant doors were sealed and their windows shuttered. The pub was open, but it had few patrons. Two tense security guards stood in the doorway. The few pedestrians scuttled past and avoided eye contact.

Amber increased her pace. Her eyes darted around the street. It was the opposite of the morning's walk, when she'd been unsettled by the dogged normality.

Her neighbour Dan was smoking outside the apartment complex, his large backside taking up three quarters of the front step, encased in loose polyester shorts that had seen better days. He had pulled his thick, prematurely-greying hair into a man bun. Beneath some small holes around the collar, his black T-shirt declared It's not illegal to seek asylum. Behind Dan's back, Bec sneered about people whose activism didn't extend past politically correct statements on shirts - virtue signalling, she called it. Amber, whose activism wouldn't have extended even that far if it wasn't for Bec, argued that it was better than not caring at all.

'Amber,' Dan said, exhaling a puff of smoke. His backside remained fixed between her and the door.

'Has anything happened, Dan? It's very... quiet.'

He squinted up at her, his eyes red and glazed. Dan always looked tired. He was a software developer for an American firm, which meant working overnight. 'Everyone's freaking out that the country's been taken over by monsters. They're all hiding in their homes praying or preparing for the apocalypse or something. Zhou,' he mangled the pronunciation of her friend's

23

name, 'Bought a carload of tinned food. He won't be able to move in his apartment.'

'Zhou is hoarding food? I didn't think he could cook.'

'He reckons he saw a monster,' Dan snorted. 'I wonder what he was on at the time?'

'You're not worried?'

'Come on, monsters? Those videos were faked.'

No they weren't. Amber didn't say the words out loud. Mahogany horns and black eyes filled her mind. She shivered.

Dan raised his eyebrows. 'You're not freaking out too? Didn't your mumma ever tell you that there's no such thing as monsters?'

'Well, sure, but she also told me that 'other kids' got 100 on every test.'

Dan laughed, his bottom and belly jiggling. Amber squeezed past him and put her key in the door. 'Bye,' she said, letting the door slam shut on anything further he had to say.

Upstairs, she deadlocked her door and kicked off her shoes, gliding in her socks over the polished wooden floorboards. She switched on the air conditioner and slumped on one of the dark grey couches, breathing in the smell of the apartment. It was her sanctuary. A large white breakfast bar separated the kitchen, with its white cabinets and stainless steel appliances, from the living area. One couch faced a wide television fixed to the long white wall adjoining the apartment next door. The other looked out wide glass doors onto the grey concrete balcony. A small outdoor setting and stainless steel barbeque were positioned to the far left of the balcony, so they didn't impede the view through the glass balustrade of the street below. The remaining apartment walls, all white, were broken by a few selected artworks. Five wooden steps, matching the floorboards, led to a split level with two bedrooms and a bathroom.

Oliver mouthed at her breast. 'Not already?' she said, but pulled her shirt up and unclipped her bra. She fumbled for the TV remote.

A woman in a tailored suit appeared on the screen. 'Our reporter, Mike Davies, is on the scene in Canberra. Mike, what messages are we hearing from the Government?'

The picture shifted to a clean-cut blonde in a crisp, checked shirt. He appeared to be in front of Parliament House, but Amber noticed that no breath of air tousled his bleached hair. Mike Davies had been in the news about twelve months earlier. His squeaky-clean, up-and-coming news reporter image had been tarnished by the leaking of a video of his sexist diatribe at a university college party a few years earlier. Bec had ranted that the reason it hadn't impacted his career long-term was because he was a white male.

'Well, Carina, a few minutes ago the Prime Minister's office released a statement advising that, due to ongoing unrest in some areas, the Government has brought in outside assistance to uphold the law and protect the Australian public. He wishes to reassure all Australians that far from being monsters that people need to fear, these Law Enforcers will ensure our safety. He emphasised that no law-abiding Australian should have anything to fear from the Law Enforcers.'

'And what about the rather dramatic stories we've been hearing from Martin Place? Any updates on that situation?'

'Absolutely, Carina. We've been advised that a small number of protesters turned out to a demonstration at Martin Place this morning. Most of the protesters were peaceful, but some terrorists with semi-automatic weapons opened fire in the mall. The Law Enforcers were forced to respond with force to protect the other protesters, and some of the terrorists were killed. The Government has hastened to reassure everyone that, contrary to the stories circulating on social media, no innocent citizens were killed. In fact, we've been hearing some stories of heroic acts by the Law Enforcers to protect the protesters.'

Amber slammed her hand on the remote, making Mike's face disappear. She was shaking. No innocent citizens were killed. An image filled her mind - the child she'd watched shot from behind as he fled with his family. Tears leaked from her eyes and dripped onto the black hair that covered Oliver's head like a cap. He raised a clenched fist.

She stared into space, trying to find the words to pray for the child, and the others who had been killed. Oliver finished feeding and fell asleep on her chest. She put him into his cot, easing her arm out from under him and exhaling through pursed lips when he didn't wake.

She hit Adam's number again. 'Hey, this is Adam -'

She hung up and leant on the breakfast bar, staring into space. She needed a drink. She'd been avoiding alcohol while breastfeeding, but Oliver wouldn't need another feed for a while. She extracted a bottle of gin from the cupboard above the stove and half filled a glass, topping it up with elderflower cordial. She downed it in a few swigs, and poured herself another, glad that Adam couldn't see her. He didn't like her drinking while breastfeeding.

She sipped the second glass. The comfortable fuzzy feeling settled over her. She switched the television back on, flicking over to a streaming service before Mike Davies could reappear, and settling on a documentary about sniffer dogs. As the credits rolled, she drifted to sleep under the influence of the gin.

Voices woke her. The comforting warmth from the gin had gone, leaving her feeling seedy. The peephole in her door showed two of her Chinese neighbours talking in the stairwell. She hid a smile at the contrast in their outfits as she opened the door. Helen, her hair a deep black that indicated regular use of dye, wore a bright red dressing gown and slippers with a yellow cartoon character on them. Vertical grooves in her forehead and deep creases around her chin hinted that her life had not been easy. It was common to see her trailed by several of her eight young grandchildren, but today she was by herself. Wendy, half a head taller than Helen and about two decades younger, was dressed in a formal business suit with a tight skirt and maroon high heels, which matched the maroon dye she put in her hair.

'I think Dan's right,' Helen said, 'The whole thing's a hoax.' Wendy nodded.

'They're real.' Zhou climbed up the stairs hugging three large boxes to his chest. He dropped them with a bang on the step just below the women, tight black jeans flaunting his lean legs as he leant over. Thick, messy spikes of hair fell diagonally across the crown of his head above the shaved sides. 'I've seen them.'

The women stared at him. 'Where?'

'In the city. My mate and I were having drinks at Silenus, that wine bar that just opened on Castlereagh Street, and three of them walked past. We shat ourselves.'

'I've seen them too.' Amber stepped into the hall and pulled the door behind her, leaving it open a crack, so she would hear if Oliver woke up. 'I was at Martin Place. There were monsters, and they weren't law enforcers. They killed everyone they could.'

Wendy stepped back, her hands finding and gripping the railing. Helen frowned, her face falling into the position of the creases on her brow and chin. 'What did they look like?'

'They had this bone on their heads.' Amber described the shape of the bone with her hands. 'Ending in six horns. And their eyes were totally black.'

'Boneheads.' Wendy looked nonplussed.

'Boneheads,' Zhou repeated, testing the word. 'Can I use that in my next post?' Zhou, Australian-born and in his mid-twenties, had amassed a fortune as an influencer on Chinese social media.

He didn't need to work anymore, but Amber doubted he'd ever give it up. He lived for attention.

Wendy shot him a look of disbelief. 'If you want.'

'You should be careful,' Helen said, her voice clipped and her accent stronger than usual. 'What you put on social media - anyone can see it.'

'That's the idea,' Zhou said.

Helen shook her head. 'The PM - the monsters - this isn't your nice safe country anymore. You can't assume that you can criticise those in power without consequences.'

'Yeah, okay, I get it. I'll be careful.'

Helen nodded, satisfied, but Amber gave Zhou a sidelong glance. She didn't believe he'd forgo posting something that would attract attention. Although she'd never have picked him for a prepper, either. She eyed his boxes.

Zhou's eyes were on Wendy's head. 'The bone is a similar colour to your hair.'

Wendy patted her hair with some discomfit. She squared her shoulders and pushed herself away from the railing. 'If the monsters are real, we need to get ready.'

'How?' asked Amber.

'I've been stockpiling food,' Zhou said, tapping the top of the pile of boxes.

'It's not just food you need.'

'Toilet paper?' Amber grinned, remembering the panic buying at the start of the coronavirus pandemic.

'We should change all our money to US dollars, in case the Aussie dollar collapses.'

Wendy was a stockbroker with a major superannuation fund, so they respected her financial knowledge. Zhou looked worried. He had a lot of assets. 'What about shares?'

'Get them out of Australian companies. Invest in something overseas. Do it quick, though, before the market crashes.'

He bit his lip and picked up his boxes again. 'Thanks for the advice.' He continued up the stairs.

Oliver wailed. Amber nodded to Wendy and Helen and slipped inside, locking the door behind her. She lifted Oliver and rocked him on her hip to calm him.

Her phone had slid down the side of the couch while she slept. She extracted it and tried Adam's number, still rocking Oliver. 'Hey, this is Adam -'

She hung up, frowning. Adam didn't usually ignore phone calls. She opened her web browser and googled Dubbo. Several tourist websites popped up, and some news articles; all from more than a few months ago. Nothing to suggest any current problems in Dubbo.

She tried his office. 'Thrive Payment Systems, Megan speaking.'

'Hi Megan, it's Amber Yu, Adam Taylor's wife. Can I speak to Stephen West, please?'

'Putting you through.'

Instrumental music filled her ear for a moment, before being replaced by Stephen's syrupy voice. 'Ammmber, sweetheart, how's it hanging?'

Amber winced at the familiarity from Stephen, who she had met twice. 'Hi, Steve. I was wondering if you'd heard from Adam. I'm struggling to get onto him.'

'Ohh, sorry to hear that. I haven't spoken to him today, but if you hold on a tick, I'll see if I can get him for you.'

'Thanks.'

The same instrumental music filled her ear again. She waited a few minutes, then put the phone on speakerphone and propped it up against the side of the wooden change table while she changed Oliver's nappy. She had finished and washed her hands before Stephen picked up again.

'Ammmber, honey, so sorry to keep you waiting.'

'No problems, Steve. Did you manage to get onto him?'

'No, and it's odd.'

Oliver chose that moment to babble.

'Aww, is that Adam Junior?' Steve asked.

'Yeah, that's Oliver.'

'Aww, how lovely. Does he look like you or Adam?'

Amber gritted her teeth. 'People say he looks like me. Steve, what was odd when you tried to get onto Adam?'

'Oh, I couldn't get through to anyone in the company he's contracting for. It seems to be a problem with the phones. Can you leave it with me? I'll let you know when I get onto them.'

'Of course, thanks Steve.'

'No worries at all. So, what do you make of this monster thing?'

The image of the child being shot from behind filled her mind again. 'Uh, I dunno Steve, I've got to go. Let me know if you hear anything.'

'Sure, will do.'

She jabbed the red icon on her phone. Steve was probably right - it was just a phone problem. She put Oliver down on the floor with some toys and looked at the bottle of gin. She splashed more into her glass, added elderflower cordial and swirled the drink around her mouth to remove the bitter taste left from her conversation with Stephen. She pulled together an easy salad for dinner, trying to ignore the feeling that something was very wrong with Adam.

Three

After a sleepless night, several unsuccessful attempts to call Adam and another fruitless conversation with Stephen, Amber strapped Oliver into the baby carrier and trotted down the stairs.

Dan was ensconced on the front step again, wearing the same clothes as the day before. Zhou was standing in front of him, waving his smartphone. One of his posts must have gotten lots of interest. It was the only thing she'd ever seen Zhou get excited about.

'Amber,' he said, brandishing his phone in her direction, 'My post went viral - and not just in China. The whole world is calling the monsters 'Boneheads'.'

'Oh,' Amber said, squinting at the phone as he waved it in front of her face. His post was in Mandarin. Despite the best efforts of her grandmother, she'd never learnt to read more than a few characters. 'You haven't made yourself a target, have you? You heard what Helen said.'

Zhou tossed his head back. 'Helen worries too much. I think the Boneheads have bigger fish to fry than some blogger, even if my post did go viral!' He finished in a cheer, raising an open palm to high five Dan.

Dan patted it without enthusiasm, stabbing his cigarette out on the step with the other hand. 'Monsters, bloody hell. I was sure it was a hoax, but every bloody news channel says they exist.'

'I told you I saw one, man,' Zhou said.

'Yeah, but I thought you must have been on something.'

'You trust the news, but not me?'

She left the two men bickering. It was just before nine - peak time for parents in four-wheel drives to race to school - but Carlingford Road was quiet. There was so little traffic she risked crossing the four lanes to the bus stop, rather than walking up to the pedestrian crossing two blocks away.

The lack of traffic hadn't improved the punctuality of the buses. A light wind had sprung up overnight and cleared the worst of the smoke haze, but the smoky smell lingered on. The wind had died down and the humidity was increasing, raising droplets of sweat where Oliver's warm body touched hers. She moved into the patchy shade cast by a spindly tree in the front garden of the house behind her and checked her and Adam's bank accounts on her phone. Adam hadn't spent any money from their joint accounts since breakfast the day before. She tried to decide what to do. 'I'll just withdraw half, so Daddy can get the other half,' she said to Oliver, adding a quick prayer that Adam would be able to.

The bus, when it arrived, was packed. Amber pulled her mask over her face and squeezed on. The air conditioning was fighting a losing battle against the heat from so many bodies. A young man with his hair in a man bun like Dan's glanced up from his phone and saw her carrying Oliver. He stood and motioned for her to take his seat.

'Thanks,' she said. She perched on the hard vinyl cushion, reflecting that the man bun looked better on this man with his tousled blonde hair than it did on Dan. 'Can't believe how packed it is.'

'Something's wrong with the buses. We were waiting more than an hour for this one to show up.'

'It's those damn Boneheads,' a man with short grey hair said, 'Everyone is terrified.'

'Boneheads?'

'The monsters,' the man said, 'That's what everyone is calling them. It's all over the internet.'

'The TV's still calling them Law Enforcers,' the young man said.

The grey-haired man snorted. 'Whose law are they enforcing?'

Amber frowned, wondering if she should be worried about Zhou. She shook her head. Zhou's post had been in Mandarin, on a Chinese platform. Even if he'd been the source of the name - and it was an obvious name for the monsters - it wasn't likely that the authorities would know it had come from him.

She jumped off the bus outside a small shopping centre and walked through the undercover carpark to the lifts. It was even hotter in the carpark. Several people were waiting for the lift. They tried to rush in as soon as the doors opened, blocking the people trying to get out with overloaded trolleys. The lift doors beeped as the scrum of people sorted itself out. Amber squeezed onto the lift as the doors closed, earning herself a glare from a lady with two whining children. The lift groaned as it rose and stopped with a violent bump.

The cool air inside the shopping centre was a relief. The centre was busier than usual for a weekday. Most of the customers had masks and trolleys full of groceries. She saw a middle-aged woman pushing one full trolley ahead of her and pulling another behind her.

Amber walked past the packed supermarket and franchise coffee shops to the bank. She withdrew half of her and Adam's savings, and took the money straight to the currency exchange booth.

'The rate isn't too good,' the young man behind the glass window told her, 'It was ten cents higher a week ago. You still want to go ahead?'

Amber nodded. 'I reckon it'll get worse before it gets better.'

He pulled a face in agreement.

She tucked the wads of US dollars into a money belt she usually reserved for travelling, and wiggled it around so that it was covered by Oliver's carrier. She grimaced. She'd never carried so much money in cash before.

She stopped in front of the supermarket. She should emulate Zhou and stockpile food. She hadn't forgotten the start of the coronavirus pandemic - she'd laughed at all the people panic-buying toilet paper, and later had to borrow from Wendy because she couldn't find any.

Her shoulders drooped. Each checkout had a long queue of people with full trolleys. Her body felt heavy and achy. 'I can't face it,' she said to Oliver, 'We'll do it tomorrow.' She bought a takeaway coffee instead, and sipped it on the way to the bus stop. She passed several women pushing trolleys down the street, piled high with tinned food, pasta, rice and toiletries.

The next day was even hotter - the air laden with smoke and moisture. It pressed down on Amber's shoulders as soon as she stepped outside. Sweat gleamed on Oliver's hair. He had been restless overnight; waking every hour demanding a breastfeed. Adam hadn't returned her increasing number of phone calls.
'Did you see the news?'
She blinked at the sickly red sun, wondering why she'd gotten out of bed. Dan was twisting his head to look up at her. He was wearing another well-worn T-shirt, this one with an Aboriginal flag on the back. She moved down the step and read Always Was, Always Will Be, Aboriginal Land on the front of his shirt.
'Just the late news last night. That sexist bastard Mike Davies was eulogising about the Boneheads. I had to turn it off before I broke Adam's precious large-screen television by throwing something at him.'
Dan sucked on his cigarette. 'I hope he's being paid well for being such a crawler. But I meant on social media. The TV news is bullshit.'
Amber shook her head. 'I was too tired to go down that rabbit hole this morning.'
'The army bombed the crap out of Dubbo last night.'
Amber felt as though the ground dropped away beneath her feet. Her stomach dropped with it.
Dan didn't notice her reaction. 'Nobody seemed to know why. There were heaps of memes this morning joking about the Dubbo zoo animals being a threat to national security.'
A chill ran down her body. She wrapped her arms around herself.
Dan frowned. 'Are you okay?'
'Adam's in Dubbo.' The words seemed to come from someone else.

'Oh, shit.' He covered his mouth with his hand, as though trying to push the words he'd said back in. 'I didn't know.'

She stumbled back up the step and fumbled with the door. Dan heaved himself up and helped her open it. 'Can I do anything?'

She couldn't find any words to answer him. She tripped up the stairs, leaving him standing in the doorway watching. Inside the apartment, she strapped Oliver into his bouncer. He bounced up and down and reached for the toys dangling above him, trying to pull a purple giraffe into his mouth. She brushed away the tears that filled her eyes and pressed Adam's office in her recent call list. Megan didn't even wait for her to say her name. 'I'll put you through to Steve.'

Stephen had lost his syrupy tone. 'Amber. I was going to call you. I've been on the phone all night trying to find out about our staff.' The exhaustion in his voice attested to this statement.

'And?' Amber didn't bother to hide her desperation.

'Nothing. I'm sorry. Apart from those clips on social media, it's like a black hole in communications. I can't get hold of any of the team, or the guys they were working for - Downunder Technology. I don't even know if the office is still standing.'

The chill she'd felt when Dan told her that Dubbo had been bombed seemed to settle deep inside her. The oppressive heat couldn't touch it.

'I'll keep trying. You'll be the first to know if I hear anything.'

Amber mumbled her thanks and hung up. She dialled Bec's number. The phone rang twice and then stopped. Bec likely rejected her call. After any fight, Bec stayed offended for days, until Amber apologised. Amber tried to dredge up some anger at Bec for not answering, but she couldn't sustain it - the flames snuffed out by the chill that had taken over her body.

She leant her head on her hands and prayed that Adam was okay, then switched on her tablet and swiped through her social media feeds. Dubbo, a small city about three hundred kilometres north west of Sydney, best known for its large open-plain zoo, featured heavily. Images showed piles of rubble - all that remained of the heritage buildings on one of the city centre streets - and residential streets where only one or two houses remained. A few wobbly mobile phone videos replayed the bombing - the ground lit by sudden flames, large clouds of dust and smoke rising into the sky.

There was a timid knock at the door. She didn't move from the couch, scrolling faster and faster, her teeth clenched and back and arm muscles strained. Maybe if she kept going she would find a post that said it was all a prank. Someone getting in several months early for April Fools' Day.

The door, which she'd forgotten to lock, swung open. Helen and Wendy marched in. Zhou hovered behind them, his cheeks red. Wendy's hair had changed to a bright emerald. Her shoes and scarf were a similar colour. Amber wondered whether she had changed her entire wardrobe to match her new hairstyle.

'Dan told us about Adam,' Helen said, dropping into the chair opposite Amber as though she hadn't just invaded Amber's home. Zhou stayed near the door, fidgeting.

'You may as well come in,' Amber said.

'I'll get drinks.' Wendy walked to the kitchen. Amber hoped she was going to pour gin and tonics, even if it was only nine am.

Zhou perched on the edge of Helen's chair. He looked at the phone on the couch next to her. 'Have you heard anything -'

Amber shook her head. 'He's not answering his phone. His office doesn't know anything.'

Zhou bit his lip. Then his eyes brightened. 'Bec,' he said, 'She might be able to find out something.'

'I tried to call her. She didn't answer. We had a fight the other day.'

'Oh, for fuck's sake.' Zhou pulled out his phone and tapped for a minute. 'I told her she needs to call you.'

'You still have her number?'

'Yeah, we still talk. A fair bit lately, actually.'

Amber was surprised. Zhou and Bec had met a few years ago at a barbeque she had hosted in the backyard. They'd had a brief love affair that had ended in a blazing row where the phrases 'manipulative cow' and 'phony, attention-seeking bastard' were thrown around. Bec had never mentioned that they'd kept in touch.

Wendy plonked cups of strong green tea in front of them. Amber grimaced. Tea, not gin. Adam would approve.

'Why would Bec know anything about Dubbo?' Helen asked.

'She's got contacts, through some group she's involved in - they organised the protests on Saturday.'

Amber nodded. 'We went to the one at Martin Place.'

Helen frowned. 'Australians are too reckless.'

'Don't you think we should protest?' Zhou was indignant.

'Australians don't know how bad it can get.'

Oliver interrupted with a squall. He mouthed Amber's breast when she picked him up. Seeing that she was about to breastfeed, Zhou leapt up and beat a hasty retreat to the door. Wendy stacked the teacups in the dishwasher while Helen checked that Amber had plenty of food, and they took their leave.

She returned to her obsessive scrolling while she nursed Oliver, the television news playing in the background. Several social media groups had coalesced of people trying to find friends or relatives in Dubbo. She posted photos of Adam and begged people to instant message her if they knew where he was, praying for a quick response.

Images of empty supermarket shelves were dotted among the images of Dubbo streets. Amber felt a twinge of remorse that she still hadn't bought any groceries. 'Tomorrow,' she promised Oliver, 'If there's anything left.'

The day and night melted away while Amber wallowed in social media, only coming up to look after Oliver's needs or watch a segment of television news. She ate cold baked beans out of the tin and a family block of milk chocolate. She didn't dare go to sleep in case she missed something that could rescue Adam.

Twelve hours after the news had first appeared on social media, the news media acknowledged the bombing, in the scantest possible terms. Even Mike Davies admitted that there had been an 'incident' in Dubbo, and assured his viewers that the Prime Minister and Law Enforcers were investigating. Amber growled at the screen like an irritated animal.

Photos of Dubbo on her social media feeds were replaced by other news. Protests sprang up around the country. The smaller ones in regional areas were dispersed with minimal violence by soldiers; larger ones in state capitals like Adelaide and Perth were brutally suppressed by Boneheads.

The national broadcaster reported on some of the protests, even showing footage of the deaths. At two pm. with no warning, it stopped broadcasting. The main channel played reruns of British comedy shows; the 24-hour news channel showed nothing at all. One by one, the other networks stopped broadcasting news, until only one television news program remained. Amber snarled as her screen filled with Mike Davies' face. Of course, it would be the one with him on it.

Zhou dropped by late the next morning. He took in her rumpled clothes, the tablet in her hands and the television, now showing a young female reporter, Charlotte Lee. Charlotte wasn't any more informative than Mike. 'Have you been up all night?'

Amber yawned in response.

'I'm going for breakfast. You should come.'

Amber opened her mouth to refuse, but before she could say

anything her stomach let out a large growl. She dumped Oliver in his arms. 'I'll need a minute.'

Oliver's face crumpled. He howled. Zhou jiggled Oliver up and down over his shoulder while she ducked into the bedroom, dragged on a clean pair of shorts and tank top, and ran a brush through her hair. She took Oliver back and slipped him into the carrier, smiling at the identical relieved sighs from Oliver and Zhou.

Dan was smoking on the step, his eyes red-rimmed again after the night's work. For a change, he was wearing a new T-shirt - so new it still had creases from being packaged for delivery. Amber and Zhou absorbed the sketch of a Bonehead inside a red circle with a red diagonal line through it and the words No Boners.

'Not very subtle, is it?' Zhou said.

'It gets the point across.' Dan gave Amber an awkward look. 'I'm sorry about yesterday.'

The sun glare through the smoke haze made Amber squint. Her temple throbbed. She resented being expected to reassure Dan. 'You didn't know,' she mumbled. She nudged Zhou. 'I need coffee.'

They walked in silence to their favourite Epping cafe. All the tables inside were taken. Ignoring the smoky air, they sat down at a spindly outdoor table, shaded by a large umbrella. The waitress brought a white plastic high chair for Oliver, who banged one fist against the table and tried to fit the other into his mouth. Amber gave him a rusk. He gnawed on it, dribbling debris onto his shirt.

Zhou waited until she had drunk half a large coffee before speaking.

'Has Bec called you?'

'Nope.' She pursed her lips.

He frowned. 'I sent her some instant messages and she hasn't read them. I can't get her on the phone at all.'

'Oh.' Amber dragged her mind away from bleak speculation of Adam's fate. 'Are you worried about her?'

'Nah. Nah, I'm sure she's fine. It's just Helen getting to me. She keeps harping on about Australians being reckless.'

Amber snorted. 'Bec is the dictionary definition of reckless.' She bit her lip. 'I don't suppose you had a fight with her, too?'

Zhou shook his head. 'Not recently.'

The waitress plonked a plate of bacon, eggs, avocado and toast in front of Amber. Amber devoured the greasy bacon, the throbbing in her head subsiding. Zhou picked at a bowl of granola and honeyed yoghurt, his brow furrowed.

A young Chinese woman approached the table. 'Are you Zhou Hui?' Her voice was breathy, as though she had been running.

Zhou bestowed a dazzling smile on her. 'That's me.'

'Can I get a picture with you?'

'Sure.'

The woman proffered her phone to Amber. 'Do you mind?'

Zhou put his arm around the woman. 'Smile,' Amber said. Zhou beamed, but the woman's serious expression didn't change. Amber handed the phone back.

'Thank you so much,' she said, backing away and nodding several times before she disappeared onto the street.

Amber frowned. 'Does that happen a lot?'

'Never. Most of my fans are in China. So cool!'

A wide smile remained on his face as they walked inside the cafe to pay.

They waited in a short queue of people ordering takeaway coffees. Zhou's eyes were drawn to a small television on the wall. The smile slid off his face. Amber followed his gaze. Charlotte Lee's face filled the screen. The television was muted; the news displayed in a scrolling news ticker at the bottom of the screen.

Amber grasped Zhou's arm as she read. Terrorists bomb Governor Macquarie Tower in the Sydney CBD... Several Federal politicians killed in unprecedented vehicle bombing...

The screen showed a skyscraper collapsing in slow motion. The north side caved into the rest of the building - each floor crumpling one after the other like odd vertical dominos. The east side followed - the top floors sagging before the last of the floors on the north side collapsed. A huge plume of dust rose into the sky and blotted out the view. The dust cleared to the strange sight of half a building standing.

'Can I help you?'

The queue had cleared. The young woman at the counter tilted her head and raised her eyebrows at them. She'd been too busy to notice the news. Zhou pulled out his phone, ignoring the woman. Amber hastened to the counter and paid. She pulled him out of the cafe. He tapped the phone in a frenzy, not lifting his gaze as they walked back to the apartment. Amber seized him before he walked into an electricity pole. He didn't seem to notice.

'What does it say? Was it the Boneheads?'

'Far as I can tell, the TV news was telling the truth for once. A group has claimed responsibility - they say they're the resistance.' He chortled. 'The Bonehead Resistance.'

'Never tire of your own jokes, do you?' Amber pulled him back before he walked out into the Carlingford Road traffic. 'Let's wait for the little green man, shall we?'

Zhou raised his eyebrows at her aggressive tone, but he was too absorbed by his phone to retort. 'It was a suicide bombing - no, wait, not a suicide, they used some kind of remote control to position the vehicle.' He looked up and met her eyes. 'They say they've killed the Prime Minister.'

'They have?'

'If Walker's dead - does that mean they'll let all those politicians out of jail, and hold the election?'

'What about the Boneheads - will they just piss off?'

'Back where they came from? Does anyone even know where that is?' He returned his attention to the phone without waiting for an answer.

Amber was relieved when they made it back to the apartment without Zhou injuring himself. They met Helen and Dan in the stairwell. Helen was wearing her fluffy yellow dressing gown again, despite the heat. Two of her grandchildren, preschoolers in grubby dresses, were wrestling on the floor behind her. She ignored them.

'The PM's dead!' Zhou whooped in greeting.

Helen shook her head.

'You're a bit behind the times, my friend,' Dan said.

'He's not dead?'

'They got it wrong. They thought he was at some meeting in that tower, but he was still in Canberra.'

Zhou's shoulders drooped. 'Bummer.'

'They took out a bunch of politicians and hapless public servants.' Helen's tone was censorious.

'At least they tried.' Zhou was defensive.

'The PM won't ignore this. They'll be dead by morning,' Helen predicted. She rounded on the children. 'Olivia, that's enough. Stop punching your sister!'

Four

Amber continued her social media vigil for another half hour while she fed Oliver, but Dubbo was old news. Her feed was consumed with chatter about Governor Macquarie Tower, and the self-proclaimed resistance.

The Government announced a curfew - nobody could leave

their homes between eight pm and six am. 'In light of increased tension,' Mike Davies said. No other explanation was given. Amber took it as a positive sign that the Government was jittery about the resistance.

She threw her tablet onto the couch. 'If they're bringing in curfews, we have to stock up on food,' she said to Oliver. He blew a spit bubble.

She tucked him into the carrier. He fell asleep as she walked to the bus stop. The humidity had risen since she'd returned from breakfast. Her headache returned.

Her phone rang as she boarded a bright red bus. She fumbled with it, praying it was Adam, or Stephen. No caller ID.

'Hello?'

'Amber!'

'Bec?'

Bec spoke in a rush. 'Tell Zhou to run and hide. There's soldiers coming to arrest him.'

Amber felt breathless. 'Zhou? But - why? How do you know?'

'A mate in the army.'

Amber wrinkled her forehead. Since when did Bec have friends in the army? 'I'll call him.'

'I tried - he never answers. And he hasn't read my messages. There's not much time.' Bec's voice quivered.

'I'll find him.'

'Thanks.' Bec hung up.

Amber pulled the cord to tell the bus driver to let her off at the next stop. A man seated across the aisle was staring at her. He leaned forward. 'Are you okay?'

'I'm fine.' Now the woman next to him was staring at her. She ducked her head and rubbed her sweaty palms on her shorts.

The bus squealed as it pulled up to the stop. She struggled off, escaping the curious looks from her fellow passengers.

She ripped off her mask and scrolled through her address book to Zhou's number. Her fingers shook, making her clumsy. The phone rang several times and went through to his voicemail. 'Yo, this is Zhou. Text me.'

Amber lowered her voice. 'Zhou, it's Amber. You need to get out of the apartment - Bec says there's soldiers coming for you.'

She hung up and searched the other side of the road for the nearest bus stop. Two trucks pulled up at the lights on the corner. They were painted in green and brown camouflage, their cargo beds shrouded in digital camouflage canvas covers. Her eyes widened. A breath later she was sprinting towards the apartment, her arms pumping back and forth, all her attention focused on her sandshoes slapping the footpath. The carrier bounced up and down with each step.

Dan was tipping a box of empty soft drink bottles into the recycling bin.

She gulped air. 'Have you seen Zhou?'

'No.' He stared as she vaulted over the steps. 'In a hurry?'

She took the stairs two at a time and hammered on Zhou's door.

The door swung open. Zhou stood barefoot in the doorway, his eyebrows scrunched together.

'You need to get out of here,' Amber babbled. 'There's soldiers coming to arrest you!'

'Too late.' Helen poked her head up from the stairs below. 'They're out front.'

'My apartment.' Amber seized Zhou's arm and pulled him to the stairs.

'I'll delay them.' Helen disappeared.

'Wait.' Zhou pulled his arm free. 'How do you know they're here for me?'

'Bec.' Amber leapt down the stairs and fumbled her key in the door. 'Why don't you answer your fricken phone?'

'Nobody answers their phone anymore.'

They heard banging on the complex's security door. 'Quick!'

The key turned, and they fell into the apartment. Amber wrenched the key out and slammed the door shut. She pushed Zhou towards the bedrooms. 'Hide!'

She leant against the door, gasping for air and trying to think. With a sharp nod, she jogged to the bathroom. She splashed water on her face and dried it, removing the sweat from her mad dash from the bus stop, then slid Oliver out of the carrier, unzipped his pants and ripped off his nappy. He yelled at this treatment. She grabbed a dirty nappy out of the bin and opened it. The stink permeated the apartment. For good measure, she threw a spew-stained wrap over her shoulder.

She jumped at a loud bang on her door. Taking a deep breath, she opened it, holding the dirty nappy in one hand and the squealing Oliver in the other.

Two men in their early twenties, dressed in army camouflage pants and shirts and white face masks, leant back at the sight and smell of the dirty nappy. The younger soldier had a tanned face and dark, curly hair. The other had a shaved head and a dinosaur tattoo on his face. 'We're looking for Zhou Hui. You seen him?'

Amber wrinkled her brow. 'Zhou Hui.' She pretended to rack her brain. 'I think there's a Zhou who lives upstairs somewhere.'

'We checked his apartment. He's not there.'

Amber shrugged. 'I don't know where he is, sorry. I've never really spoken to him.'

The tattooed soldier handed her a card. 'If you see him, please call this number.'

'Why, what's he done?'

'Just call if you see him, please.' The tattooed soldier nodded at Oliver. 'We'll leave you to get on with your day. Thank you for your time.'

Amber closed the door and rested her face on Oliver's head. Her heart rate slowed. His sobs eased as he burrowed into her neck.

Zhou appeared in the doorway of the bedroom. 'Fuck,' he said in a flat tone. Amber sucked in a shaky breath, and nodded in agreement.

She stumped up the two steps to the bathroom. Zhou watched as she dropped the nappy back into the bin and the wrap on the floor. 'Clever,' he said, 'Scaring them off with poo.'

She washed her hands and returned to the kitchen. Zhou followed. She rummaged one-handed in the fridge and held up a half-empty bottle of pinot gris. 'Drink?'

Zhou frowned. 'Isn't it a bit early?'

Amber shrugged. 'If you say so.' She splashed the wine into a large wine glass.

'Alright, hit me up,' Zhou said. She handed him the glass and poured another for herself.

Taking a sip, she peered down at the street from behind the balcony blinds. The two trucks she had seen earlier were parked in the middle of the road. Half a dozen soldiers milled around.

She turned to Zhou. 'What's going on? This can't all be for some dumb social media post calling the monsters Boneheads.'

Zhou didn't meet her eyes. 'Guess the monsters are thin-skinned.'

'Zhou.'

He sighed. 'I told you I'd been talking to Bec a fair bit lately. She reached out to me to help her seek some - resources - for the resistance. I don't just have my followers on social media, you know. I have other contacts in China. Some of them agree with Bec that the Boneheads are a threat to the world, not just Australia.'

Amber's mouth fell open. She felt light-headed and dizzy. Helping Zhou might have put her - and, worse, Oliver - in danger. 'Why is Bec organising resources for the resistance?'

Zhou shrugged. 'You know Bec - she's always fighting someone.' He turned back to the street. 'You're not going to be able to scare them off with pooey nappies forever. I need to get out of here.'

'You can't go now. There's soldiers everywhere.'

He rubbed his fingers on his temple. 'I haven't got anywhere to go, anyway. What am I going to do?' His words ended with a wail.

'Can't you stay with one of your friends?'

'Them? They're worse than I am. They'll dob me in to the soldiers just so they can post the arrest. With a picture of themselves in designer clothes in the foreground.'

Amber blinked. 'You live in a very strange world.'

He wasn't listening. 'Something's happening.'

'What?' Amber looked at the street. A black four-wheel drive had pulled up on the curb behind the trucks. A man with distinctive short, red hair and a matching short red beard got out of the back, pulling a black mask over his face. He wore a black collared shirt, well-cut black pants and large sunglasses. There was nothing in his outfit to suggest that he was military, but the nearby soldiers stood to attention. The two soldiers who had banged on her door walked out of the complex and spoke to him. He motioned to another two soldiers and the four of them followed him into the complex.

Amber and Zhou exchanged glances. 'Hide,' Amber said. He disappeared into the bedroom. Amber inhaled the rest of her wine and stood in the centre of the room, jiggling one foot up and down. There was a loud bang on the door.

'Open up!' a voice yelled.

She had expected they would work their way through all the apartments, like the last time. It didn't bode well that they'd come straight to her apartment. As she walked to the door, she saw Zhou's wine glass sitting on the coffee table.

She glanced at the empty glass in her hand and cursed under her breath. She ducked into the kitchen and tossed the glass into the bin with a crash.

'Army! Open up!' the voice called again.

Amber jogged towards the door, but before she got there a loud bang echoed around the apartment. Smoke filled the room. Oliver shrieked. She squeezed him tight against her chest and backed up until she hit the kitchen bench.

The red-haired man pushed the door aside. Bits of wood and dust fell onto the carpet. He took his time looking around the apartment. The soldiers stood in the doorway with rifles in their hands.

'I was just coming. You didn't need to blow up my door.'

The red-haired man ignored her. Her breathing raced. She struggled to take slower breaths.

'So,' he drawled, turning to her at last. His eyes were so pale and hard they were like stones. 'Private Jerome, here,' he jerked his head towards the young soldier with curly hair, 'Tells me that when asked about the fugitive, Zhou Hui, you said,' - he switched to a falsetto voice that made her cringe - ''I've never really spoken to him'.'

She lifted her chin. 'That's right. I haven't.'

'Huh,' he said, 'That's surprising, given that we recorded this call to his mobile.' He held up his phone, and pressed play.

Her own voice spilled out into the apartment. 'Zhou, it's Amber. You need to get out of the apartment - Bec says there's soldiers coming for you.'

He pressed pause. 'Seems like an odd message to leave for someone you've never really spoken to. And who is Bec, I wonder? Could it be Rebecca Williams, who also left several messages for Mr Zhou? Someone else who we are very interested in speaking with.'

A chill spread through Amber's body. She pressed her lips together, too scared to say anything.

The red-haired man beckoned the soldiers. Three of them took a different room each. The one with the serpent tattoo remained just inside the doorway.

There weren't many places a man could hide in the three-bedroom apartment. Zhou stumbled out of the bedroom less than a minute later. One of the soldiers was right behind him, pressing a rifle into his back. Zhou met Amber's gaze, his eyes huge.

The red-haired man didn't show any sign that he was pleased they had found Zhou. 'Take him downstairs.' Two soldiers pushed Zhou out of the apartment. The red-haired man turned his stone eyes to Amber.

'I have to thank you.' His voice was as hard as his eyes. 'We need some examples to discourage people from standing in our way.' His words went over Amber's head. She clenched and unclenched her shaking hands. He turned to Jerome and the tattooed soldier. 'Take the child.'

'No!' This Amber understood. She turned side on and wrapped both arms around Oliver. 'No, please!'

Before she had time to think about running or fighting, the tattooed soldier grabbed her from behind. He held her while Jerome wrenched Oliver out of her arms.

'Please,' Amber begged, tears streaming down her face. Jerome avoided meeting her eyes. His face looked pale despite his tan.

There was no emotion in the red-haired man's eyes. He motioned for Jerome to precede him out of the room. The tattooed soldier let go of Amber's arms and backed out of the apartment, his rifle pointed at her.

She stood frozen for several minutes after he left, unable to think. Her whole body was shaking.

She had to get Oliver back. She ran into the stairwell. Some of her neighbours had congregated on the stairs. Ignoring them, she hurtled downstairs, almost falling at the bottom. More neighbours crowded around the doorway, including Helen, in bright, flowery pyjamas. She pushed past them. Oliver and Zhou had disappeared. The tattooed soldier leant on the window of the lead truck, chatting to the soldier in the driver's seat. The red-haired man was climbing into the four-wheel drive. Amber bounded over the steps - straight into a new type of monster.

This one was a large, wombat-shaped animal, as big as a Labrador. It opened its mouth wide, showing a mouthful of razor-sharp teeth. Predator's teeth - more like those of a dingo than a wombat.

'Get back!' The animal was on a lead, held by a soldier. 'The wombat's bites aren't nice.'

'That's no wombat,' she said, her eyes fixed on the animal.

'You don't say.' The soldier's eyes above his mask looked grim. 'Just stay back.'

She backed into the steps.

'They put Oliver in the four-wheel drive,' Dan said into her ear. Amber blinked at him. Helen's yellow dressing gown was stretched tight across his chest. 'Go,' he said, nodding at the four-wheel drive as its engine started, 'I'll distract that... thing.'

The oversized wombat bared its teeth. Dan put his hands around a star picket that was stabilising a young wattle tree next to the steps. He wrenched it out and brandished it at the wombat, ignoring the soldier's shouts. Amber stared at Dan, her eyebrows pulled in tight, wrinkling her forehead.

'Go!' Dan yelled over his shoulder.

She dived across the road. She could make out Oliver's small face through the tinted windows of the four-wheel drive. The vehicle eased away from the curb. She wouldn't reach the door in time to free Oliver.

A spare tyre hung on the back of the vehicle, with a cover over it. She yanked her phone out of her shorts pocket and thrust it into a gap between the tyre and cover. The vehicle sped up and she stumbled backwards, sitting down hard.

The vehicle accelerated around the corner. Oliver was gone.

Dan knelt on the step, his hands on his head and the star picket on the ground in front of him. The soldier holding the wombat's leash held a rifle to his head. Helen's dressing gown had split open, flaunting the Bonehead picture and the words No Boners.

Amber's stomach clenched with guilt. She jogged over to him, ignoring shooting pain from her bruised bottom. The wombat growled and bared its teeth.

'Please,' she said to the soldier, 'He was just trying to help me. They took my son.' She waved a hand in the direction the four-wheel drive had disappeared.

The soldier looked her up and down. She searched his eyes for emotion or sympathy, but couldn't see any. She clenched her fists. After a long moment, the soldier gave her a nod and lowered the rifle. He tugged the wombat to the lead truck.

Dan looked up at Amber. 'You didn't get him,' he said, sinking onto the step.

Amber wanted to tell him that he'd given her a chance, but there were too many soldiers and other residents around. She shook her head. 'They took off too fast.'

'I'm sorry,' he said.

She ducked her head and trotted inside. Her neighbours in the doorway moved back, out of her way. A teenager pulled out her phone and lifted it to take a photo of herself with Amber and Dan in the background. Helen reached forward and pushed the girl's arm down. The girl swung around in a fury, wilting when she met Helen's steel gaze. Amber ran up the stairs.

She found her tablet between the two couch cushions. Breathing a prayer, she opened a phone tracking app. A map appeared. On the map, a dot that represented her phone moved from Carlingford Road onto Pennant Hills Road. She whispered a thank you prayer.

The dot flew down Pennant Hills Road and James Ruse Drive and came to a stop in the grounds of a university. She waited, eyes glued to the screen, to see if it moved again.

If she could retrieve Oliver, where could they go?

The dot didn't move.

Could she stay with a friend? She listed her friends in her mind, followed by Adam's friends, and mentally crossed off their close friends - as the soldiers might track her to them - and those who she thought unlikely to be willing to hide her. There was no-one left.

'Amber?' Helen's voice came from the doorway. 'Are you okay?'

Amber shoved her tablet under the cushions. Helen and Wendy peered in through the door frame. Tears leaked out the side of Wendy's eyes and ran down her face. Amber had never seen the tough stockbroker cry. Her own eyes welled up.

'I'm okay,' she said, 'I just - want to be on my own. Thank you, though.'

'Of course,' Helen said, 'If you need anything, let us know. Even if it's the middle of the night. Yeah?'

Amber nodded.

Helen looked at the mess the soldiers had left when they blasted the door. 'You want us to call someone to fix the door?'

'Later. I'll sort it out later.'

They cast concerned looks behind them as they left. She resisted the urge to call them back and tell them her plan. She knew they'd worry when she disappeared, but she didn't dare trust anyone.

Hiking had been her and Adam's favourite pastime before she got pregnant, so the hall cupboard was full of lightweight hiking gear. She stuffed her bike panniers with the gear, always watching the tablet in case the dot moved.

In the kitchen, she filled what space was left in her panniers with cereal, coffee, dried soup and pasta. She was delighted to find an almost-full packet of powdered milk at the back of the cupboard under the sink; past it's best before date, but still usable. She pulled an old cask wine out of its box and dropped it on top of the pack.

She looked around the apartment, taking a deep breath. She wasn't just leaving her sanctuary. She was leaving her connection with Adam. Her phone was gone, so he wouldn't be able to call her. She picked up her panniers, and reminded herself that she could track him down on social media. When it was safe.

Five

The stairwell was quiet again. A young couple were standing in their doorway, talking. She didn't know them well; they'd moved into the apartment beneath hers a few weeks before. They averted their eyes and pretended not to see her as she trotted down to the garage.

She rolled open the door to her unit's garage, revealing Adam's old surfboard, a mouldy mattress, a fridge and piles of cardboard boxes full of old clothes, university textbooks and car parts. Her turquoise touring bike was leaning against Adam's black bike. She'd had a child seat installed on the bike two weeks before, with visions of taking Oliver for leisurely rides. Her throat thickened at the thought. She swallowed and hastened to clip her panniers onto the bike rack. She dug an old octopus strap out of one of the cardboard boxes and used it to tie a hiking child carrier to the top of the rack.

She rolled the door closed again, locked it and walked up the stairs and out the front door. Dan was smoking in the gap between the brick wall and the porch column, next to the door. He just fitted in the small space, which was usually the refuge of spiders and empty beer bottles. Some spider webs had rubbed off the wall onto the plain white shirt he'd changed into - one he usually reserved for work teleconferences. He saw her looking at it and grimaced. 'I didn't want Helen to have to sacrifice another dressing gown trying to save me from being arrested.'

His reason for hovering behind the column became apparent when she shaded her eyes and looked at the street. Two soldiers were standing in the direct sun opposite the building, their eyes on the door. They must have been sweltering in their heavy uniforms. She wondered why they hadn't moved under the trees a few hundred metres down the road.

'I thought they'd all gone,' she said, 'What are they doing?'

'Stopping us leaving? Maybe they don't want us to tell our story to the news. Oh, that's right, they've cancelled any half decent news.' He glared at them.

'Zhou could post it on his socials.' Dan flinched, reminding her that Zhou had been abducted. She swallowed again. 'Only one way to find out, I guess.'

He frowned. 'You going somewhere?'

'Assuming they let me.'

He shifted his weight from side to side, his ears turning red. 'It's just… you won't do anything… stupid?'

Definitely something stupid. But not what he was thinking. 'I'm just going to the supermarket.'

'Oh. Right. Good.'

The soldiers watched as she walked down the street, but didn't try to intercept her. So, whatever they were there for, it wasn't to stop the residents from leaving. She plodded towards the large supermarket on the main street. A few hundred metres from the door she halted, taking in a sharp breath. Four soldiers stood on the footpath outside.

Eyeing the soldiers, it took her a moment to notice that the supermarket's electronic glass doors were hanging off their hinges. She looked in the windows. Almost all the shelves were bare. She could see the odd can of vegetables lying on the floor. The rest of the tinned food was gone. The fresh food aisles were untouched, apart from two tomatoes that had been stepped on, their insides strewn across the floor. Two trolleys were on their sides in the walkway.

Amber didn't want to push her luck by passing the soldiers. She ducked across the road to the small Asian grocer opposite.

A short Chinese man in a disposable mask balanced on a blue plastic stool at the counter, reading a Chinese language paper. The aisles here had also been cleared of tinned food, but she didn't want tins: too heavy. There was enough lightweight, non-perishable food left to satisfy her, including a whole shelf of muesli bars. She put all of them in her basket. She would have to survive without the things that the Asian grocer didn't stock - like nappies.

She plonked her basket on the counter. 'What happened over there?' she asked, nodding towards the supermarket, as the shopkeeper added up the cost of her groceries on an old-fashioned calculator.

'Riot,' he said, 'People fighting over groceries. A whole bunch of stuff was stolen.'

Amber raised her eyebrows. 'A riot in Epping?'

He shrugged. 'Everyone's frightened.'

The final amount was three times what she would have paid for similar items at the supermarket. Amber tapped her card without comment. As she waited for the system to process the transaction, movement out the window caught her eye. One of the soldiers was crossing the road towards them. Amber caught her breath - it was Private Jerome, the soldier who had taken Oliver out of her arms.

There was a screech of tyres and two large, black four-wheel drives pulled up next to the supermarket. Amber's mouth dropped open. She covered it with her hand. Four Boneheads erupted from the vehicles.

'What... the... fuck?' As the shopkeeper spoke, shots rang out across the street. The shopkeeper fell off his plastic chair and ducked behind the counter. Amber dived behind some shelves full of seaweed and wasabi-flavoured snacks. She peered around the corner of the shelves and through the open door into the street.

People in a mix of military uniforms and ordinary casual clothes appeared from either side of the supermarket, firing at the Boneheads. The soldiers she had seen out the front of the supermarket scattered. Jerome leapt down the concrete stairs into the Asian grocer. Amber slid backwards and hid behind some large boxes piled with jelly cups. Her heart was beating so fast it hurt. Her stomach clenched and she felt a sudden need to go to the toilet.

There was a large bang as a bullet hit a green electricity pillar box on the footpath. Jerome jumped and scuttled behind the counter, almost knocking heads with the shopkeeper. The shopkeeper looked unimpressed. He grabbed Jerome by the shirt and yanked forward with far more strength than Amber would have expected from his small stature. 'What the fuck is happening?'

Jerome's body shook, even though he was the one with the rifle. 'It's some kind of resistance group,' he gasped.

The shopkeeper slammed him back. 'And why the fuck aren't you fighting with them instead of the monsters?'

Jerome gaped at him. Any reply he might have made was drowned out by gunfire. The resistance fighters were firing rounds of bullets at the Boneheads, but the Boneheads walked through the bullets as though they were nothing.

Several egg-shaped metal balls bounced at their feet. There was a series of explosions. Dust billowed up from the road. Pieces of metal smashed into nearby buildings and cars. A car alarm wailed.

'Frags,' said Jerome, looking over the shopkeeper's shoulder.

'What?' the shopkeeper demanded.

'Grenades.' Jerome spat out the response, his eyes on the street.

Amber held her breath. Through the dissipating smoke she could see the four Boneheads. They were still standing, untouched by the pieces of metal. They fired a continuous stream of bullets. Many of the resistance fighters fell: some dead, others screaming. Amber averted her eyes.

The sounds of fighting continued on the street behind, fading as it moved further away. Amber's ears rang from the gunfire and grenades. Pain thumped in her forehead.

The shopkeeper turned to Jerome. 'Get... out... of... my... shop.' Jerome scrambled to his feet. His eyes begged for understanding, but the shopkeeper's gaze was cold. He stumbled back into the street.

Amber waited for ten minutes, then crawled out from behind the jelly cups. She stared at the shopkeeper. His eyes looked as haunted as she felt. She tried to think of something to say - some way to acknowledge what had happened - but no words were adequate.

'Thanks,' she said, hefting her shopping bags as though it had been an ordinary shopping trip. The shopkeeper didn't reply. She slipped out the door, checking both sides of the road for soldiers or Boneheads.

The car alarm was still wailing. She could hear gunfire echoing from the other side of the building. She jogged across the street towards Boronia Park, a local park that backed onto the supermarket carpark.

A bridge spanned a fenced canal into the main part of the park. On the other side of the canal, a concrete path was flanked by tall stands of eucalypt trees. Approaching the bridge, Amber saw three soldiers. They strode away from her, every muscle tense. She wasn't close enough to be sure, but one of them looked like Jerome. She ducked and hid behind a bush.

'Psst,' whispered someone behind her. She jumped, her heart thumping. A woman was standing in the canal wearing a large, olive-green pack. Her face was hidden beneath the hood of a thin cotton hoodie and a black face mask. Water covered her sneakers and socks and lapped against dark leggings. She pointed at the canal fence.

'Slip through there.'

Without waiting to see if Amber followed her suggestion, she jogged away, keeping her head well below the canal wall.

Amber looked where she had pointed. Someone had hacked off two bars in the canal fence. The fence was low enough to climb, but the hole made it possible for a small adult to crawl into the canal without anyone seeing. Amber bit her lip, wondering whether to trust the strange woman.

She glanced back at the soldiers. They had reached the playground. As she watched, they turned around and strode back in her direction. She scooted over to the fence and slid through the bars. The bars scraped and bruised her hips. Dirty water covered her ankles. She pulled the shopping bags one at a time through the bars and hung them on the inside of her elbows, holding her arms high to keep them out of the water.

The canal snaked past the supermarket, between office buildings on the right and scrub and apartment buildings on the left, before heading into a tunnel under Carlingford Road. Amber trotted along the canal, her arms aching from the weight of the swaying shopping bags. She resisted the urge to glance back to check if the soldiers had caught sight of her and bolted the last metre into the dark hole of the tunnel. Blinded by the sudden darkness, she almost ran into the woman she'd followed. She grabbed onto the woman's arms to keep from falling over.

'Sorry.' She jerked away.

'That's alright,' a familiar voice replied, 'It's not the first time I've had to hold you up. Although not usually this early in the day.'

Amber's mouth dropped open. 'Bec?' She squinted into the darkness.

'Hi,' Bec said, her voice as calm as if they were meeting at their regular bar in the city.

Amber's cheeks started burning. Her heart raced. She clenched her fists. 'Bec.' She spat the name out. 'You asked Zhou to help the resistance! You told me to warn Zhou!'

Bec recoiled, splashing backwards deeper into the tunnel. 'Amber? What's wrong?'

'The soldiers took Ollie! They took Zhou, and they took Ollie, because I tried to help Zhou. They took my little boy from me.' Her sentence ended in a wail.

She couldn't see Bec's face, but she heard her intake of breath.

'They took Ollie?' Bec said in a small voice, very different from her usual brash tone.

'That's what I said.' Tears dripped onto Amber's T-shirt. She rubbed her face on her sleeve. 'What are you doing here, Bec? How did you even get here?'

'Train,' Bec said, 'I thought - Zhou might need help.'

'He did,' Amber snapped.

Bec was silent.

Amber let her breath out in a deep sigh. 'You couldn't have helped him. There were tons of soldiers. And the weird wombat thing.'

'The weird wombat thing?'

'They had this animal on a leash. It looked like a carnivorous wombat.'

'Strange.' Bec frowned. 'What are you going to do?'

Amber didn't hesitate. 'I'm going to get Ollie back.'

'Of course you are.' Bec regained her usual airy confidence. 'I'll help you.'

'You will?' Tears filled Amber's eyes again.

'Of course,' she said, 'But let's get out of this canal. My toes are cold.'

Bec bent down as she led the way out of the tunnel, her eyes darting everywhere. Amber followed, her eyes on Bec's legs. She couldn't remember seeing Bec wear leggings before.

'Why the pack?' she called.

Bec didn't stop sloshing through the water. 'Soldiers came to my apartment too - last night,' she said over her shoulder, 'I had enough warning to grab a few things and get out of there, but I can't go back.'

The canal skirted behind Amber's church, a plain brick building that hid a convoluted rabbit's warren of stairs, hallways and rooms. It continued between two older red brick apartment blocks, before dividing in two. One channel led under a side road and ran past the back of Amber's apartment complex.

The canal was unfenced here. Amber swung the shopping bags onto the bank before scrambling up herself. Bec did the same with her pack. It was easy to slip into the garage area without anyone seeing. Amber opened the garage door, wincing at the screeching sound it made. She swung around, expecting the soldiers she'd seen out front to appear at the top of the driveway.

Several tense breaths later, Amber relaxed and pointed at her bike. 'I was planning to go after Ollie on this.' She pointed at Adam's bike. 'Want to take that one?'

Bec nodded and slipped her pack off her shoulders onto the bike rack. Amber searched in a dusty cardboard box and handed Bec a couple of octopus straps to tie it on.

She checked her tablet. Her phone was on the move again. 'Shit. Now I don't know if he's at the university or they're taking him somewhere else.'

Bec pushed back her jacket hood and took the tablet. She frowned at it. There were shadows under her eyes that hadn't been there on Saturday. 'Looks like it's heading back towards the city. They were stopped at the university for ages?' Amber nodded. 'Let's go there first. If he's not there, we'll check the next place your phone gets to, and keep going until we find him.'

Amber clenched her teeth. Helping her was the least Bec could do. But she couldn't silence a niggling voice. What if she got Bec killed?

'Are you sure you want to come? If we succeed, the Boneheads will be after us.'

'The Boneheads are already after me.' Bec tightened the octopus straps around her pack and fiddled with her phone for a few minutes, before slipping it into her pocket. She looked at Amber. 'Shall we go?'

Amber's jaw and shoulders relaxed. She slipped her tablet under the octopus strap that was wrapped around the child carrier, where she could keep an eye on her phone's movements as they rode. They wheeled the bikes out of the garage. She hesitated, looking around the garage. The contents were mostly trash, really. But it was her and Adam's history. She didn't know when, or even if, she'd be back. Breathing a sigh, she closed and locked the door.

Amber took the quietest back streets she knew to Meadowbank, riding alongside Bec. She tried to keep her breathing shallow to avoid sucking in too much smoky air. Regular glances at her tablet confirmed that her phone was still heading towards the city. She picked up their earlier conversation. 'I'm sorry you can't go back to your apartment.'

Bec laughed. 'Come on, how many times have you said I should move out of that dump?'

For years, Bec had commuted two hours every day so she could live in a rundown apartment in the inner west furnished with items she'd found for free on social media. Amber had never understood why she didn't move to Parramatta, where she worked as a marketing manager for an environmental lobby group.

'Oh well. I know you liked the location.'

'I'm just going to miss Stingy Brent,' Bec referred to her landlord, who she'd had an ongoing battle with. 'Imagine if I get a landlord who fixes the broken aircon the first time I ask? I won't know what to do with all the free time.'

Amber settled into a comfortable rhythm on the bike, leaving her mind free to concentrate on other things. She started praying. For the first few minutes her prayer was reverential, and wouldn't have been out of place at a service in her church, but it soon disintegrated into a mixture of pleading and bargaining for Oliver's safe return.

She was interrupted by something dropping out of the sky and hitting her helmet. Her bike swerved. 'What the hell?'

'Magpie!' Bec shot away down the road. Amber hurtled after her. The black and white bird struck her helmet a second time.

'Those birds are a menace,' Bec said once they were out of range of the magpie's attack.

Amber's eyes were on her tablet. Her phone had stopped in the CBD. She dragged the tablet out from under the octopus strap. 'Any idea where that is?'

Bec shrugged. 'Just a street full of office towers, as far as I can remember. And the odd cafe.'

Amber took a screenshot of the address and replaced her tablet on the bike.

At Meadowbank, they left the road and joined a cycleway that wound its way along Parramatta River. Amber was very familiar with the route; she'd ridden it many times with friends to get brunch at Parramatta Park. It had never felt so exposed before. Sections of the concrete path travelled past wide open sports fields, with no cover at all, while other sections ran under high-rise apartments. Amber hunched forward over the handlebars, convinced that every window housed an enemy. She almost expected soldiers or Boneheads to leap out from behind the trees.

'Gees,' Bec said, 'Any Boneheads will know we're up to something just by looking at you. Can't you look ordinary?'

'Paranoid is the new ordinary. The Boneheads will think we're up to something because you look too relaxed.'

'At least I'm not jumping about like a fricken kangaroo.'

The path turned into a metal boardwalk that wound its way through a mangrove swamp. The bikes clattered on the metal slats, making conversation difficult. Amber looked over the side of the boardwalk. The roots of the mangroves poked up out of the mud like little worms, seeking air.

The boardwalk joined another concrete path. Amber sped up. She felt edgy. Her breasts were uncomfortable and itchy after missing Oliver's afternoon breastfeed. She could hear Bec panting behind her. They were silent for a long time, their legs pumping hard.

The path led through the back of an industrial area and over a small bridge. Ahead were two grey metal truss bridges - a wide railway bridge and a narrower bridge carrying cement pipes.

Amber stopped to wait for Bec. 'We're almost there.'

Bec took gulps of air.

They rode under the metal bridges. Amber looked to the right, and stopped in surprise.

A new chain link fence had been installed up the hill, enclosing the university buildings. The fence was topped with barbed wire coils. There was no visible break in the fence, but she guessed that any entrance would be on the road on the other side of the university grounds.

Worse, two soldiers were patrolling the fence.

Six

Amber ducked down behind a low stone retaining wall, dropping her bike against it. Bec was a heartbeat behind her. After a long moment, Bec risked a glance over the wall. The soldiers were walking away from them, holding rifles across their bodies.

'That's a good sign,' Bec whispered.

'What?'

'The fence and soldiers.'

'A good sign?'

'Yeah. Something's going on in there. It's a good sign that Oliver might be there.'

Amber looked up at the fence with its vicious barbed topper. 'I don't know how we're going to get in, though.'

'Easy.'

Amber wrinkled her brow. 'Seriously?'

'Yep.' Bec rummaged in her pack and pulled out a pair of bolt cutters. 'We'll cut the fence.'

'What on earth are you carrying those things for?'

She shrugged. 'Just a precaution, in case I need to get in somewhere, or leave somewhere fast.'

'It was you who cut the hole in the canal fence at Boronia Park.'

'I thought it might come in handy. And I was right, wasn't I?'

'Yes, yes.' Amber rubbed her eyes. They felt dry and scratchy. 'I still can't believe you're carrying bolt cutters in your pack. Aren't there lighter tools for cutting fences?'

'Yeah, but I couldn't go into a hardware store and buy a pair of side cutters with the soldiers on my tail, could I? I stole these from a building site.'

'Speaking of soldiers - even if you cut open the fence, we'll still have to get past them.' Amber nodded at the soldiers.

'We can go in after dark. And wait until they're out of sight.'

Amber nodded, though a voice in her mind was screaming that she needed to retrieve Oliver now. The two soldiers skirted around a cottage on stilts, and disappeared out of sight. Bec dragged her bike further along the stone wall, where the water pipe bridge rose from the ground on a wide cement pylon, creating a small hiding space under the bridge. She settled down cross-legged in the grass next to the bike.

Amber copied her, trying to ignore the small black ants climbing on her shoes. She propped her tablet against the retaining wall. Her phone hadn't moved from its location in the CBD.

She freed the hiking child carrier from the bike rack and squished the contents of her panniers into the bottom of the carrier. They wouldn't be able to take the bikes through the hole Bec cut in the fence. She hoped they'd be able to come back for them.

Bec tossed Amber a muesli bar and bit into one herself. Amber hadn't felt hungry, but her stomach started growling when she saw the bar. She gulped it down in a couple of bites. Bec handed her a second bar.

On the water, a Rivercat ferry slid downstream. Amber watched it for a moment. It was turning in wide circles. She couldn't see any people on board. 'Is it just me, or is there something odd about that ferry?'

Bec followed her gaze. 'It's not you,' she said after a moment, 'I don't think anyone's driving it. It's just drifting.'

'Why would the ferry master abandon it? Not even tie it up?'

Bec pulled a face as though she could imagine why, and didn't like what she was thinking.

Amber turned back to the university grounds, squinting into the setting sun. A single-story, grey rendered building with a sloping silver roof rose above them. Beyond that she could make out some tall, red brick buildings with similar silver roofs. The other buildings were hidden behind the fence and grey building. A rabbit scurried across the lawn, then a second and a third. Amber watched them with fellow feeling. She and Bec would soon be scurrying across the same lawn. She rubbed her eyes again, her stomach churning.

The Rivercat had stopped its slow drift downstream and was now almost stationary, indicating that the tides had changed.

The soldiers meandered past again about half an hour later.

The sun crawled its way below the hills, adorning the sky in brilliant pinks and purple - richer than a normal sunset because of all the smoke in the sky. Amber jiggled her legs and ground her teeth. Even after the sun disappeared, the last rays of light and the humid heat in the air lingered. A swarm of mosquitos feasted on their bare arms and legs.

'I wish it was winter,' she muttered, slapping a mosquito on her leg and smearing blood down her thigh.

'We'd be freezing our arses off,' Bec said, her eyes on the university.

'I'm not sure that would be worse.'

The cottage and drifting ferry vanished as the summer twilight gave way to night. Lights shone in the university buildings, making a patchwork of shadows and light within the fence. Outside the fence it was pitch black.

A small, gnarled banksia clung to the edge of the retaining wall. Its flower spikes were black against the night sky, reminding Amber of the baddies in a childhood book, but there was nothing scary about this banksia. The baddies were on the other side of the fence.

The soldiers didn't reappear. Amber couldn't bear to wait any longer. 'Perhaps they've gone for dinner.' She slung the hiking child carrier over one shoulder and picked up her tablet with the other hand.

Bec looked unconvinced, but followed as Amber slid around the retaining wall and up the grass slope. Amber stopped in front of the fence where it was hidden behind the grey building. Bec dropped to her knees and began cutting the wire.

The sound of voices drifted to them. Amber grabbed Bec's arm as the soldiers approached. It was too late to return to the retaining wall. They flattened themselves against the grass. Amber sent up an urgent prayer that the darkness would hide them.

The soldiers were deep in conversation.

'Ahhh, he's a complete wanker,' said one, with a broad north Queensland drawl.

'You want to watch who you say that to,' the other replied, 'You don't want to attract the Boneheads' attention.'

The soldiers were close enough that Amber could see the Queenslander shiver in the lights from the buildings. 'They give me the willies.'

'They give everyone the willies.'

'Ever seen them fight?'

'Yeah, once. Just in training, not for real.'

'Fucking scary, ay.'

'Shit yeah. Faster than any human I've ever seen. And strong, too. Everyone reckons they can't be killed.'

'Yeah, but if I was them, I'd tell everyone I couldn't be killed, too. Stop people from trying to kill me, ay.'

'I'm not sure any human could kill them anyway.'

The soldier's voices receded as they passed on.

Bec took a deep breath and returned to her cutting. 'Done.' She dropped the bolt cutters in her pack. 'Where are the soldiers?'

'Nowhere in sight.'

'Good enough.' She tossed her pack and the carrier through the hole, then slid through. Amber swallowed as she followed, her impatience replaced with fear.

They shouldered their bags and crept up the hill, past a roundabout with a small tree growing in the centre, surrounded by low plants.

'Where to?' Bec asked.

Amber stared at the collection of buildings nearby. Her stomach clenched. How would they find Oliver? 'Don't know.'

'Let's start searching, then.' Bec lifted her chin and strode towards the tall, modern building in front of them. The wall facing them was raised above the ground and made of glass panes. Light flooded out onto the cement and asphalt in front of it. Bec walked to the left of the building, skirting the lit area, and squinted into the light. Amber trotted to catch up. The windows showed several desks in front of shelves of books - a large library. All the lights were on, but the room was devoid of life. It struck Amber as creepy.

They moved around the building, past a cafe on the corner with large white umbrellas shading small outdoor tables and chairs. On this side, large blinds covered the library windows. Light spilled from the edges and underneath the blinds. In contrast to the light-filled library, an older brick building opposite was swathed in darkness. Amber stepped into the surrounding garden beds to peer into the windows, but couldn't see anything. Bec risked stepping closer to the library and ducked down to peek in the bottom of a window where the blind wasn't fully closed. She hissed at Amber, beckoning her over.

Amber crossed to her side. 'What?' she whispered.

'Oliver's not the only child they've taken.'

Amber snuck a glance in the window. Six rows of three children slept in sleeping bags on gym mats on the red carpeted floor. Some were restless, but most seemed to be fast asleep. She wasn't familiar with children older than Oliver, but they looked primary school age. Two soldiers sat on desk chairs near low bookshelves, frowning at something on the ground between them.

'What the hell?' Amber breathed.

Bec bit her lip. 'It's one way to gain control of the population. Make sure no-one with kids dares to resist you.'

'Or grandkids,' Amber croaked.

Bec nodded. 'Then you just need to find a way to terrify the rest of us.' She took another peak in the window.

'Don't suppose you saw Oliver?'

'Those kids are older than him. Maybe he's somewhere else in the library.'

Amber slid around the building, checking two more windows. A long porch roof with a wave design extended out over a tall, glass-panelled entrance. It was as bright as daylight under the porch. Diagonally opposite was another brightly lit brick building. A verandah with a glass roof and glass balustrade jutted out from the building and an old chimney rose high above it.

Bec put a hand on her arm. She jumped, and bestowed a furious glare on Bec, who didn't notice.

'Let's keep away from the light,' Bec breathed into her ear.

They skirted around the lit areas, between two low, sculpted hedges. The sound of children's voices cut through the silent night air, and the light from a large torch shone towards them. They jumped backwards and tripped up the stairs of another darkened building with a steeply sloping roof on one side.

The voices increased in volume. Bec paused outside a brown painted door with the stylised female picture on it to indicate a toilet. She pushed the handle, and it opened. They ducked inside. To their left was a sink with two basins. A wall hid the toilets. They put their ears to the door, straining to hear.

Amber jumped when a male voice spoke just outside.

'I'll wait for you here.'

Amber cursed under her breath. They were trapped. She and Bec ran to the back. There were two brown toilet doors. They squeezed into the one furthest from the door and held their breath. They heard the sigh of the heavy door being pushed open and then swinging closed. Amber hugged her tablet to her chest and stared at a bare noticeboard on the back of the door. She prayed that they wouldn't be seen.

There was silence for a long time. Then the door of the cubicle swung open. A pre-teen girl with unruly, thick blonde hair looked at them; a younger girl with tight red curls and similar facial features clinging to her side. The blonde had the awkward, bony look of a child going through a growth spurt. They had bare feet and identical cheap cotton pyjamas with cutesy cartoon characters on them - too young for the older girl.

The redhead's eyes were wide and fearful, but the blonde tilted her head and gave them a calculating look. She extracted her arm from the younger girl's grip and pushed her towards the other cubicle. 'Go to the toilet, Lucy.' Lucy opened her mouth to argue. The blonde narrowed her eyes in a glare that was even more fearsome than the one Amber had given Bec. Lucy did what she was told.

'What are you doing here?' the blonde demanded in a whisper. Bec glanced at Amber, who hesitated. The blonde gave her a similar glare to the one she'd given Lucy. 'There's a soldier waiting for us just outside. I can call him anytime, you know.'

She seemed too smart to buy any lie that Amber could make up on the spot. 'I'm looking for my son, Oliver. He's a baby.' She swiped her tablet and held up a picture of Oliver. 'Have you seen him?'

'No.' She tossed her wild hair. 'There's a lot of kids here. But I can tell you which building the little kids are in.'

'That would be wonderful,' Amber gushed, 'Thank you!'

She lifted her chin. 'I'll only tell you if you take Lucy an' me out of here. And help us find our mum and Nick. And if you don't, I'll tell the soldier that you're in here.'

Amber stiffened. 'What?'

The blonde met her gaze. 'You heard me.'

Amber turned to Bec, her eyes wide. Bec met the blonde's calculating look with one of her own. 'Do you have a name?'

'Alice.'

'And your Mum and - who was it, Nick?'

'Our stepdad.'

'Your Mum and Nick, where are they, then?'

Alice's face crumpled for a moment, but she regained her self possession and glared at them. 'The soldiers took them. They put them in a four-wheel drive, and us in a car, and brought us here.'

Amber's voice squeaked. 'You don't know where the soldiers took them, but you expect us to find them?

'Yes.' Alice clenched her fists. 'You promise, or I'll call that soldier.'

Amber and Bec exchanged glances. Amber had no desire to be saddled with two children - or a futile mission to track down their parents - but Alice didn't seem to be bluffing.

'We might not be able to find them.' Bec was blunt. 'But we can promise to do our best to look for them.'

Alice bit her lip, then nodded.

'Deal,' Bec said, 'I'm Bec. She's Amber.'

Amber couldn't believe they'd been outgunned by a pre-teen. She scowled at Alice as Lucy came out of the cubicle, giving them a scared look on her way to the basin to wash her hands. There was a bang on the door. 'You finished yet?' Lucy jumped and scuttled back to Alice without washing.

Alice raised her voice. 'Coming!' She spoke so fast that Amber had trouble understanding her. 'Lucy an' me will go back with him to the room where we're supposed to be sleeping. You follow, and we'll double back and meet you.'

'How are you going to get away from the soldiers?'

She looked scornful. 'Any idiot could get away from them. They don't think any of us have the guts to escape.' She tossed her hair again, gathered up Lucy and left the toilet.

Amber took a deep breath. The situation was getting out of hand. Bec pushed her towards the door. 'We'd better follow.'

Amber eased the door open, scared that the soldier might be waiting outside, but he and the two girls were heading back towards the library. Bec and Amber watched from the shadows as they walked towards the glass doors under the porch roof. The soldier tapped a card against a card reader. The doors slid open and they disappeared inside.

Amber had a long drink from her water bottle. 'How the hell are we supposed to find their parents?'

'I'll put out some feelers through my network.'

Amber squinted at the white light blazing out from the glass entrance. What if they didn't come back again? 'We're wasting time.'

'They've been all of two minutes.'

'What if they can't get away, and we run out of time to find Ollie?'

'We have to wait. If they come and we're not here, that Alice will tell the soldiers we're here.'

'Little shit,' Amber growled, sitting down to wait for the second time that night. Where had Alice learned to negotiate like that? She wished she'd been that self-possessed at Alice's age.

Twenty interminable minutes later the doors slid open again. Alice and Lucy dashed out, holding hands, and ran straight towards them down the lit pathway. Bec grimaced and pulled Amber deeper into the shadows as the girls joined them.

After agonising about how long the girls were taking, Amber

now felt suspicious about how quickly they'd come. 'How did you get away?'

'We're sleeping near the door. We pretended to go to sleep, and nicked out when the soldiers stopped watching. They were playing cards.' Her voice was full of disdain.

'They didn't lock the door?'

'I told you those soldiers don't think we'll try to escape. And I don't even know if they can lock it from the inside. Are you going to keep blabbering all night?'

Bec made a sweeping gesture with her hand. 'Lead on.'

Alice trotted back the way they'd come from and around the corner of the library. Bec and Amber had to jog to catch up. Alice halted at the edge of the library and pointed across the road at a small building with a curved flat roof and red brick wall. 'The little kids are in there.'

Amber narrowed her eyes, thinking about how to approach the building.

'Amber!' Bec's voice reeked of pure desperation. Amber swung around. A rifle was pointed at her head.

At the other end of the rifle was a beefy soldier who reminded Amber of a nightclub security guard. A younger, well-muscled soldier with a dragon tattoo on his neck was pointing an identical rifle at Bec. A third soldier stood further back, pointing a high-powered torch in their direction. The light made her eyes water. Amber put one hand over her eyes and turned away. Her gaze fell on Alice. She had moved back, out of the light, her arms wrapped around Lucy's chest.

A noise made Amber turn back towards the light. She could just make out four more figures approaching, three of them taller than any human. Her breath caught in her throat. Boneheads.

The Boneheads stopped just outside the circle of light, but the smaller figure approached. Amber gave a start as the light fell onto his face. It was the red-haired soldier who had taken Oliver away.

The beefy soldier stiffened. 'Lieutenant Colonel Nichols.' His voice oozed dislike.

Nichols surveyed them with his flinty eyes.

'I know her,' he said, pointing his index finger at Bec, 'She's one of the terrorists.' He smiled at Bec. 'We already caught your friends.'

'We don't have any friends,' Bec said, wrinkling her brow.

Nichols gave her a disbelieving sneer.

'And her?' The soldier with the dragon tattoo nodded at Amber.

He shrugged. 'If she's with the other three, she's a terrorist too. Put them in with the others.' He started to walk away, then turned back, waving at Alice and Lucy. 'And deal with the brats.'

'We're not terrorists!' Amber said, 'You know me! You took my son! We came to get him.'

The red-haired soldier didn't turn around. Dragon and Beefy prodded them with their guns.

'Move!' Beefy said. Amber looked for Alice and Lucy. They melted back into the shadows. The soldiers seemed to have forgotten them.

Beefy hit her on the back of the head with the rifle. 'I said, move!' Pain exploded in the back of her head and her eyes filled with tears. She stumbled. The tablet slipped out of her hands, smashing on the ground.

Amber reached for it - her only way of tracking Oliver if they'd taken him elsewhere. The soldier with the torch beat her to it. He pressed some keys. 'Broken. Nichols'll be pissed - it might have had evidence on it.'

'So don't tell him,' Beefy grunted.

He forced Amber ahead of him across the campus. One large hand squeezed her neck and pushed her forward, so hard she had to focus all her attention on keeping her feet under her. She didn't have a chance to think about escaping. The light from the high-powered torch bounced in front of them. She was aware of being forced past the library. The torch light fell on a giant chessboard, its pieces still in position from the last game, with the white queen, a white knight and a white rook holding the black king in checkmate.

Beefy forced her past an open, wood-panelled pavilion attached to the side of the building with the tall chimney that she'd seen earlier. Most of the buildings around and behind it were in darkness, but lights shone in a long, brown brick building with a verandah at the front. A soldier was guarding a green painted door. He was thin and weedy compared to Beefy and Dragon, but he had a firm grip on his rifle and an alert gaze.

Beefy stopped in front of him. 'Another couple for you.'

The guard grunted and put a key into the door behind him. Beefy propelled her through the door, followed by Dragon, Bec and the soldier with the torch, who flicked it off as they entered.

The room was strange. The floor was raised in parts, with wooden barriers along the raised parts, and seating in front. It took Amber a moment to realise what she was looking at - a pretend courtroom, probably for the law students to practice in.

The soldier with the torch was still fiddling with her tablet. Shrugging, he tossed it into a wastepaper basket near the door. Amber moved towards it, but Beefy stopped her.

'Drop your packs and take off your shoes,' he barked.

Amber let the carrier fall to the floor and pushed one sneaker off using the other foot, maintaining a wary eye on Beefy. Once she had both sneakers off, he patted her down. Dragon did the same to Bec. Amber cringed as Beefy's large hands touched her body. Surely only women were allowed to do this to women? The PM seemed to have done away with ordinary laws.

Amber met Beefy's eyes. 'We don't have any weapons. We're not terrorists. We just came to get my son. That red-haired man took him.'

Beefy shrugged and turned to the guard. He unlocked another green painted door behind them, pushing it open to a bare room. All the furniture had been removed. An Asian man and Caucasian woman were sitting on the floor inside the enclosure. They jumped up as the door opened, their eyes narrowed. A large, red bucket was wedged in the corner, with a single roll of toilet paper next to it. Even if she hadn't seen the toilet paper, Amber would have known the bucket was serving as a toilet, from its smell. The ceiling sported two cameras, and there were metal bars on the windows.

Beefy pushed Bec and her inside, and locked the door behind them.

Amber rested her head against the door. She'd failed Ollie. If they killed her, he'd be stuck here. Adam wouldn't know where he was. There'd be no-one to rescue him.

'Here.' The blonde woman held out a rag. Amber stared at it. 'For your head,' she said.

Amber realised that her head was throbbing. She patted the back of her head with the rag. It came away with patches of red blood. 'Thank you.' She pressed the rag harder against her head.

The woman nodded. She wore her blonde hair parted on the left and pulled back into a low bun at the back of head. Her skin was pale, except for her plump cheeks, which were sunburnt. She was frowning, but the wrinkles that emanated from the side of her eyes suggested that it was more common for her to smile. She was wearing a thick, high vis shirt, long pants and bare feet.

The Asian man wore similar clothes. His dark hair was cut short, like a cap around his head. A large bruise marred his long, thin face. Amber's eyes were drawn to his thick eyebrows. They seemed too large for his face and its matching long, thin nose. There were puffy bags under his eyes. He was tall for an Asian man, with a straight back. He sat back down on the floor and leant against the wall. He exuded a relaxed, confident air; not what she would expect from a prisoner of monsters.

The woman joined him on the floor. Unlike the man, she seemed aware of their precarious position. Her eyes danced around the room, resting on the security camera above them, on Bec and on Amber herself.

Amber pulled the rag away from her head, staring at the blood. She thought about curling up into a ball and wailing, but the despair was leaving her and fury taking his place. I will get Ollie back. Amber pulled herself upright, clinging to the thought. I will get Ollie back.

Amber rattled the door hard. It didn't give. Glass panels surrounded the door. She kicked the one next to the door, then rammed her body against it, hard, but only succeeded in adding bruises to her hips and shoulders.

She turned to the window. Bec moved out of her way, giving her a wary look. The bars on the window weren't new, but they were solid. She checked each bar in turn, then turned to the walls. The outer wall was solid, painted brick. It seemed unlikely to have any flaws, but she systematically checked every brick anyway.

'There's no way out,' the Asian man said after a while, 'Do you think we'd be sitting here if there was?'

She ignored him and continued her careful circuit of the room.

'Stubborn, isn't she?'

'Pig-headed, more like,' Bec said. She sat down on the floor next to them and picked at a loose thread in the industrial beige carpet.

'I'm Ren. She's Josie.' He pointed his chin at one of the cameras. Bec nodded to show she understood his warning.

'Bec, Amber.'

Amber checked the interior walls, which seemed much less solid, but no amount of kicking made a dint on them. She had to concede that there was no way out. She threw herself down next to Bec.

'No escape?' Bec said.

Josie gave her a sympathetic look.

Amber lay down on the well-worn carpet, turned her back to them and pretended to sleep.

'We should follow her lead,' Ren said, 'Get some sleep while we can.'

Josie sighed. 'I'll never be able to sleep.' She gave Ren a glare. 'I know you can sleep through everything.'

'You worry too much.' Ren stretched out on the ground and closed his eyes.

Josie stuck her middle finger up at him, but she followed his lead. Bec did too.

There was silence for a long time, then Bec whispered into Amber's ear. 'That was interesting, what that soldier said.'

'Huh?'

'The one patrolling the fence. That if he was a Bonehead, he'd tell everyone Boneheads couldn't be killed, so that people wouldn't try.'

Amber sat up, directing the cold fury inside her at Bec. 'We know they can't be killed,' she hissed, 'Or are you forgetting the gunmen at Martin Place? And I saw some resistance group try to blow them up with grenades, for fuck's sake.'

'Yeah, but maybe there's another way to kill them?'

'I can't believe you're thinking about that now! They're probably going to kill us in the morning.'

Bec shrugged. Amber curled into a ball. Tears leaked out of her eyes. Once she started crying, she couldn't stop.

'They're probably not going to kill us,' Ren said, breaking the silence, 'They could have done that already, instead of locking us up.'

Amber gritted her teeth. If she wanted the opinion of

overconfident eavesdroppers, she would have asked for it. She curled into a tighter ball. Her eyelids closed and she couldn't force them open again. She slipped into a light sleep.

Seven

Amber woke to aching breasts. It was still dark. She crept over to the toilet bucket, frowning at the security cameras. There was no way to do this modestly. The smell from the bucket made her retch. She turned her face away, pulled up her shirt, unclipped her bra and hand expressed the excess breastmilk into the bucket. She blinked back tears, trying not to think about Oliver crying for his milk.

The others woke over the next couple of hours. They spoke in brief grunts, conscious of the security cameras. Amber's stomach growled. She paced around the room, hoping a soldier would bring them food. Not long after ten am four soldiers slammed their way into the room, but they had other things than food on their minds. Each soldier strong-armed a prisoner out of the room. Dragon grasped Bec's arm, but this time Beefy took charge of Ren, leaving Amber to a young, wiry soldier with shaved blonde hair.

The soldier had a lighter grip than Beefy. Amber relaxed her muscles and dropped her head forward, every inch the abject prisoner. As they reached the wastepaper basket where Dragon had thrown her tablet, she wrenched free and dived towards it. The soldier cursed and lunged to grab her again. She knocked the bin flying and fell on her knees, staring at the hole in the top as the bin rolled back and forth on the carpet before coming to a stop. It was empty.

Beefy stopped and raised his eyebrows at the soldier, keeping a firm grip on Ren. 'What the hell?'

The soldier yanked Amber up by one arm, his grip burning her skin. 'Don't ask me.'

Beefy bared his teeth at Amber. 'You want to cause problems? You can go first.'

The wiry soldier didn't give her a chance to worry about what Beefy meant. He pushed her out of the building. The hot bitumen seared her bare feet. The smoke had cleared at last, and the full strength of the sun beat down on them, glinting off the silver roofs and blinding her. She tried to walk on her toes, but the soldier kept pushing her off balance.

The university grounds looked very different in the daylight. Buildings were dotted among extensive green lawns - more than twenty, of assorted sizes, shapes and designs, from tall, modern multi-story buildings, to colonial-style heritage buildings and small cottages. Most had walls in similar earthy colours - red or brown brick, yellow sandstone - and silver metal roofs. The effect was soothing, but Amber's stomach clenched. She wished she'd used the bucket in the prison room before the soldiers had come.

The soldiers walked around the pavilion that Amber had noticed the day before, with the antique chimney stack rising above it, and stopped out the front. Amber blinked at the darkened area inside. The building had been turned into a restaurant. The pavilion was empty, apart from some chairs and tables that had been moved to the back, out of the way. As she watched, three Boneheads walked out of the restaurant to the front of the pavilion - just metres from her. Her whole body shook. The bony plates rising from their noses and alien black eyes were even more terrifying up close. The Bonehead closest to her was as intimidating as the ones she'd seen in Martin Place and Epping, with a rich mahogany bony plate. The other two were about half a head shorter and their bony plates were the same dull grey colour as their skin. Females? Or juveniles? Their clothes were identical to the ones she'd seen before, down to the long, thin, black sword scabbards. They weren't carrying automatic weapons; she assumed it was because they had soldiers to do the shooting for them.

The two smaller Boneheads unfurled what looked like a long, coiled rope, with a cable running behind it into the restaurant. The large Bonehead beckoned someone out of sight.

'I want this to go out live.' The Bonehead spoke with an odd, flat accent.

A blonde man moved into view. Amber stiffened. Mike Davies - Bonehead collaborator, and sexist bastard. He turned and met her eyes. Her contempt trickled away. In person, he didn't look so young and fresh. His eyes held a haunted look and there were dark shadows underneath. There was a bruise on the side of his face that someone had tried to cover with make-up.

A young cameraman followed him, with long hair in a topknot and a neat beard that jarred with the lines etched into his face, making him look older. He pointed the camera towards the prisoners. Amber ducked her head, regretting the short hairstyle that didn't hide her face.

She lifted her head again as the cameraman pointed his camera at Mike, who spoke clearly. 'Last night, after a fifteen-hour manhunt, the Law Enforcers apprehended four of the terrorists responsible for the bombing of Governor Macquarie Tower in Sydney.'

Amber's mouth fell open. Were they really pinning the bombing on her and Bec? She turned to give Bec an incredulous look, but Bec didn't meet her gaze. She was standing straight, her chin lifted, glaring at the Boneheads. Dragon had one of her arms in a firm grip.

Amber turned back. The cameraman was pointing the camera at Mike, but looking at Amber. He gave her a sad smile.

She missed the last of Mike's introduction. The cameraman

turned the camera towards the large Bonehead. 'The four terrorists were apprehended breaking into a secure government facility,' the Bonehead said with his strange accent, 'Our intelligence indicated that the terrorists were planning another attack on this facility. To anyone else who might think to commit such acts on Australian soil, I say think again. If you don't, we will find you, and you will receive the same treatment as these terrorists you see before you.'

Treatment? A queasy feeling rose from Amber's stomach.

Beefy nodded at the soldier holding Amber. 'I said she could go first.'

The soldier pushed Amber forward into the pavilion and down onto the ground. She winced as her knees scraped the concrete, but her breath eased in the cooler air. The large Bonehead held out its hand, and one of the smaller ones put the rope in it. Behind the Boneheads, she made out Nichols, standing at the edge of the pavilion, past the chairs and tables. He was a picture of nonchalance, with his arms crossed in front of him and a small smile on his face.

A soldier led out a snaking line of children. The children lined up in rows in front of the chairs and tables. Amber estimated there were at least thirty children of all ages.

The large Bonehead didn't wait for the last of the children to settle. It swung the rope down against her upper back, flicking it in the way a stockman would flick a stock whip. As the rope landed on her back, fire ripped through her body. She couldn't think. She couldn't breathe.

Then it was gone, as the Bonehead flicked it back into the air. Now she could think again, but she wished she couldn't. Where the rope had touched her back, the skin was on fire. The Bonehead was getting ready to swing the rope again, and this time she knew how much it was going to hurt.

The rope landed. Her whole body was flooded with pain.

As the rope lifted again, she gasped for air. Tears streamed down her face. Through the tears, she could hear a commotion. The large Bonehead turned, irritation on its face. Someone was pushing through the neat lines of children. Some of the children were complaining, and others were moving back out of the way. She lifted her head, blinking, trying to focus through the pain and tears.

A girl had pushed her way to the front, directly in front of Amber. Amber barely noticed that it was Alice, with Lucy holding on tight to the back of her infantile pyjamas. Amber's entire focus was on the chubby, black-haired infant that Alice was holding up.

Oliver. Somehow, Alice had found him.

She had to get to him.

The large Bonehead turned away from the children, and brought the rope down again.

Please help me! Amber wasn't sure who she was crying out to. In her mind, she reached out. Through her fear and pain, she felt a sense of timelessness and strength, somewhere just outside her reach. Time seemed to slow down. The rope landed on her back, but this time it moved as though it was pushing through a thick liquid. There was only a dull sense of pain across her back. She twisted around. The rope swung back up as though on a slow-motion replay on television. She grabbed it with her right hand. She could see the shock appear on the Bonehead's face as she pulled the rope out of its hand. She flicked the rope with all her strength towards the Bonehead, but it sidestepped out of the way. The side of the rope caught one of the smaller Boneheads, who was knocked over, curling in on itself in pain.

The large Bonehead lunged for her, baring its teeth in anger. She flicked the rope again, making it writhe like a snake across the ground. The Bonehead jumped back, trying to avoid the rope.

The third Bonehead drew its sword in a single, smooth

movement and charged her from behind, but time was still moving slowly. She had more than enough time to turn and face it. The blade of the sword reared up in her face. It was almost a metre long, slightly curved and sharpened along one side. It swept up and ended in a sharp point. The Bonehead held the hilt with both hands.

She flicked the rope and coiled it around the Bonehead's feet. It fell with a shriek, and dropped the sword. She swooped forward, dropped the rope to seize the sword and swung around as the largest Bonehead leapt at her with its sword drawn.

It raised the sword above its head, but before it could swing, she dove at it, stabbing the sword where its heart would be if it was human. It screamed as she pulled it out and hunched forward over the wound, letting its sword trail on the ground. It was still standing, so either Boneheads were nothing like humans or she'd missed its heart, but it was enough to stop it for a moment. The other two Boneheads came at her together, still in slow motion, one with a sword and the other holding the end of the rope. She jumped over the rope as though she was playing a skipping game from her childhood, and slashed the sword from left to right across the waist of the Bonehead that was wielding it. Its eyes went blank and it slumped to the floor.

The last Bonehead roared in fury, but it had learnt from the others, and approached with its sword held low across its body. She backed away, and almost tripped over the rope again. The Bonehead continued to stalk her. She bent, switched the sword to her left hand, scooped up the rope with her right hand and threw it with all her strength. The Bonehead jumped over the rope, but was off-balance when it landed, and she took the opportunity. Raising the sword above her head with both hands, she drove it into the Bonehead's throat. Red blood sprayed out, splattering her. The Bonehead dropped and didn't move again.

Time sped up. Her vision blurred and her legs wobbled. She retched, and swallowed down vomit. Her back was on fire, but the rest of her body was icy cold. Pain seared through her right hand, which still gripped the black, leather-wrapped sword hilt. She tossed the sword away. It clattered on the ground. She wanted to collapse on the ground herself, but forced herself to take off, her bare feet slapping on the concrete.

People were shouting on all sides, but nobody stopped her. She snatched Oliver out of Alice's arms. She heard the crack and thump of gunfire, and ducked, but it wasn't directed at her. Risking a quick glance behind her, she saw Ren and Josie sheltering on the edge of the pavilion and firing at several soldiers. She couldn't fathom how they'd overpowered the soldiers guarding them, until she realised that some of those soldiers were firing alongside them. She couldn't see Bec.

Bec will get herself out, Amber told herself, but she felt a hard knot of guilt in her stomach.

'Stay with me,' she shouted to Alice and Lucy, shouldering her way through the lines of children and knocking over several chairs. She sprinted back towards the building where they'd been held overnight and through a gap between it and the building next to it, leaping down a short flight of stairs. Alice and Lucy pounded behind her.

She found herself in a small, tree-lined courtyard. She could hear shouts and gunfire behind them, but nothing close. She guessed that the soldiers were distracted by Ren, Josie and their friends. She tried to think of a brilliant escape plan, but the only thing that came to mind was the hole Bec had cut in the fence. She ran through the courtyard to a wide lawn. Across the lawn she could see the side of the library.

The shouting increased in volume. She tried to speed up, but her legs felt weak. She zigzagged to her left, onto the verandah of a small, grey-cement rendered building with the ubiquitous sloping silver roof. Bullets slammed into a wall ahead of them, sending chips of render flying. She felt a sharp pain and blood trickled down her left leg. She dragged Alice and Lucy around the corner. Through the windows, she could see at least three soldiers firing in their direction.

The soldiers stopped firing. The sudden silence was shocking. 'Amber Yu!' Her name reverberated through the university's public address system. 'You have no chance of surviving this. Surrender now, and we may let the children live.' Over the whining speaker, she could hear the sneer in Nichols' voice.

Lucy whimpered. Amber looked down into her scared eyes, and clutched Oliver to her chest. For the first time since Nichols had taken Oliver, her determination deserted her. Her shoulders slumped. She had to surrender. For the kids. For Oliver.

'Will these help?'

She looked down and swore. Alice was holding two grenades. 'Where the hell did you get those?'

Alice shrugged. 'Lying around.'

The lie was so brazen that Amber was speechless. She held out her left hand. Alice placed the grenades in it. She stared at them - receptacles of death. Bile rose in her throat and her face paled.

'Last chance, Amber Yu. You don't really have a choice, do you?' Nichols was almost chortling.

She couldn't let them take Oliver again. Balancing Oliver against her left side, she ripped out the ring on the grenade, and flung it around the corner towards the soldiers. As soon as it left her hand, she pulled out the ring on the second. There was a deafening bang and the building's windows shattered. She flung the second grenade after the first.

'Let's go,' she screamed before it had even landed, and erupted out from behind the building, zigzagging towards the hole in the fence. She heard another large explosion. She dared a glance over her right shoulder. Alice and Lucy were keeping pace with her. The grey building was swathed in smoke and dust. She couldn't see the soldiers.

As she scrambled through the hole in the fence, a figure stepped out in front of her. She bit back a shriek.

'Fuck, I'm glad to see you.'

Bec. Amber sucked in mouthfuls of air, her heart rate slowing.

Bec was looking behind her. 'What the hell happened? Did the resistance fighters blow something up?'

'Must have,' she lied, heaving Lucy and Alice through the hole.

Bec thrust the hiking child carrier into Amber's arms. Her shoes and socks were stuffed in the top.

'You got our bags!' She strapped Oliver into the carrier, fumbling with the straps in her haste, and pulled her shoes onto her battered feet without socks.

'They were still in the room next to our prison. I don't think the soldiers even bothered to search them.'

Amber glanced at the grey building. Smoke and dust still hid it from sight. Several rabbits belted past them down the hill.

She swung the carrier onto her back and almost screamed as the straps hit the welts from the rope. Gasping, she swung the carrier around so that it was on her front. It wasn't designed to be worn frontwards - so tall she couldn't see past it. Oliver howled.

She could hear gunfire. The resistance fighters were busy.

'That won't slow them down forever.' Bec had turned away from the university and was scanning the river.

'Ferry.' She pointed to the Rivercat they had seen bobbing around earlier.

'You've got to be kidding,' Amber said, but Bec was gone - bounding down the hill. 'How the hell are you going to start it?' she called.

Alice and Lucy hesitated, looking at Amber. She didn't have a better plan. She waved at the hill. 'Go, go!' They flung themselves down the hill. Amber caught up to them a heartbeat later.

'Can you swim?' she gasped.

Alice nodded. 'Lucy's not that good.'

'I am, too,' Lucy said. Amber blinked, as surprised as if one of the rabbits had spoken. She'd almost forgotten that Lucy and Alice were separate people.

Bec waded into the water, then flung herself forward and swam with long, confident strokes, unhindered by the pack on her back. The two girls eased themselves into the river, sinking into the thick mud.

Amber pulled a rain cover out of the pocket of the carrier and wrapped it around the bottom of the carrier before following. Thigh deep in water, she sank into the river, slipping the child carrier off her arms and holding it upright in front of her. 'You can hang on to this,' she said to Alice and Lucy. Alice nudged Lucy, who put an arm on the side of the carrier. Alice threw herself into the water and swam after Bec. Amber held the carrier like a kickboard, kicking her legs to propel them forward. Lucy copied her. Oliver stared at the water, his mouth open, the tears drying on his cheeks.

Cold river water splashed the welts on her back, offering bursts of respite from the scorching pain. She turned her right hand so it was under the water and gave a small moan of relief.

Bec reached the Rivercat and gripped the port bow, clambering up onto it. She dropped her pack into the ferry and waited for Alice, dragging her up onto the bow.

Amber's teeth were chattering. An engine revved behind her. What now? An army truck rounded the fence. Bec dropped down flat on the bow and Alice disappeared inside the cabin. Amber kicked harder, reaching the bow. Treading water, Amber pushed the carrier up the bow for Bec to grab, followed by Lucy.

She scrambled up herself.

Soldiers leapt out of the truck. They weren't looking at the water. 'Quick.' Bec seized the carrier and flung herself into the cabin. Amber and Lucy tumbled in after her. Oliver bawled.

There was a bubbler in the cabin. Amber fell on it and gulped water.

Bec knelt between two green, fabric-covered seats next to the port side cabin windows, and lifted her head just high enough to peer out the window. 'They haven't seen us. They're searching the bank.'

Alice and Lucy sat cross-legged on the grey carpet in the aisle, where they couldn't be seen through the windows. Amber wiped water off her chin and joined them, lifting Oliver out of the carrier. 'How can they have failed to notice a massive ferry?'

'Maybe they're used to seeing it bobbing about? The ferry's drifting downstream - the tide must be going out.' Bec checked the window on the starboard side of the cabin. 'No-one on the other bank. I'm going up to the bridge.' She ducked out the cabin door.

Amber fumbled with her bra strap and put Oliver on her breast. He stopped shrieking and gulped. His body was warm against her skin, which still felt icy cold. She buried her face in his hair, drinking in his smell. Tears ran down her face. She had Oliver back.

When he finished drinking, she reached around him to open the bottom of the child carrier. Some water had seeped in, but not as much as she had feared. The rain cover and heavy nylon of the pack had kept most of the contents dry. She extracted a wrinkled T-shirt. Balancing Oliver on her knees, she slid her tank top over her head. She bit back a scream when it caught against one of the burns on her back, and swore under her breath. The Bonehead's rope had cut the back of the tank top into ribbons. The cold river water had diluted, but not removed, the blood splatters on the front. They had turned a light brown colour. She screwed the top up, dropped it on the floor and eased the clean T-shirt over her back.

An icy chill had seeped into her bones. She pulled a fleece jacket over the T-shirt and crawled over to the port side window that Bec had been looking through earlier.

The ferry was drifting closer to the bank. The noise from the university had died down. Sporadic gunfire and the occasional shout drifted across the water. She could see a few soldiers up and downstream of the university.

'I'm going to check on Bec.'

'We can mind the baby,' Alice offered.

Amber didn't think she would ever let Oliver go again. 'Thanks, it's fine.'

She slithered out of the cabin with Oliver nestled under her chin. The bridge door handle was hanging at a funny angle. She pushed and the door swung open.

Bec was sprawled on the floor, her back against the wall, staring at the console. The bolt cutters were on the floor in front of her. Her voice was hollow. 'I was hoping the ferry master might have left the keys in the ignition if he was in a hurry. Or maybe he'd been killed, and his body would be here. But no luck.'

Amber's mouth dropped open. 'You were hoping to find a dead body, so you could pick its pockets?'

'Oh well.' Bec waved a hand. 'I don't think we'll be able to get it started. Unless you know how to hotwire a ferry?'

'I guess we could search the cabin for keys.'

Bec rubbed both hands over her face, but she picked up the bolt cutters and got to her feet to follow Amber. Alice and Lucy helped them search the cabin, with no success.

Bec started to laugh.

Amber glared at her over the top of Oliver's head. 'What on earth is funny?'

There was a slight edge of hysteria to Bec's giggles. 'This has got to be the worst getaway vehicle ever,' she managed to spit out.

Amber clenched her fists. 'You're the one who thought we should escape on this floating death trap. We're sitting ducks here!'

Bec's giggles trailed off. 'Have you looked out the window? We would have been sitting ducks out there, too.'

'So now what? We just wait for the soldiers to come and pick us up?'

Bec's face reddened. 'And what was your plan? Escape on bicycles? Dinking Alice and Lucy, I presume?'

Amber knew they were only fighting because they were scared, but she couldn't seem to stop. 'We wouldn't be here at all if you hadn't convinced Zhou to piss the Boneheads off!'

'Oh sure, this is all my fault.' Bec's voice dripped with sarcasm. 'I didn't kill Boneheads. Nobody has killed Boneheads. Congratulations - you just made yourself enemy number one.'

Amber's legs wobbled. The fight went out of her. She slumped on the floor. 'You can't kill a Bonehead. They were probably just injured.' Her voice was weak.

Bec, Alice and Lucy just looked at her. Her eyes were drawn to the tank top crumpled on the floor, with its damning light brown spatters. In her mind, she saw the two Boneheads falling over.

She was a killer. A murderer. It seemed impossible, unimaginable. 'But we saw Boneheads being shot at, and it didn't hurt them. I saw some hit by a grenade, and they survived. How can I have killed them?'

Bec shrugged, the anger leaving her eyes. She let out a deep breath and sat down next to Amber.

'The big one might be okay,' Lucy said.

Bec stared at her in surprise, then nodded. 'Yeah, it might.'

Eight

Amber rummaged in the bottom of the child carrier for a damp box of chocolate-coated biscuits. She took several and passed the box around.

Her breathing slowed as she crunched the biscuits, savouring the chocolate flavour. 'What now?'

Bec picked biscuit crumbs from her teeth. 'Keep an eye out. Get off this 'floating death trap' as soon as we get a chance.' She crawled over to the port window.

Amber took the starboard side. The sun reflected off the water, blinding her. She shaded her eyes and gazed at the opposite bank. It was overgrown and deserted. 'It's still clear on this side.'

'It's too far to that bank. The ferry keeps drifting this direction. There's still soldiers on this side, though.'

They drifted towards the two bridges upstream of the university. Amber stared out the window with glazed eyes. Her hand and back were throbbing. She pulled the fleece jacket tighter, still feeling cold. She nibbled on her last biscuit, her eyes half closed.

Bec tossed a question over her shoulder, her eyes still on the water. 'How did you move so fast?'

Amber was jolted out of her torpor. 'What?'

'When you fought those Boneheads. You were like a blur.'

Alice looked up, a biscuit halfway to her mouth. 'I've never seen anyone move as fast as you.'

Amber shoved the last of her biscuit into her mouth and rubbed her hands on her pants. She took her time swallowing.

'It felt like when you have a car accident,' she said after a moment.

Bec turned away from the window and gave her a blank look.

She tried to explain. 'When I first got my licence I had an old car without ABS brakes. I was driving to Armidale one time and a tyre blew on my car, and I remember time slowing down and I had enough time to think to myself 'I need to pump the brake' and do it. It's a thing - time slowing down like that when you have a car accident.'

Bec looked unconvinced. 'I think that's just your brain - working faster in an emergency, or creating more memories, or something. This was different. You moved fast.'

Amber shrugged. She remembered the sense of timelessness she'd felt. What was that? She'd always believed on an intellectual level that there were supernatural forces - she was a Christian, after all. But it was another thing to admit she'd personally experienced something supernatural. And if that thing had helped her to kill the Boneheads, did that mean it was evil? It hadn't felt evil, but it hadn't felt good, either - just neutral. She shivered, and rushed to dismiss the idea.

'It was probably just strength I didn't know I had that came out in a moment of stress. I've heard of that - like people picking up cars to rescue someone trapped undreneath.'

Her eyes back on the water, Bec hadn't noticed her shiver, but Alice had. She narrowed her eyes.

Amber changed the subject. 'Tell us about your mum and stepdad. What are their full names?'

This time Alice didn't lose her self-control. Her voice was wooden, as though she was talking about strangers. 'Elise Nicole Taylor and Nicolas Peter Christou.'

'What work do they do?'

'They're engineers.'

'Working on what?'

Alice bit her lip. 'I don't know. They've got their own company. Sometimes they do projects for the government. And sometimes for other companies.'

'Do you know the name of their company?'

She shook her head. 'They didn't talk about it much.'

'Why did the soldiers take them?' Bec asked, 'Were they involved in the resistance?'

'I don't think so. I don't know why.'

'The soldiers kept shouting at them,' Lucy said, 'About thongs.'

'Thongs?'

'Yeah,' Alice nodded, 'It was strange. They kept asking where the thong was. Mum and Nick didn't seem to think it was a strange question, but they said they didn't know. I don't think the soldiers believed them.'

Amber looked at Bec. 'Any idea what that's about?'

Bec shook her head, looking as bewildered as Amber. 'None whatsoever.' She felt in her pack and pulled out a smartphone. 'I'll see what I can find out.'

Amber's eyes widened. 'Should you do that? What if the soldiers track your mobile?'

'They won't track me on this.' Bec's voice was confident. 'I got it from a friend. It's got burner software on it, they can't link it to me, and everything I do is encrypted. What were their full names again? Elise?'

Bec typed while Alice repeated the names. She kept an eye out the window while searching on her phone. Amber turned back to her own window. A 'friend' had given Bec the phone, she'd been working with Zhou - what else had Bec been up to in the few days since they'd met at Martin Place? Nichols had called her a terrorist - but then, the Boneheads clearly intended to pin Governor Macquarie Tower on them, so that could have been a lie.

Her eyes closed. She blinked them open. They closed again.

'I can keep watch.' Alice was next to her. 'You're falling asleep.'

Amber blinked her eyes open again. Bec was still dividing her attention between the window and the phone.

'Thank you,' she said. She lay down in the aisle with Oliver tucked into her chest and was asleep in minutes.

Bec nudged her awake. 'The ferry's drifted near the bank. I don't think we'll get a better chance to get off.'

Amber struggled to sit up. 'The ferry's near the bank? Soldiers?'

'None that I can see.'

'How long have I been asleep?'

'A couple of hours.'

She looked around. 'Oliver?'

He was sitting on Lucy's lap, giggling as Lucy ran her finger around his palm. 'Round and round the garden, goes the teddy bear -'

'Lucy's entertaining him.'

She forced herself to get up, wincing at the pain. The burning in her back and hand had lessened, but the wounds had stiffened up. Her head spun for a moment. She waited for it to pass, then stumbled to the bubbler and gulped water.

A glance out the window confirmed what Bec had told her - the Rivercat was within a couple of metres of the bank - almost touching the fleshy leaves of the closest mangroves. Beyond the mangroves was a wide grassed area. The cycleway they had ridden along the day before wound through the grass. Behind it, she glimpsed a chain link fence enclosing a grey steel shed. She couldn't place where they were. She doubted they were far from the university - the Rivercat's drift had been slow.

She zipped up the carrier and wrapped it in the rain cover. Lucy brought Oliver to her, and she slipped him into the carrier. Bec shrugged her pack on her back. 'Ready?'

One by one, they slipped over the port bow and half-walked, half-swam through the mud and mangroves to the bank. Bec scouted ahead, keeping within the shrubs and trees, while

Amber struggled out of the mud with the carrier in her arms. Mud covered her shoes and legs, and stuck to the bottom of Alice and Lucy's pyjamas.

'We're right near Rydalmere wharf,' Bec said when they caught up to her. She pointed through the trees to an aqua green sign with Rydalmere in large white letters. 'I can't see any soldiers.'

They crept through the trees. A gangway led to a pontoon with a silver canopy, enclosed by glass panels. There was a shelter on the shore with a canopy in the same aqua green as the sign.

Oliver wriggled, stretching his arms towards Lucy. Amber held onto the carrier, and he wailed. Amber tried to rock him without dropping the carrier, praying that his yells didn't bring soldiers down on them.

Bec looked upwards. 'Do you hear something?'

'I can't hear anything but him,' Amber said, as Oliver continued to cry. But she heard a faint thumping sound in the distance.

'Everyone, under the gangway. Run!' Bec sounded so panicked that they ran, slithering off the riverbank and splashing into the water under the gangway. Oliver howled.

The thumping got louder - a helicopter approaching. Lucy clutched Alice, looking like she wanted to wail like Oliver.

'Can't you make him shut up?' Bec demanded.

Amber glared at her. She put the carrier down on the solid ground under the end of the gangway and took Oliver out, holding him up to her breast. He started sucking.

'Effective,' Bec muttered.

Amber was fuming that Bec had told her to shut Oliver up. 'Is there some reason why you're making us stand knee-deep in water? I don't think anyone in the helicopter would have spotted us under the trees.'

'They've got thermal imaging cameras; they can pick up body heat from the air, even through trees. They shouldn't be able to see us under here.' She knocked the metal gangway above her and shivered. 'I hope. The Boneheads used one of the cameras to capture some friends of mine.'

Amber winced. 'Your friends -'

'They've disappeared.'

The thumping grew louder. The helicopter sounded like it was almost above them. Amber ducked her head, as though it would help hide her. Oliver fell asleep. She clipped her bra back up and held him against her shoulder. Her feet began to go numb from standing in the cold water. She wriggled her toes.

She balanced Oliver with her left arm and plunged her right hand into the water, closing her eyes as the cold water numbed her hand. She considered lying in the water to ease her back, but she still felt so cold, she didn't want to get any colder.

The helicopter noise faded. Bec helped herself to the contents of the carrier. Using the carrier as a table, she spread vegemite on crackers and passed around cracker sandwiches.

The thumping from the helicopter increased. Amber stared up at the gangway, relishing the salty vegemite flavour on her tongue. The helicopter noise faded again. She swallowed her cracker and spoke to Bec in a low voice. 'How did you go finding out about their parents?'

Bec looked disgusted. 'Nothing. No social media or internet presence at all. I've put out some feelers through my networks, but no hits so far. What kind of business owners aren't on the internet?'

'People who don't need to be? They get their contracts through networks?'

'People who 'sometimes do projects for the government'?' Bec pulled a face. 'I tried searching for thongs, too, but couldn't find anything beyond a million sites selling footwear, or g-strings. It doesn't help that Alice and Lucy don't know the name of their parents' company, or anything else. All they could tell me was their address - they live in Thornleigh.'

'Maybe we should go there.'

Bec's eyes widened and her voice rose to a squeak. 'That's nuts! After your and my apartments, it's the first place the soldiers will look for us.' She lowered her voice even further. 'Look. I say - we've done what we could to find their parents. We need to get out of Sydney. The girls can come with us if they like.'

Amber pulled back from her. There it was - the ruthlessness that Amber had always hated, the readiness to discard people and promises if it would further whatever cause Bec had decided to support today. Amber gritted her teeth. 'So we just use them to get what we want, and then discard them? The same as you did to Zhou?'

Bec's eyes narrowed. 'I came to Epping to help Zhou, remember? I didn't discard him.'

Amber looked at the girls with mixed feelings. The way Alice had negotiated with them in the toilet - threatened them - left a bitter taste in Amber's mouth. But she'd been instrumental in reuniting Amber with Oliver.

'If it wasn't for Alice and Lucy, I wouldn't have gotten Ollie back. I'd probably have let that Bonehead beat me to death.' And maybe they'd have beaten you to death, too. She didn't say the words out loud, but she didn't need to. Bec's face paled, and she gazed down at the water, seeming engrossed in watching a school of small, silver fish dart around her legs.

The helicopter flew overhead for a third time. When it passed, Bec let out a long breath and lifted her head. 'You really want to do this?'

Amber just looked at her.

Bec spoke in her most airy, confident voice. 'I guess we're going to Thornleigh, then.' She frowned, wrinkling her forehead. 'Whenever that damn helicopter pisses off.'

The helicopter made one last pass. They didn't hear it again, but Bec insisted they remain in the shelter of the gangway for another hour.

'And then where are we going?' Alice lifted her chin and glared at Bec.

Amber's mouth twisted. Alice wasn't stupid. She'd seen them talking, and she knew she didn't have leverage over them anymore.

'Your house, to search for info about your parents,' Bec said, as though she'd never considered anything different.

Alice swallowed, and her lips curved upwards. It was the first smile Amber had seen on her face.

When the hour was up, Amber eased Oliver into the carrier. He woke, looking around with his wide brown eyes. Amber ran her hands over her head. Her back was a mass of pain, and she couldn't imagine how she would carry the child carrier. Her brow wrinkled as she looked at Bec, who had been known to drive to the local shopping centre that was ten minutes' walk from her apartment, and Alice and Lucy, who didn't have shoes. 'It's a bit of a walk,' she said.

'Walking,' Bec said, with a distaste that Amber reserved for cockroaches. She elbowed Amber out of the way and lifted the carrier onto her back. Alice saw, and splashed over to pick up Bec's pack.

'Can you manage the weight?' Amber asked.

She shrugged. 'You can't carry it.'

Bec waved them up the bank. Out of the water, the summer heat enveloped them again. Bec looked at Amber. 'Aren't you sweltering in that jacket?'

'No,' Amber said. The cold seemed to have seeped into her bones, and even the summer heat beating against her skin didn't seem to warm her.

Shrugging, Bec led the way, keeping within the treeline adjacent to the cycle path where she could. Alice and Lucy followed, looking pale and tired. Amber took up the rear, gritting her teeth as her shirt rubbed against the welts on her back with every step. Oliver babbled in the carrier for half an hour until the motion rocked him to sleep. Nobody else had the energy to talk. In the silence, Amber couldn't escape her thoughts. She saw again the sword slicing open the Boneheads. She clutched her stomach as though her anguish was a physical pain.

Bec dropped back to join her, letting Alice and Lucy take the lead. 'Are you okay?'

'I killed two Boneheads. I'm a murderer!' The words came out in a quiet wail.

'If you hadn't, they would have killed us. And Ollie would have been left to their mercies.'

'But I'm a Christian. It's like the biggest rule of all - thou shalt not kill.'

'That's about killing people. The Boneheads aren't people.'

'What are they, then?'

'Monsters.'

Amber ran her hands over her head again. She wanted to believe Bec, but Bec was the last person she'd trust for spiritual advice. She couldn't imagine Adam, who was a committed Christian, being so blasé about killing Boneheads. They might be monsters, but they bled red blood, just like humans. And she hadn't told Bec about the grenades. She didn't know if those explosions had killed anyone.

It took them about an hour and a half to get to Meadowbank Wharf, but it felt like days to Amber. She counted her steps to take her mind off the pain and exhaustion, getting to eight hundred before giving up.

Through the fog of pain, she kept an eye on Alice and Lucy. Alice didn't voice any complaints about the heavy pack, but Amber saw her flinch when she stepped on something sharp. Lucy stayed close to Alice and avoided making eye contact with Amber or Bec. She gave the sleeping Oliver an occasional pat when Bec wasn't looking.

Bec stopped them twice, once to eat muesli bars under a concrete picnic table, and once at a toilet block, where they all used the toilet and had a drink of water from the sink. She scanned the sky every few minutes. Amber had never seen Bec so spooked.

Amber took the lead when they left the cycle path. Oliver woke and started crying as they slunk up a steep suburban street surrounded by three- and four-storey apartment towers. His soft cries echoed around the silent streets.

Bec jumped. 'What's wrong with him?'

'He wants a feed,' Amber said, 'Quick, give him to me.'

Bec's eyes darted around the street. The only sign of life in the apartment towers was the washing hanging on clothes horses on the balconies. 'I'd rather we stopped under cover.'

'He'll get louder,' Amber warned.

Bec sighed and swung the carrier off her shoulders. She searched for helicopters while Amber sat on the edge of the gutter to feed Oliver.

'And you complain about me jumping around like a fricken kangaroo,' Amber said.

Bec gave her a sideways glance. 'That was before. When we weren't important enough for them to send helicopters after us.'

Before she'd killed Boneheads. Amber looked away and fixed her eyes on Oliver, her voice defiant. 'I got Ollie back. It's worth it.' She wielded the words as a shield against the uncertainty that threatened to overwhelm her.

'Never said it wasn't. I'm not shedding any tears over those Boneheads.'

'Me, neither,' Alice said.

The sun was low in the sky when they trudged through Epping, passing within a few hundred metres of Amber's apartment.

Her gaze was drawn towards her home. She pictured herself walking in to find Adam making his signature lasagna, his eyes lighting up as she kicked off her shoes and sank into the leather couch. Her eyes filled with tears.

What if the Boneheads went after Adam because of her? She hugged herself and breathed a silent prayer for his safety. Focusing on her prayer, she didn't notice the long line of stationary cars on Carlingford Road, until Bec flung out an arm to block her way.

She looked up. 'What's going on?'

Bec ducked into the shadow of a vine-covered fence, motioning for them to join her, and opened a web browser on her phone. Oliver tugged at some leaves growing over the wooden fence, trying to pull them into his mouth. 'Checkpoint on Epping Road,' Bec read, 'Soldiers are searching cars.'

'For what?' breathed Amber.

Bec shook her head. 'It doesn't say. It says they've been setting up checkpoints all over the city, since the tower bombing and shoot-out at Epping. And - other things.'

Amber noticed the pause. Her brow wrinkled and she snatched the phone out of Bec's hand. The words leapt out at her.

...public servant and Epping resident Amber Yu killed two Boneheads and critically injured a third...

She clutched her stomach with her free hand. 'I really did kill them,' she whispered.

Bec's mouth twisted. 'I saw the footage and reports when I was searching for Alice and Lucy's parents. The official news tried to downplay it, but they couldn't cover it up, because Mike Davies was broadcasting live. So it was all over social media within minutes.'

Amber looked down at the phone.

...known links to activist Rebecca Williams, who has been implicated in the Governor Macquarie Tower bombing...

'I think it's good. Now everyone knows it's bullshit that the Boneheads can't be killed.' Bec slid the phone out of Amber's unresisting hand. 'Have a nervous breakdown about it later. We need to keep moving.' She turned to leave.

Amber didn't move. 'Bec?'

Bec raised her eyebrows in a silent question.

'Did you have anything to do with bombing that tower?'

Bec looked Amber in the eyes. 'No.' Her voice was firm. 'They're trying to pin it on me because some other members of my group were involved. I had nothing to do with it.'

Amber swallowed and nodded. She backed away from Carlingford Road - worried the soldiers would be searching it too. She led the way down silent suburban streets to Beecroft Road, just south of where it ran over the M2 Motorway on its way north.

A businesslike fence separated the road from the land surrounding the M2. Amber eyed the fence.

'Can you cut a hole in that one?' she asked Bec.

Bec wrinkled her nose at the weedy patch of land behind the fence. 'Why would you want to?'

'I used to start bushwalks in there before they stuck up that fence. There's two tunnels under the M2. They lead to a bunch of walking tracks - that mostly connect up to the Great North Walk.'

Bec gave her a blank look, reminding Amber that she was not a fan of walking. 'It's a massive walk that runs from the Sydney CBD to Newcastle.'

'Sounds ghastly.'

Amber shrugged. 'Thornleigh is one of the suburbs on the route.'

Bec sighed, and surveyed the fence. 'Yes.'

'Yes, what?'

'Yes I can cut a hole in it.'

Bec extracted her bolt cutters from the pack and cut a hole in the fence. They squeezed through and sloshed through the creek water in the smaller tunnel. Amber expected complaints about the dirty water, but Alice and Lucy walked through like zombies, their eyes glazed and red-rimmed. Bec touched the side of the tunnel with her fingertips, looking relieved to be under cover. An artificial bank, created from large stone blocks covered by wire mesh, ran along one side of the creek in the second tunnel. They clambered out of the creek.

Alice and Lucy slumped on the hard stone ground. Alice leant against the pack, not bothering to slide it off her shoulders. Lucy put her head in Alice's lap.

Amber swayed on her feet, squelching in her wet shoes. On the other side of the tunnel, a dirt track led through grass choked with lantana and other weeds. She looked up at the roof. 'There must be tons of concrete over us. This would be a safe place to camp.'

Bec's eyebrows rose. 'I don't think we should stop in Epping. They know you live here.'

'It's not like we're going to my apartment. They're not going to look for us in some dank tunnel under the M2.' Amber nodded at Alice and Lucy. Lucy's eyes were closed. Alice was staring into space. 'They're asleep on their feet, I'm in agony, even you look wrecked. We need a break.'

Bec rolled her eyes, but squatted down on the rocks herself.

Amber exhaled and sagged to the ground. She wasn't sure she'd have been able to keep going if Bec had refused to stop.

Nine

Bec emptied the contents of the carrier over the rocks. Amber assembled and lit the hiking stove while Bec pulled together the ingredients for a simple spaghetti bolognese. Alice and Lucy fell asleep where they sat.

Bec held up the bag of cask wine. 'Shall we have some of this?'

Amber's eyes lit up - she had forgotten she'd packed it. 'Please!'

Bec slopped wine into two plastic glasses. Amber sipped. The wine warmed her throat and body. It was the first time she'd felt warm since they'd left the university. She listened to the birds making the most of the last of the daylight. A flock of rainbow lorikeets chattered in the trees outside the tunnel, then took to the air with loud screeches.

Bec spooned spaghetti and bolognese sauce into a mix of bowls, plates and a saucepan and woke Alice and Lucy. Amber devoured her serve with Oliver on her lap, dribbling sauce on his head. Slurping the remains of the tomato sauce, the comfort of the pasta filling every corner of her stomach, and washing it down with the wine - it was better than a meal from the finest Sydney restaurant.

'We should pack up camp before dawn, in case there's early morning joggers or dog walkers around,' Bec said, 'If we meet them on the track, we can pretend we're out for a morning walk.'

'Only from a distance,' Amber said, surveying her and the girls. She couldn't imagine what a passerby would make of them - the girls in pyjamas with no shoes, Alice laden with a large pack while she carried nothing, all of them with rumpled clothes encrusted in mud. Bec's hair was a knotted cloud around her head. Alice's was even worse - she had leaves and twigs caught in it. Lucy's pyjama top was torn from where it had caught on a tree branch. 'A really long distance.'

The food brought some energy back into her limbs. While Bec rinsed the dishes with water from her water bottle, Amber unrolled two self-inflating air mattresses and sleeping bags that had been in the carrier and slid a third sleeping bag from Bec's pack.

'Should we erect the tent?'

Bec shook her head. 'We don't need it - it's so warm. And we don't want to be seen by someone walking past.'

'Anyone walking past shouldn't trouble us - they'd have to be curfew-breakers themselves.' Amber shot Bec a sidelong look. She'd changed overnight from her usual cocky self to the more paranoid of the two of them. 'The mosquitoes'll get us.'

'Better than the Boneheads getting us,' Bec said with finality.

Amber gave one mattress to the two girls, and unzipped a sleeping bag to spread over them.

Bec pushed the other mattress at her. 'You're injured.' She spread out the tent as a rough ground cover for herself.

Amber changed Oliver's nappy and clothes, fed him and collapsed with him onto the mattress, pulling her sleeping bag over them. Bec and the girls were already asleep. The cicadas launched into a piercing chorus. She frowned at a mosquito buzzing around her head.

She closed her eyes. Images filled her mind of the Boneheads she'd killed. She saw again the sword slicing into them, the blood spurting out, their eyes going blank. She'd killed them. She shivered.

She opened her eyes and gazed out the tunnel entrance. The night sky was tinted with orange from the city lights. She could hear the roar of trucks on the M2. 'I'm not a killer,' she whispered.

She longed for Adam - picturing him wrapping his arms around her and telling her everything was okay.

Except he'd probably give her a pained look and ask why she did something as stupid as killing Boneheads.

Oliver rolled over and buried his face in her chest. Breathing in his scent, she relaxed enough to fall asleep.

In her dreams, she was at the university again. The three Boneheads lurched after her, covered in blood. She could hear the steady thump thump thump of the helicopter. She swam to the ferry, but it floated out of reach. Helen appeared on the deck. 'Australians are too reckless,' she berated Amber, as the ferry floated further and further away.

Treading water, she turned around. The thumping from the helicopter grew louder and louder. Bec, Alice, Lucy and Oliver were standing on the shore. The Boneheads raced down the hill, swords raised. She tried to swim back to shore. The water dragged at her, pulling her back. Unable to move, she watched as the Boneheads killed Bec... Alice... Lucy... and Oliver.

Oliver's cries roused her, blocking out the pounding helicopter noise. Her heart thumped. Tears ran down her cheeks. She took deep breaths until her heart slowed.

Sharp pains flooded her back as she moved sideways so Oliver could feed, making the tears run again. After feeding, Oliver rolled over and babbled. Bec groaned and pulled her sleeping bag over her head. Oliver picked up a loose stone and tried to put it in his mouth. Amber sat up, grimacing in pain, and snatched it out of his hand. Bec reached out from her sleeping bag and pressed the power switch on her phone: 4.45 am.

Her stomach queasy, Amber boiled water on her hiking stove and made coffee, stirring powdered milk into it. Bec pulled the sleeping bag off her head and reached for her cup without sitting up. Birds filled the air with noise. Amber identified the distinctive cries of kookaburras and screeching of cockatoos.

Once they'd had a caffeine hit, Amber poured muesli into bowls and the saucepan. Alice and Lucy ate without speaking, their eyelids heavy. Bec cradled a bowl in her hands and stared at the dark sky outside the tunnel.

They packed up as the first smudge of light appeared on the horizon.

Bec clipped a black box about the size and shape of a mobile phone to the top of the pack. The front was covered in small solar panels. It had two USB ports for charging phones.

'Wow. You came prepared,' Amber said.

'Not me,' Bec said, 'The friend who gave me the phone. He said it's a bit slow to charge, but better than nothing.'

She gave the pack to Alice. Alice winced when she pulled it onto her shoulders.

'Are you okay?' Amber asked.

Alice gave a terse nod. 'Fine. Just a bit bruised from the pack.'

Amber's right hand was red and blistered. She held it half open, like a claw. Her back was stiff and painful. She tried not to imagine how it looked.

Amber and Bec's feet squelched in their shoes, still wet from the night before. Amber looked at Alice and Lucy's bare feet under their soiled pyjama bottoms. At least she and Bec had shoes.

They followed engraved timber Great North Walk signs along eroded, rocky trails. The heat and humidity rose with the sun. Tall, straight eucalypt trees reached high above them, shading the trails and offering some relief from the heat. Birds called in the trees above them and flitted on the ground. The bellbirds maintained a chorus of chimes. They didn't see any other people, to Amber's relief. She pointed out a large rock shaped a little like a whale. 'Whale rock,' she said, recognising the landmark from previous bushwalks. Bec glanced at it without interest. Alice and Lucy didn't even look up.

After four hours of walking, with three short rest breaks, they popped out of the bush at Thornleigh oval. Amber's shoulders stiffened and her stomach muscles clenched together. The bush had given her a sense of security.

An unwarranted sense of security. There was nowhere safe for her and Oliver anymore.

Bec slid the carrier off her shoulders and opened a map on her phone.

'We need to cross the train line at Thornleigh station,' she said.

'We can't walk through Thornleigh station looking like this!' Amber objected.

'We have to. Unless you want to wait until after dark, but then we'll be breaking the curfew.'

Amber grimaced.

'I'll look up the train timetable and we'll aim for when there's no trains coming,' Bec said. Amber gave a resigned nod.

The fifteen-minute walk down suburban streets to the station was uneventful. Two middle-aged men sped past with their heads down, avoiding eye contact. They didn't seem to notice Amber, Bec and the girls' disheveled state.

Amber clenched shaking hands as they approached the major road artery of Pennant Hills Road. Switchback concrete ramps led to an uncovered pedestrian overpass over the road, exposed to any watchers from the air or on the ground. She and Bec debated crossing the overpass or at the lights up the road. Settling on the overpass, they climbed the ramp, passing a heavily pregnant woman with a toddler's arm clutched in her hand. Her eyes widened. She squeezed the toddler's arm tighter and hurried past.

Bec had timed their arrival at the station well. It was ten minutes after the last train had departed the station and twenty minutes before the next arrived. The station was deserted. A second overpass took them over the platforms and train lines and down the other side. Amber let out a sigh as her feet touched the ground on the other side. Her lips were curving up in the beginning of a smile when she heard a sharp intake of breath from Alice and a low squeak from Lucy. She swung her head up. A line of eucalypt trees separated the station from the road. Two soldiers were approaching from within the trees, their camouflage uniforms blending into the dappled light.

Bec grabbed Alice and Lucy's wrists and dragged them into the shadows under the steps. Amber dived after them. They hunkered down behind a large square rubbish bin, trying not to breathe in the distinctive smell of overheating garbage.

The soldiers ambled, deep in conversation. Amber clenched her fists so hard her nails bit into her palms, praying Oliver would stay silent.

'I'm so fucking bored,' one of the soldiers said, 'When will they let us go back to the real action?'

'Dickhead. This is the real action. Catch them, and I reckon we'll be set up for life.'

'What are you talking about?'

'You need to pay more attention.' The soldier lowered his voice.

'No fucking way! I thought they couldn't be killed!'

'Keep your voice down. Of course they can. Why do you think they need -' he lowered his voice again. Amber thought she heard him say 'Dubbo'. Her eyes filled with tears.

'Shut the fuck up!' The first soldier looked over his shoulder, his eyes flickering everywhere. 'Let's get the coffees.'

The soldiers trotted up the steps over their heads. When they'd disappeared along the ramp, Bec leant over and breathed into Amber's ear. 'You still want to do this?'

Amber swallowed. She might have imagined that he said Dubbo. She rubbed her hands on her pants, gave a sharp nod and stood, without meeting Bec's eyes. 'Let's go.'

Alice took the lead. 'I know the way from here.'

Twenty minutes later they arrived at an attractive, tree-lined street of small, unassuming brick houses and cottages. Amber knew that their modesty was misleading - any one of them would sell for more than a million dollars. The street ended in a Y-shaped intersection.

Shouts and laughter drifted to them from a school at the top of the Y. Amber had almost forgotten that normal life continued, with schools and work and shopping - so far removed from their bubble of fear and pain and flight.

Lucy let out a small sob. Amber's head swung up, her stomach clenching. She scanned the street, sensing Bec doing the same. She couldn't see any danger. Lucy had buried her face in Alice's pyjama top. Alice swallowed several times. Amber raised her eyebrows.

'It's our school,' Alice answered the unspoken question. She swallowed again. 'All our friends are there.'

Amber's stomach muscles relaxed. Bec let them stare at their school for a few minutes, then cleared her throat. 'Let's go.'

Alice pulled Lucy upright. They averted their eyes as they took the street to the left of the school. A sign warned that it was a no through road. The street headed down the hill to a turning circle with bush behind it. Alice pointed at the second last house on the right side of the street - a double storey, grey weatherboard with two large eucalypt trees in the front yard and a hedge covering the front fence.

Oliver started fussing in the backpack. 'Another feed?' Bec wrinkled her brow at Amber's nod. 'People will notice if we spend too long on the street.'

Alice pointed at a bus stop opposite the school. 'We could pretend we're waiting for a bus?'

Bec raised her eyebrows. 'Good idea.'

They backtracked to the corner and Amber settled herself against a low brick wall that separated the footpath from the house behind. She helped Oliver to latch onto her breast. 'I hope the bus doesn't come.'

Bec eyed Alice and Lucy's house down the street. There was no sign of danger: no parked cars on the street nearby.

'Is there a less obvious way in?'

Alice dragged her eyes from the school. 'Mrs McKenzie around the corner backs on to us.' She pointed to the street that ran to the right of the school.

'Show me?'

Bec and Alice mooched down the street as Amber switched Oliver to the other breast. Alice reappeared as she strapped Oliver back into the carrier, and waved for them to follow.

Bec was hovering in the shade opposite a brick house, smaller and older than Alice and Lucy's house. A low grevillea hedge bordered the front lawn. Two large hydrangeas splashed their blue and purple flowers on either side of the front door. A battered car stood in a cluttered carport on the left side of the house. When they caught up, Bec led them down the right side.

The blank brick wall was broken by a small bathroom window, above head height. A white wooden gate halfway down separated the front from the backyard. Bec inspected the locked gate handle. She motioned to Alice to turn around, and retrieved her bolt cutters from the pack on Alice's back. Standing side on to the gate, she swung the cutters up and brought them down hard on the handle. With a loud crack, the handle broke. Bec removed the mechanism, and the gate swung open. They crept into the backyard.

A verandah ran the length of the house, with an inbuilt barbeque and sink on one end and a weathered, wooden outdoor table with matching chairs in the middle. Fairy lights had been strung along the roof of the verandah, and potted ferns hung from each corner. A well-kept lawn swept down to the back fence. Through screening bamboo, Amber could see the back of Alice and Lucy's house.

A screen door slammed. They swung around. A weathered woman in her late seventies walked onto the verandah, her hands on her hips and eyes narrowed. 'You could have knocked. Didn't need to break my gate.'

To Amber's surprise, a flush crept across Bec's cheeks, and she rubbed the back of her neck.

Lucy hid behind Alice. 'Hi, Mrs McKenzie,' Alice said, sucking in her lips.

'I've seen you on television,' Mrs McKenzie said, her sharp eyes taking in Bec's face. 'And you,' she said to Amber. 'Terrorists, they called you.'

'We're looking for their parents,' Bec said, 'Do you know anything about them? Elise and Nicolas?'

Her eyes softened. 'Nothing, I'm afraid. I knew them to say hello on the street, and these two sometimes came over to retrieve balls that had flown over my fence, but that's it.' She spoke to Alice. 'Soldiers were swarming your place for days. I heard them banging around. They might have left the place in a bit of a mess.'

Alice bit her lip.

Mrs McKenzie's glittering eyes returned to Bec and Amber. 'You chose a good time to come, anyway. They just left last night. Asked me to call if I saw anyone suspicious. Gave me a card and everything.'

A chill ran down Amber's body. 'Please - don't call them.'

'Why would I? You think I want a friendly chat with one of those monsters?' She frowned. 'I suggest you make it quick, though. I can't speak for all the neighbours. Some of them'd sell their own grandmothers for peanuts.'

Bec waved a hand towards the back fence. 'Is it okay -'

Mrs McKenzie glared at her. 'Be careful with my bamboo. You're lucky I don't make you pay for the gate.' One corner of her lips twitched. 'There's a stepladder in my carport if you need it.'

Amber ducked out the front to retrieve the stepladder, hearing the screen door slam as Mrs McKenzie went inside. They could have scaled the fence without the ladder, but it would be easier for Bec with Oliver in the carrier. She held the stepladder while Bec, Alice and Lucy clambered over the fence.

Mrs McKenzie returned. 'Hey,' she called, raising a green reusable shopping bag in one hand. Amber's stomach clenched, but she walked back to the verandah, not wanting to upset Mrs McKenzie. She wouldn't put it past the woman to call the soldiers in vengeance.

Mrs McKenzie handed her the bag. It held an odd mixture of food - bread, spaghetti, some tinned tuna, and several boxes of biscuits. A tube of aloe vera gel lay on top. 'The aloe will help your burns.' Mrs McKenzie nodded at Amber's hand, but Amber suspected she knew about the ones on her back, too. No doubt she'd seen what had happened at the university on television.

'Thank you,' Amber said, tears pricking her eyes at the unexpected kindness.

Mrs McKenzie nodded at the stepladder. 'You'd better get going.'

Amber nodded, and followed the others over the fence.

A square swimming pool, surrounded by tan tiles and a glass fence, took up most of Alice and Lucy's backyard. An old swing set with cracking paint filled a small square of grass between the house and pool, flanked by paved walkways and manicured hedges.

An outdoor bench seat stood on the small verandah under a wide window. The inside of the house was hidden from view by white vertical blinds. Between the seat and the back door, a variety of lettuces sprung from a half wine barrel. Bec eyed the back door, hefting her bolt cutters, but Alice raised a hand to stall her. She put her hand into the lettuces and pulled out a key, brushed it on her pyjamas to remove the loose dirt and unlocked the door. It swung open, and she gasped. Bec pushed her aside. 'Fuck.'

Amber peered over their heads. The back door led straight into an open plan living and kitchen area, with polished wooden floorboards and an all-white kitchen. Amber could picture what it would look like immaculately clean - a sanctuary, like her apartment. But it was the opposite of immaculate. Every cupboard in the kitchen had been emptied, their contents strewn over the floor. A large sideboard and a television cabinet in the living area had been emptied too, and a piano stool knocked over, music books cascading onto the floor. A Persian rug - the only spot of colour in the neutral tones of the room - had been tossed aside.

'What were they looking for?' Bec asked.

Alice lifted her hands high, a bewildered look on her face. Lucy's mouth had formed an O shape. She looked as confused as Alice.

Bec gave the girls a firm look and spoke in a business-like tone. 'I need you to pack a small bag, some clothes, anything you can't live without. Small. Amber and Lucy can't carry much, and you and I already have enough to carry.' She looked at their feet, which were almost black from all the dirt and grime they'd collected. 'And find some shoes.'

Alice took a deep breath, and nodded. 'Come on,' she said to Lucy. A tear leaked from Lucy's eye. She swatted it away.

The girls disappeared through a door on the right. Amber trailed them up a set of floating wood stairs. Beyond the stairs, she could see what looked like a rumpus room, with toys and art supplies strewn over the floor.

Upstairs, several rooms opened into a hallway, all carpeted with a cream wool. Alice dumped Bec's pack near the stairs. She and Lucy disappeared into the two rooms at the far end. Amber dropped the shopping bag next to the pack, removed the aloe vera gel and smoothed it onto the burn on her hand, closing her eyes and exhaling as the gel reduced the pain. She checked the first room - a large, sunny bedroom overlooking the pool. The mattress and blankets on the king-sized bed had been upended and thrown onto the floor, and the contents of a large walk-in wardrobe tossed on top. Even two large pictures had been removed from the wall - an abstract painting that she suspected was an Australian Aboriginal artwork, and a photo of a laughing woman, who had the same tight red curls as Lucy, with her arms wrapped around a stocky man with thick dark hair, brown eyes and a wide smile. The man was in a suit with a light blue shirt that matched the light blue dress the woman was wearing. She dangled a bouquet from one hand. Elise and Nicolas' wedding.

On the other side of the room, a door opened into an ensuite. Amber peered in, her eyes widening at the large spa that took up most of the space. A small bathroom cabinet had been emptied of its contents - half empty bottles of perfume and hair and body products.

The room opposite was a study with a large oak desk and three in-built bookshelves. Unlike the other rooms, nothing in this room had been thrown on the floor. The desk and bookshelves were bare. Amber opened the desk drawers - also empty. A computer cable ran from a power point under the desk to the top of the desk, indicating that a computer had once stood there, but it was gone. Even the small wastepaper basket was empty.

The next door was a large linen closet. Amber picked through the contents, which had been left on the floor. There was nothing unusual. She extracted two sleeping bags and a large air mattress. She squished the mattress into the bottom of the green shopping bag that Mrs McKenzie had given her, and forced the small sleeping bags into the top of Bec's pack. She grimaced, hoping the extra weight wouldn't be the straw that broke Alice's back.

Beyond the linen closet was a bathroom and separate toilet. The toilet held a toilet brush, plunger and rubbish bin with two empty toilet rolls and two tissues. Amber picked through the contents of the bathroom cupboards, which had been thrown into the bath - toiletries, beauty products, hairbrushes - nothing unusual.

She used the toilet while she was there, then stepped around Bec's pack to the girls' bedrooms. Alice's walls had been covered with an eclectic mixture of pictures - photos of her with various girls the same age, or standing in front of tourist attractions, drawings of animals and cartoon characters, pictures of musicians and tv stars printed from the internet. They had been torn from the walls; bits of the pictures still stuck to blobs of blue tack on the wall.

Alice knelt on the floor, still dressed in pyjamas, smoothing two crumpled photos. One was a recent photo of Elise, Nicolas, Alice and Lucy dressed in ski gear, next to a misshapen snowman with a muesli bar nose and a light blue beanie - probably Elise's, since she was the only one without one. Elise's red hair was marred by some grey strands, and Nicolas' body was heavier, but they had the same beaming faces as in the wedding photo. The other photo showed Alice posing in front of the Sydney Harbour Bridge with three girls the same age. Both photos had torn corners.

Alice looked up and met her eyes. Tears dribbled down her cheeks. She rubbed them with one hand. 'I haven't packed, I'll do it now,' she muttered.

'Want some help?'

She jerked her head in a firm no and began sorting through the clothes that had been dumped on the floor. Amber retreated. Lucy had left a pile of summery garments in the hall outside her bedroom. She was staring out the window, dressed in denim shorts and a yellow T-shirt with a picture of a unicorn disco dancing in front of a rainbow, and holding a battered blue teddy. She had put a cheap, rainbow-coloured watch on one wrist. A branch of one of the eucalypt trees stretched almost to her window, dappling the light that fell into the room.

'You should pack some warm stuff, too, and a raincoat,' Amber told her, 'The weather might change.'

Lucy blinked. 'Okay.' She rummaged in the mess on the floor and added some clothes to the pile.

Alice dropped a backpack covered in coloured cats next to Lucy's pile of clothes. She had changed into black shorts and an oversized black T-shirt with Girls Can Do Anything scrawled in silver writing on it. She scrunched the cutesy pyjamas into a ball and slammed them into the bathroom rubbish bin with a small, satisfied smile.

She began shoving Lucy's clothes on top of her own, looking up at Lucy's bear, her eyes narrowing. 'Why have you got that?'

Lucy's face reddened. 'Ollie might like it.'

'Have you got a raincoat, and warm clothes?' Amber asked Alice.

She slouched back into her room. Bec came up the stairs, Oliver asleep in the carrier on her back. 'Find anything?' she asked Amber.

Amber shook her head. 'Nothing useful. The office has been cleared. There's not a single thing left.'

'I couldn't find much downstairs.' Bec held up a small photo, similar to the large one in the bedroom. This time Alice and Lucy flanked Elise and Nicolas, in matching white dresses with blue sashes, holding smaller versions of the woman's bouquet. They looked about five years younger. 'I got this. So at least we know what Elise and Nicolas look like.'

'I think Alice has a more recent photo of them.'

Alice reappeared with a waterproof jacket and a thick black coat.

'Either of you see anything unusual in your rooms? Any hints about what happened to your parents?' Bec asked. Lucy and Alice shook their heads. Bec pulled a face, and ducked into Lucy's room, picking through the mess on the floor.

Amber helped Alice ram her jacket and coat into the pack and zip the pack closed.

Bec barrelled out of the room. 'We have to go. There's a black four-wheel drive out front.'

Ten

Alice threw the cat pack at Amber. She caught and hugged it with both arms. 'We should have left someone on guard.'

'Too late.' Bec hurtled past and down the stairs. The others followed, scooping up Bec's pack and the shopping bag on the way.

The kitchen door slammed. Bec froze, holding one foot in the air above the bottom step.

'The garage,' Alice breathed. She pushed past and led them through a small door at the back of the rumpus room.

Empty shelves lined each side of the garage - their usual contents of hardware, sports equipment and pool toys carpeting the floor. Glass glittered on the ground near an orange sports car and a red four-wheel drive. The driver's side window on both cars had been smashed. A motorboat sat on a trailer behind them.

They picked their way through the mess to another small door on the front wall, next to the garage doors. Bec turned the deadlock and inched it open. The door opened into the front yard, behind the trunk of the tree that shaded Lucy's window upstairs. Bec waved them through and eased the door back into place.

Amber clenched her teeth. Bec had said there was a four-wheel drive out front, and whoever had slammed the kitchen door must have come in from the back. That left the side fence closest to them. She slid along the weatherboards and peered around the edge of the house, holding her breath. Nobody was there. The side of the house was windowless: the bottom floor taken up with the garage, and Alice and Lucy's bedroom windows on the top floor facing the backyard and street respectively. Three bins - rubbish, green waste and recycling - leant against the house. Several stunted bushes grew in the permanent shade between the house and the fence. Bec raised the bin lids in turn, but the bins were empty. Amber pulled the recycling bin between two straggly banksias and up to the fence. She motioned for Alice and Lucy to climb it. Alice tossed Bec's pack over the fence and scrambled over herself, Lucy a silent shadow in her wake. Bec clung with her fingertips as she let herself down the other side so that Oliver didn't notice the bump. Amber let the cat pack and shopping bag fall to the ground and slithered over.

By the time she landed, Bec was sprinting across the overgrown garden towards a gate set in the fence opposite, Alice on her heels and Lucy behind. Amber absorbed that they were in the yard of another weatherboard house, this one a small one-storey with peeling paint and a wraparound verandah. Grasping the handles of her bags with her good hand, she leapt over the weeds that had taken over the vegetable garden and were advancing on the lawn.

She caught up to Lucy as Bec flung the gate open onto a thin dirt track into the bush.

'Freeze!' a young male voice roared.

Amber whirled around. A soldier balanced his rifle on the fence. He had to be standing on the rubbish bin. His face was hidden by sunglasses and a helmet, but the tanned skin and curls escaping the helmet were etched into Amber's memory: Private Jerome.

'Stay where you are, or I'll fire!' His voice cracked on the last words, robbing them of authority.

Bec propelled Alice through the gate. The movement galvanised Amber - she seized Lucy's arm and leapt at the gate.

There was a succession of cracks. Amber's eyes widened as several bullets hit an invisible barrier in front of her and fell to the ground. Jerome lowered his rifle, his mouth dropping open. Bec wasn't looking at him. She was staring at Lucy. Amber followed her gaze. Lucy clutched the teddy she'd picked up at her house in one hand. Its stomach was lit with a series of small lights in a circular pattern - coming from inside the bear.

'Go!' Amber yanked Lucy through the gate.

They sprinted through the bush. Bec crashed past her and Lucy and caught up to Alice. The track petered away, disappearing in the scrub, but they kept running, branches and leaves whipping against their bare legs and arms. Small dots of blood welled up from small scratches and scrapes. They ran without any plan or direction - spurred on by crashing sounds behind them. Amber gulped mouthfuls of air. Bile rose from her throat into her mouth.

Above the sound of their feet pounding the ground Amber felt, rather than heard, the sound that had haunted her nightmares the night before - a distant thump thump thump. It was so faint that she wasn't sure if it was real or a memory from her nightmare.

She paused in her flight and strained to listen. Thump thump thump. A chill ran down her back. It was increasing in volume. 'Bec!'

Bec turned her head towards Amber, risking a fall by not watching where she placed her feet. 'What?'

'Helicopter.'

Bec stopped still. Alice, following close on her heels, dodged at the last minute, crashing into a prickly bush on her right. Her cheeks and forehead reddened, and she turned her worst glare on Bec. Bec didn't notice.

'We have to hide.'

Amber swung around. Trees, bushes... nothing that would hide them from a thermal imaging camera.

Bec had made the same assessment. She met Amber's gaze, her lips trembling.

'We'll find somewhere.' Amber copied Bec's usual airy tone. 'Keep moving.'

Bec swallowed and nodded. She led the way again - the thump thump thump creeping closer. The helicopter sounded like it was overhead. Amber squeezed her eyes closed. It was over.

'There!'

Her eyes flicked open. Lucy pointed at the hill above them. In one small patch the rock was bare of trees and scrubs; the sandstone eroded by wind and rain into a shallow cave.

'I can't believe it.' Bec's eyes shone.

Thump thump thump. 'Quick!' Amber said.

They scrambled up the steep slope. The soil crumbled beneath them and made them stumble. Lucy slipped back down the slope. Amber slid after her, grabbed her by the wrist and yanked her back up. The helicopter appeared overhead, the thumping giving way to a roar. Bec and Alice ducked under the narrow overhang, flattening their bodies against the soft stone. Amber dragged Lucy over the top and they threw themselves down next to Bec and Alice.

Amber's heart hammered against her chest - so hard that she thought the helicopter's instruments would be able to pick up the vibrations. It flew over and out of sight, but the thumping noise continued to echo around the valley.

Oliver woke, sobbing. Bec handed Amber the carrier, and she soothed him with another breastfeed. While he sucked, Bec inched her way along the cave, one hand against the stone wall. Amber looked down the hill. Thin eucalypt trees with blackened bark sprouted high into the sky. They were widely spaced, allowing an array of smaller trees and shrubs to spring up underneath them. Amber rubbed her arms where the shrubs had scratched them. She felt exposed. The overhang protected them from searchers from above, but they would be visible to anyone in the valley.

Bec slid around the side of the cave, keeping an eye on the sky above. She returned a few minutes later and slipped the carrier on her back. 'There's a better hiding place further along.'

Amber followed, with Oliver in one arm and the cat bag in another. Lucy carried the shopping bag. Beyond their cave, several more areas of cliff had weathered away into a series of shallow caves. Under the furthest overhang, a large piece of rock had fallen from above and leant against the overhang. One by one, they slid into the small space behind the rock, where they wouldn't be seen.

Amber finished feeding Oliver and placed him down on his stomach next to her. He pulled himself into a crawling position and rocked back and forth on his knees. Lucy rubbed her wrist where Amber had grabbed her. Amber looked away, feeling a sharp pang of guilt. She hadn't had time to be gentle.

Amber made vegemite sandwiches. The bread that Mrs McKenzie had given her had been squashed out of shape, but nobody complained.

Bec shoved the last of her sandwich into her mouth and brushed her hands on her clothes. 'Can I check out your bear?' she said through the sandwich.

Lucy clutched the teddy close to her chest, wrapping both arms around it. Alice gave her a withering look. Her shoulders sinking, Lucy handed the teddy to Bec.

Bec squeezed the bear all over, stopping at its chubby stomach. 'There's something in here,' she said. She looked at Lucy, her face reddening. 'Do you mind if I cut it open?'

Alice's eyes glittered, daring Lucy to complain. Lucy shook her head.

Amber wiped vegemite from the pocket knife she'd used to

butter the sandwiches. Bec used it to cut a small incision in the bear's stomach. She wiggled her fingers inside and pulled out a round, black ball, about the size of a tennis ball, with smaller rotating balls set into its surface. When she rubbed her fingers over it, the small balls lit up. 'It looks like a puzzle,' Alice said.

'I don't think it is,' Bec said, 'It lit up when the soldier fired at us, and the bullets didn't reach us. I think it's the device the Boneheads use to stop bullets.'

Alice's eyes widened. 'I didn't know they used a device. I thought they had magical powers.'

Bec rolled the device in her hands. The look in her eyes was as close to reverence as Amber had ever seen on her face. 'People have speculated that they're protected by some kind of advanced technology, but I don't think anyone knew for sure. Until now.'

'Can I see?' Amber asked.

Bec handed it to her. She rotated it in her hand, noting the way each ball lit up if she touched it. A word was engraved in tiny capital letters on one ball. She crawled past Alice and Lucy to the edge of the crevice and held it up to the light. 'THONG,' she read.

Alice's mouth dropped open. 'The soldiers kept asking Mum and Nick where the thong was.'

'That must be what they were searching the house for,' Bec said.

Amber stared at the glinting ball. 'I guess they didn't think to look inside the teddy bear.'

The helicopter traced lazy circles overhead, reminding Amber of a patient eagle waiting for its prey to make a wrong move. She gave the THONG back to Bec.

'I wonder why they called it a thong?' Bec said.

Amber noticed Lucy pick up the teddy and stroke its stomach. Her eyes softened, and she combed through the carrier for a small travel sewing kit. In silence, so that Alice didn't notice, she drew the teddy from Lucy's hands, sewed up its stomach and handed it back. Lucy rewarded her with a brilliant smile. The fear that had lurked in her eyes since they'd met evaporated. Amber found herself grinning back.

Oliver slipped back down to a lying position and yawned.

'We should get some rest.' Bec slipped the THONG into a small pocket on the inside of her hoodie and zipped it shut. 'It might be our last chance for a while.'

The rock crevice was too tight for them to stretch out on their mattresses. They blew up one of the self-inflating mattresses and used it as a shared pillow, either lying half upright against the wall or flat with their knees bent.

'At least it's so warm we don't need sleeping bags,' Bec said.

'Thank goodness.' It would be impossible to squirm into a sleeping bag in the narrow space.

Bec unclipped the solar panel power bank from her pack and laid it in the sun outside the crevice to charge. Amber tried to dab aloe vera gel onto her back.

'I'll do it.' Bec took the tube. She lifted the back of Amber's shirt and drew in a sharp breath. Amber closed her eyes. She didn't want to know what her back looked like. Bec smoothed the gel onto the wounds. Amber let out a deep sigh as the throbbing lessened.

She lay down, struggling to find a comfortable position next to Oliver. When she drifted off, it was into more nightmares, where the sound of the real-world helicopter mingled with the dream helicopters.

It was a relief to wake. She listened for the thump thump thump. The only sounds were the hum of insects and the chimes of bellbirds. She climbed over Bec, who didn't wake, and slid out of the crevice to go to the toilet.

Oliver woke when she returned, babbling. She fed him, then

placed him on the ground and watched him struggling to crawl through half-closed eyes.

'I can watch him for you, if you want to sleep,' Lucy said. She sat up and wrapped her arms around her legs, pulling them tight into her chest. She nestled the teddy in the gap between her legs and chest. Alice was asleep next to her.

'Thanks,' Amber said, 'But I can't sleep anyway. I keep having nightmares.'

Lucy hugged her knees tighter. 'I have them, too. I dream that something bad has happened to Mum and Nick.'

Amber wanted to say something reassuring, but there was a good chance that something bad had happened to Lucy's parents. Her eyes followed a large red ant that was dragging a crumb from one of their sandwiches over the stony ground. It stumbled on a loose stone. 'My husband is missing, too,' she said, 'I pray that he's okay. I'll pray for your parents, too.'

Lucy's eyes were on the ant too. She picked up a leaf and smoothed the ground in front of it, so it could continue on its way. 'That would be good,' she said.

Bec cracked an eye open. 'What's the chance of a coffee?'

'No problem, if you find us a bigger crevice to hide in,' Amber said, 'If we try to light the stove in here we'll end up with more burns to deal with.'

Bec pulled a face, and yawned.

'I think the helicopter's gone. Should we move soon?'

Bec shook her head. 'Let's wait until it's dark.'

'You said the dark won't protect us from the infrared cameras.' Their quiet words had woken Alice.

'It won't. But it'll stop us being seen by other things, like people's eyes.'

'Where are we going?' Lucy asked, moving a stone out of the ant's way.

Alice sat up, her eyes on Bec's face. 'You didn't find out where

Mum and Nick are.'

'No, but we did find the THONG. I have some - friends - who might be able to figure out where it came from.'

Amber narrowed her eyes. 'Friends?'

Bec wriggled her shoulders. 'Alright, contacts in the resistance. I think we should give them the THONG anyway. It could be a game changer.' Her eyes sparkled. 'Imagine if the resistance fighters couldn't be shot, like the Boneheads.'

Amber's mouth tightened. Of course Bec would be more concerned with giving the resistance the THONG than helping Alice and Lucy. 'So where do you want to go? Resistance headquarters?'

'There isn't a headquarters. It's a bit of an overstatement calling it the resistance at all, but I guess they had to call themselves something. It's not one group, just a bunch of like-minded groups and people with loose connections. They're dotted around the place.' She looked at the empty sky. 'First we need to lose the soldiers and helicopters. I'm not going to lead the enemy to them.' She looked at Amber. 'Any ideas?'

Amber rubbed her eyes. 'I'm not even sure where we are.'

Bec opened a map app on her phone and passed it to her. Amber pinched the screen to zoom in. 'Okay, we're not far from the Great North Walk,' she said. She met Bec's eyes. 'We could walk out of Sydney, to Newcastle.'

Bec's brow furrowed. 'That's a crazy long way. We won't have enough food.'

'We'll have to pick it up on the way. The Great North Walk goes through a bunch of towns.'

'How about, instead, we walk to some other suburb and take a car.'

Amber raised her eyebrows. 'Take? Do you mean steal? Are you telling me that you know how to get around a car security system? Something else you got from your friends?'

Bec's mouth twisted. 'No. Wish I did. We could hire one.'

'You need ID to hire a car. The Boneheads will be onto us in minutes. And there were all those roadblocks, remember?'

Bec lay down with her head resting on the mattress. 'Once this is all over, I'm never walking anywhere again. I'm driving everywhere.'

'I thought you already did that,' Amber said, turning back to the phone. 'There must be a website about the Great North Walk.' She opened an internet browser to search. 'Bingo. Detailed track notes and everything. Do we have a pen and paper?'

Bec rolled over and reached into the front pocket of her pack. She handed Amber a pen. 'I don't have any paper.'

Amber searched for something to write on. She settled on tearing open the cardboard boxes of biscuits that Mrs McKenzie had given them, leaving the biscuits in their plastic wrappers.

The Great North Walk wasn't one single, clear track. The route took in many different bush tracks and trails and suburban streets. It was signposted, but Amber knew from experience that it was easy to miss the signs. Especially in the dark. She scrawled notes about the route in small writing on the inside of the cardboard boxes.

'Why not use the phone?' Bec sounded drowsy.

'Some of those bush tracks won't have service. And we might run out of battery, even with your solar power bank.'

Bec dozed. Alice and Lucy crawled out of the crevice to go to the toilet. When they returned, Alice threw stones at a small sapling that was clinging to the overhang. Lucy played peek-a-boo with Oliver, covering her teddy bear's eyes with its hands and filling the quiet space with Oliver's giggles. Tears pricked Amber's eyes as she smiled at them. Her throat felt dry and thick, and she swallowed hard, thinking about how close she had come to losing Oliver. His eyes met hers, crinkling up at the sides like Adam's did when he laughed. She bit the corner of her lip and turned back to her notes, trying not to think about Adam.

It took more than an hour to jot down enough details to feel confident that she wouldn't get lost. Bec looked over her shoulder, yawning. 'We'd better make sure nothing happens to you, because none of the rest of us have any chance of understanding your notes.'

She stashed the notes in the carrier, gave the phone back to Bec and lay down. The hot, humid air was suffocating; no breeze reaching their cramped hiding space. She stared at the patch of blue sky she could see through the crevice above her.

Bec scrolled on her phone. 'You and I are still trending,' she told Amber, 'You especially.'

'I don't want to know,' Amber said, 'Anything on the girls?'

'Nothing. I'm not sure anyone even knows they're with us.'

'Damn.' Amber looked at Alice. 'I was hoping someone on the internet might find out where your parents are for us.'

'This is from the news media,' Bec said, 'A manhunt is underway to find fugitives Amber Yu and Rebecca Williams, who were last seen in the Thornleigh area of north-western Sydney. Authorities advise that Yu and Williams are dangerous and may be armed. Anyone who sees Yu or Williams or knows of their current whereabouts is warned not to approach them but to contact triple zero immediately.'

'Fuck.'

'I wish you were armed,' Alice said.

'I don't.' Amber gritted her teeth as images of the Boneheads she'd killed filled her mind again. The crevice felt even more suffocating. Manhunt... fugitives... dangerous and may be armed... She couldn't believe these phrases were being used about her. News stories like these were about desperate, disadvantaged people - not her, with her university education, high-paying public service job and million-dollar apartment.

Bec kept scrolling. 'Listen to this. It's from a group I follow.

129

They're a bit fringe - they're into conspiracy theories - but they do have government informants. It's talking about the Boneheads trying to find us. It says that they're using helicopters - we know that - but this is the interesting bit: A worrying development in the hunt for Yu and Williams is the deployment of a large, carnivorous animal with a keen sense of smell believed to be being used for tracking, like a police dog. Observers note that the animal looks like a large wombat. It is unknown where these animals have come from. Theories include that the Boneheads brought them from wherever they came from - also unknown - or that the animals are the result of genetic experimentation on native marsupials.'

Amber shuddered, seeing again the mouthful of razor-sharp teeth on the animal the soldiers had brought to her apartment building. 'Do you think they can track us?'

Bec shrugged. 'They haven't found us yet.'

Amber thought about Dan attacking the animal with a star picket. She wondered what he, Helen and Wendy were making of the news reports about her. Did they know she got Oliver back?

She looked at Bec. Her eyes were closed, and she was squeezing her hands together. 'Are you okay?'

Bec opened her eyes. There was moisture in them. 'I just read - Tasmania is still free. The PM hasn't even tried to take it over.'

Amber put her hand on Bec's arm. 'So that means your parents and sister are okay.'

Bec nodded. 'I was worried that they might be in danger - because of me. You're lucky your parents are in China. You don't have to worry about your family.'

'Except Adam.'

'Yeah, of course, except Adam. I'm sure he'll have the sense not to tell anyone that he's married to you, though. He's the sensible one in your relationship.'

Amber hit her on the arm, and she grinned, but her eyes were still moist.

'I wonder why the PM isn't bothering to take over Tassie?'

'Not worth the effort, is it?' Bec said, taking pleasure in insulting the place she grew up in.

'I'd invade it for the pinot.'

'He's probably a beer drinker. He looks like one.'

'Bet he doesn't drink at all. Not even coffee. That's why he's a miserable bastard.'

They ate crackers and the tinned tuna that Mrs McKenzie had given them for dinner, and waited for night. The sun seemed to hover above the horizon for hours.

'What time is it?' Alice yawned.

Bec tapped her phone. 'About eight.'

'It's still as light as anything.'

'That's summer for you.'

At last it was dark enough to satisfy Bec. They emerged from the cave, stretching cramped muscles. Amber's back had stiffened after the day in the small space. She gritted her teeth and shuffled sideways down the hill to the valley floor, placing each foot with care, Bec's phone with the map app clutched in her sweaty left hand. Bec took up the rear with Oliver in the carrier, his eyes big and round with excitement and tiredness.

The moon hadn't risen yet; the darkness broken only by the light spilling from Bec's phone. Amber dimmed the phone and confined herself to quick peeks at the map to make sure they didn't change direction and miss the main spine of the Great North Walk. Thorny branches, sharp grasses and tree roots seemed to leap out of the dark and snare them, adding more scratches and bruises to the ones they'd collected earlier in the day. Oliver's head drooped up and down as he fought to stay awake, before succumbing to the darkness and rocking movement.

Amber dragged her leg free from a clinging vine, and found herself standing on a wide, well-defined track. She looked up at the stars and breathed a quick prayer of thanks that the map app had led them the right way. The others appeared on either side of her, smiling to be out of the scrub. They had a quick snack of biscuits and water. Amber took the first biscuit box with her notes about the route out of the carrier, and strode with confidence down the formed track.

The route that night varied, from concrete paths, flat management trails and tracks to steep tracks and stairs. Amber led the way, flicking the torch on Bec's phone on to squint at her cramped handwriting on the piece of cardboard. Great North Walk signs at intervals gave her confidence that they were on the correct route. The night air was cooler than the day, but the humidity was high. Sweat stung the wounds on her back and the cardboard was damp from her sweaty hand. They stopped every couple of hours for drinks and snacks and to go to the toilet, plus an extra time when Oliver woke demanding a breastfeed.

Just after midnight, a perfect half circle moon with a slight concave slid above the horizon. It lit the bush with a grey light, making it easier to avoid uneven ground and tree roots. At two am they ate vegemite sandwiches near a small creek, swatting mosquitoes. Amber filled their water bottles from the running water in the centre of the creek and dropped iodine tablets from her first aid kit into the water to purify it. Once she'd finished, Lucy took off her shoes and socks and paddled in the shallow water near the creek edge.

They trudged on. Alice and Lucy were yawning. Amber's back ached, and she stumbled, the pain sapping her energy. After a while she noticed that the owlet nightjar calls had been replaced by the twittering of small daytime birds. She was tempted to suggest they crawl under a bush and go to sleep, ignoring the risk from helicopters, but the thought of arguing with Bec was more exhausting than continuing to walk.

As the sky began to lighten on the horizon, a large bridge with steel, triangular trusses and wooden slats came into view. Amber stopped in front of the group. 'Will that stop helicopters seeing us?'

Bec's eyes were on her feet. She looked up and blinked. 'Oh, it's getting light.' She looked at the bridge, biting her lip. 'I don't think the wood will. But we could hide under the foot of the bridge. I think that would be okay.'

Amber jumped down the side of the bridge, into a small gap under its foot. The bank had been cut into to create a rough stone wall on one side. They squeezed in together, with the three mattresses side-by-side, touching each other. Amber didn't even have the energy to squirm into her sleeping bag. She pulled the open bag over herself and Oliver and was asleep in minutes.

Eleven

The empty pit in Amber's stomach woke her. The light was grey, and the air heavy with moisture. She pushed the sleeping bag away. Sweat clung to her body. The usual cacophony of birds was muted. She eased herself onto her knees, trying not to bump Oliver or wake the girls sleeping next to her, while she mixed powdered milk with water for breakfast.

A loud crack of thunder made her jump. As though it was a signal, black clouds filled the sky and rain fell in sheets to the ground. Oliver woke in tears. Bec, on the other side of the girls, swore and sat up, pulling her sleeping bag out of the water splashing up from the ground. Small hailstones battered the ground. Lucy crawled onto Amber's mattress and reached out to catch them, the rain dribbling down her arms.

Lightning lit the sky, followed by ominous, rolling thunder. The hailstones disappeared, but the heavy rain continued. Lucy dried her arms on her clothes and crawled back to her own mattress, where Alice lay gazing at the storm with red-rimmed eyes.

Bec took over making breakfast while Amber fed Oliver. The thunder and rain were too loud for them to speak without shouting, so they sat cross-legged on their mattresses with bowls of muesli, watching flashes of white light illuminate the bush like strobe lights at a nightclub.

When they finished eating, Bec collected the dishes and rinsed them in the rain, which was already easing. It stopped a few minutes later and the clouds moved on. Sunlight brightened the bush, heating up the air, which was even more humid after the rain. Water dripped from the trees. The occasional crack of thunder echoed around them.

Amber moved into the open, carrying the pieces of the camping stove.

Bec sat up. 'What are you doing?'

'I figure they're not going to put any helicopters in the sky while there's storms in the area. So I'm going to make coffee.'

'Oh.' Bec was silent for a moment, her concerns about safety warring with her desire for coffee. Amber hid a smile, guessing which would win. 'Good.'

Amber made the coffee, passing Bec a cup, and sitting on her mattress to drink hers. She closed her eyes as the warm liquid ran down her throat. When the coffee was gone, she felt more relaxed than she had in days.

They spent the day resting. Amber struggled to sleep. Her body was drenched with sweat and the damp air pressed down on her. She drifted into a light doze and was woken by a helicopter circling overhead. She stared up at the bridge above them, thinking how much she hated the sound of helicopter blades.

Oliver rocked back and forth on his hands and knees, moaning and trying to reach the camping stove. He collapsed, screaming in frustration. Lucy tried to distract him by playing peek-a-boo.

It was a relief when the long afternoon came to an end. Bec made sandwiches for dinner, not willing to risk the stove twice. They ate in silence, preparing for another long night of walking.

The air was cooler than it had been the previous two nights. Bec led the way along a wide management trail. Amber trailed behind, looking at the sky. The clouds had cleared, revealing a trail of flickering stars. After about an hour of walking, they had to leave the easy management trail and feel their way in the dark down a steep, rocky track flanked by large boulders. Amber took the lead, her eyes aching from trying to stare into the darkness.

The track came to a sudden halt at the edge of a tall rock. She froze, telling the others to stop.

'Are we lost?' Bec asked.

Amber checked her piece of cardboard with the torch on Bec's phone. 'There's meant to be a ladder.' She shone the torch down the face of the rock. A rectangular piece of metal stuck out of the side. Below it were several more, evenly spaced. 'Yep, here it is. Stay there a sec.'

She pushed the cardboard into her pocket, swapped the phone to her right hand and put her right foot on the first step, reaching out with her left. Once she felt the second step under it, she moved her right foot down, using her uninjured hand to hold the first step. She continued this way, feeling awkward climbing with the phone in one hand. Reaching the ground, she stepped back and pointed the torch at the ladder to light the way for the others.

As soon as they were all on the ground, she switched the torch off, worried that someone might see the light. They stayed still for a while, waiting for their eyes to adjust to the darkness, then continued to a creek under a huge concrete bridge.

The air was full of the crick-crick-crick sounds of frogs calling. Alice picked up a stone and tossed it into the water.

Amber flashed the torch across the water. Swollen from the earlier rain, the creek raced under the bridge.

Lucy shrank back. 'I don't want to go in there.'

'Do you think we should take the bridge?' Amber nodded at the concrete arches stretching far above their heads.

Bec followed her gaze. They heard the roar of a car. An artificial white light lit the tall trees nearby for a moment, and the car screamed over the concrete bridge. Bec shook her head. 'Definitely not.'

She pulled the THONG out of her zipper pocket. Amber gave her the phone and she put it and the THONG in a pocket at the top of the carrier, just below Oliver's head.

Amber took the shopping bag from Lucy and slung it over her left shoulder, and the cat pack over her right. She directed them to link arms, with Bec and herself in the middle, Alice on her left and Lucy on Bec's right. Linked together, they stepped into the creek. The water rose midway up her thighs, and waist height on Lucy. It pushed against them, trying to dislodge their feet and send them tumbling downstream. Lucy's foot slipped out from under her, and she dragged down on Bec's right arm. Bec struggled to keep her feet, Lucy and the carrier pulling her backwards. Cold water splashed onto Oliver's head, and he screamed. Amber held tight to Bec's arm, gasping as burning pain ran up her arm from her injured hand. Bec found her footing and pulled Lucy up.

Amber relaxed her grip. 'Right to keep going?'

Lucy took a shaky breath and nodded. She took a cautious step.

Amber spoke in a singsong voice to Oliver. 'You're okay, you're okay. I'm here. You're okay.' His wails lessened.

One slow step at a time, they reached the other side. Lucy

flopped down on the stony ground. Her shirt was soaked, and even the back of her hair was dripping. She shivered. Alice dropped down next to her and wrapped her arms around her, wetting her own shirt.

Bec dumped the carrier on the ground and scrambled in the top pocket. Water gushed out of the pocket as she opened it. She pulled out the THONG and ran her hands over it. The lights glowed over its surface.

'Have you got somewhere dry to put this?' She held out the THONG. Amber took it and slipped it into the top of the cat pack.

Bec pushed buttons on the phone. Nothing happened.

'Fuck!' She rounded on Lucy. 'Clumsy idiot, why couldn't you have been more careful?'

Lucy buried her face in Alice's shirt. Alice's face turned red and she opened her mouth.

Amber stood upright before she could speak. 'Don't you yell at her! You insisted we go across the creek - she didn't even want to.'

'What do we do now? I can't contact Ren without the phone.'

'Ren?' Amber's brow furrowed. She knelt and searched for her hiking towel in the bottom of the carrier. 'That guy who was a prisoner with us at the uni? How do you even know how to contact him?'

Bec's mouth twisted. She lifted her shoulders. 'I've been meaning to tell you about that - he's our explosives expert.'

Amber pulled out the towel and handed it to Lucy. 'Huh?'

'You know - my group. He's a member of one of the larger resistance groups - I think Josie is, too - but he helped other groups out with explosives, including mine.'

Amber's mouth dropped open. 'You knew him before that night?'

'Yeah.'

Amber's face paled. 'And - why was he there that night?'

'I asked him to meet us there.'

'But - you didn't know I was planning to go there.'

'I texted him. Just before we left.'

'You texted him,' Amber's voice was icy cold, 'And you didn't think to mention that to me?'

'I thought we might need help. I couldn't ask anyone from my own group - we were scattered everywhere by then. He was the only person I could think of. It was lucky I texted him. We wouldn't have got away if he and Josie hadn't kept the soldiers busy.'

'We might not have been caught at all if they hadn't been there! They got caught first. The soldiers' guards were up - because of them.'

'You don't know that.'

'You don't know that I'm wrong! I can't believe you contacted them without telling me!'

'I was trying to protect us.' Bec drew her brows in tight. 'Look, I'm sorry I didn't tell you. But I still think it was just as well I contacted them.'

Amber gasped in air. She'd never felt so angry. 'It was just as well? Because we got caught, I had to kill two Boneheads, and now we're on the run from helicopters and Boneheads and wombats and who knows what the fuck else! And you think that was just as well?'

Oliver let out a loud wail. Filled with guilt that she'd ignored him to yell at Bec, Amber pulled him out of the carrier and held him against her shoulder. He buried his head in her chest.

'What else aren't you telling me? Why are you still in contact with him?'

'Oh, well,' Bec wriggled in discomfort, 'His group want to help us. Make sure we don't get caught.'

Amber let out a long breath. 'You need to promise me,' she said,

'That you won't contact them again without asking me first.'

Bec frowned, then shrugged. 'O-kay, I promise.'

Amber turned away. Her anger was a hard knot in her stomach. Lucy's eyes were on Amber and Bec, the towel clutched in her hands. She hadn't moved to use it.

'You should dry off and get changed.' Amber shoved the cat pack closer to Lucy. 'You, too,' she said to Alice. She knelt at the edge of the creek and submerged her sore hand in the water.

Bec shoved the broken phone in the carrier and opened one of the packets of biscuits that Amber had taken out of the box for her notes. She took one and handed the packet to Lucy. 'You were right,' she said, 'We should have taken the bridge.'

It wasn't much of an apology, but Lucy took it as one, and gave her a smile.

Alice glared at Bec. She wouldn't forgive so easily. Amber knew how she felt.

When Bec and the girls had changed, they kept walking along narrow bush tracks. Exhaustion settled over Amber, her limbs and muscles heavy and slow. She walked with her shoulders hunched forward and her eyes on the ground.

The moon rose just after one am, another half-circle lighting up the bush. Amber straightened, feeling the weight ease. The light made walking seem easier.

Bec glared at the moon. 'Where were you earlier?' Lucy giggled, the rippling sound of genuine laughter startling. Alice scowled.

They passed open picnic areas, wetlands and followed a boardwalk through the bush. Amber imagined that during the day, under less stressful circumstances, it would be a beautiful walk. Adam would like it. She felt a pain in the back of her throat, and swallowed. She had been avoiding thinking about Adam. There was nothing she could do for him. She rubbed her hand on the trunk of a casuarina, using the feel of the rough bark to stop the thoughts flooding her brain.

The next two days followed the same pattern. They hid during the hot, humid days in small overhangs under rocks, and walked all night. Amber managed without the phone torch. Each day she tried to memorise her notes for the following night, so she wouldn't need to look at them in the dark. The few times that she wasn't sure, and the moon hadn't risen yet, she used one of the matches that she'd packed to light the hiking stove. She held the match above her piece of cardboard until it burnt down, burning her fingers a couple of times. At regular intervals she checked with Lucy what the time was, to work out how far along the route they were. After a while, Lucy took off her watch and gave it to Amber.

Amber avoided speaking to Bec unless she had to. The hard knot of anger seemed to grow rather than fade. Alice also retreated into a sullen silence.

The nights of walking strengthened them, and they adjusted to sleeping during the day. Amber's wounds improved every day, until she could walk without pain, but she still couldn't carry a pack. Helicopters continued to circle overhead during the day, but the length of time between helicopter overflights increased, until there was only one pass each day.

'We're running out of food,' Bec said on the second morning as she poured cereal into bowls.

Amber blinked. 'Already?' She'd known the food she bought from the Asian grocer wouldn't last long with four people living off it, even with the additional food Mrs McKenzie had given them, but she'd been trying not to think about it. 'How much do we have left?'

'Another day? Maybe two if we're careful.'

Amber pulled one of her pieces of cardboard from her pocket and stared at the scribbled words. 'We should get to Brooklyn tonight. There'll be food there.'

'We'll have to be careful,' Bec said, 'We're recognisable -

remember Mrs McKenzie? She said she'd seen us on television. We might have to steal the food rather than buying it.'

Amber pulled a face. Thou shalt not murder; thou shalt not steal. At least there wasn't any chance of committing adultery right now.

She looked back at her scribble. 'The guide notes said to take a water taxi to Patonga.'

'I don't think we should do that.'

'I don't know if there's a better option. There's a train, but people might recognise us on that, too.'

Bec pulled a face. 'Let's worry about it when we get there. Where do we go after Patonga?'

Amber read from her notes. 'Wondabyne, Somersby, Yarramalong, Basin Campsite, Congwai Valley, Watagan, Teralba, Glenrock Lagoon, Newcastle.'

'Gees,' Bec groaned, 'We're going to be walking forever.'

'You got something better to do?'

Lucy had her hands wrapped around her teddy. She released one hand, reached out from the overhang they were camped under and ran her hand down the squiggly lines etched into the bark of a scribbly gum.

'I don't mind,' she said, 'This is nice.'

Alice gave her a look of disbelief. 'Nice?'

'Well, it is. I like the bush. It's peaceful.'

'You're bonkers.'

Lucy turned away, her face turning red.

'It is nice,' Amber said, 'My husband would love this. He loves spending time in the bush.'

'Not me,' Bec yawned, 'I can't wait to get back to civilisation. And have the longest shower in the history of the world.'

'Me too.' Alice spoke to Bec for the first time since the creek crossing. 'And pizza.'

Amber had to agree with her, especially when Bec handed out

half-servings of cereal. She surveyed her bowl in disgust.

Bec was watching her. 'Just in case we can't get food in Brooklyn, for some reason,' she said.

Their route that night led them to Jerusalem Bay. The air temperature dropped as they neared the water. Amber zipped up her light jacket. In the still, moonless night, the water was almost invisible. Only the stars glinting on the ripples indicated the threshold between land and sea. Amber was drawn to the timeless, black expanse of water. She started walking towards it. She felt hypnotised.

'Where are you going?' Bec's voice was loud in the silent air. 'The track is that way.'

Amber blinked, and turned back towards her. She shook her head. 'Right. Sure.' She followed Bec, her brain muzzy. She was tired. How long had it been since she'd had a proper night's sleep? But she couldn't shake the feeling that there was something familiar about the water - not the familiarity of a friend, more like an old, half-forgotten acquaintance.

As they trotted down sandstone steps, she realised why it had seemed familiar. It felt the same as at the university, when time slowed down. She shivered, and kept her face turned away from the water as they continued, resisting the urge to turn towards it. When they left it behind, she felt a sense of relief, but also a sense of loss. A missed opportunity.

The moon rose as they stumbled down a very steep, cement management trail. Alice, with the weight of Bec's pack on her back, struggled to stop herself from rushing headlong down the hill, despite the corrugations in the cement. Bec trotted down sideways with an odd, jerking movement. They breathed a sigh when they reached a low metal gate. The grey moonlight reflected on the metal roof of a house beyond the gate.

'This is it?' Bec asked, 'Brooklyn?'

Amber nodded. She leant against the gate, staring at the house with glazed eyes. Her body felt weighed down. She couldn't dredge up any interest in their problems with food and getting to Patonga.

The sight of Brooklyn had the opposite effect on Bec. She bounced on the balls of her feet, her eyes sparkling. 'Why don't you stay here with Ollie and the girls and I'll have a look around? I'll see if I can get some food, and check out options for getting to Patonga. I'll be less noticeable on my own - they'll be looking for two women, not just one.'

Amber narrowed her eyes. Why did Bec want to go on her own - so she could contact the resistance again? She clenched her teeth. 'No - we'll all go.'

Squaring her shoulders, she ploughed past the gate and houses. Bec shrugged and followed. Amber turned right towards town. Cars lined the street on both sides. Streetlights made the roads a patchwork of light and dark. Darkness shrouded the brick and weatherboard houses they passed. A cluster of small shops lined the main street - a motel, pharmacy, real estate agent, post office, cafe and pub.

'What are we going to do about food?' Amber asked in a low voice, 'The shops don't look very promising. And they might be alarmed.'

'Houses?' Alice asked.

'The owners might be home.'

Bec pulled a face. 'Let's keep looking. Something might come up.'

They passed a brightly-lit, modern overpass and lift tower to the train station, which seemed out of place among the Brooklyn shacks and cottages. Tall palm trees grew in two lines behind a carpark, rising even taller than the station lift tower. A large grey building stretched along the shore - the marina.

Bec wandered in one of the openings to the centre of the marina. The shops and cafes were locked or shuttered for the night. A mast, complete with crow's nest, ship's wheel and bell, rose from the centre of the room and out the top of the domed ceiling. A gangway led down to a floating dock, surrounded by motorboats in a variety of sizes.

Bec squinted down at the water. 'I wonder if any of the boaties would have left food on their boats?'

Amber stared at the boats, quivering on the still water. 'It's worth a look.'

Bec dumped the carrier on the wooden slats. Oliver opened his eyes and yawned.

Bec turned to Lucy. 'Can I take the shopping bag?'

Lucy deposited the air mattress on the ground, along with the tube of aloe vera gel and one box of biscuits; all that remained of the food Mrs McKenzie had given them. She handed Bec the empty bag.

'Wait here,' Bec said, 'I won't be long.' She hurried down the nearest gangway.

Amber dropped the cat pack and squeezed the aloe vera gel and packet of biscuits into the bottom of the carrier. Bec hopped onto the first motorboat and rummaged in the gear compartments. Amber could just make out her shaking her head. She climbed back onto the dock and jumped into the next boat. This time she held up a small packet. She put it in the shopping bag and moved to the next boat.

Amber stared out at the water, waiting while Bec worked her way through the moored boats. Amber's breath formed clouds in the cool morning air. Listening to the slap, slap, slap of the water lapping against the boats, tension that she hadn't known she was carrying left her shoulders. A lone cormorant flapped its wings on a pylon, then settled down again.

Bec climbed out of the last boat, the shopping bag bulging in her hands. She lifted her fist above her head.

'She must have found some,' Alice said.

They watched as Bec jogged back towards the gangway.

A large figure ducked its head under the entrance to the marina. Amber whirled around. Black eyes, with no whites at all, met hers. She flinched and bit back a scream.

Twelve

'And here they are.' The Bonehead showed rows of sharp, white teeth, the sides of its mouth curving up in the semblance of a human smile. It spoke with the same flat accent as the Bonehead at the university. It was the shortest one she'd seen, with a dull grey bony plate and a sword strapped to its left side, but no rifle.

Amber felt dizzy. Her legs wobbled.

Alice didn't hesitate. Flinging Bec's pack on the ground, she grabbed Lucy's hand to flee out a second entrance. 'Don't move.' The Bonehead's words were like a whip crack. 'Or I'll tell Private Jerome to fire.'

Amber's eyes darted around the scene. Bec had frozen halfway up the gangway. Jerome was standing behind her, his body stiff and lips pressed together, holding a rifle to her head. She'd dropped the shopping bag. Packets of biscuits, chips and muesli bars tumbled out of it onto the gangway.

Alice's body went rigid, but she stayed on the balls of her feet, a calculating look on her face. An icy coldness gripped Amber. Alice was going to run. She only cared for her own family - she wouldn't care if Jerome killed Bec. Amber was paralysed.

Lucy yanked her hand free of Alice's and moved out of her reach. Alice blinked, her mouth falling open in an O shape. She looked as surprised as if her own shadow had refused to follow her. She dropped so that her feet were flat on the ground, but her body remained tense, reminding Amber of a cat waiting for an opportunity to pounce.

The Bonehead bared its teeth again. 'We intercepted your messages to the resistance. Thank you for making it so easy for us to find you.'

Amber looked at Bec. A roar filled her mind. Bec's messages had gotten them captured. She was so consumed by fury she barely noticed the Bonehead stalking around her, or Jerome directing Bec at gunpoint up the gangway.

''Where's the THONG?' the Bonehead snapped.

'Don't.' Bec's voice was a squeak.

Amber gave her an incredulous look. Bec had put them all in danger, and the only thing she cared about was giving the THONG to the resistance. Amber's body was shaking, but she couldn't tell if it was in fear or anger.

The Bonehead let out a deep sigh. 'Let me make this clear. I will be taking the THONG. You can give it to me, or I can kill your friend, your baby, and you, and take the THONG from your dead body.' It wrapped its right hand around the hilt of the sword, sliding it out of the scabbard so that the top of the silver blade showed. 'The THONG might protect you from Private Jerome's bullets, but it won't protect you from this. Of course, you know that.'

Amber didn't care about the THONG - the Bonehead could have it. But she didn't trust the Bonehead. She was sure it would kill them whether she gave up the THONG or not.

'I'll get it.' She knelt next to the cat pack and fumbled with the zip, exaggerating how much her hands were shaking to give herself time. She reached out with her mind, searching for the power that had helped her at the university. She could almost feel it on the edge of her mind, but it skittered away, staying out of reach.

'I'm losing patience,' the Bonehead said.

Amber tried again. Please help me, she begged, as she had at the university. But this time she couldn't feel the timelessness and strength at all.

Amber's hands were really shaking now. It took a few tries to unzip the pocket. She drew out the black ball. Lights flashed across its surface where her fingers touched it.

She held it out. Bec let out a small moan. The Bonehead took it from Amber's hand. 'We got what we came for,' it said to Jerome.

Jerome was unmoved. 'You want me to call for help to bring them in?'

'And let one of those bastard Red Bones take the credit? We'll bring them in ourselves.'

'They're killers!'

The Bonehead gave Amber a contemptuous look. 'I think we can handle them.' Its mouth curved up again. 'I want to see the look on that Red Bone's face when I return the THONG and the two hostages.'

A splash drew its attention to the water. Two men in their early thirties paddled identical blue sea kayaks towards the marina, to Amber's left. They were clad in bright yellow life jackets, their kayaks laden with fishing gear. Amber couldn't believe anyone was voluntarily on the water at this time of morning.

'He keeps leaving early,' one of them said, tossing a waterproof sack onto the pontoon and hauling himself after it, 'And I have to cover for him.' He wrapped a rope tied to the front of the kayak around a cleat on the floating dock.

'And you've told your manager, yeah?' The second man pulled himself onto the pontoon, flinging his rope around another cleat. 'Yeah, several times. He couldn't give a fuck.'

The Bonehead stalked towards them. They saw it at the same time, and froze, their eyes widening.

'Go away.' The Bonehead jerked its head towards the edge of

the marina. The men didn't need telling twice. With furtive glances at the women and Jerome, they scuttled away, leaving the waterproof bags and kayaks without a second glance.

The Bonehead turned back to Jerome. It nodded at Oliver, still seated in the top of the carrier, his large, round eyes on Amber. 'We don't need the baby. Kill it, and we'll take the other four with us.'

'No!' Amber's anger was swept away in a flood of terror. She knelt to scoop up the carrier. The Bonehead grabbed the back of her jacket and propelled her onto the wooden slats in front of Lucy.

'Do it,' it said.

Jerome stared at Oliver, his mouth opening. He stumbled backwards, shaking his head in long, slow movements.

'Useless.' The Bonehead drew its sword in a single movement. 'I have to do everything myself.'

Amber lunged to her feet and cast about for something - anything - to stop the Bonehead. Alice was ahead of her. She wrenched the bolt cutters from the top of Bec's pack and threw them to land at Amber's feet. Amber seized them.

Help me! This time, something responded. Once again, time slowed. The Bonehead started to turn, swinging its sword towards her. She dodged the sword with ease, lifted the bolt cutters above her head and swung them down with every ounce of her strength onto the Bonehead's head. The Bonehead's sword clipped her arm as the bolt cutters landed. The bone on its head cracked with a sickening crunch and the bolt cutters sliced into the soft flesh beneath.

Time sped up again. Blood sprayed out of the Bonehead's head onto Amber and Oliver. Oliver wailed. The Bonehead crashed to the ground. The THONG dropped from its hand and rolled across the slats to Jerome's feet.

Jerome raised his rifle and pointed it at Amber. This is it. She felt numb, waiting for the bullet to rip into her. At least she'd stopped the Bonehead killing Oliver.

The bullet didn't come. Jerome was motionless, his finger on the trigger.

'Let's get out of here,' Bec said.

Amber blinked at her, still expecting Jerome to shoot. Bile rose into her throat. She leant over her knees and vomited on the cement floor.

Bec pushed past Amber, scooped up the carrier and the cat pack and bounded down the gangway. She dropped the cat pack and the carrier, with Oliver still strapped into it, into the front kayak.

Alice scooped up Bec's pack and the air mattress and grabbed Lucy's hand. 'Come on.' She dragged Lucy towards the kayaks and dropped the pack and mattress into the back kayak. Oliver wailed louder. Alice let herself down in the front kayak and undid the carrier straps to release him. Oliver clutched her with his small hands and sobbed.

Amber stared at the bloody bolt cutters, unmoving. She opened her hand and they landed on the floor. She continued to stare at her hand. Her body was icy cold again.

Bec shovelled the food into the shopping bag and swung it over one shoulder.

She moved towards Jerome, her hands held out wide to the side. 'I just want the THONG.'

Jerome's eyes narrowed. He lifted a foot and brought it down onto the THONG, crunching it into pieces.

Bec's eyes were like saucepans. 'What are you doing?'

'Making sure no-one gets the damn thing.'

Bec lunged at him. He swung his rifle up and she drew back, baring her teeth. 'Nah uh,' he said, sounding more like a schoolboy than a soldier, 'You're not immune to my bullets now.'

'I was going to take that to the resistance.' Bec didn't move, but the words dropped from her mouth like icicles. 'That could have given us a fighting chance. Whose side are you on?'

'I'm not on a side! I joined the army to protect the country I love, and its people, not to fight for monsters.'

'Then why destroy the THONG?'

'Not all monsters have bones on their heads.' Jerome's mouth twisted. 'Do you even know how many people died in Governor Macquarie Tower?'

Bec met his gaze, her chin held high. She didn't reply.

He snorted. 'Didn't think so.' He fumbled at a hand-held radio strapped to his chest, pressing a button on the side of it. 'Other soldiers will be on their way. You'll want to paddle fast. I'm not sure you'll make it.'

Bec looked like she wanted to keep arguing. Amber shook her head, clearing it, and stood. She grasped Bec's arm and spoke through chattering teeth. 'Leave it. Come on.'

Bec shook her off and scooped up the bolt cutters. She bent over the Bonehead's body and straightened, holding its sword. Amber followed her down the gangway, twisting her head to keep an eye on Jerome.

Bec threw the shopping bag, sword and bolt cutters into the back kayak. 'Come on,' she said to Lucy, jumping in. Lucy climbed into the front and crouched on the floor. Bec pulled the rope free of the pole and let it drop into the kayak.

Alice released the rope as soon as Amber sat down in the front kayak, pushing the kayak away from the jetty. Oliver still sobbed in her lap. Amber looked back at the marina. Jerome had lowered his gun. His face was pale in the moonlight, his curls again escaping his helmet, making him look younger. Amber felt a sudden urge to mother him, as though he was an older version of Oliver.

'Come with us,' she called.

'Amber.' Bec's voice was loud in the quiet morning air. 'We

need to go.'

Jerome didn't move. His lips curled up in snarl, but his eyes were moist. He looked lost.

Bec started paddling hard. Alice thrust a paddle into Amber's hands, and she followed Bec out onto the Hawkesbury River.

Oliver reached for Amber. Alice passed him back, into her lap. He buried his head into her clothes. Something dripped down her back. She reached behind to check it. Her hand came back streaked in blood. Not the Bonehead's blood, which had hit her front, but her own blood. She'd reopened her wounds. She shook her hand in a vain attempt to get rid of the blood, and kept paddling. Oliver stopped crying and fell asleep, still covered in the Bonehead's blood.

They paddled past a cluster of fishing boats, moored to an oyster-encrusted jetty. Amber looked back towards the marina. From here, the domed central room looked like a UFO that had landed on the top of the building. She couldn't see Jerome.

To her left, a wide land bridge crossed to a long, thin island. A road and a train line ran along the land bridge, both empty of vehicles. In the dim light, she could make out empty train carriages, vehicles and storage buildings along the shore. A large transmission tower stood sentinel above the island. They rounded the tip of the island. A railway bridge with eight steel trusses crossed the water high above them.

Amber opened her mouth to pray, but the prayer died on her lips.

'I killed another Bonehead,' she moaned between strokes, 'I really am a murderer.'

Alice looked surprised. 'Of course you did. It was going to kill your baby.'

Amber shook her head. She wondered if Alice had always been so nonchalant about killing, or only since her parents disappeared.

'Keep paddling,' Bec called, her soft voice carrying across the water, 'I wouldn't have thought it possible, but we've found worse get-away vehicles than the ferry.'

Bec was right. Amber pushed the Bonehead out of her mind and concentrated on paddling. Bec steered her kayak into the shadow of the railway bridge.

'Do you know where you're going?' Amber called.

Bec looked back and shrugged. She nodded her head towards a tall, dark hill in front of them. 'I just want to get off the water. That shore looks closest.'

The bridge towered above them. At intervals huge, concrete supporting pylons reared up out of the dark, fell behind and disappeared into the night. Amber put her head down and concentrated on dipping one side of her paddle into the water, drawing it through the water and lifting it high, dipping the other side into the water. Cold water splashed onto her head and shirt as she switched from side to side, cooling her skin to match the cold she felt inside.

'A train's coming,' Alice said. Amber lifted her head and stopped paddling for a moment. Alice was right. She could hear the soft roar of a train. Bec pulled her kayak further under the bridge and kept paddling. Amber followed suit. The roar increased to a deafening screech overhead that seemed to go on and on - a freight train. With a final metallic shriek, the last wagon passed overhead, the roar of the train echoing over the water for a long time after it squealed off the bridge and into the bush on the other side.

They had almost reached the rocky shore as a passenger train rasped overhead, quieter and shorter than the freight train. A few minutes later another passenger train hurtled past in the opposite direction. They pulled the kayaks onto the rocks and waited for it to pass.

A smudge of light appeared on the horizon. Invisible birds

twittered in the trees and three large pelicans soared over the water towards Brooklyn. A large motorboat roared out from behind the long, thin island and turned right, just visible against the sky.

Amber's arms ached from paddling, and her back was bleeding even more. She still felt cold. There was a dull ache from her stomach, reminding her that she hadn't had breakfast, and had thrown up any food left from the previous night. She slid Oliver into the carrier. He whimpered without opening his eyes, and went back to sleep.

Bec rinsed the bolt cutters in the water lapping at the shore and dried them on her leggings. Amber turned away and squeezed her eyes shut, but images of the Bonehead collapsing on the ground filled her mind. Bec pushed the bolt cutters into her pack and lifted the Bonehead's sword. 'Do you want this?'

Amber stared at it in horror, holding her hands up in front of her body. 'No.'

Bec strapped the sword to the side of her pack and handed the pack to Alice. She swung the carrier onto her back. 'We need to hide the kayaks, or the Boneheads will know exactly where we are.'

'I think they'll guess,' Amber said, 'It's the closest shore to Brooklyn.'

'Well, we don't have to confirm their guess.'

Bec wrapped her hand around the small handle at the front of the kayak. Amber took the handle at the back. The slope rose steeply from the water, covered in rocks and shaded by tall, twisted gum trees. They placed their feet with care on the rocky ground as they carried the kayak up, to the right of the train line. The girls trailed behind them.

'Let's dump them in those weeds.' Bec pointed at a large stand of lantana that had taken over the bush next to the train line. The weeds had grown well over head height, their branches twisting and turning on each other, creating a strong barrier.

Amber pulled the shopping bag and air mattress out of the kayak and dropped them on the ground. Bec swung the carrier off her back and left it with Lucy. She and Amber pushed their way through the lantana, the branches scratching them and grabbing their clothes as they passed.

They returned for the second kayak, dumping it next to the first one. An image of the two young men in their bright yellow life jackets appeared in Amber's mind. Sorry, she thought to the image. She felt a heavy weight on her chest. What was she turning into? She let out her breath in a sigh and turned her back on the kayaks.

Bec moved the branches back into position as they pushed their way out. The lantana was so dense that there was little evidence of their passage.

They returned to find Lucy sitting on the ground, her teddy clutched to her chest, tears running down her reddened cheeks. Alice was standing at the edge of the bush, ignoring Lucy and staring out at the blue-black sea. The tip of the sun was visible above the hills.

Amber gave Alice an accusing look. 'What happened?'

Alice glared back. 'I don't know. She just started crying and saying she doesn't want to do this anymore.' Her face reddened. 'And she told me to go away and leave her alone.'

Amber knelt next to Lucy. 'What's wrong?'

'I want to go home,' Lucy wailed. Snot dribbled out of her nose, and she tried to sniff it back up. Her eyes were swollen. 'I want my mum.'

'I know.' Amber spoke in the soothing voice she used when Oliver was upset. 'We're all tired and frightened.' Lucy sniffed again. Amber pulled a tissue out of her pocket and gave it to her. She blew into it, her shoulders shaking.

Amber sat back on her heels, considering her and Alice. Alice's back was rigid, her neck and shoulders tense. Amber's lips curved in a grim smile. Lucy was finding her voice - and Alice didn't like it.

Bec had her eyes on the sky, looking for helicopters. She crossed her arms over her waist and frowned at Lucy. 'We learnt one thing today,' she said, her tone abrupt, 'One of your parents is probably alive. Maybe both.'

Alice scowled at her. 'What makes you say that?'

Amber flashed Bec a warning look, worried Bec was giving the girls false hope. Bec ignored her.

'That Bonehead said it was going to return the THONG and the two hostages. That has to be you two. I can only assume that they're keeping you hostage to make your parents behave. Unless there's anyone else who cares that much about you?'

Lucy turned her reddened eyes to Alice, the tears still running down her face. Alice bit her lip, her face pale. 'I doubt it.' Her voice was hoarse. She turned her face away.

'It's getting light,' Bec said, 'We need to move. Find somewhere to hide before they get a helicopter in the air.'

Amber stood and held out a hand to Lucy. Lucy wiped her eyes and put one soggy hand in Amber's. Amber pulled her to her feet.

Bec opened one of the boxes of muesli bars from the green shopping bag and handed them each a bar. 'Which way?'

'I don't know,' Amber said, 'I don't really know where we are. But the Great North Walk goes past Wondabyne station. If we follow the train line I guess we'll meet up with it.' She bundled the air mattress in her arms. There was no room in the bags for it until they ate some of the food Bec had stolen.

Bec set a fast pace. Lucy and Alice stumbled after her, picking bits of muesli bar from their teeth and yawning. Amber's shirt rubbed her reopened wound with every step. She cast a bitter glance at Bec's back, wondering how she still had energy. She must be full of adrenalin.

The train line wound to the edge of a wide creek and snaked along it. Forested hills rose on the other side of the creek, about half a kilometre from them. A rumble warned them that another passenger train was approaching. They ducked into the scrub next to the train line and kept walking. Another train in the opposite direction passed soon after.

Bec scanned the landscape as they went, her brow furrowed. After ten minutes, she stopped and slipped behind an acacia tree, at right angles to the train line. Amber and the girls exchanged glances.

'Maybe she needs the toilet?'

'I don't.' Bec's voice came from the other side of the tree. 'Come here.'

Shrugging, Amber followed. The scrub opened out into a clearing. Bec was standing near a large piece of corrugated iron. It was red with rust. 'It's the remains of an old shed.'

Beyond her, Amber could see rusty wire fencing and an old stone chimney from a building that must have predated the shed.

'This should do to hide us from helicopters,' Bec said, 'Help me move it.'

Alice moved to help her lean it against a tree.

'Don't cut yourself,' Amber said, 'We can't take you for a tetanus shot.'

They crawled into the space that Bec and Alice had created. Amber found some baby wipes and wiped the Bonehead's blood off herself and Oliver, wrinkling her nose at the tangy smell.

Alice craned her head to look. 'Monster blood. If you drink it, you'll probably turn into a monster too.'

'Ewww!' Lucy said.

Oliver mouthed at Amber's chest. She wrapped her sleeping bag around her shoulders, unhooked her bra and fed him. For a while the only sounds were his sucking, the twittering of small birds and the screech of cockatoos far away.

'No helicopters,' Lucy said.

'They'll come.' Bec spoke with complete conviction. She rummaged in the shopping bag and pulled out a block of milk chocolate.

'Ohhh, wonderful,' Amber said. Bec broke off four rows of chocolate and handed them out, wrapping up the remains of the chocolate and putting it back in the shopping bag.

Amber bit into the chocolate, savouring the sweet taste. The chill in her body seemed to lessen.

She finished feeding Oliver and adjusted her clothes. Lucy reached out her hands to Oliver. Amber relinquished him and turned to Bec. She didn't bother to keep the accusation out of her voice. 'That Bonehead found us because of your messages to the resistance.'

Bec's face reddened. 'Those messages should have been secure. I don't understand how the Boneheads hacked them. Maybe someone sold us out.'

Amber gritted her teeth. 'They wouldn't have been able to if you hadn't sent them in the first place.'

Bec rolled her eyes. 'I promised I wouldn't contact the resistance again without asking you, didn't I? I can't anyway, now that the phone is trashed.' She narrowed her eyes. 'And while we're on the subject, what the hell was that, asking that soldier to come with us? You didn't think killing another Bonehead would complicate our lives enough, you thought, hell, why not bring one of the enemy along for the trip?'

Amber's face grew warm. 'I could have let the Bonehead capture us, if you'd preferred.' She picked up a stick and drew a spiral in the dirt, not meeting Bec's eyes. 'I just thought - Private Jerome reminded me of Ollie. I thought if Ollie was in that situation, I hope someone would save him.'

'He's not Ollie, you -' Bec waved her hand around, trying to think of an appropriate insult, 'Knucklehead! You don't know anything about him. He's probably killed heaps of people.'

'Of course he hasn't. He could have killed us, easily, and he didn't. He didn't even try.'

Bec let out a disgusted snort. 'That time. He was happy enough to shoot at us in Thornleigh.'

Amber drew two more spirals. 'I hope he didn't get in trouble for letting us get away.'

'For fuck's sake! Would you feel better if he'd shot us?'

Amber glared at her. 'He's just a kid. You're just pissed because he destroyed the THONG.'

'Too right I am.'

Lucy interrupted their argument. 'Here's the helicopter.'

Bec stopped with her mouth open ready to fling another insult. In the sudden quiet, they could make out the familiar sound of helicopter blades approaching.

Bec's mouth twisted. 'I knew they'd send one eventually.'

Thirteen

'I think there's more than one helicopter,' Alice said.

'There's at least two,' Bec said, 'Maybe three. Must be costing them a fortune.'

Amber gazed at the wrinkled metal above her, listening to the thump of helicopter blades and picturing a whole flock of angry helicopters. She sunk back into the dirt, her body numb. 'They're going to catch us, aren't they?'

Bec snorted. 'They haven't caught us so far.'

Amber heard the rustle of a chip packet.

'Have something to eat,' Bec said, 'You'll feel better.' She forced some corn chips into Amber's hand and held out an open jar of salsa. Amber struggled up out of the dirt, letting out a shaky breath, and dipped the chips into the salsa. Bec passed the chips and salsa to the girls. The salty flavour filled Amber's mouth, and her spirits lifted.

They napped after eating. Helicopters buzzed overhead, and every hour a passenger train rattled past towards Wondabyne station, followed by another heading back towards Brooklyn. Freight trains screamed past at random intervals.

The sun beat down on the corrugated iron, heating up the small space underneath and driving away the cold from Amber's bones. She threw off the sleeping bag. Sweat formed on her skin, stinging the open wounds on her back. She gave Oliver extra breastfeeds to keep him hydrated. Breastfeeding made her even hotter, and she gulped water from her water bottle. By mid afternoon, the bottle was three quarters empty. Amber frowned at it. She looked around. She couldn't see Bec's water bottle, but Lucy's had less than hers. Alice had a third of a bottle left.

An hour later, the helicopters disappeared. Alice, Lucy and Amber hurried to the bushes to go to the toilet, leaving Oliver with Bec. While Alice and Lucy finished, Amber searched the area for a freshwater creek. They'd built buildings here, so she thought there must be fresh water somewhere near, but it wasn't obvious. She walked further into the bush, scanning the vegetation for changes that might signal water.

The roar of yet another helicopter filled the air. She sprinted back to the iron sheet. Alice and Lucy flew back from the bushes, yanking their undies and shorts up as they ran.

Amber stared out the triangle hole of their shelter at the stunted banksia bushes growing out of the hard, grey dirt. 'What if the helicopters keep searching all night?'

'We'll just have to stay here for another day,' Bec said. 'We've got enough food.'

But not enough water. They needed the helicopters to leave.

Amber stared at the serrated leaves on the nearest banksia. At the back of her mind, something stirred - the sense of timelessness and peace that she'd felt each time she'd killed the Boneheads. What are you? She reached out to it with her mind, but it skittered away. She reached out again. It was gone.

She gave up, blinking at the banksia until its leaves came back into focus. The leaves seemed to quiver. She frowned, wrinkling her forehead. The dirt and leaves in front of the banksia were spinning in circles on the ground.

'The wind's getting up,' Alice said.

'Good.' Bec nudged Amber. 'If it gets too windy, they'll have to ground the helicopters.'

Amber shook her head. Now the larger trees were tossing in the wind. It had to be a coincidence. Nobody could control the weather.

Or make time slow down? She shivered. The shiver turned into a second shiver, as cold seeped into her body, in a feeling she was growing to recognise. She wrapped the sleeping bag around her.

The wind rose further, whipping dust into their shelter. She turned away from the entrance, covering her eyes and pulling a wrap over Oliver's head.

The sky darkened with clouds. The helicopters disappeared to the north as rain battered down on their iron sheet, making the metal rattle and shake. The air temperature plummeted.

'I think we should move while we have the chance,' Bec shouted into her ear.

'It's not dark yet,' Amber yelled above the noise of the rain.

Bec shrugged and started packing. The girls followed her lead. Amber frowned as she shoved her sleeping bag into its cover. She wasn't looking forward to walking in the heavy rain.

One of Adam's favourite sayings surfaced in her mind: be careful what you wish for. Her frown deepened. She forced the sleeping bag into the bottom of the carrier with more force than usual.

The rain didn't ease while they packed. In silence, they pulled on their raincoats and Amber slotted the rain cover into the top of the carrier over Oliver's head. The train line continued to follow the edge of the creek. They trudged, heads down, in the cleared area next to it. Water flowed in sheets on the hard, compacted ground, drenching their feet. Lucy's rainbow-coloured raincoat, and Alice's more subdued navy-blue raincoat, seemed designed to look good in a light rain shower rather than protect them from heavy rain. Even Amber's hiking raincoat leaked as the rain beat down on her.

They ducked into the scrub as a train approached. The cold seeped into their skin as soon as they stopped walking. Amber's body was racked with shivers, and Lucy and Alice's teeth chattered.

After about an hour, the land zigzagged in and out in a large M shape. The train line took a shortcut, skimming over a land bridge in a half-circle shape.

'What do you think?' Bec asked.

Amber squinted through the rain. She estimated that the land bridge was a bit over half a kilometre long. It was impossible to tell whether the forested hills surrounding the M hid large rivers or impassable cliffs. She pulled a face. 'I think we should stay with the train line.'

Bec lifted her head, listening. She couldn't hear anything above the sound of the rain. She pointed her chin towards the creek side of the train tracks. A large rock wall ran at a 45-degree angle from the train tracks to the creek. Amber nodded, raising her eyebrows at Alice and Lucy to check they'd got the message. Together, they dashed over the tracks.

'How long since the last train?' Bec kept her voice low.

Amber checked Lucy's watch, shielding it from the rain with

one hand.

'About twelve minutes.'

Bec nodded. 'Let's do it.'

She climbed halfway down the rock wall and then stepped from rock to rock, her movements inhibited by the wet rocks and Oliver's weight on her back. The girls overtook her. Amber trailed behind.

Alice and Lucy had almost reached the other shore when Amber felt the vibrations in the ground. 'Bec,' Amber called, but her words were drowned out by a metallic screech.

Bec glanced backwards. 'Come on,' she yelled. She sped up, trying not to slip on the rocks. Alice and Lucy reached the shore and looked back, the whites of their eyes showing. Bec waved her arm at the bush on the other side of the track. The girls dived across the track and disappeared into the trees.

The screech became deafening. They weren't going to make it. Amber hugged the wet rocks, pressing her chest into them. Bec slid down towards the water and flattened herself against the rocks. Her silhouette was thrown into sudden blinding clarity as the bright white lights from the train hit her, the carrier sticking out above the rocks. Amber pushed herself further into the rocks, sure that the driver must see them, but as fast as it had come the light raced away. Wind buffeted her clothes. The rocks she was lying on shook, and she was overwhelmed by the thunderous shriek of the train, which seemed to go on and on.

She stayed frozen against the rocks as the last of the wagons squealed away around a bend. Bec unpeeled herself from the rocks and started climbing back up. Amber lifted her head, sure that she'd heard the shriek of another train, but then realised that it was Oliver, wailing his unhappiness at being woken by the screaming train. She took a deep breath and clambered after Bec. They slipped across the train line and into the bush. Alice and Lucy were huddled behind a knotted red gum tree, its trunk thick with rough, hairy bark. Hearing Oliver, they peered around the side of the trunk.

'Can I have Ollie?' Amber asked.

Bec slid the carrier off her back. 'With pleasure. He's more deafening than the train.'

Amber snorted, and settled her back against the red gum to feed Oliver. He stopped crying and sucked.

Once Oliver had fed, they trudged on through the rain, stopping to fill their water bottles at a small waterfall gushing down the hill next to the train line. Amber threw an iodine tablet in each water bottle to purify the water.

Fifteen minutes later they reached another railway bridge. Amber wasn't keen to cross another one, but Bec was bullish. 'There's at least another twenty minutes until the next passenger train, and I doubt we'll see another freight train so soon after that one. We'll be fine.'

They crossed without incident and continued. Amber plodded with her head down, her arms wrapped around her in a vain attempt to warm her body. Her sneakers splashed through water running in sheets off the side of the train line. They hid in the bush as a passenger train flew past towards Wondabyne station, followed by another speeding in the opposite direction. The cool air on their wet clothes seemed to whip through their bodies, chilling them inside.

The second train disappeared around the corner and its screech was replaced by the patter of rain and loud calls of several frog species. Amber shooed Alice and Lucy back into the cleared area next to the train line. They kept walking, their shivers subsiding as the movement warmed them. Bec and Amber agreed that they would get too cold if they stopped for dinner, so Bec opened two large packets of chips and they gobbled them as they walked.

They crossed two more land bridges. Not long after seven pm, the land curved to the left. Rounding the corner, Bec clutched Amber's arm. 'Shit,' she breathed.

Amber squinted into the rain, pushing strands of wet hair off her face. Wondabyne station, the only train station in the country without road access, was about two hundred metres in front of them. The station comprised two tiny platforms - less than one carriage long - one perched on stilts next to the river, the other cut into a flat, grassy area in front of a scrubby hill. Each platform held a bus station-style shelter protecting a blue-painted, three-person wooden seat. Instead of the deserted station she had expected, three soldiers huddled under the left-hand shelter. Several large, olive-green tents had sprung up on the grassy area.

On the river side, a white, bow top metal fence separated the platform from the water. At the far end of the platform, a public wharf jutted out over the river. Two large motorboats were tied to the wharf.

A strange howl rang out, echoing around the hills. It was a mix between the sound of a donkey braying and a dingo howling. A shiver ran down Amber's spine.

'We're too exposed,' she breathed, and plunged into the treeline. She struggled up the steep slope, slipping on the muddy ground and tree roots.

The howl was cut off, leaving silence. Even the frogs stopped calling.

Amber stopped, a metre up the hill. 'What the hell was that?'

'Dog?' Alice suggested.

'Not like any dog I've ever heard.'

Bec wrapped her arms around herself. 'They know we're here. They're waiting for us.' She turned wide eyes on Amber. 'We'll have to go a different way.'

Amber sank down into the mud. She felt light-headed, filled with a fear stoked by childhood stories and movies about children lost in the Australian bush. 'We can't. We don't have a map. We have to go around the station to find the Great North Walk, or we'll end up lost in the bush.'

'We could go back.'

'You think they won't be waiting for us in Brooklyn, too?' She pulled herself up using a small tree and took a deep breath. 'We'll just skirt around the station. They won't even know we're here.'

Bec frowned, her brow wrinkling. Amber didn't give her time to argue. She started sliding around the slope, impeded by bushes and vines, and the relentless rain.

Bec caught up to her. 'Can't we go deeper into the bush?'

'I want to keep the train line in sight.'

Near the station, the slope curved to the left. Amber peered through the trees at the army green tents. In the dim light, she didn't notice two soldiers standing on the edge of the scrub until she was within a couple of metres of them. She flung herself down on the ground. Bec and the girls copied her without question.

The soldiers wore identical heavy, olive-green raincoats. One of them clutched a leash in his hand. At the end was one of the strange, wombat-like creatures Amber had seen in Epping. As she watched, the wombat flung up its head and made the braying, howling sound they heard a few minutes before. Amber's hands shook. She clasped them in front of her.

'I think it's got a scent,' the soldier holding the leash said.

'Come on, in this weather?' the other replied. Amber started at the sound of the voice, almost giving away their position in surprise. Private Jerome. He pushed back his hood, revealing his dark curls, and searched the bush. 'I doubt it can smell anything.'

'We should check.'

Amber felt Bec, behind her, tense her body; ready to flee.

Jerome snorted. 'We can go bush-bashing tomorrow. It'll be dark soon. If it's actually got a scent, which I doubt, we'll be able to pick them up in the morning.'

The other soldier cast him a sideways glance. 'Your heart's not really in this job, is it?'

Jerome stiffened. 'I'm just as keen as you to see those women captured.'

'If you say so,' the other soldier said, his eyes back on the bush, 'But some of the others have questioned why you let them get away in Brooklyn.'

'So what, Commander Haliena was fucking bleeding to death in front of me, and they think I should have just left her there while I chased the fugitives? They were escaping in kayaks, for fucks sake. If the backup had bloody well come as soon as I called it in, they could have picked them up on the water.'

'Yeah, alright, mate, calm down.'

'I just think they're more dangerous than anyone is giving them credit for. You didn't see what I saw. That Yu girl - when she took out Commander Haliena - I've never seen anyone move that fast. Inhumanely fast.'

'You still on about that? She looks pretty human to me.'

'Sure. And three months ago, would you have believed that there were Boneheads, or even that creature you've got there?'

The soldier looked at the wombat. 'I take your point.' He peered into the gloom. 'Nah, you're probably right. We'll do a proper search tomorrow.'

He tugged at the wombat's lead, and the two soldiers returned to the tents. Amber lay flat, shivering in her wet clothes, until Bec tugged at her foot. Bec jerked her head up the slope.

Amber followed without argument. Her mind kept throwing up pictures of what might have happened if the soldiers had decided to check the bush. Her body was shaking. She didn't know if it was from fear or cold.

At the top of the hill, Bec paused. Alice and Lucy stopped next to her. Amber gritted her teeth as she caught up, expecting Bec to berate her for taking them so close to the soldiers.

Instead, Bec looked at her with wide eyes, her brow furrowed. 'Did you hear those soldiers?'

Inhumanely fast. Amber shivered.

'They're going to use that wombat thing to track us.'

Amber blinked.

'Amber?'

'Do you think it'll be able to find us?'

'I don't know.' Bec slammed a fist against her thigh. 'I don't know anything about them. I've only seen that one reference on social media, which said they were using them to track.'

'There must be a reason they're using them. Maybe they're better trackers than dogs?'

'Maybe. Or they're cheaper, or easier to train than dogs.'

'Maybe the Boneheads just hate dogs,' Alice said.

Bec shrugged. 'Whatever, we need to lose that thing. Do you think we should walk along a creek or something? Sniffer dogs can't track you if you walk in water, can they?'

'Actually, they can still smell you on the air,' Amber said.

'Damn. I don't suppose we have any pepper. I think that stops sniffer dogs.'

'No, it doesn't.'

Bec glared at Amber. 'What, you're an expert on sniffer dogs now?'

'I saw a doco on them.' She'd watched that documentary to distract herself, that first day she'd seen Boneheads - and watched them kill. Was it really less than ten days ago? Amber wrapped her arms around herself. A roaring filled her mind. It seemed like a different life - a time when it would never have entered her mind that she would kill anyone, and end up on the run. A time when she thought Adam was just too busy to answer his phone.

'So what did the doco suggest we should do?' Bec's tone suggested she was unimpressed with Amber's source of knowledge.

'Just keep moving so they can't catch us.'

'Great. And then the helicopters can catch us instead.' Bec lifted both arms up towards the sky. 'Or maybe -' She dropped her arms, staring down the hill towards the army camp and train station, invisible through the trees.

'What?'

'There's a way to move much faster.'

Amber frowned. 'Like what?'

Bec gave her a bright smile. 'Catch a train.'

Amber let out a bark of laughter. 'You're insane. You saw the soldiers on the platform.'

'I'm not suggesting we catch it from the platform.'

Fourteen

Bec led them in a wide semi-circle through the bush, around the soldiers' camp and behind an old quarry. The rain eased, but so much water dripped from the trees and brushed onto them as they pushed their way through the scrub that Amber didn't think it was much of an improvement. They crossed a leaf-covered track with stone steps set into it.

Amber clutched Bec's arm. 'That's the Great North Walk.'

Bec shook her off. 'Give it up. The soldiers'll catch us before lunch if we follow the track.' She plunged back into the bush.

Amber cast a longing look down the path before following.

The last of the daylight trickled away. They continued in the dark. Invisible branches and thorns whipped them as they passed, adding to the scratches that adorned their legs and arms. Bec led them back down the slope towards the water, their feet sinking into the wet, muddy earth. They broke free of the bush where it met the train line, on the opposite side of the station. Amber could just make out a glow from bright lights at the station and the soldiers' camp.

'This'll do,' Bec said, 'The train should slow as it goes past the station.'

Amber gripped her hands together. They were sweaty. 'Are you sure about this? Remember that train that went past us on the bridge? It was like a monster! And we've got children with us!'

Bec met her gaze, her eyes fierce. 'We can't keep walking. The Boneheads will catch up eventually, with their helicopters, or their wombats, or something else. And the kids won't be any safer if they do. You saw how ready that Bonehead was to kill Ollie in Brooklyn.'

Amber looked at Alice and Lucy.

'If you can do it, we can,' Alice said.

'I'm not sure that I can,' Amber muttered.

'I'll go first. Alice and Lucy go next, and copy what I do. And you last, okay? There's plenty of time, you know how long those freight trains are.' Bec's voice was full of confidence. Amber squeezed her hands tighter. So much could go wrong with Bec's plan.

They stayed standing, bouncing on the spot to warm themselves. A passenger train squealed past first. They didn't move. There was nothing to grab onto on the outside of the passenger trains.

It felt like a long time later that they heard the unmistakable screech of a freight train.

'Here we go,' Bec said, pulling the carrier straps tight. As the rattling and screeching of the train grew louder, Oliver woke up. He stared at the approaching headlights, his eyes huge. Amber opened her mouth to make reassuring noises, but at that moment the train arrived.

The ground shook as the engine passed: a yellow and blue blur. Bec didn't hesitate. She raced towards the train, ran alongside it for a moment then grabbed the step on the side of a wagon and pulled herself up. Alice pushed Lucy after her and followed a split second later, swinging herself up onto a wagon further down. Amber waited until they were aboard and then raced at the train. She ran alongside until there was a metal step next to her. She leapt, grabbing the metal bars above the step with her hands and trying to swing her legs onto it. It was harder than she expected to hold on. The momentum of the train pulled her sideways, the muscles in her arms screaming. Her injured hand felt like it was being burnt all over again. For a moment she was afraid she'd lose her grip on the step and be thrown onto the track below. Swinging her legs back under her, she scrambled with her feet on the side of the wagon for a minute before her feet touched the step. She pushed with her legs until she was standing, then climbed onto the wagon.

The back of the wagon had a flat section with a small roof hanging over it, and some rusty metal equipment. She had no idea what the equipment did, but it was a good place to sit. She crawled along the wagon to the back and sat down, gasping for breath and shaking.

The noise of the train was deafening. Amber clutched her injured hand. She wondered how the others were faring on their wagons, and prayed that Oliver wasn't scared or hungry. There was a flash of lights and houses to her left - a coastal town - a brief black stretch of water and then a long stretch of houses. Lights shone in the windows and on the streets. Amber felt like an insect, clinging to the back of the train and staring out at a world she wasn't a part of.

The wind rushed past her as the train screamed its way through the night. It forced its way through her wet clothes and into her bones. Shakes racked her body. Numbness spread over her toes and fingers, and they started to ache. She wrapped her arms around her legs and hid her head in her arms. The constant squeal of the train pounded in her head.

It felt like the train screeched its way through the night for hours, but it was only an hour and half from when she'd climbed onto the train that it slowed and squealed through the suburbs of Newcastle, slowing further and then halting with a yelp in the middle of several lines of wagons. The engine had stopped next to a rectangular brown metal building. Closely spaced streetlights lit the entire area as though it was daytime.

Amber squeezed her eyes shut as the sudden light blinded her. She opened them with care, peering through the lashes. Some flashes of orange moved around the engine - people wearing high vis jackets - but nothing moved near her. She scrambled down the steps and jumped the short distance to the ground. She huddled against the wagons as she walked towards the front of the train, feeling vulnerable under the bright white lights.

She spotted Lucy leaning over the edge of her wagon, her face looking small and pale above her rainbow-coloured raincoat. Lucy saw her and started climbing down the ladder. Bec and Alice appeared, panting for breath. Amber's stomach twisted as she saw Oliver looking out over Bec's shoulder. He wailed when he saw her. She hurried to Bec's side and wrapped an arm around him without taking him out of the carrier.

'What the fuck are you doing?'

Amber swung around. A sandy-haired man in an orange high vis jacket appeared from behind a coal wagon on the next train. He looked only a little older than her. Amber let go of Oliver and stepped back, ignoring his cry. Her muscles tensed. The man's eyes widened in recognition. 'You're Amber Yu!'

Amber gripped sweaty hands together. Lucy landed on the ground next to her.

'Run,' Bec said, as soon as Lucy's feet touched the ground.

Amber stretched out one of her hands and took Lucy's arm. Bec took off across the freight yard with Alice at her heels. Amber followed, towing Lucy.

The man yelled something and gave chase, catching up to them. Amber could hear his deep breathing behind her. It spurred her to run faster. Lucy gasped as she tried to keep up.

Bec leapt over train tracks and around wagons. She reached a corrugated iron fence and swerved left, following the fence.

Amber could hear the man behind her. He was right on her heels - within touching distance.

A gate, made from the same corrugated iron panels as the fence, came into view. A large, thick padlock was clipped around the handle. Bec pulled up next to the gate and swung around. Amber wasn't expecting her to stop and almost ran into her. She dodged to the side.

The man also hadn't expected Bec to stop. He pulled up just in time, his face almost touching hers. Her hair swirled in a tangled mess around her face. She bared her teeth.

'Why are you chasing us?'

The man jumped back. 'I -'

'Are you working for the Boneheads?'

'What? I've never even seen a Bonehead!'

'Lucky you,' Amber muttered.

'Then why?' Bec demanded.

'I -' he pulled himself upright, 'You shouldn't be here!'

'Fine,' she spat, 'Open this gate, and we'll go.'

'I - I can't.'

She thrust her face closer to his. 'Why not?'

'I don't have a key.'

'Argh.' She swung around to Alice. 'I need my bolt cutters.'

Alice dumped the pack on the ground and withdrew the bolt cutters. Bec positioned the lock's shackle between the blades.

'What are you doing?' The man's voice rose an octave.

Bec ignored him and squeezed the blades together. The lock didn't break easily. She clenched her teeth and kept squeezing until it snapped. She removed the pieces and pushed open the gate.

'Let's go.' She ducked out, followed by the girls.

'The government's looking for you.' The man spat the words out in a rush.

'What?' Amber paused.

'They've flooded the TV and social media with your pictures. Just you two - not the kids.' He ran his hand through his mane of hair. 'I just thought you should know.'

'Yeah, thanks. We know,' Amber said. She slid through the gate.

The gate led into a quiet cul-de-sac. The corrugated iron fence ran along their side of the road. Small, aging, weatherboard houses lined the opposite side of the road.

Bec urged Amber and the girls into a brisk pace. 'I don't trust that guy,' she muttered, looking over her shoulder at the gate.

The street was deserted. Light pooled underneath the sparse streetlights, leaving the rest of the street shrouded in darkness. The moon wouldn't rise for another few hours. Squinting into the shadows, Amber could make out more small weatherboard houses.

Amber's eyes ached and her face burned. The pace Bec set left her breathless. Lucy kept tripping on the lumpy ground, clumsy with tiredness.

After fifteen minutes of brisk walking, Bec led them onto the highway and across a bridge over the railway line. Small shops and mechanics replaced the houses.

Amber caught up to Bec. 'What do you think we should do?'

'Find somewhere to buy a phone, and call the resistance,' Bec replied.

'Why? We don't have the THONG to give them anymore.'

A car rushed past, illuminating them with bright white light for a moment. 'Not for them - for us,' Bec said.

'What?' Amber frowned.

'We need help, Amber. It's been - what - less than a week since we went to rescue Ollie? And the fact that we're alive - that we haven't gotten Ollie and the girls killed - is more good luck than good management. We're out of our depth.'

Amber's shoulders slumped. Bec was right - they were out of their depth. But what would the resistance want in return for their help? She shivered.

'Amber?' Bec prompted.

'No.'

Bec scowled. 'Are you serious?'

'Why would the resistance help us? What's in it for them?'

'They're desperate to be able to kill Boneheads. They can't win this fight if they can't kill the enemy. And as far as I'm aware, you're still the only person who's ever killed one.'

'Exactly. I'm not interested in helping them kill anyone. I wish I'd never killed those Boneheads. If I could take it back, I would. I just wanted to keep Ollie safe.'

'And if we can't keep him safe on our own?'

Amber was silent.

Bec sighed. 'You're the most pigheaded person I've ever met, you know that?'

Amber rubbed her aching eyes. 'Pot, meet kettle,' she muttered.

On the street, historic shopfronts were interspersed with squat modern buildings and garish fast-food outlets. Bec came to a stop next to an empty carpark. Behind the carpark was a supermarket. Bright fluorescent light blazed from the windows.

'We need to stock up on food,' Bec said.

The supermarket was a squat rectangular box. A portico stuck on the front of the box, its roof raised above the height of the rest of the building, was the sole nod to aesthetic appeal. Large white shades had been erected over some of the car parks.

'It's closed,' Amber said, yawning. 'We'll have to wait until tomorrow.'

Lucy wasn't looking at the supermarket, but at the 24-hour fast-food restaurant across the road. 'I'm so hungry.'

Amber followed her gaze. After two days of living off the chips, muesli bars and chocolate Bec had stolen at Brooklyn, she could almost taste the fresh burgers. She swallowed and shook her head. 'We can't risk it. They might recognise us. It's dangerous enough going to the supermarket.'

'That guy said the government had only shared your pictures - not ours,' Alice said, 'I can buy the food.'

'No way. Someone your age buying food on your own in the middle of the night? You'll raise way too many questions.'

'I'll go,' Bec said, 'I'll wear a mask - pretend I'm paranoid about germs.' Amber bit her lip. 'It'll be fine,' Bec added.

Bec propped the carrier against a low hedge between the highway and the carpark. She motioned for Alice to drop the pack and dug down into the bottom of it, pulling out a plain, black mask. She settled the mask on her face as she strode across the highway and disappeared into the restaurant.

Oliver woke from a nap and started crying. Amber took him out of the carrier and leant against the hedge to breastfeed him. She stared at the patterns the supermarket lights made on the bitumen.

Bec reappeared, laden with brown paper bags. She pulled the mask off her face and gave Amber a grin. 'No problems at all.'

She and the girls joined Amber on the ground behind the hedge. Amber nestled Oliver against her chest as she bit into a burger, closing her eyes in pleasure.

It didn't take them long to finish the food. Alice and Lucy argued over the last few chips. Amber yawned, her stomach full and comfortable.

'Let's find somewhere to sleep until the supermarket opens,' Bec said.

Amber stared at her with bleary eyes, exhausted. She dragged herself upright. Bec led them away from the highway. There was a small, grassy park at the back of the supermarket, with small clumps of trees, picnic tables and a wide, cement drain running through it.

'Can we just stop here?' Alice's voice was a wail.

'There's nowhere to hide,' Bec said.

Amber knew how Alice felt. 'We might not find anything better. This is suburbia.' She pointed at a patch of spindly trees in a circle. 'Let's just sleep over there. No-one's going to see us before sunrise. We'll just have to leave early.'

They stumbled into the circle of trees and wrapped themselves in sleeping bags. Amber was asleep in minutes.

Bec nudged Amber awake the next morning. The sun was hovering above the horizon. 'We should go back to the supermarket carpark.'

Amber yawned. 'The supermarket won't be open for another hour.'

'Still.'

Amber sat up. Her injured hand ached from when she'd used it to pull herself into the wagon, but her back was less stiff than the day before. She twisted from side to side. She felt a stretch, but no pain. They packed up the sleeping bags and returned to their spot near the hedge.

Bec leant the carrier against the hedge. Oliver reached out and tried to pull the leaves into his mouth. He seemed content, so Amber left him in the carrier. She watched the supermarket. There were a few cars in the carpark, and she could see staff moving around inside.

Bec was watching the road over the hedge. It was quiet at this hour of the morning. Each time a vehicle approached, Bec stiffened, fixed her gaze on it, then relaxed as it kept going.

'What's biting you?' Amber asked.

'Nothing,' Bec muttered. She turned away from the road to face Amber, and yelped. Amber swung around. A giant wombat bounded straight towards Bec. Bec sprung up to run, and tripped on the cement gutter. The wombat leapt at her. As it landed it opened its mouth wide, showing a mouthful of razor-sharp teeth, and sank them into Bec's left shoulder.

The Bonehead's sword was still attached to the side of Bec's pack. Fumbling with the straps, Amber pulled the sword out. Holding it two-handed, like she would hold a tennis racket to hit a tricky backhand shot, she whacked the wombat on the side of its head. It fell over on its side.

Bec's shoulder was a mess of blood. Amber grabbed her right hand and pulled her to her feet. Her face was white and she was breathing hard. The wombat rolled over and picked itself up. It bared its teeth, but seemed hesitant to attack again. It turned its head towards the girls, snarling, then saw Oliver in the carrier.

The wombat snarled again and braced to leap at the carrier. Amber screamed, lifting the sword above her head, but she knew she'd be too late.

A voice yelled a command. The wombat hesitated and turned. Amber dropped the sword and scooped Oliver out of the carrier with shaking hands. Holding him to one side, she grabbed the sword again and pointed it in the direction the voice had come from.

At least fifteen soldiers, in full combat gear, had their rifles trained on Amber, Bec and the girls. The wombat bounded back to one of them, who opened his hand to feed something small to the wombat.

The soldier standing next to him screamed at them. 'Get on the ground!' Amber recognised him: Private Jerome.

Bec and the girls flung themselves onto the bitumen. Amber hesitated. She reached out with her mind towards the power. This time, it filled her straight away. Time slowed. She stared at the row of soldiers, rifles pointed at her, their fingers on the triggers. Somehow, she knew that the power wouldn't slow time enough to avoid a bullet. This time, it wasn't enough.

She released most of her hold on the power, but kept a loose touch on it. Time sped back up, but she still felt a sense of strength and comfort from the power in her mind.

Jerome's face twisted in fear and anger. 'Get down! Now!'

Protecting Oliver, Amber knelt on the ground. In a moment, the soldiers were on top of her. Oliver was wrenched from her grip, and her arms forced behind her. Lucy was sobbing.

Jerome knelt, looking from her to Bec. 'What, were you expecting the resistance?' His voice was triumphant, but Amber sensed fear behind it. 'We intercepted your phone call last night. Nobody is coming for you, but us.'

Amber froze as she took in what he was saying. A roaring anger filled her mind, burning away her connection to the power.

Jerome continued, speaking to Amber. 'I suggest you don't try to fight. We've got orders to kill your son if you cause any trouble.' His face twisted. 'This time, I won't hesitate.'

Rough hands hauled her to her feet. Her eyes darted. She couldn't see Oliver. Bec was still on the ground, with two soldiers holding her down. One soldier was holding Lucy. Another was trying to hold Alice, struggling as she kicked and bit. The soldiers forced Amber to a truck and flung her into the back of it. She hit a metal bench. It bit into her side. The fall winded her. She gasped, struggling to breathe. She looked up as the soldiers tossed Bec in after her and slammed the truck doors shut.

Amber gulped air and threw herself at the truck doors, but they were locked tight. The truck lurched into motion. She lost her balance and landed on the hard metal floor. The truck engine roared.

Bec was clutching her left shoulder with her right hand. Blood escaped through the sides of her hand and ran down her arms. Sweat glistened on her face.

Amber's heart pounded and her body felt burning hot. She couldn't think above the roar in her mind. 'You called the resistance. Behind my back.'

Bec grimaced and rubbed her face with her free hand. 'I had to. You were so stubborn about not accepting their help, you were going to get us all killed.'

Amber's mouth dropped open. 'You're the one getting us all killed! They've taken Ollie, and the girls, because of you!'

Bec dropped her eyes, clenching her hand into a fist and rubbing it against her lip.

They've taken Ollie. The words echoed in Amber's mind. She pulled her legs into her chest and buried her head in her arms. She'd lost Oliver again. Tears dribbled down her face. She tried to swallow, but her throat felt thick.

'We'll get them back. I'll figure it out.' Bec's words were confident, but her voice quivered.

Amber pulled her head further into her arms, covering her ears. Her anger with Bec fizzed in her body and settled into her bones.

Fifteen

The truck lurched to a halt. The doors were flung open. Amber ducked her head, blinded by the sun.

A rifle was thrust in her face. 'Move!' Jerome's voice barked the order.

She slid out of the truck. A soldier grabbed her from behind and forced her towards a nondescript one-storey brick building. Two other soldiers flanked her, either side, their fingers on the triggers of their rifles. A small carpark ran along the front of the building. A tall, metal fence surrounded the building and carpark, edged with flower gardens. She sensed other soldiers behind her pull Bec from the truck, but she didn't turn around or try to make eye contact with Bec.

The soldiers forced her into the building and into a small, airless room with cream walls and a grey, vinyl floor. The only window was a small rectangle high above her head, shut tight. Sweat beaded on her body. The room had absorbed weeks' worth of heat, which couldn't escape.

Four hard, green plastic chairs stood around a small grey table. The soldiers thrust her into the chair furthest from the door. Bec was pushed into the chair next to her. Amber wrapped her arms around herself.

The soldiers remained standing, their rifles aimed at her. She stared at them through glazed eyes. A tremor shook her body. Her eyes rested on Jerome. He was standing closest to them. He saw her look at him, and his hand on the rifle shook. She looked away. They were really scared - of her. The power had disappeared, as though it had never been there. Reaching out, she felt nothing.

She looked at the soldiers again and twisted her mouth. Nothing to be scared of, boys.

The door opened, and a red-haired soldier with a short red beard entered. Lieutenant Colonel Nichols. He was followed by a Bonehead. Nichols jerked his head to dismiss all the soldiers apart from Jerome. Looks of relief flashed on the faces of the soldiers who had been dismissed. They took the widest berth possible around the Bonehead and escaped the small room.

The Bonehead sat down on a chair opposite Amber. It looked almost comical on the too-small chair, its knees at chest height. Scowling, it stretched its legs out under the table. Nichols sank down onto the chair next to it, edging the chair to the right as he did so.

Despite the heat, an icy cold washed over Amber's body. The contents of her stomach seemed to roll over, like clothes in a washing machine.

She forced herself to look at the Bonehead's eyes. It wasn't true that the Bonehead had no iris or sclera. The point where its pupil would be was blacker than the rest of the eye, which this close looked more like a dark grey than black. The skin on its face was so grey and wrinkled that it made Amber think of a dead body - a zombie, maybe. But its bony plate was a bright splash of colour - more red than mahogany. She remembered the Bonehead at Brooklyn talking about 'the Red Bone'. Did the colour of their plates mean something to the Boneheads, then? Was it more desirable to have a redder plate?

Nichols' face was shiny with sweat within moments of entering the hot room, but the Bonehead showed no sign of being bothered by the heat.

To her surprise, the Bonehead ignored her, and looked at Bec.

'Tell us about Governor Macquarie Tower.'

Bec clasped her hands together in her lap and pressed her lips together.

'We know you drove the truck with the bomb,' Nichols snapped.

Amber ground her teeth. She'd been fairly sure Bec was lying about her involvement in the tower, but - she drove the vehicle? Did she ever tell Amber the truth about anything?

The Bonehead bared its teeth, its lips curling upwards in the same odd smile that Amber had seen on the Bonehead's face at Brooklyn. 'It was a set-up. The President never intended to leave Canberra. We spread the rumour that he'd be there, to draw your resistance out so we could pick you off one by one. It worked, too. Every other person involved in the attack is dead -

you're the only one left.'

Bec became very still. Her hands in her lap tightened.

Amber glanced at Jerome. His shoulders tensed and he clenched his teeth. He concentrated and they relaxed, but his hands trembled.

The Bonehead leant back in its seat. 'We know you're still in touch with the resistance. I want names. Addresses. All of it. And you're going to give them to me.'

Bec met its eyes and pressed her lips together even tighter. The Bonehead's smile broadened. It switched its gaze to Amber, the smile disappearing as though it had never been there. 'How do you move so fast?' it barked.

Amber gaped at it, stunned by the change of subject.

The Bonehead bared its teeth. 'I got a human martial arts expert to look at the footage from the university. She confirmed what I thought - you moved faster than you should be able to. Faster than anyone she's ever seen. And Private Jerome here says you did the same at Brooklyn. I want to know how you did it.'

'I - I don't know.'

The Bonehead slapped her face. 'Wrong answer.' Amber's head snapped to the side. The side of her face went numb, then burned. Her jaw ached.

'I really don't.' Tears ran down her face.

The Bonehead leant over the table. 'Aren't you forgetting something?' Amber looked up into its dead eyes. For the first time, she noticed that it didn't have any eyebrows. 'We have your son. Give me the answers I want, and I'll consider sparing his life. Keep quiet, and he can die with you.'

Amber remembered Nichols saying something similar over the public address system at the university, a week ago. She squeezed her hands into fists. It felt a lot longer.

There was a loud explosion and the walls shook. A whooping sound filled the building, and loudspeakers boomed a recorded message. 'Evacuate. Evacuate. Evacuate.'

The Bonehead scowled. 'What now?'

The alarm and recorded message were cut off, leaving a silence that seemed more shocking than the noise.

The Bonehead flung itself up. The green plastic chair skidded across the room to hit the wall behind it. It slammed the door open. 'Get in there,' it said, 'I'll find out what's going on.'

It stalked away as two of the soldiers who had been in the room earlier trooped back in.

Nichols narrowed his eyes at Amber and Bec. 'You know anything about this?' Another explosion shook the building. He stood and walked to the doorway. 'Don't let them out of your sight,' he ordered the soldiers, 'If they move, shoot them somewhere that's not lethal.' He looked back at Bec and Amber and gave a small smile. 'A leg should do it.' He disappeared, closing the door behind him.

The oldest soldier ran his eyes over Bec and Amber. His large body and arms reminded Amber of Beefy, but his stomach had a slight bulge and his arms were not as well defined, indicating that he had been fit when he was younger but was now overweight. He clutched a handgun in his right hand. Amber frowned. Attached to his waist was a black leather sword scabbard, with a sword nestled in it - the same as the ones the Boneheads carried.

Bec followed her gaze. 'What are you doing with that? Fancy being one of the monsters?'

He sneered at her and swaggered over to Amber. He leant over her, planted a wide, hairy hand on the table and ran the handgun down the side of Amber's face.

'What the fuck do you think you're doing, Jonno?' Jerome demanded.

'Fuck off, Jerome. This is none of your business.'

Bec jumped up, but the other soldier pointed his rifle at her.

'Stay where you are.'

Distracted by Bec, Jonno removed his arm from the table. Amber took advantage of his distraction to jump up herself, knocking over the plastic chair. She backed away from Jonno, but he grabbed her left arm, forced it behind her back and pushed her flat down on the table. She felt a rush of fear and reached out with her mind to the power. This time it filled her in a rush of heat.

Where were you before, when they took Ollie from me? There was no response to her furious thought. Railing against the power felt as effective as railing at the sea, or a mountain.

Jonno's movements slowed. An image flashed in her mind - a memory, of a self-defence course she and Bec had done when they were at university. She lifted her left foot and stepped down hard on his inner leg. He swore and eased the pressure on her arm. She ripped her arm free. Jonno turned and raised his gun - in slow motion. The handle of the sword he was wearing stuck out at right angles from his side. Amber seized the sword handle and tugged it from the scabbard. Before Jonno could react, she plunged the sword into his throat. He fell to the ground.

The other soldier pointed his rifle at her. She dived across the room and leapt on top of him, knocking him to the ground. Before he could recover, Bec tugged his rifle out of his hands and slammed it against the side of his head. His head thumped against the ground and his body went limp and still.

Bec swung around to Jerome. 'Drop it!' she screamed, pointing the rifle at him. He stared at her with wide eyes, his mouth open. He knelt and placed his rifle on the ground, holding his hands above his head.

Time sped up again. Amber started shaking and slithered as fast as she could off the unconscious - possibly dead - soldier.

Bec offered her a hand, but Amber scrambled on all fours past

184

her and vomited onto the floor. She felt icy cold and couldn't stop shaking.

'I killed a human,' she whispered. The words rang in her mind and seemed to echo around her head.

'Are you okay?' Bec's voice came from somewhere above her.

'I killed him,' she babbled.

'Good thing, too.'

Amber stared at the sword clutched in her hand. Blood. Sickened, she tossed the sword away. They weren't monsters, they were humans. She'd killed a human.

'We need to get out of here,' Bec said. She yanked Amber to her feet one-handed, keeping the rifle trained on Jerome. 'Have a nervous breakdown later.'

The shakes and sickness were already disappearing, and she was able to stand.

Bec knelt and picked up the sword, wiping the blood off on the unconscious soldier's pants. 'You should keep this.'

Amber opened her mouth to refuse it, and hesitated. They still had to escape. And find Oliver. She took the sword from Bec, straightened and met Jerome's eyes. His lips and chin trembled, and spots of sweat appeared on his face. She lifted her sword and pointed it at his chest. 'Where is my son? Where are the girls?'

'I don't -' he stopped, fidgeted, and glanced away. He took a deep breath and met her eyes. 'Lieutenant Colonel Nichols sent them back to the university.'

'He's lying,' Bec said.

Jerome's mouth twisted. 'Terrorist,' he spat at her, 'Murderer.'

Bec met his eyes. 'Don't talk to me about murder. You heard that Bonehead - they set us up at Governor Macquarie Tower. All those innocent people you're so concerned about? They could have gotten them out. They chose to sacrifice them.'

Jerome's face turned white. Amber touched his chest with the sword, not hard enough to hurt, but enough that he would feel it. 'Where - is - my - son?'

His shoulders dropped. 'I don't know. Not the university. Lieutenant Colonel Nichols gave them to the Mule to take somewhere, but I don't know where. That's the truth.'

'What do you mean, the Mule?' Amber was almost screaming.

'Mueller, Jacinta Mueller, she's one of the officers. But we all call her the Mule - because of her name, and because she's as stubborn as one.'

The sound of another explosion ripped through the building. Bits of plaster fell from the ceiling onto the floor and into their hair.

'We need to get out of here,' Bec said again.

Amber put more pressure on the sword. Jerome drew in a quick breath. 'How can I find out where the Mule went?'

He raised his hands in a shrug. 'Lieutenant Colonel Nichols' office?'

Bec jerked the rifle towards the door. 'Show us where that is. No tricks - or I'll get Amber to cut off your arm.'

Amber's eyes rested on the rifle. Bec's hold on it was confident. No doubt something she learnt from her group - the one she'd insisted she didn't help to blow up Governor Macquarie Tower. A bitter flavour rose in Amber's throat.

'You going to get the door?' Bec asked.

Amber shook her head to clear it. It was not the time to worry about Bec's lies. She cracked open the door. The room was one of several that opened into a long corridor. It was empty. She opened the door and stepped out. Bec thrust the tip of the rifle into Jerome's back and propelled him out the door. He pointed down the corridor, in the opposite direction to the door that they'd used to enter the building.

They passed three large rooms with painted wooden doors and frosted glass walls. Another explosion shook the building. As the noise disappeared, Amber heard footsteps. 'Someone's coming.'

She thrust open the next door. It was an empty office. White desks with large screens and docking stations lined the walls in a U-shape. A few desks held files - stacked in neat piles in trays or scattered across the desk. Some had photos of children or pets blue-tacked to the wall behind them. There were several pot plants - all dead. If the office was still being used, it wasn't by anyone who cared enough to water the plants.

Bec pushed Jerome into the room. 'Keep quiet.'

Amber pulled the door closed, leaving a small gap to peer through. Two young soldiers rounded a corner, holding the arms of a young Asian girl, who was wearing handcuffs. On an impulse, Amber pushed open the door and stepped out in front of them, her sword raised.

'What are you doing?' Bec hissed behind her.

The soldiers froze.

'You know who I am?' Amber screamed at them, her sword trembling. 'I just killed your buddies. Let her go, or I'll kill you too.' The soldiers' eyes widened as they took in the blood splatters on her clothes and sword.

Out of the corner of her eye, she saw Bec push Jerome out the door. 'Do as she says,' she said.

The soldiers let the girl's arms go, stepped back a few paces, and ran.

'Take these cuffs off me first!' the girl yelled after them. The soldiers disappeared down the corridor. She turned back to Amber and her eyes narrowed. 'You're Amber Yu. They brought me here to give them my 'expert opinion' on you.'

Bec ran her eyes up and down the girl. 'You're the martial arts expert?' Her voice made it clear that she wasn't impressed.

The girl shrugged. 'According to them, not me. I guess they couldn't find anyone else.'

'Got a name?'

'Kim.'

Amber couldn't tell if it was her given name or surname. When the Bonehead had mentioned a martial arts expert, Amber had pictured someone who looked like Mr Miyagi. Kim was nothing like him. She was even shorter than Bec, a full head shorter than Amber, with a slight frame and blonde highlights running through her black hair. She looked just out of her teens, an impression increased by her hairstyle - a ponytail with two bangs on either side.

'Let's go,' Kim said, turning towards the exit, 'Those soldiers will have gone for reinforcements.'

'No,' Amber said, 'We need to find Nichols' office.'

Kim narrowed her eyes and looked at the exit.

'You go, if you like.'

Kim clenched her teeth. 'No. You helped me - I'll help you.'

Amber thought it unlikely that Kim would be much help with her hands still in cuffs, but she shrugged and turned to Jerome. 'Where?'

They continued down the corridor to a smaller room with frosted glass windows. Amber pushed open the door. Whatever privileges Nichols' position may have afforded him, they didn't extend to a luxury office. A single white desk sat in front of the room's only window, with a battered office chair in front of it. The desk held two large screens and a docking station with a laptop attached to it. Two large filing cabinets stood against the opposite wall. There was no other furniture, and no personal belongings. The explosions had battered the room, and a pile of ceiling plaster had landed on the desk, covering the laptop and screens with a white powder.

Bec again pushed Jerome into the room with her rifle. Kim followed. Amber closed the door behind them and made a beeline for the filing cabinets. She tried the drawers, but they were locked. 'Know how to break into a filing cabinet?' she asked Bec.

Bec shrugged. 'I don't think they're difficult. You need a paper clip or something.'

Amber checked the desk for anything useful, but apart from the laptop and plaster dust, it was clear.

'Someone's outside,' Kim hissed.

Amber swung her head up. Too late. Giving up on the filing cabinet, she wrenched the laptop charger out of the wall and bundled the charger and laptop under her left arm, keeping the sword in her right. She gritted her teeth. Her arm was getting tired from the weight of the sword.

The door burst open. Five soldiers stood in the doorway, their rifles trained on Bec, Amber and Kim.

'Fuck,' Kim said.

Jerome struck, smashing his fist into Bec's injured shoulder. She gasped and fell back against the wall. He wrenched the rifle from her hands and swung it towards Amber and Kim.

'Now,' he said, 'You can put that laptop down and come with us.'

Sixteen

Amber froze. Her head spun. She lifted her arm to put the laptop back on the desk, and a wall of sound hit her. Pressure beat down on her body, and a bright light blinded her eyes. She hunched over on the ground. Then the pressure was gone. Her ears screamed. She blinked, trying to see through bright spots. Her head pounded.

The soldiers who had been outside the doorway were strewn around the floor. The doorway had become a gaping hole - the wood surrounding it gone. The ceiling was caving in.

Ren appeared in the doorway, a rifle in his hands, his mouth stretched in a wide grin as he took in the destruction that he'd caused. He spoke, but none of them could hear what he said. He thrust his rifle in Jerome's face.

Jerome seemed as dazed as she was. He let his rifle fall to the ground. Ren picked it up and slung it over his shoulder.

Keeping his rifle trained on Jerome, Ren met the women's eyes and jerked his head towards the corridor. Amber stood, shaking. Bec clutched her injured shoulder, her face pale. They stumbled out of the room after Ren and Kim, leaving Jerome behind.

In a daze, Amber didn't realise they'd returned the way they'd come until Ren and Kim halted in front of her. She looked up and realised they were at the exit. The ringing in her ears had lessened, and she could hear sounds again. Ren inched the door open.

Another explosion boomed from the other side of the building. Amber flinched. Ren glanced at her. 'Josie,' he shouted, so she could hear his words over the ringing in her ears, 'She's keeping them busy.'

He led them to the edge of the building. Burn marks stained one wall, and the ground was covered in shattered window glass.

There was a squeal of tyres, and a battered, white, single-cab ute without plates barrelled around the corner. It screeched to a halt in front of them and filled the air with the smell of burning rubber.

Ren pushed Kim into the tray. She tumbled in, her hands still bound by the handcuffs. Ren was gentler with Bec, whose shoulder was oozing blood. Amber tossed the sword into the tray and climbed up, clutching the laptop and cord with one hand. Ren swung himself into the tray and pointed his rifle towards the building.

Amber pushed the sword out of her way and sank down next to Bec. Bec nudged her. To her surprise, Bec was grinning. 'We finally got a proper getaway vehicle.' Amber didn't smile back.

Josie appeared around the corner of the building and ran towards the ute.

Out of the corner of her eye, Amber saw three Boneheads running around the side of the building. 'Boneheads!' she shrieked.

Ren had already seen them. He fired rounds of bullets at them, but the Boneheads didn't even slow their stride.

Josie reached the ute and dived into the tray.

'Go!' Ren yelled.

The driver floored the ute as one of the Boneheads grabbed the back of the tray. The Bonehead pulled itself into the tray so fast that no-one reacted in time to stop it. It swung its sword at Ren. He lifted his rifle to block the blade, but he was at a big disadvantage sitting on the floor with the Bonehead standing over him. There was a clang as the two weapons met, and the rifle flew out of his hand and over the side of the ute.

The driver swung the steering wheel hard, causing the ute to skid across the street. Somehow the Bonehead kept its feet. It swung its sword at Ren again. Ren tried to swing Jerome's rifle around to meet it, gave up, and dived at the Bonehead's legs. The driver sped up again, and the Bonehead fell on top of Ren.

Amber dropped the laptop and seized the hilt of the sword. She stood, placing one foot in front of her body and one behind, balancing on the moving tray as though it was a surfboard. Holding the sword in two hands, she pushed it into the Bonehead's back. The ute hit a bump, and she fell back onto the floor of the tray. The Bonehead let out a wild screech, and staggered up, turning to face her. Josie hit it over the face with her rifle and it fell back onto the side of the ute, pushing the sword in deeper. Blood stained the back of its shirt. It groaned, and its eyes went blank. Its sword fell from its hand. Josie and Ren rolled it over and Josie pulled the sword out of its back.

Then they tipped its body over the side of the ute, and it disappeared behind them.

The ute swerved around a corner. Amber was thrown sideways into Josie. She lurched back.

'Sorry.'

Josie dropped the sword next to the one the Bonehead had dropped and pointed her rifle at the road behind her. 'Our driver, Tev - Tevita - doesn't care about his passengers' comfort. But he's fantastic if we're trying to outrun trouble.'

Bec grabbed the edge of the tray as the ute spun around another corner. 'Does he know the ute comes with brakes?'

As though in answer to Bec's question, Tevita screeched to a sudden halt as a small, blue hatchback pulled out of a driveway. He whipped around it. Amber caught a glimpse of the hatchback's driver - his face white, a terrified look in his eyes. He gave a belated toot of his horn.

Amber could hear sirens wailing in the distance, but there was no sign of a pursuit.

Ren held a mobile phone to his ear, and shouted instructions to Tevita through the open side window. Amber wondered how Tevita could hear above the noise of the engine and squealing tires. 'Avoid the Pac Highway and Main Road - University Drive! Turn here! - ah, no keep going - yes, here! Take Moore Street -'

Amber wedged herself in a corner of the tray, bent her knees and planted her feet, and lifted the lid of the laptop. The screen showed the Australian Government logo and requested a password.

Amber bit her lip and closed it again. She wrapped her arms around her body, pushing the laptop into her stomach. Her chest felt tight. Ideas for how to find Oliver and the girls rushed into her mind in quick succession, each less likely to succeed than the previous one.

She closed her eyes and tried to pray. An image of the soldier rose in her mind. She snapped open her eyes. How could she pray, after what she'd done? She squeezed her eyelids together again. 'Please,' she begged silently, 'Please keep the kids safe.'

Fifteen minutes later, Tevita braked hard left twice, then swerved into a driveway and straight inside a large warehouse. The cab door swung open and Tevita, a short, stocky Tongan, jumped down from the right side. He pulled a large roller door closed.

Metal arches, painted green, supported the building at evenly spaced intervals. A forklift held a pile of packing crates. Sunlight fell through small gaps in the roof, but someone had covered any larger gaps. It was still early, but the air inside the warehouse was warm and stuffy.

Ren jumped off the tray and opened the back of the ute. Josie lowered her rifle and helped Bec and Kim to slide off the tray. She looked back at Amber. 'You coming?'

Amber stared at her. Maybe the resistance could break into the laptop. Maybe they could help her find Oliver. She nodded, and slid down from the tray, the laptop and power cord cradled in her arms.

Large sheets of metal and blankets shielded the corner of the building. At night, it would stop any light escaping from the warehouse. A metal shelving unit ran along one wall, bursting with cardboard boxes. More boxes lined the floor in front of the shelves. A variety of sleeping bags, mats and bivy bags lay on the floor in front of the shelves.

A man in long, olive-green shorts and a blue checked shirt with the sleeves rolled up was sitting on one of the air mattresses cleaning a rifle. He was one of the more attractive men she'd seen. He had dark brown hair cropped to his head. Matching dark brown eyebrows and eyes were set in clear olive skin. A short, trimmed moustache edged the top of his mouth, with a short line of hair beneath and a thicker beard below. Deep grooves ran from the edges of his mouth to the side of the nose. On some people his wide nose might have been considered too large, but it was a perfect match to his face.

Radio and computer equipment covered two trestle tables leaning against the far wall. Above them, three screens played different television channels. On two that were muted, Amber recognised old nineties comedy shows. The third, its volume turned up, showed Mike Davies speaking to a camera. On screen, his appearance was flawless. There was no hint of the haunted look that Amber had seen on his face at the university. The camera shifted and showed Prime Minister Walker, looking relaxed in his usual uniform of white shirt and blue tie.

Two men on folding chairs stared at the screen. Amber realised that they were wearing camouflage uniforms.

'Soldiers!' she shrieked.

The two men glanced at her. They had weather-beaten faces. One had short, bristly, blonde hair, and the other was bald. The bald one raised an eyebrow at Amber.

Ren looked back over his shoulder. 'Don't worry about Glenn and Dave. They're deserters to the resistance.' He directed Bec to sit down on a folding chair.

The man on the floor spoke in a strong New Zealand accent. 'You think there's any chance you'd still be alive if we were working for the Boneheads?'

'Lay off, Sam,' Josie said, coming to Amber's side, 'They've been through hell and back. Wariness is sensible.'

'I know they've put us through hell,' he grumbled.

Josie flashed her teeth at him. 'You're just pissed that the MG yelled at you because the Boneheads got to them before we did in Brooklyn and Newcastle.'

'The MG?' asked Bec.

Sam glared at her. 'Never you mind.'

'The boss,' Josie said.

Amber took three deep breaths, trying to halt the rush of thoughts in her mind. 'What does your boss want with us, anyway?'

Sam looked at her as though she was stupid. 'What do you think? The resistance is yet to succeed in killing a single Bonehead. And yet you have killed three.'

'Four,' Ren said.

Amber narrowed her eyes. 'I don't know what you're expecting,' she said to Sam, 'But I'm not staying. I'm leaving as soon as I can to find my son, and the two girls we've been travelling with. And I think Josie killed the fourth Bonehead.'

'Three and a half,' Josie said, 'It was a joint effort.'

A ute like the one they'd arrived in was parked to one side of the radio and television equipment. The tray was open, with a small electric stove, kettle and portable fridge resting near the edge. Ren retrieved a first aid kit and a tool bag from the cab.

'Give me a hand, would you, Dave? Bec's shoulder needs some first aid.'

The bald soldier joined them. He slid on gloves from the first aid kit. Bec removed her hand so he could look at her shoulder. Her T-shirt sleeve was soaked in blood. He pulled the sleeve away and dabbed at her shoulder with a damp cloth. Amber looked over his shoulder. Underneath bits of dried blood, there was a large chunk of flesh missing.

Amber had no sympathy. Bec had only been bitten because she tried to contact the resistance. It was her fault Amber had lost Oliver. She clenched her hands and teeth.

Bec closed her eyes while Dave wiped her shoulder with antiseptic and bandaged it.

Ren inserted two pieces of metal wire into the lock on Kim's cuffs. After a few minutes, there was a click, and the cuffs fell off. She rubbed her wrists. 'Thank you.'

'Where do you fit into this? We were only expecting to retrieve these two.'

Kim shrugged. 'The soldiers came to my house a few days ago, pretty near knocked down the door, ignored my housemates and nabbed me. The Bonehead said he wanted a 'human martial arts expert' to give an opinion on her.' She nodded at Amber. 'Then the soldiers kept me locked up until you guys started blowing the place up. A couple of them came to take me somewhere else, but she leapt out at them like an avenging butcher, and they split.'

Dave disappeared to wash his hands, and Glenn flicked the switch on the kettle. He pulled out a box of mismatched, dusty mugs, a carton of milk and a packet of plain biscuits, and waved at a packet of teabags and a jar of instant coffee. Bec, Kim and the resistance fighters helped themselves to tea and coffee and sat down on the floor or folding chairs. Sam stayed on his feet, leaning back against the tray of the ute, looking more like a movie star than a resistance fighter. Kim kept casting surreptitious looks at him. Bec didn't even try to be subtle - she just stared.

Amber stayed where she was. She was full of energy, and bounced her weight from one foot to the other. Oliver was out there, somewhere, and they were wasting time with tea. 'I'm not staying,' she repeated.

Sam took a sip of coffee. 'You said.'

Dave spoke through a mouthful of biscuit. 'You can't leave now.'

He pointed at the television that he and Glenn had been watching when they arrived. The screen showed images of soldiers wrestling people to the ground. The news ticker at the bottom of the screen read Snap 48-hour lockdown - Newcastle and surrounds.

'The city is crawling with soldiers,' Dave said, 'They're arresting anyone who moves out there.'

Amber's eyes widened. 'Why?'

Dave drew his brows in and tilted his head to one side. 'Uh - I expect they're looking for the person who killed three and a half Boneheads.'

She stiffened.

Sam shook his head. 'What the hell did you expect?'

'It's a good sign,' Josie said, 'If they're resorting to a lockdown, it means they have no idea where you are.'

'But I won't be able to go after my son.' Amber's voice rose in a wail.

'So you may as well have a cup of tea,' Dave said.

Amber stared at him. Ideas rushed around her mind again.

The silence dragged out. Dave broke it. 'How about I get you one?'

Dave nudged a chair in her direction. She slumped onto it, placing the laptop on the ground, and took the tea and three biscuits he handed her. As she sipped the tea her mind settled. She dunked a biscuit in the tea and chewed. Her shoulders relaxed.

Sam watched her through narrowed eyes. She frowned. 'Is there something you want to say?'

'How did you kill those Boneheads? All our attempts have failed.'

'It's the THONGs,' Bec blurted.

Sam raised both his eyebrows this time. 'The thongs?'

'They have these - devices,' Bec made the shape of a ball with her hand, 'They stop bullets, but not swords. Or bolt cutters.'

Ren and Josie exchanged glances. 'That explains more than it doesn't,' Ren said.

'Why the Boneheads always carry swords, and only sometimes rifles.' Josie sounded breathless.

'They must block shrapnel from grenades, too,' Ren said, 'But it's not metal they're blocking, or swords wouldn't work. What do they block then - flying objects? Objects travelling at high velocity?'

Glenn looked at Bec, wrinkling his brow. 'Bolt cutters?'

Sam waved a hand, silencing them. 'You alluded to these devices in your messages. Did you say you have one?'

Bec pulled a face. 'We don't have it anymore. That blasted soldier destroyed it in Brooklyn.'

Sam rolled his eyes. 'Well that piece of news will fill the MG with joy.'

Ren looked at Amber. 'These - thongs - are only part of the explanation, though. I watched you at the university, and again in the TV footage. You moved - fast.' He glanced at Kim. 'Correct me if I'm wrong, but I would have said - too fast.'

Kim nodded. 'If the footage that Bonehead showed me is real, I've never seen anyone move that fast.'

'How did you do it?'

They all looked at Amber. She wriggled, pulling her shoulders towards her ears. 'It just happened. I didn't do anything.'

Sam narrowed his eyes, as though he didn't believe her. 'Has it 'just happened' any other time?'

'I don't know.'

'Yes,' Bec said, 'At Brooklyn. And this morning, before Ren showed up, when she killed a soldier.'

'A soldier?' Sam raised his eyebrows.

'Jonno.' Amber's voice sounded too loud in her ears. 'His name was Jonno.'

'How?' Ren kept his eyes on Amber.

'It just happens,' she repeated.

When it was clear she wasn't going to say anything else, Sam turned to Bec. 'You organised the Martin Place massacre?'

'No.'

He drew his eyebrows in. 'What?'

'No, I organised the protest. The massacre was all the Boneheads.'

He rolled his eyes again. 'Right, yes. The protest. And Governor Macquarie Tower?'

'Just a bit player,' Bec said.

Glenn snorted.

Bec kept her eyes on Sam. 'The Bonehead said that everyone else involved in the attack is dead. Is that true?'

'As far as we can tell, yes. But there might be some who have gone to ground.'

Bec hunched her shoulders. Her eyes were moist, but no tears escaped.

'I think,' Sam said, flinging himself down on a folding chair, 'That you had better tell us the whole story. We know about the university - Ren and Josie were there - but where the hell have you been since then?'

Bec raised her eyebrows at Amber. Amber kept her mouth closed. After a moment, Bec launched into their story. The resistance fighters gave her their full attention. Glenn picked up a laptop from the trestle table and tapped at it while she spoke, taking notes.

Amber was glad that Bec was the focus of the resistance fighters' attention, not her. Bec didn't seem bothered by the attention, but Amber noticed that she told the story factually, without any of her usual embellishments. Amber helped herself to more biscuits and a cup of instant coffee, and walked over to the television, listening to Mike Davies' voice describing the Newcastle lockdown. He glossed over the reasons for the lockdown with the word 'unrest'. He didn't mention her. Small mercies.

She turned back to the group as Bec finished speaking, and Sam turned to Kim.

'Exactly what kind of martial arts expert are you?'

Kim rolled her eyes. 'I wouldn't use the term expert - that was the Boneheads. I just do it for fun and fitness. I started with Taekwondo as a kid, then various other styles as I got older, particularly Japanese sword fighting. Which I guess is why the Boneheads were interested in me - their swords are like the ones we use.'

Sam stood. 'I'd better brief the MG.' He looked at Amber, raising his voice. 'You want to give that laptop to Glenn and Dave, see if they can crack it for you?'

Amber returned to the group and handed the laptop to Dave.

'These THONGs -' Sam continued.

'On it,' Glenn said.

Sam nodded. He glanced at Kim.

'Also - confirm Kim is who she says she is, please.'

He dragged a folding chair over to the trestle table with its computers and began typing on a laptop. Glenn and Dave joined him. Dave put a CD into the laptop that Amber had given him, while Glenn continued to type on the one he'd been taking notes on. He wagged a finger at Kim to join them.

Bec stared into her coffee cup. Amber pressed her lips together. Bec was distressed - she'd had friends killed - but Amber couldn't dredge up any sympathy.

Ren laid out loaves of bread and a variety of spreads on the kitchen ute for an early lunch. Eating the biscuits had made Amber realise how hungry she was. They helped themselves to sandwiches. The bread tasted a few days old, but it was fine washed down with more coffee.

Tevita drained his coffee cup. 'I'm going to have a nap.'

Josie yawned. 'Good idea.' She beckoned Amber. 'If you come with me, I'll find you some sleeping gear.' She ran her eyes over Amber's blood- and dust-spattered clothes. 'And some clean clothes.'

Amber followed her to the metal shelves.

'I think there's some around here.' Josie tugged a box out. It was full of army ration packs. She shoved it back and tried the next one. Toilet paper. Another was full of canisters of the same instant coffee they'd just been drinking. At last, Josie found one with several sleeping bags in it. She deposited three on the floor.

'Thanks,' Amber said.

Josie yawned again. 'I don't think we've got any mats or anything for you to sleep on.' She checked a few more boxes. 'Oh, here.' She dumped a large box on the floor. It was full of blankets. 'Take as many as you need.'

She deposited a second box next to it, which was overflowing with folded pants and shorts. A third box joined them, with shirts and T-shirts. The clothes were worn, practical, in dull colours. Clothes for wearing when you didn't want to be noticed.

Josie pointed out of the shielded area. 'There's a toilet out there you can get changed in.' She yawned wider than ever. 'I'll leave you to it.'

Amber found an empty patch of floor in front of the shelves, to the right of the other sleeping gear. She spread blankets out on the floor, laid the sleeping bags on top, and selected a pair of shorts and a yellow T-shirt.

She returned to what she'd started thinking of as 'the kitchen ute'. Bec was still sitting in the same position. Kim joined them.

'So I am who I thought I was. That's a relief.' She started buttering herself a sandwich.

'I set up some sleeping gear for us.' Amber pointed at the sleeping bags. 'And those boxes have clothes we can use.'

'Thanks.' Bec struggled to her feet.

'Awesome,' Kim said.

Amber slipped out of the area protected by the metal sheets. The sun was high overhead. Light slipped through every hole and crack in the roof and walls, covering the concrete floor in a chaotic, mottled artwork. In the dancing light the empty market building looked rundown and uninviting. She hurried to the toilets.

Once she had changed and used the toilet, she washed her hands, splashed water on her face and ran her fingers through her matted hair; grateful, for once, for the short style. She expressed milk from her breasts into the basin, her eyes filling with tears as images of Oliver rose in her mind. She squeezed her eyes shut and prayed the same prayer as before. 'Please keep the kids safe.'

When she returned, she found Bec asleep on top of one of the sleeping bags. Bec hadn't bothered to change her clothes. Kim was rummaging in the clothes boxes, searching for clothes small enough to fit her.

Amber sank onto the top of the sleeping bag next to Bec. It was too hot to get inside the bag. Kim disappeared and returned wearing a T-shirt so long it covered her shorts, looking more like a dress than a shirt. She lay down on the third sleeping bag. Her breath slowed.

Amber's eyes burned with tiredness, but she couldn't lie still. She wriggled and rolled from side to side, tangling her sleeping bag around her legs. Sweat sprang from her body. Her mind threw up pictures from the morning - the wombat leaping at Oliver, teeth bared - Jonno pushing her down on the table, his breath warm on her cheek - Jonno dead on the ground, his sword in his throat - the soldiers standing in the doorway of Nichols' office one minute, then dead on the ground the next. And through all the pictures the gnawing absence of Oliver, her whole body aching to hold him in her arms.

Amber squirmed her way out of the sleeping bag. Her bladder felt overfull - too much crap coffee. She walked to the toilets, the concrete floor hard against her bare feet.

Her eyes took a while to adjust when she slipped back into the darkened area protected by the metal sheets. Glenn and Dave hadn't moved from the trestle table. The other resistance fighters had retired to their sleeping bags.

Amber found her cup, gave it a half-hearted rinse and made another cup of instant coffee. She sipped it looking over Dave's shoulder. Glenn was squinting at a webpage showing three half-naked girls with large smiles and perfect teeth. Dave was leaning back in his seat watching the news on low volume. The laptop Amber had taken from Nichols' office was open beside him, blinking.

The news showed pictures of cranes and diggers working on the main street of Dubbo. Amber's chest tightened. She wondered if Adam was there somewhere. She imagined seeing him again, and having to explain to him that she'd lost Oliver. Tears filled her eyes. She clenched her hands, her nails pressing into her palms.

Dave sensed her behind him and turned the volume up. A young blonde woman was gushing about the government rebuilding Dubbo. Her intonation and the way she enunciated each word reminded Amber of Charlotte Lee.

'Bastards,' Dave said, 'Dubbo wouldn't need rebuilding if they hadn't bombed the crap out of it. You can bet that whatever rebuilding they're doing there, it's in their best interests, not the people who live in Dubbo.'

'Dubboans?' Glenn suggested, without taking his eyes off his computer, 'Dubbosiders?'

'Arseholes.'

'O...kay; bit harsh.'

'Not the - Dubboans - the fucking government.'

'I don't know why you watch that crap,' Glenn said, 'It just pisses you off.'

'You know why,' Dave said to him. He glanced at Amber. 'It's propaganda, but it's still based on truth. I watch it in case they let something slip that they didn't mean to tell us.'

'Like that they're up to something in Dubbo?' Amber asked.

Dave beamed at her. 'Exactly!'

'Which we knew more than a week ago, when they bombed the town, where there was no resistance presence,' Glenn said, his eyes still on the screen in front of him, 'And then followed it up by sending several truckloads of soldiers there, where sure, now there were a number of pissed off Dubboans, but they weren't organised enough to cause the Boneheads any real headaches.'

'They're starting to organise now,' Dave said.

'My point is, you've learnt nothing by torturing yourself with propaganda.'

Dave rolled his eyes at Amber. Amber glanced at the laptop next to him. Lines of code appeared in white text on the black screen. 'How are you going with the laptop?'

Dave glanced at it. 'No joy so far, but I've got a few tricks to try.'

Amber squinted at it. 'What are you doing now?'

'Trying to access his files through a backdoor. I'm not holding my breath - it won't help if the files are encrypted, which they probably are. But it's the easiest thing to try first.'

Amber finished her coffee and washed the mug. Her body was tense, full of energy. She left the shielded area and prowled around the warehouse. A small door was set into one corner, with a green exit sign above and a fire hose on the wall next to it. She pushed open the door and shaded her eyes.

The sun beat down on the road outside. A ticket booth stood at the entrance of the compound. A small stretch of grass separated the road from a large carpark. A few seedlings had been planted in a line in the grass, each protected by a wire mesh cage wound around three star pickets. An image of Dan wielding the star picket at the wombat rose in her mind. She smiled at the memory of the ridiculous dressing gown stretched across his chest to hide the 'No Boners' T-shirt. The smile slid off her face as she remembered the soldiers driving away with Oliver. And now they had him again.

She returned to her sleeping bag. Bec and Kim were fast asleep. Amber lay down again and closed her eyes. This time, exhaustion overcame her, and she slept.

She woke a few hours later, her stomach growling. The warehouse was even hotter. A layer of sweat had glued the nylon sleeping bag to her skin.

Bec was gone from her sleeping bag. Amber lifted her head and found her near the kitchen ute, eating another sandwich. She'd changed into clean clothes. The bandage that Dave had wrapped around her shoulder was stained red.

Amber peeled herself off her sleeping bag and walked over. Avoiding eye contact with Bec, she helped herself to a couple of slices of bread and started spreading butter on them. Bec opened her mouth to say something, then changed her mind and sank onto one of the folding chairs.

The heat woke the resistance fighters. Ren poured himself a coffee. He'd changed out of his battered high vis clothes into a worn army uniform. Josie joined him, looking half-asleep. She threw two heaped teaspoons of coffee powder into her cup, then hesitated. 'Ugh, I still haven't had enough sleep.' She added two more teaspoons of coffee powder.

'That is going to taste horrible,' Tevita said, walking over and leaning on his forearms over the ute.

Sam came from the toilets, looking fresh and wide awake. He stopped at the trestle tables, where Glenn and Dave were still hunched over laptop screens.

'Any luck?' he asked Glenn.

Glenn sighed and ran his hands over his face. 'Nothing. There's no reference to THONGs anywhere - other than the traditional types. I've spent the entire day looking at footwear and G-strings. If anyone's tracking my search history, they'll think I have a serious fetish. And Dave can't get into that laptop Amber stole.'

Amber left her bread on the ute tray and hurried over to them. Bec followed her.

'You can't?' Amber's chest tightened and her heart raced. That was her only plan for finding Oliver. She didn't have another one.

'Sorry.' Dave looked at her, 'We're not hackers. We've got a few programs that let us create a backdoor, but like I told you before, they don't work if the files are encrypted. And there's a program we use to crack passwords, but it only works on simple passwords. It doesn't work if the guy uses a decent, long password. You need a real hacker for this.'

Amber's head shot up. 'A real hacker?' The image of Dan with the star picket flashed in her mind again. 'I know one!'

Sam raised his eyebrows at her.

'My neighbour, Dan. Daniel Scott.'

Bec frowned. 'Isn't he just a software developer?'

'Now. He has a disreputable past. He was arrested for hacking in his twenties.'

Bec blinked. 'Wow. My opinion of him has just gone up about a hundred notches.'

Seventeen

Sam refused to let her contact Dan until Glenn had checked him out. Amber gave Glenn his address, then watched as he searched, bouncing her weight from one foot to another.

'That's not helping,' Glenn snapped.

Bec dragged her back to her sandwich.

She had finished eating when Glenn trotted over from his

computer. He spoke to Sam. 'His story checks out. Arrested in 2003 for hacking into his old university system, and a couple of state government departments. They gave him a suspended sentence, community service, a good behaviour bond. Hasn't been caught doing anything since then. Working as a software developer, as Bec said, for a US company.'

Sam looked at Amber. 'Alright, you can message him, but I want Glenn to check each message before you hit send. There's a good chance the Boneheads will be monitoring your contacts.'

'Can't you stop them hacking my messages?'

'Sure. But what we don't know is if they're standing behind him. Or if they've locked him up somewhere and are pretending to be him. Or if they've offered to pay him a squillion dollars if he tells them you've contacted him.'

'Plus, we're trusting that the encrypted messaging app is doing what it says on the box,' Dave said, 'It wasn't that long ago that a bunch of organised crime networks were smashed because the encrypted messaging app they were using was controlled by the FBI.'

Glenn motioned for her to sit in the chair he was using. He dragged another chair over next to it and clicked on an app on the laptop screen in front of him. 'Alright. Type your message and I'll check it before you hit send.'

Amber hesitated, nervous after all their warnings. Glenn raised his eyebrows. Turning to the screen, she typed a short message. Glenn read it and clicked send.

For a long time, nothing appeared. Amber clenched her teeth. It was daytime, so Dan might be asleep, or outside, rather than online.

Piss off whoever the fuck you are

Amber let out her breath. He was online.

I said it's Amber Yu

Two words appeared on the screen.

Prove it

Amber bit her lip, trying to think. She typed two sentences.

Last year I banged on your door in the middle of the night 'cos Adam was away and there was a giant spider

A couple of months ago I told you that I'd never watched any of the Star Wars movies, and you told me that I was dead to you

She glanced at Glenn, who nodded. She hit send.

Fuck me

It really is you

Amber took a deep breath.

I need a favour

Can you hack a laptop for me?

His response wasn't encouraging.

You've got to be fucking kidding. I don't do that shit anymore

Not to mention, you're like public enemy no. 1

There was a pause. The chat box indicated that Dan was typing.

You know Zhou hasn't come back? Nobody has heard from him

Amber felt guilt hit her in the chest. She hunched her shoulders. When had she last thought about Zhou? Not for days. She stared at the screen, feeling helpless.

Glenn gave her an impatient look. 'Convince him.'

Dan, they've got Ollie. I think the laptop will tell me where they took him

There was another pause.

I thought you got him back

A tear rolled down Amber's face.

I did, but they got him again

She waited.

Fucking hell, Amber, you ever heard that once is misfortune, twice is just careless?

Amber slumped down in her chair.

'Arsehole,' Bec said, reading his message over her shoulder, 'Let me talk to him.'

Dan, this is Bec. You're always wearing those T-shirts. This is your chance to be a revolutionary

She waited.

It's a fucking massive jump from wearing some damn T-shirts to helping two of the most wanted people in the country

There was a long pause.

I must be fucking insane. Where am I meeting you?

Amber sat upright, surprised.

'Right,' Glenn said, pulling the laptop towards him, 'This is where I come in.'

Glenn arranged to meet Dan in the largest shopping mall in Newcastle.

9am Thursday. We'll see you there

'Thursday!' Amber's heart raced and her face turned red. 'Why not today? Or tomorrow, at least!'

Glenn raised his eyes to the ceiling and sighed. 'Lockdown, remember? None of us can move around Newcastle until it's over.'

Amber paced the length of the shielded area. Her body was hot, her face flushed. At the shelving unit, she pulled out boxes, looked in them, and pushed them back. She felt suffocated. She walked outside the shielded area, making a beeline towards the small door to the outside. As she passed the back of the ute that they'd arrived in, she heard Sam speaking from near the cab.

'Sorry, Ren, but you haven't convinced me. That girl moves too fast - it's like she's not - not human. And she didn't even attempt to give us an explanation.'

Amber shrank back against the ute.

'She might have been telling the truth - that she doesn't know how she does it,' Ren's voice replied.

'Tev thinks she's possessed.'

Ren snorted. 'I might have had to accept that monsters are real, but I'm not going to start believing they have superpowers. The Boneheads are flesh and blood, like us. If what Bec says is true, even their seemingly magical ability to stop bullets is just an electronic device. There's no evidence that they or anyone else can possess someone.'

'Well, there's something that girl's not telling us.'

'Come on, Sam,' Ren said, 'She could give us an edge in this fight. I don't think we can afford to throw any potential advantage away. And the MG must think the same, or he wouldn't have sent us chasing her across the country.' There was silence for a moment, and Ren added. 'It'll be fine.'

Sam sighed. 'Why is it every time you say that it ends up anything but fine? Alright. Talk to them both. But I'll be keeping an eye on Amber. I suggest you do the same.'

Amber waited until they'd gone back into the shielded area before she walked outside. She stared at the ticket booth without seeing it, the conversation she'd just heard replaying in her mind. Not human? Private Jerome had said something similar; he'd called her inhumanely fast.

'I am human,' she said aloud. But the power she kept reaching out to - what was that? 'Not human, for sure,' she whispered. She closed her eyes and reached out with her mind. She felt the slightest sense - almost an echo - of the timelessness, but nothing more.

It wasn't possessing her. Of that, she was sure. She was still herself. She was just - leaning on it, for support. But - it chose when she was allowed to. Did that mean it was sentient? Shivering at the thought, she hurried back into the shielded area.

Glenn cooked a simple stir-fry with freeze dried meat, vegetables and couscous for dinner. Nobody spoke much as they ate, lost in their own thoughts.

Ren finished first. He put his bowl on the ground in a deliberate movement, and went to the cab of the ute.

Sam cleaned the last of the stir-fry from his bowl with his finger and stretched his legs out. His eyes followed Ren.

Ren returned with a sword in each hand - the one the Bonehead had used to attack him in the ute, and the one that Amber had taken from Jonno. Amber was relieved to see that he'd cleaned the blood from the latter. He spoke to Kim. 'Given what Bec's told us about the THONGs, the resistance is going to need people with your skills. Will you join us?' He proffered one of the swords.

Kim took it. She ran her finger down the blade with care. 'I never thought I'd use my sword fighting skills for anything other than fun.' She gave a small shrug and met his eyes. 'But I'd love to send those Boneheads packing. And it's not like I've got anything better to do.'

'You won't be alone. The MG is going to try to recruit other people with sword fighting experience. And to try to train up new people. Speaking of which -' Ren turned and met Amber's eyes.

'No,' Amber said, 'No way. Like I said this morning - I'm leaving as soon as I can.'

He frowned at her, drawing his brows in. 'Fine. But since we're stuck here for at least another day, I want Kim to teach you how to use a sword - properly.'

Kim looked as startled as Amber felt. 'Years of martial arts training in one day?'

'Of course not. Just - as much as you can teach her.'

Amber's mind filled with an image of the sword in Jonno's throat. She never wanted to touch a sword again. Ever.

'Ren -' Kim started.

Amber gave a firm shake of her head. 'I'm good, thanks.'

Ren glowered at her. 'So, you're going to find out where the

Boneheads have taken your son, and then what? Rush in swinging a sword around like a tennis racket?'

Bec tilted her head up at him. 'She's killed three and a half Boneheads and one soldier that way.'

Ren bared his teeth. 'As Ms Williams reminds me,' he turned his glare on Bec, 'You have had some success. But you have been lucky. They've underestimated you. Assuming they can add as well as Ms Williams, they won't make that mistake again. If you want your luck to hold long enough to retrieve your son, it will help to know how to use a weapon.'

He pushed the hilt of the second sword into Amber's hand. Her conviction of a moment before crumbled. What if he was right, and she needed to use a sword to rescue Ollie? She wrapped her fingers around the hilt.

'Ren -' Kim said again, 'I've never taught martial arts.'

Ren shrugged. 'You're the only one here who knows anything about it. You'll have to do.'

Kim screwed up her face. 'Thanks for the effusive vote of confidence.'

'Me too,' Bec said, 'I want to learn too.'

Kim drew her brows in. 'You can't lift your arm.'

'I'll use the other one. I'm right-handed anyway.'

Kim let out a deep sigh. 'I'll need some things,' she told Ren.

The resistance fighters finished eating and dispersed - to work, or to sleep. Ren and Kim moved to the shelving unit, taking both swords with them. Bec washed the dishes and Amber dried them, avoiding eye contact with Bec.

Bec washed the last cup and placed it upside down to drain. 'That's it. I might go to bed, too.'

'How's the shoulder?' Amber asked, still avoiding eye contact.

'I'll live.' Bec hesitated for a moment. 'Well - good night.'

'Night.'

212

Kim shook Amber awake the next morning. 'Get up.'

Amber looked at her through slits in her eyes. Her head ached. She had laid awake until early in the morning, worrying about Oliver.

'Why?'

'Sword fighting lessons, remember?'

Amber dropped her head back into the pillow with a groan.

'You agreed to this,' Kim reminded her.

'Nobody said anything about the middle of the night.'

'It's not the middle of the night. The sun's up. You can't see it because of the shielding.'

Amber groaned again, but she slid out of her sleeping bag, giving Bec a kick as she did so. Bec blinked sleep out of her eyes and scrambled out of her sleeping bag.

They trained in the space between the shielded area and the ute. Amber peeked out of the small door. The sun was up, but only just - it hovered above the horizon, sending blinding rays across the carpark towards her. The western sky was a light pink colour. Wispy clouds floated on the horizon - the kind that would disappear by mid-morning. She shut the door again, blinking as coloured streaks flashed in front of her eyes.

Kim handed her a belt fashioned out of hiking straps. 'We don't have any sword belts, so I had to improvise.' She had a similar makeshift sword belt around her own waist. 'You can have this one once I've shown you how to draw from it,' Kim told Bec. 'We've only got two swords - we'll have to share.'

Once Amber had clipped it around her waist, Kim handed her the sword that she'd taken from the soldier. A thick, dark green material had been wrapped around the blade and secured with electrical tape. She passed a second wrapped sword to Bec. 'I had to cut up a canvas tarp that Ren found for me. Don't rely on the wrapping - hopefully it'll stop you from cutting yourself, but those swords are sharp. I expect they'll rip through the material.'

Amber frowned, her brow wrinkling.

'Don't worry,' Kim said with a small smile, 'If you kill yourself today, you'll just save the Boneheads the trouble of doing it later. First, let me show you how to hold the sword. Are you right handed too?' she asked Amber.

Amber nodded.

'So your right hand goes just below the guard, and your left beneath it. No, further down the hilt than that.' She guided Amber's hands into the correct position. Amber felt the weight of the sword and bounced it up and down, getting a feel for it.

Once they were both comfortable, she showed them how to draw the sword out of the makeshift sword belt. She drew it with her right hand in a single, sharp movement, which looked deceptively easy. Amber could copy the move in slow motion, but when she tried to speed it up the sword caught in the straps and she struggled to control its weight with one hand. She winced as it bumped against her legs, grateful for the canvas covering.

Kim gave her sword belt to Bec, and made them both repeat the move over and over until sharp pains ran up Amber's wrist and arm. Her right hand burned, as though the Boneheads had hit it with their rope again.

Kim took the sword belt back from Bec and added a second movement. After drawing the sword with her right hand, she brought it over her head with both hands. 'From here, you can swing it down on your opponent.' She stepped forward as she swung so that she added her body weight to the movement.

Amber was relieved to use her left hand to help wield the weight of the sword, but the relief was short-lived. After several repetitions of lifting the sword over her head, both arms were aching.

Kim had no mercy. 'Keep going!' she called if Amber slowed.

Bec couldn't lift her left arm above her head, but she put the sword down on the ground and practiced the movement with her right hand.

Kim showed them an alternative second movement. She again drew the sword with her right hand, then brought it up to neck height with both hands and held it horizontally. She stepped forward and swung the sword forward at the same time, slicing into an imaginary opponent.

She gestured for Amber to try the move. Amber lunged forward, feeling the weight of the sword slice through the air, propelled by the weight of her body. Despite the ache in her arms, the move felt good.

Kim made Amber repeat the moves over and over until Amber was struggling to lift the sword. Bec's shoulder forced her to give up, but she stayed and watched.

Amber's stomach growled. Kim called a halt. 'Let's have breakfast. I'll teach you some defensive moves next.'

Amber followed Kim and Bec inside, wondering how she would be able to manage any defensive moves when her arms were in agony.

Dave had plugged a toaster into a powerboard running from the generator and was making toast. Josie was finishing a bowl of cereal.

Amber made herself a strong mug of coffee.

'How's the sword fighting going?' Dave asked.

Amber pulled a face. 'I don't suggest relying on me to save us from the Boneheads.'

'Just stab them in the back, like last time,' Josie said, standing up and rinsing her plate in a bowl of dirty, soapy water. Amber winced.

Dave handed her a plate with two slices of toast on it. She spread apricot jam on the toast and devoured both slices. Dave passed her another two slices.

As soon as they'd finished eating, Kim bounced out of her chair, ready to go again.

'Leave the plates,' Dave said, 'I'll wash them.'

'Thanks,' Amber and Bec chimed in unison.

He shrugged. 'I've got nothing else to do, apart from watch endless propaganda on TV.'

With food and drink in her stomach, Amber felt better than she'd expected. Kim started by asking Amber to attack her in slow motion so she could demonstrate several defensive moves. It wasn't like the sword fighting Amber had seen on medieval television shows. Kim didn't use her sword to block Amber's sword, she caught the strikes on the side of the sword and let it slide off while moving her body out of the way.

They switched, and Kim attacked Amber, still in slow motion. Unlike Kim, who had pivoted her body away from each attack with ease, Amber felt clumsy. She tripped over her own feet, fumbling with the sword and dropping it. Kim, shaking her head, made Amber put the sword to one side and showed her how to stand with one foot in front, bouncing on her feet. Bec joined in, pleased to be able to do something that didn't bother her injured shoulder.

The sun rose higher in the sky, heating the inside of the warehouse. A layer of sweat covered Amber's body. Damp locks of hair fell around her face and sweat dripped into her eyes.

They continued, with only a short break for a snack and drink. The resistance fighters came out at different times to watch. She gritted her teeth and tried to ignore them.

Just before lunch, Kim revised all the moves that she'd taught them so far. Amber was so exhausted that her fighting went downhill rather than improving. Shaking her head, Kim called it a day, finishing with a session of stretching. Instead of holding the stretch, like Amber had done at the gym, Kim pulsed, releasing the stretch and then stretching further forward.

Amber stumbled inside when they were done and collapsed on top of her sleeping bag, ignoring the sweat dripping onto the bag. She wondered if there was any muscle in her body that didn't ache.

Bec came and sat down on her own bedding, rubbing her injured shoulder.

'This is stupid,' Amber said, 'I'm not going to become a sword fighter in a day.'

'Ren's not stupid,' Bec said, continuing to massage her shoulder, 'He doesn't expect you to become an expert. You don't need to be - you've killed Boneheads without any skills at all. But maybe if you can hold the sword correctly and know a few moves you'll be more effective.'

Amber pulled a face. 'Or not.'

'Besides, what does Ren have to lose by getting Kim to teach you? Apart from pissing her off a bit?'

'Is she pissed off? I think she's enjoying torturing me.'

'So it's a win for everyone.'

'Except my poor arms.'

Amber had to admit that there was one benefit of the day's training - she had a sound sleep that night. She woke early. The lockdown was ending. She could go after Oliver at last. She slithered out of the sleeping bag, pain running up her arms from the training the day before. At the kitchen ute, she switched the kettle on, massaging her right hand. She was drinking a coffee when Kim and Bec came to find her.

'I'm going with Ren and Josie to get Dan this morning,' Amber said.

'They're still asleep,' Kim said, 'So we've got time for a bit more training.'

Amber's brain felt fuzzy, and she wasn't sure she could remember the moves Kim had taught her the day before, but her body remembered them. She settled into the training. This time, she didn't need to concentrate as much. She let her mind wander as she repeated the moves over and over.

Ren came to find her. 'We need to leave in half an hour. Have you had breakfast?'

Amber shook her head.

'You'd better have some. And bring your weapon, just in case.' He glanced at Kim. 'You can have her back once we've picked her friend up.'

Kim flashed her teeth in a predatory grin. 'Good.'

Amber groaned. She pulled the electricians tape and tarp wrapping off the sword as she followed Ren back to the kitchen ute. Tevita and Josie were eating breakfast. Glenn and Dave were hunched over their computers.

Glenn swung around as they passed the trestle table. 'We've got a problem.'

Ren raised his eyebrows.

'They've put up roadblocks. All over the city.'

'Not a huge surprise. I didn't really think they'd give up after forty-eight hours. Do we know where they are?'

'Dave's pulling together a list.'

Dave looked up. 'I can't guarantee I'll get all of them.'

Ren narrowed his eyes, considering. 'I think the risk is worth it. Let Tev know where the roadblocks are, please.'

'Will do.'

Amber removed the last of the wrapping from the sword and slid it into the sword belt. She was conscious of its weight swinging at her side. So presumptuous - as though she was some kind of swordsman. Tevita and Josie looked up as she and Ren approached, and her cheeks reddened, but they looked back down at their bowls, more interested in cereal than in her.

They ate breakfast in silence, standing up at the kitchen ute. As soon as they'd eaten, Ren herded them out of the shielded area.

Kim and Bec were still outside; Kim demonstrating a new move that Amber hadn't seen before. Sam strode after them and stopped Ren, speaking to him in a low voice, while Tevita opened the roller door.

Bec approached Amber. 'Hey, good luck. I hope that dickhead turns up.'

Amber looked away, towards the ute. Her anger with Bec no longer fizzed inside her - it had solidified into a large, unmovable ball inside her stomach. 'I thought you'd raised your opinion of him.'

'He's still a dickhead.'

Bec looked like she wanted to say something else, but Ren and Sam finished their conversation, and Ren strode towards the ute, waving at Amber to come.

He directed Amber to sit in the passenger seat, next to Tevita. He and Josie hunkered down in the back of the ute, keeping their heads below the sides of the tray wall to avoid attracting attention. They rested their rifles just below the tray wall, ready to fire.

Amber pulled the sword out of the sword belt and climbed in, resting the sword on her lap. Tevita had stuck a list of roads to the dashboard with electrical tape. He saw her looking at it and flashed his teeth at her. 'Ready to dodge some roadblocks? I hope your friend is worth it.' He started the engine and released the park brake.

Amber had a flash of fear. What if Dan couldn't hack the laptop? She only had his word for it that he was a decent hacker.

The ute rumbled out of the warehouse and onto the street. Sam pulled the roller door shut behind them. This time, Tevita stuck to the speed limits, avoiding attention. He took a convoluted route, making so many turns up and down small roads that Amber wondered how he knew where they were.

It took them about three quarters of an hour to arrive at the shopping centre, a sprawling concrete building with a mishmash of architectural features. On one side, vines covered the concrete wall. Amber smiled at the juxtaposition of nature against this bastion of consumerism. Tevita drove under the plant-covered wall and into a carpark.

The shopping centre was due to open at nine. It was about a quarter to, and the carpark was busy with people who had been taken by surprise by the unexpected lockdown.

Tevita drove around the carpark in a circle, dodging an elderly lady with an armload of reusable shopping bags. A younger woman lifted a pram out of the back of a large SUV and unfolded it. Amber's chest tightened, and she looked away. Tevita pulled into a park facing the exit lane. He kept the engine running. A few spaces down, two men were talking over the top of each other, each explaining why they had been the more inconvenienced by the lockdown. Amber clenched her fists. A wave of envy flooded her. All these people's lives were unaffected by Boneheads or soldiers. She stared at the sword in her lap, as though it was a foreign object she'd never seen before.

Ren slid down from the tray and opened the passenger door. 'Tell me if you see him.' Amber climbed out of the ute, leaving the sword on the seat. More cars pulled into the carpark. She scrutinised each one as it entered. Nine am came and went, with no sign of Dan. Ren noticed Amber checking Lucy's watch.

'Think he's coming?'

Amber shrugged.

Just after nine thirty a silver, luxury hybrid car drove into the carpark. 'That's him,' she said, stepping away from the ute.

Ren put a hand on her shoulder. 'Wait.' He gripped his rifle, his knuckles white.

Dan cruised around the carpark. Josie peered at the car down the scope on her rifle. 'He's alone,' she said.

Ren lifted his hand from Amber's shoulder. 'Okay. Wave him over.'

Amber stepped forward and waved at the car. Dan pulled into an empty space two spaces down from the ute. He opened the drivers' side door and pulled himself out of the car.

He wore his usual uniform of shorts and an old, faded T-shirt. This one was less overtly political than usual, but the company name splashed across the front of it was a well-known fair-trade company. She recalled hearing that the company went bankrupt in 2020. He had a small, canvas backpack slung over one arm.

She felt a rush of affection for Dan, surprising herself, because she'd never felt a particular attachment to him. But he was someone from home - from her life before all this.

Dan ran his eyes over her, looking unimpressed. For a second she saw herself through his eyes - the sweat from the morning's training still sitting on her skin, the faded shorts and T-shirt rumpled from being slept in, days' worth of dirt caught in her fingernails, her hair unwashed and unbrushed.

'Living on the lam doesn't suit you,' he said.

'Nice to see you, too.'

'Let's get this over with.'

He looked over her shoulder at Ren, his eyes resting on the rifle.

Ren gave him a nod and jerked his head towards the passenger door. 'Let's go.'

Amber climbed in, moving the sword out of the way. Dan hesitated, then pushed his car door closed and squeezed in after her. His eyes narrowed as he took in the sword, but he didn't say anything. Ren slammed the door shut and climbed into the tray.

Dan's thigh muscle pressed against Amber's and his arm dug into her side. 'Sorry,' he said, trying to shift his weight away from her.

'Don't worry about it.'

Tevita jabbed at the park brake again and eased out of the carpark.

Amber crossed her arms in front of her, holding her body straight, trying to ignore the discomfort of being jammed between Dan and the centre console. She stared at the traffic out the front windscreen. They left the shopping centre behind.

Tevita slammed on the brakes, causing her body to jolt forward. She blinked at the road ahead. Blue and red lights flashed. A line of cars stood motionless in front of them. A red metal sign commanded PREPARE TO STOP. A row of six, bright orange barricades made of thick plastic blocked the road, with space for a single car to slip through. A long metal sign stood in front of the barricades, painted with yellow and black lines and the words ROAD CLOSED. Orange witches' hats were strewn across the road.

'Oh no.' Her voice came out in a whimper.

Dan gave her a sidelong look. 'It's just roadworks.'

'No, it's not. Dan, they're looking for me.'

Dan squinted into the sun. Soldiers in camouflage approached each car, checking inside before waving them through one by one.

'Fuck,' he said.

Eighteen

Amber sunk down in the seat as the line of cars inched forward. Dan muttered swear words under his breath.

Tevita gripped the steering wheel, his eyes on the car ahead. He waited until it had moved forward, leaving a gap between the two cars, then turned the steering wheel all the way to the right. He changed gears and slammed on the accelerator at the same time as letting out the clutch partway. The ute swung out of control. Amber shrieked and gripped the dashboard in front of her.

A red sports car drove up behind them. The driver braked and slammed the horn.

Just before the ute had swung a full one hundred and eighty degrees, Tevita let go of the clutch and straightened the steering wheel. The ute lurched forward. He sped around the sports car and down the road, back the way they'd come. Amber looked back, worried about Ren and Josie in the back, but they were holding on.

Two unmarked, dark blue sedans pulled out from the side of the road and sprinted after them.

Tevita gritted his teeth. He twisted the steering wheel and hurtled into one of the side streets. The tyres squealed. His neck was rigid; his eyes fixed on the road. He flew down suburban streets. With every turn the ute rolled in the opposite direction. Amber pushed her body down into the seat, flattened her feet on the floor and leaned away from Dan.

She craned her neck to see out the rear vision mirror. The sedans were still on their tail.

Tevita's knuckles on the steering wheel were white. He swerved back onto another main road and raced down it, the sedans right behind. He slammed the brakes on and swung the steering wheel. The ute slid across three lanes of traffic. Screeching tyres and car horns filled Amber's ears. The sedans overshot the turn. As the ute careened down another suburban street, Amber caught a glimpse of the sedans braking and swinging over a painted island into traffic, causing cars to brake and swerve around them.

Tevita swung the ute down a side street to the left. He raced down it. The end of the street came into sight - a turning circle. A sign with black and white lines marked the end of the road.

'It's a dead end!' Amber yelled. Dan swore again.

Tevita ignored them. He slowed as they approached the end of the street and turned left onto a wide, concrete footpath with a metal handrail on the left side. Amber glanced behind. There was no sign of the sedans. Tevita bumped down the footpath, the right side wheels digging into the dirt verge. He turned left onto a wide cycle path.

A group of cyclists on the path ahead waved and shouted at them. Amber made out one of them screeching, 'This is a cycle path, you fuckwits!'

Tevita ignored them and kept driving, forcing the cyclists off the path and into the bush on the side. The cyclists screamed obscenities after them.

A brick tunnel reared up in front of them. Two brick pillars rose on either side of the tunnel. Five rings of bricks decorated the outside of the arch. Plants and moss grew around and on it. It felt magical - like you could enter and be transported to another world.

Tevita drove into the entrance. Bricks lined the inside. A row of electric lights on the roof lit the tunnel, colouring the bricks orange. The tunnel curved. Tevita parked near the exit. Looking back, Amber couldn't see the entrance, which was hidden by the curve of the tunnel.

'Stay there,' Tevita said. He left the engine running, swung his door open and jumped out. He grabbed the lever to push the seat forward and dragged out a large, metal box that had been hidden behind the seat. As Tevita pulled it out, Ren clasped one handle. He had a wide smile on his face. Tevita took the other handle, and they disappeared around the back of the ute.

Amber slid over the centre console and out the driver's side door.

'He said to stay,' Dan said.

Amber ignored him. She walked to the back of the ute. Ren, Tevita and Josie were placing round, flat metal boxes around the tunnel. They reminded Amber of old cinema film boxes.

The roar of a car engine echoed around the walls of the tunnel.

'We're going to be too late,' Tevita yelled.

'Just another second,' Josie said.

They didn't have a second. The roar was getting louder. Amber ran past the resistance fighters to where she could see the entrance. A blue sedan appeared in the entrance, blocking the light. Amber stepped into the centre of the tunnel. A piercing shriek of car brakes reverberated off the tunnel walls. She held her hands up.

'I give up,' she yelled above the noise, 'I surrender.'

The car kept coming. Amber's heart raced. They weren't stopping. She leapt sidewards. The car halted inches from her, and the driver and passenger's side doors swung open.

A hand gripped her arm and yanked, almost pulling her off her feet. 'Come on!' Ren's voice screamed in her ear. He pulled her back to the ute, his fingers burning into her skin. Shouts rang out behind them.

Tevita was back in the driver's seat. He started driving the ute forward. Josie, in the tray, helped Ren and Amber tumble into the back. As soon as they were in, Tevita sped forward, slamming them against the back of the tray. They clutched the sides.

Tevita flew out the end of the tunnel. Amber heard a deafening crack, then a roar like a wave crashing on the beach. She ducked her head beneath the back of the tray. A huge dust cloud billowed out from the tunnel. Tevita flew down the path, leaving the tunnel behind.

Ren had a huge grin on his face. He put his head back and yelled. 'Woo-hoo!'

Josie grinned too, her eyes sparkling. 'Lost those bastards.'

Amber couldn't breathe. She closed her eyes and gasped in lungfuls of air. Her heart was beating hard and fast.

There was a break between houses on the right side of the path, where the road next to the path curved in a tight V-shape. Tevita yanked the steering wheel to the right, scraping against an open white gate, and bumped over the grass to join the road. The ute roared down the quiet street.

The metal from the side of the tray bit into Amber's hands. She loosened her grip, shaking her hands out. The left side of her torso ached from being thrown against the side of the tray.

Tevita slowed to the speed limit and took a long, winding route back to the warehouse. He switched the engine off. Amber let out her breath in a deep sigh. Her heartbeat and breathing slowed. Ren and Josie jumped out of the tray and opened it for her to scramble down. Ren gave Tevita a high five.

Amber walked around to the passenger side and opened the door. Dan was staring out the windscreen, a glazed look in his eyes.

'Are you okay?'

He turned the glazed look on her, then slid out of the ute and stood frozen where he landed.

'That was a wild ride.' Josie looked at Dan. 'How about we get you a cup of tea?'

'I don't drink tea,' he said, but he followed as she led the way into the shielded area.

Bec bounced over. 'Heard you guys had some excitement.'

'Just the usual,' Josie said, 'We got to blow up a tunnel, so that should keep Ren happy for a couple of days.'

'That tunnel looked really old.' Dan sounded breathless.

Josie shrugged.

'1880s,' Dave said, turning from the computer trestle table to look at them, 'Fernleigh tunnel. Used to be a railway tunnel.'

Dan's brows drew together in concentration. 'You just blew up a tunnel that was more than a hundred and thirty years old!'

Ren tilted his head on one side. 'Would you prefer we'd been caught by the Boneheads?'

'That's, like, our historic heritage!' He met Ren's eyes and his shoulders drooped. 'No, I guess not.'

They continued to the kitchen ute. Tevita caught up as Sam walked over.

'Mr Scott,' he nodded to Dan, 'I'm Sam. Thank you for helping us.' He looked at Tevita. 'Well done.' He nodded to Ren and Josie to include them in the praise.

'We almost didn't manage it,' Ren said, 'Amber distracted them.'

Sam narrowed his eyes at Amber. 'Well done,' he said again.

Josie looked at Dan. 'Tea or coffee?'

'Do you have any soft drink?' Dan asked.

She shook her head.

'I'm fine,' Dan said, with a sigh, 'Can we just get this over with?' He looked at Amber. 'Where's this laptop you want me to hack?'

'Over here.' Dave waved him to the computer table.

Amber made a coffee and sank down on one of the plastic chairs. Her legs felt shaky. She'd been able to forget that Oliver was gone while the sedans were chasing them, but now his absence came crashing down on her like a dumping wave at the beach. Every bone in her body ached to hold him. Tears formed in the corner of her eyes, and one trickled down her cheek.

She brushed the tear away and jumped up, dumping the half-drunk cup of coffee on the tray of the kitchen ute. Josie was telling Kim and Bec about the explosives they'd used on the tunnel.

'Can we do some more sword fighting?' Amber blurted to Kim, interrupting them.

Kim raised her eyebrows. 'Don't you need time to recover?'

'I'm fine. Once Dan cracks into that laptop, we might not have any more time.'

Kim didn't move. 'You were never this keen before.'

227

'Only because you keep wanting to train at the crack of dawn.'

Kim grinned, and led the way out of the shielded area. As they passed the computer trestle table, Amber stopped. 'You'll tell us if you find anything?' she asked Dan.

Dan didn't look up from the laptop. Dave nodded to her. 'We'll let you know.'

'I left my sword in the ute - I'll just grab it,' Amber said.

Bec followed Amber. She leaned against the side of the ute. 'I didn't know you were so keen on sword fighting, either,' she said in a low voice, 'Anything to keep your mind off Oliver?'

Amber gritted her teeth and concentrated on retrieving the sword.

Bec gave her a sidelong look, but bounced towards Kim without saying anything further.

Amber did her best to focus on the moves Kim was teaching them, but her attention kept drifting. How long did it take to hack a laptop?

Tevita came out with a toolkit. Amber's eyes followed him. He unscrewed the number plates from the ute, replacing them with a new set.

Kim noticed that Amber was distracted. 'Let's try something different. Amber, attack me, using any of the moves I've taught you so far. I'll block.' She gave Bec an apologetic look. 'Sorry, but you'll have to wait for your shoulder to heal.'

Amber hefted the sword and struck. Kim blocked and let the sword slide off. 'Again - harder. I'll block the attack; you don't have to hold back.'

Amber tried, but her strikes were ineffective. Every instinct told her to pull back before the strokes landed. Kim frowned.

Ren called them in for lunch. The bread was even more stale than the day before. Dan drifted over long enough to spread peanut butter onto one slice of bread and honey onto another, not speaking, his mind focused on the puzzle of the laptop. He slapped the two slices together and returned to it, dropping breadcrumbs onto the keyboard while he typed with one hand.

Kim, Amber and Bec returned to sword fighting.

Mid-afternoon, Kim called a halt. Amber let the sword fall to the ground. An image of Oliver filled her mind.

'I can keep going,' she said, trying to force the image away.

Kim raised an eyebrow.

Amber tried to heft the sword again, but her arms felt like jelly. The bruise on her torso was a dull throb. Her back ached. Even the quad muscles in her legs were aching. She let the sword fall again. 'Maybe not.'

Amber searched the clothes box for clean clothes and walked out to the toilet. Locking the door, she stripped off, and splashed water out of the sink over her body: removing days' worth of grime and sweat. She even put her head under the tap, giving her hair a wash. She used the old T-shirt to dry herself, and pulled on clean underwear, T-shirt and shorts, feeling fresh for the first time since she'd left her apartment. She rinsed out the old clothes in the sink and carried them in a wet ball into the shielded area.

Bec, Kim and the resistance fighters were standing in a circle around Dan. Ren looked up as she walked in. 'He's in,' he said.

Amber ran over, dumping her wet clothes on a plastic chair. 'Does it say anything about where Oliver is?'

'No-o,' Dan was frowning at the screen, 'But I found this.'

He tapped at the keyboard. An image filled the screen.

'Look familiar?' Bec asked.

Amber squinted at the grainy image. It showed two women standing outside a large shed - one with blonde hair, in a military uniform, and one with short red curls, in jeans and a T-shirt. Amber's eyes widened. 'That's Alice and Lucy's mum!'

Dave tapped the caption at the bottom of the image. 'And you said that your son was taken by someone called Jacinta Mueller, didn't you?'

'If Private Jerome was telling the truth.' Amber read the caption. Major Mueller and Doctor Taylor, at Secure Facility D1.

She stared at the photo. The shed was made from a cream coloured steel. A portico with a green roof stuck out the front. Above the awning, the letters DT were painted in a fancy font. Underneath, the words Downunder Technology were printed in smaller letters.

Amber ran her fingers through her hair. 'That company name - Downunder Technology.' Her voice seemed to come from far away. 'Adam was doing a project for a company with that name.'

Sam wrinkled his brow. 'Adam?'

She looked up from the screen. They all had their eyes on her. 'My husband. He was doing a project for Downunder Technology in Dubbo, when it was bombed.' Her throat constricted at the thought of Adam. She swallowed. 'I haven't heard from him since.'

Dave sat up straight. 'Dubbo?' He looked at Glenn. 'That can't be a coincidence.'

'Downunder Technology,' Glenn said, staring at the screen, 'It's a pretty generic name. What does the company do?'

'I don't know. Adam worked - works -' Amber corrected herself, swallowing again, 'On payment systems, for small and medium-sized companies. He didn't tell me what Downunder Technology did.' In fact, she remembered, it wasn't him who had told her what company he was working for - that was Steve. 'His manager must know. I could contact him?'

'No,' Sam said, 'Dave and Glenn can track down the company.'

Amber thought of Steve's treacle voice. Good idea. If anyone would sell her out, it was him.

Sam tapped his fingers on the desk, thinking. He looked at Ren and Josie. 'I want you and Tev to leave tomorrow morning.'

Josie's head jerked up. 'We're going to Dubbo?'

'Unless Mr Scott can find anything else on that laptop, we need more information. Doctor Taylor seems to be our best link to these THONGs. Possibly to Major Mueller, too.'

Who had Oliver. Maybe. Amber's shoulders drooped. There were too many maybes.

Ren's eyes rested on Kim. 'We might need someone who can use a sword.'

Sam raised his eyebrows at her. 'Feel like earning your pay?'

'We get paid?' Kim asked.

'All the instant coffee you can drink,' said Glenn.

'Well, in that case, count me in.'

Sam and Ren left the shielded area to chat with Tevita, who was refilling the ute with jerry cans of fuel. Josie pulled two cardboard boxes from the metal shelving unit and extracted ration packs and ammunition. She packed them into two giant hiking packs.

Amber's stomach growled. She hung her wet clothes over the plastic chair and went to the kitchen ute. Kim was munching biscuits. She held the packet out to Amber, who helped herself to several.

Bec rummaged through the large first aid kit, clutching her shoulder. She splashed water into a coffee cup and swallowed two painkillers.

'Bad?' asked Kim.

Bec shrugged, then winced. 'It's okay. Shouldn't have done so much pretend sword fighting.'

Amber took several more biscuits and watched Josie. A thought flickered. She skittered away from it. Don't be stupid.

The thought continued to swirl around her mind.

Ren and Sam returned, and started up a discussion with Josie.

How high a priority would finding Oliver be to them? Their

priority would be the THONGs. Amber glanced at Bec, and the lump of anger hardened. She gritted her teeth.

'I got an address,' Glenn called across the warehouse.

They congregated around his laptop again.

'It's an old one for Downunder Technology - according to the records, the property is now rented by a company called P.K. Rundle, but I did some digging and it looks like it's a subsidiary of Downunder Technology. It's on the outskirts of Dubbo, north of the city, so it would have been outside the area that was bombed. And check this out.' Glenn brought up the address on a map and switched to street view. 'Look familiar?'

'It's the shed in the picture Dan found,' Ren said, 'The one of Major Mueller and Doctor Taylor.'

'Yup.'

'Good job,' Sam said.

Amber stared at the address. Yarrandale Road. She repeated it over and over in her head until she was sure she wouldn't forget it. Just in case, she told herself, but the idea that had been swirling in her mind began to solidify.

The resistance fighters began a discussion about where Ren, Josie and Kim should go and what they should do.

'There's the Dubbo resistance group,' Dave said, 'They could help.'

Sam screwed up his nose. 'Like a lot of those community resistance groups, their security is pretty lax. The MG thinks some of the members are feeding information to the military.' He spoke to Ren and Josie. 'You might want to link in with them, but I'd be wary.'

Glenn pulled up some maps of Dubbo on his computer. The discussion went round in circles.

'We don't know enough. You might just need to suck it and see,' Glenn said at one point. The others nodded in grim agreement, but then resumed their discussion.

Amber yawned and slipped away. She walked over to the metal shelving unit, glancing over her shoulder. The resistance fighters were immersed in their discussion. On the bottom of the unit were a couple of old, battered backpacks. She slid one out, hiding it behind the clothes boxes, which were still open on the floor. Working fast, she grabbed two handfuls of ration packs and dropped them into the pack. She threw in a pair of shorts, a T-shirt, long pants and a long-sleeved shirt. She glanced at the resistance soldiers again, rubbing her hair and the back of her neck. Thou shalt not steal.

She hid the backpack under her sleeping bag and returned to the kitchen ute. Tevita was dicing vegetables.

'Can I help?'

He thrust a knife and several potatoes in her direction, nodding at the other resistance fighters. They were arguing the same point they'd been arguing when Amber left. 'I thought I'd get dinner started. They'll do this for hours, and we'll end up eating toast or some shit for dinner.'

Dinner that night was quiet. The resistance fighters' discussion had tailed off at last, and they gulped the stew that Tevita and Amber had made in silence.

Bec was still rubbing her shoulder. Dan was yawning. 'I'm not used to working while the sun's up.'

Amber's limbs felt heavy. The morning's excitement and the sword fighting training had crushed the nervous energy she'd been feeling ever since the soldiers had taken Oliver. She blinked heavy eyelids.

Josie and Kim did the dishes, before following the others to bed. Amber made herself a coffee, and forced herself to sit up, until the only sounds were the quiet breathing and snores of the others. She slipped back to her sleeping bag. Retrieving the battered backpack, she folded her bedding and pushed it into the pack.

She slid the pack onto her back, clenching her teeth in anticipation of pain, but there was only a slight stiffness. She let out her breath in a sigh.

She looked at Bec, who was still fast asleep, and bit her lip. Sneaking off at night seemed a poor way to end things. But - this whole time, all Bec had wanted was to meet up with the resistance. She wasn't going to leave, and she wasn't above making that decision for Amber. Amber straightened her shoulders, righteous anger filling her chest. She was done with trusting Bec.

She snuck out of the shielded area and strode towards the small door at the back of the warehouse.

As she passed the ute, a figure stepped out in front of her. She bit back a yelp as she recognised Sam.

'You're off, then.' In the dim light, she couldn't make out his expression.

'I'm going to get my son. And Alice and Lucy.'

'On your own?'

Amber just looked at him.

He sighed. 'I'll give you some credit - you have done okay surviving so far. But, as I believe Ren has already pointed out, they've underestimated you.'

Amber shrugged.

'My money is on you getting yourself killed within the week.'

Amber clenched her hands together. 'I'm going anyway.'

He stepped out of the way and waved a hand to indicate she could walk past. She clenched her jaw, gripped the backpack's shoulder straps and stepped past him.

'Or -' he said, 'We could make a deal.'

She hesitated, tempted to keep walking.

'What kind of deal?'

'Ren and Josie are going to Dubbo anyway. You can go with

234

them - I'll even get them to help you extract the children.'

Amber's eyes narrowed. 'And in return?'

'Stop fucking around and running away. Join the resistance. Fight with us.'

Nineteen

Heat filled Amber's cheeks. 'I thought you didn't trust me. Weren't you worried that I'm 'not human'? Or was it 'possessed'?'

Sam's voice was cool. 'If you heard that, then no doubt you heard Ren's response - that we can't afford to throw any potential advantage away. Every day the PM and Boneheads are tightening their grip on the country. The resistance has been on the back foot the whole time - we can't kill the Boneheads, but they can kill us. The MG is recruiting people with sword fighting skills as we speak, but I saw the Boneheads fight with swords before I left the army. They're strong, and faster than any human I've ever seen. Apart from you.'

Amber squeezed the backpack's straps. She didn't want to join the resistance. Didn't want to fight. Thou shalt not kill. But - she didn't even know how she was going to get to Dubbo, let alone what she was going to do there. With Ren and Josie with her, there was a much better chance that she'd be able to rescue Oliver.

Getting Oliver was the only thing that mattered. She'd figure the rest out later. She pressed her lips together. 'Alright. I'm in. But not until Ollie - and Alice and Lucy - are safe.'

'Tomorrow, then.' Sam's voice was emotionless, and she still couldn't see his face. If he was happy that she'd agreed, there was no sign. 'I'm going to bed.'

Amber slept the entire night without stirring. Bec shook her awake.

'We're going to Dubbo.'

Amber blinked at her. 'You're coming too?'

'Think I'm going to let you go off without me again? I missed all the fun yesterday!'

'That's your idea of fun?' Dan's voice came from a bundle of blankets behind them. He sat up, his hair a tangle around his head.

Bec ignored him. 'Sam told Ren and Josie that they had to take you, so I said they had to take me too. He didn't argue, but Josie wasn't impressed. How'd you convince Sam?'

'I didn't,' Amber yawned, 'I don't think anyone could convince Sam to do anything he doesn't want to.'

'Mmm, good point.' She looked at the battered backpack lying on the floor behind Amber's head. 'You already started packing?'

Amber's cheeks reddened. 'Just threw a few things in yesterday. Ration packs, mainly. And a change of clothes.'

'I'll need to pack, too. You'd better have breakfast. I don't think they're going to hang around for long.'

Bec was right. Amber had time to drink a coffee and gulp down a bowl of cereal before Ren came to find her. 'You ready?'

'Just a sec.'

She hurried back to her sleeping bag, scrunched it into a ball and pushed it into the top of the pack. Dan watched her from his nest of blankets.

'What are you going to do now?' Amber asked, wrapping the makeshift sword belt around her waist.

He gave an exaggerated shrug. 'I need to finish the job - there's a couple of folders on that laptop that we haven't managed to break into yet. After that? Go home, I guess.'

Amber shoved her sword into the belt. She looked up and bit her lip. 'Thanks for coming. And for trying to help me the other day in Epping, fending off that wombat thing.'

He waved her thanks away. 'For what it's worth -' he paused. She raised her eyebrows. 'The mainstream media is keeping mum on what you guys are doing, but it's all over the dark web. You've been giving a lot of people hope. That's why I came. Not because of Bec talking about my bloody T-shirts. And - I hope you get Ollie back.'

Amber nodded. 'Thanks.'

'Just don't bloody lose him again.'

Tevita drove into the warehouse in a third, battered white ute.

'Does the resistance have an endless supply of beaten-up utes?' Bec asked.

'No,' Ren said, 'Tev's got a friend who's a used car dealer.'

'And since we're taking a whole crowd with us,' Josie paused to roll her eyes, 'We need another vehicle. I'm not riding to Dubbo in the tray.'

Sam joined them. 'Good luck. See you when you get back.' His eyes rested on Amber.

Ren directed Amber and Josie to climb into the new ute with Tevita, while he drove with Bec and Kim in the second ute. Tevita had a thick, ring-bound state road atlas open on his lap. Amber hadn't seen a road atlas like that in years.

There was a new list of roads stuck to the dashboard. This one ran over two scraps of paper instead of one.

'Glenn assures me this list is more comprehensive than the last one,' Tevita said.

'I hope so,' Josie said, 'I don't know of any other tunnels we can use to escape.'

'I'm sure I can find you something else to blow up.'

'Good. You know how twitchy Ren gets when he hasn't blown something up for a few hours.' They grinned at each other.

The morning sun flashed into their eyes as they drove out of the warehouse. The sunlight reflected off any shiny surface - other cars, metal roofs, windows. The air conditioner blasted cold air at her face, but barely took the edge off the heat in the cab. Sweat congealed on Amber's body. Heat radiated from Josie's body where their arms and legs touched. At least it was more comfortable sharing with Josie than Dan.

There were few other vehicles on the roads, and no police or roadblocks. Glenn's list must have been as comprehensive as promised. Amber glanced behind. Ren drove close to Tevita's tail.

They left the suburbs via a complicated maze of roads through patches of bush and farmland. Tevita kept one hand on the steering wheel and thumbed through the road atlas with the other; one finger following their route on the page. Amber was impressed by his map-reading skills.

The heat made Amber drowsy. She drifted in and out of sleep as the morning disappeared. Tevita continued to map out a route via country roads, eschewing use of highways and major roads.

They made a couple of stops for people to go to the toilet behind a tree. As they left the coast far behind them, the heat became drier, but no less uncomfortable. Any sweat their bodies produced to cool their skin dried at once, powerless in the face of the unrelenting heat. At about one pm Tevita and Ren pulled up in the gravel on the side of a paddock full of sheep and brown grass. Ren passed out sandwiches and Tevita produced a giant thermos of hot water for tea and coffee. The air was still. Swarms of flies buzzed around their heads. Amber could almost feel the sun burning her skin in the few minutes they stood there.

The convoluted route was longer and slower than the same trip would have been on the highway. It was late afternoon when they arrived. Dubbo arrived all at once, as though a magician had made it appear in an instant on the empty plains. One minute they were driving through flat paddocks of brown grass, tall gum trees and shorter pines, separated from the road by wooden posts, metal wires and sometimes a line of electricity poles. The next, they were driving through a typical modern suburb - manicured gardens and single-story brick houses, which wore different colours and features, yet somehow all looked the same.

Tevita kept driving north, skirting around the edge of the new suburbs and avoiding the town centre. The suburbs were replaced by large sheds that clustered along the roads, surrounded by a sea of flat paddocks. It was the end of the workday, and a stream of cars and four-wheel drives pulled out of carparks surrounding the sheds. Tevita slowed. Ren had fallen behind, and a few cars now separated the two utes.

'That's it,' said Tevita, nodding his head to the left, 'Downunder Technology.'

'Wow,' Josie said, 'Downunder Technology has expanded.'

The site had changed since someone had taken the street view photos that Glenn had shown them. It didn't just comprise the cream shed, but took in a long white warehouse to the left of the shed and several large buildings to the right. The other sheds they'd seen on the road had, at most, chain wire fencing for security. Downunder Technology's security was in another league. A tubular steel fence enclosed the site. At least two stories high, the fence had closely spaced bars, the tops of which were shaped like spears and protruded inwards at a 45-degree angle. Barbed wire coils ran between each of the spears. Multiple rectangular security cameras were positioned along the fence, surveilling the inside and outside of the site.

Tevita drove past without slowing. He took the next left turn and pulled up near a yard full of harvesting equipment. Ren pulled in behind him.

It was a relief to escape the stuffy cab. The air outside had cooled as night approached. Amber stretched her arms and back.

Tevita looked at Ren. 'What now?'

Ren checked his watch. 'We've got a couple of hours until curfew.' He looked at Josie. 'Guess we should take a look.'

Josie bared her teeth. 'Finally.'

Ren made eye contact with Kim, Amber and Bec in turn. 'Wait here. We won't be long.' He turned to Tevita. 'Be ready in case we need a quick getaway.'

Tevita waved a hand in a mock salute. Ren and Josie pulled packs from the back of the utes and shrugged them onto their backs. Shouldering their rifles, they disappeared down the road.

Amber waited until Ren and Josie were out of sight. She tugged her backpack out of the tray of the ute.

'What are you doing?' asked Kim.

'What does it look like?' Amber slid the pack onto her back.

'Ren said to wait,' Tevita said.

Amber flicked him a sidelong look. 'And I love his confidence that I'm going to take orders from him. I haven't joined your resistance.' Yet, anyway, she thought, remembering her promise to Sam.

Tevita folded his arms and leant back against the ute. 'Then I hope you won't be expecting 'my resistance' to save you when you - inevitably - get yourself in trouble.'

'I won't. I never asked you to save me in the first place.' She looked at Bec. 'Are you coming?'

Bec gave Tevita and Kim an apologetic look. 'I can't let her go alone.' She pulled her own backpack out of the tray.

Tevita shook his head and rolled his eyes. 'Your funeral.'

Amber strode down the road. The sun was low in the sky. Electricity poles lined the right side of the road, casting long shadows across it. The grass was worn in places, revealing a deep, burgundy soil. They walked across a railway crossing.

Utes and cars drove past, the occupants staring at Amber and Bec. Amber guessed that it was rare to see people walking along the road verge this far out of town.

The fence that surrounded the Downunder Technology compound came into view. On foot, it looked even more imposing than when they'd driven past.

Amber focused on the buildings past the fence, willing herself inside. It had been four days since they'd taken Oliver and the girls. What if they weren't in there?

'Let's get closer,' Bec said, 'Watch out for the cameras. Stay out of their line of sight.'

That was easier said than done. On three sides, the compound was surrounded by flat paddocks of yellow grass with a few tall eucalypts - their foliage above head height. Only the western side offered any cover from the cameras that surrounded the compound. A large, white shed sprawled on the block of land next to the compound. A square, red brick building was attached to the entrance, two stories high, with a crenellated top. Bec stared at it.

'Why the hell did someone think it was a good idea to plonk a tiny castle in front of the shed?'

'Are you seriously worried about architecture at a time like this?' Amber blinked back tears. Oliver had to be in there. She didn't know what she would do if he wasn't - she didn't think she could survive it. Please, she prayed.

The white shed had a chain wire fence, with two strands of barbed wire on top, but the gate was open.

'Let's go over there.' Without waiting to see if Amber agreed, Bec dashed across the road, through the gate and behind the red brick building. Cursing, Amber followed, sliding to a halt in the dirt behind the building.

'I told you to wait.' Amber jumped at Ren's voice from behind them. He and Josie joined them at the side of the building.

'We did wait,' Bec said, 'For at least a minute.'

Ren gritted his teeth. 'When we return to the vehicles, we'll be having a discussion.'

Bec ignored him, her eyes on the compound. 'Any idea how we can get in there?'

'Nothing we can't blow our way through,' he said.

Josie rolled her eyes and gave an exaggerated sigh. 'It's getting out that's the trick.'

Ren grinned at her. 'Nothing we can't blow our way through.' He squinted at the compound, the grin falling from his face. 'The problem is the number of objectives.'

Josie ticked off items on her fingers as she spoke. 'Oliver, Alice, Lucy, and a THONG. No way we're getting in and out quick.'

Ren's mouth twisted. 'We're going to need some help.'

'The Dubbo resistance group?'

Bec frowned. 'Sam said they might be feeding info to the military.'

Ren shrugged. 'The amateur groups are all like that.'

'Not mine,' Bec said.

Ren tilted his head. 'Really? You and Amber did a pretty good job of disappearing into the bush, but every time you tried to contact the resistance, the Boneheads were onto you like a flash.'

Bec gave Amber a wary glance. Amber clenched her hands into fists and kept her eyes on the building. Bec frowned at Ren. 'Someone from my group sold us out?'

He shrugged again. 'That would be my guess.'

It took all of Amber's self-control not to say out loud what she was thinking: I told you so.

Tevita and Kim looked unsurprised when the four of them returned together.

'I see you found them,' Tevita said.

'Civilians,' Josie snorted.

'Where to now?' he asked.

'Town centre,' Ren said, 'We need to contact the Dubbo resistance. Dave gave me the name of a pub where we can get in touch with them.'

'Why do all these groups meet in pubs?' Josie asked, 'It's such a cliche.'

'Good excuse for a drink,' Tevita said.

'Suits me,' Bec said, 'I'm dying for one.'

Ren shook his head at Bec. 'Not you. Your image has been on almost every news bulletin for the past ten days. We'll send Tev in.'

Tevita flashed his teeth. 'Awesome. A couple of schooners of icy cold beer -'

'You're the designated driver, remember?' Josie gave him a sweet smile. 'How about a schooner of icy cold lemonade?'

Tevita and Josie swung themselves back into the ute, bickering. Amber turned to follow, but Ren stopped her and Bec. Kim stopped too.

'The enemy knows we helped you in Newcastle. If you get yourselves caught, they'll come looking for us. I can't risk the resistance's chance of getting our hands on a THONG.' He made eye contact with them both. 'I need to know you'll do what I ask.'

Bec rubbed the back of her neck. 'Sure, sorry.'

Amber glared at her. She'd gone behind Amber's back countless times to call the resistance, and now she was rolling over like a good dog and promising to follow his orders.

Ren looked at Amber. Amber frowned and crossed her arms. He drew his brows in. 'I'm more than happy to use those cuffs we took from Kim to lock you inside the ute until we're ready to leave Dubbo.'

Amber glared at him. 'You can try. We both know I'm faster than you.'

He raised his eyebrows. 'Sure about that? Because I don't think you can turn that speed thing on and off at will.'

Amber ground her teeth. Bec tugged on her arm and spoke into her ear. 'Why are you trying to piss him off?' she muttered, 'I can't break into that big fuck off fence with bolt cutters. We need these guys.'

Amber wasn't sure why she was arguing with Ren. Every part of her was tense. Oliver might be in that compound, just around the corner - she wanted to go there now. She clenched her fists, and then released them, releasing the tension. 'Fine. I'll do what you say.'

Ren narrowed his eyes, holding her gaze. 'Good. Let's go.'

Ren and Bec turned to return to the vehicles. Kim put her hand on Amber's arm. 'You can't control that speed thing?' she asked, her brow furrowed.

Amber glared at her. 'No. I told you all - it just happens.'

Kim returned her glare. 'Then you need to sit down and figure out what the difference is between the occasions it 'just happens' and when it doesn't happen. What are you doing? What's happening around you? Then use those things to increase the chances of it 'just happening'.'

Without waiting to hear Amber's response, she hurried after Ren and Bec.

Amber scowled at her back and stomped back to the ute, where Tevita and Josie were waiting. She glowered out the window as Tevita drove back past the flat paddocks. When was she able to reach out to the power, to lean on it? When she felt desperate. Really desperate. But what was the difference between those times and the times when she felt desperate and the power wouldn't let her lean on it? Like when the Boneheads captured them at Newcastle? Nothing. Absolutely nothing. Amber scowled again. What would Kim know about it, anyway?

The centre of town looked much the same as it had looked on the news bulletin that Dave had been watching in the warehouse. Work had ended for the day, and cranes and trucks stood in silence near piles of rubble. It reminded Amber of the devastation after a bushfire passed through a town, with some buildings standing intact next to others that had been destroyed. The street that the pub was on had been less affected by the bombing than some of the other streets, but even here there were several blocks of rubble. Tevita and Ren pulled into a large carpark behind the pub. Tevita climbed out. He tried to brush the dust from his shorts, but his efforts just left light brown streaks that wouldn't budge.

Josie watched him. 'We're not in the city now. I doubt they'll care what you look like here.'

Tevita grimaced at her. 'Wish me luck.' Squaring his shoulders, he strode across the carpark and through the wide, automatic glass doors.

Amber slid over to the driver's side and cracked open the door, letting the cool night air circulate into the stuffy cab. How long would it take? She craned her head towards the glass doors.

Josie leaned back in her seat and closed her eyes. Amber gave her a sideways look. How could she be so calm?

It was close to half an hour before Tevita returned. He leaned in the window of the other ute to speak to Ren, then opened Josie's door.

'There's a back way you can enter through. They're waiting for you.'

'Cameras?' Josie asked.

Tevita shrugged. 'Christine assures me there aren't any. Whether you trust her or not is another matter.'

Ren came up behind him. 'The Boneheads are going to know we're here soon enough anyway.' He jerked his head towards the pub. 'Let's go.'

Josie sighed. 'Do we always have to rush in recklessly?' she muttered under her breath.

Tevita led the way through a back door into a short corridor. Amber peered through another open door into a large bistro area. Its decor favoured white tiles and wood veneer; clean, tidy and forgettable. Children ran between the tables, forging alliances among themselves and getting in the way of the adults balancing drinks and plates. Tired-looking parents downed glasses of sav blanc and schooners of beer and ignored them. It seemed an unlikely place to plot resistance activities.

'I was expecting something more grimy,' Bec said, 'Filled with unsavoury types.'

'The unsavoury types are upstairs,' Tevita said.

'It's busy,' Josie said.

'Friday night.'

'Is it?' Bec shook her head. 'I've lost track of the days.'

Ren pulled the door closed, hiding the bistro from sight. They padded past beeping sounds from a gaming area somewhere behind the wall, and up a short flight of uncarpeted stairs. A light chain crossed the stairs halfway up, with a wooden sign swinging from it. Staff only. Tevita unclipped it and clipped it back into place once they'd all passed.

At the top of the stairs was a large room that must have served as a second bar or restaurant in the past. Unlike the downstairs bistro, this area hadn't been renovated in recent years. The floor was covered in a worn red carpet with years of dirt and grime trodden into it. The walls were painted a sickly yellowy-green colour. A small bar took up the back wall, but it was being used as a storage area for all the detritus of the pub - broken chairs, old signs, two pallets of dusty glasses. The room was furnished with a mix of old, sagging couches and plastic restaurant chairs and tables.

An Aboriginal woman and a thin white man with a mop of

curly black hair sat on a low couch, looking at a sleek black laptop computer. They looked up as the group entered, and the woman stood. The man closed the lid on the laptop.

'Grimy enough for you?' Tevita muttered in a low voice to Bec.

Bec nodded. 'Much more appropriate.' She stared at the walls and shook her head. 'Whoever thought that was a good colour choice?'

The woman approached in time to hear this comment. She looked a few years older than Amber and Bec and wore her hair in a messy bun at the top of her head. 'I wondered if they had a problem with drunks vomiting on the walls, and solved the problem by painting the walls vomit colour.' She narrowed her eyes and looked at Tevita. 'You didn't mention that your 'friends' were the most wanted people in Australia.'

'This is Christine,' Tevita said. He pointed to each of them in turn. 'Kim, Ren, Josie -'

'Amber and Bec,' Christine finished for him, 'I know them. They've been all over the television. What brings you to Dubbo?'

'What does the word thong mean to you?' Ren asked.

Christine looked blank. 'Um - something you wear on your feet?'

'You haven't heard it used in any other context? To do with the Boneheads?'

Christine looked at the thin man. 'Ben?' He shook his head. 'Sorry, no idea what you're talking about.'

Ren changed the subject. 'What do you know about Downunder Technology?'

Christine shrugged. 'Small tech startup nobody had heard of until the last week or so. Based out in a shed on Yarrandale Road - probably because they couldn't afford the rents in Sydney. Since the bombing, the army has forcibly acquired several of the other sheds and warehouses nearby and whacked

247

a massive fence around them. No idea what they're producing, but whatever it is, the army wants it. Any trucks out of there travel in convoy with army troop carriers, a helicopter, the works.'

'DT used to have a small number of staff, and they've disappeared,' Ben said, 'I've got a coffee shop down the road that was lucky enough to escape the bombing. There were two DT guys I used to see every morning and lunchtime, like clockwork. Haven't seen them at all recently, and they were mad caffeine addicts, can't imagine them giving up their coffee.'

'Maybe they were killed in the bombing?' Josie said.

He shook his head. 'They disappeared before that. A couple of weeks before, I'd say.'

'We don't know if the missing staff are dead, being held on the site, or been taken elsewhere,' Christine said, 'But somebody must be making whatever goes out in those trucks.'

Josie looked at Ren. 'If they're keeping the staff inside, against their will, it would explain why the spears on the fence point inwards.' She turned to Christine. 'You haven't been tempted to check it out?'

Christine's mouth twisted. 'We're quite a new group, and our members aren't really willing to stick their necks out yet. They don't trust each other enough, especially after the bombing. To be honest, we're a resistance group in name only at the moment.'

Ren gave a grim smile. 'Maybe it's time to join the fight.'

Twenty

Christine gave a slow nod. She turned to Ben. 'Let's get our people in. Not all of them - just the useful ones.'

It took a while for the people Christine and Ben contacted to assemble. As each of them entered the room, in singles or pairs, their eyes landed on Amber and Bec and widened. Amber again wished her hair was long enough to cover her face.

Christine spoke to each of them as they arrived. Amber found herself grinding her teeth in frustration as time passed. She tried to distract herself by watching each person respond to Christine. A middle-aged couple, wearing matching wide-brimmed hats even though the sun had set, gave grim nods. A woman who looked like an older version of Christine gave her a quick hug and then pulled back, biting her lip and looking nervous. A young man, with arm muscles so large she was sure he must be taking a supplement, drew back and shook his head, until Ben placed a reassuring hand on his shoulder. Another young man and woman with round faces and wide blue eyes, clearly siblings, gave identical wicked smiles and chorused, 'About time'. A very thin middle-aged man with thinning hair gave a nervous smile and chewed on a fingernail.

The nervous man was the last. When they'd perched themselves on plastic chairs or couches, she turned to Ren. 'We're all yours.'

Ren stepped forward. 'Those of you who are our getaway drivers will stay with the vehicles. The rest of us will split into two groups - one with Josie and one with me. Both groups will blow up the fence at separate locations at three am tomorrow morning.'

'What?' The young man with the large muscles rounded on Christine, almost falling off the arm of the couch he was sitting on. 'You didn't say anything about tonight.'

The man with the hat nodded. 'Surely we should do reconnaissance for a couple of days before we go rushing in and blowing things up?'

Amber's heart beat faster. She couldn't abandon Oliver for a few more days. It had already been four days since they'd taken him.

Ren shook his head. 'We go in tonight,' he said, his voice firm,

'The sooner we move, the less likely the enemy will realise we're planning something.'

'And the less likely any traitors will be able to warn the army,' Bec muttered into her ear. 'Clever.'

Amber let out a shaky breath. She stood up, ready to go, but the Dubbo resistance members hadn't finished. They began an interrogation of every point of Ren's plan, which Amber thought was clear and simple. Ren was the epitome of patience as he answered their questions, but frustration rolled off Josie.

'Your entire plan boils down to 'blow shit up',' the man in the hat complained, 'You don't have a plan for how we get these kids we're rescuing out, let alone our own people if something goes wrong.'

'It's better to keep the plan simple and flexible, and adapt when we know what we're facing,' Josie said, 'We can't plan for every contingency.'

'We could if we did some actual reconnaissance,' he grumbled.

Amber sank down on one of the sagging couches. Bec and Kim joined her and went to sleep. Amber closed her eyes and tried to block out the incessant arguing. A few hours, and she'd be able to rescue Oliver. She tried to ignore the voice in her head reminding her that she didn't know for sure that Oliver was in the compound, or even in Dubbo at all.

She cracked her eyelids. Even Ren's patience seemed to be fraying. He cut the man in the hat off mid-sentence. 'Let's talk weapons.'

'We've got guns,' Christine said, 'Sourced from local farmers.'

'We can do better than that,' Ren said. He lifted his rifle. 'We've brought enough of these to give you each one.'

There was a palpable change of atmosphere in the room. The man in the hat sat upright, and even the young man with the muscles brightened. 'That's what I'm talking about.'

'Anyone know how to use a sword?' There was a general

shaking of heads. 'Pity. At any rate, we suggest carrying bladed weapons. The devices the Boneheads have that stop bullets - that they call THONGs - don't seem to protect against them.'

Ren didn't mention her, but Amber felt everyone's eyes on her. She ducked her head.

'So it's true?' the woman in the hat said, 'You really did kill Boneheads? Mike Davies said it was faked. He said the Boneheads can't be killed.'

'Mike Davies is a bloody liar,' Christine's relative said, 'I'd like to stick a bladed weapon into him.'

'It's true,' Ren said, 'They can be killed.'

'We've got plenty of knives,' Christine said.

The talk of weapons seemed to resolve the last of the Dubbo resistance members' reservations about Ren's plan. They stood, pushing back chairs and gathering belongings. Ben produced a crate from the back of the bar full of knives - mostly hunting knives. Some of the Dubbo resistance members were carrying knives already, and the others helped themselves from the crate. Bec and Kim opened sleepy eyes.

'We're doing this at last?' Bec asked.

'Looks like,' Amber said, 'Ren offered them all rifles, and they leapt at the chance.'

'Hope he's going to give me a rifle, too.'

'I wouldn't know what to do with one,' Amber said.

'Too easy. Just point and click.'

Josie joined them in time to hear this. She snorted. 'Don't listen to a word she says. You need practice before you use one in anger.' She looked at Bec. 'And you're still injured, remember? You'll do more damage to that shoulder of yours.'

Bec scowled. 'Better a damaged shoulder than dead.'

Josie pulled a face and changed the subject. 'Do you three have anything else to wear? You're not exactly dressed for combat.'

'In the ute.'

'Come out with us. Tev and I need to get some guns for this lot.'
The temperature had dropped while they'd been inside the pub. Stars shone in a cloudless sky. Amber shivered in her shorts and T-shirt, and goosebumps rose on her arms and legs. She, Bec and Kim retrieved their packs and helped Josie and Tevita with two crates of weapons.

Amber changed into long pants, long-sleeved shirt and a heavy leather jacket in a staff toilet. She stared at herself in the mirror. A white face with huge, tired eyes stared back at her. Her black hair fell lank and oily around her face. The enormity of what they were about to do hit her. She leaned over the basin, her stomach churning, and gulped breaths of air. Her face was burning. She pressed it against the cool basin.

When she returned to the vomit-coloured room, she was shocked at the change in atmosphere. It was like a warped Christmas morning, where everyone had received deadly weapons as their gifts. Bec waved at her and held up a rifle. Amber slipped past the muscly man, who was running his hands over his rifle as though it was a lover, and joined her.

Amber looked at Bec's gun. 'You convinced Ren to give you one?'

'He didn't need much convincing. You want one?'

Amber shook her head. 'I'm sure Josie is right about needing practice. I might miss the enemy and shoot one of us.' She looked around the room. 'Anyway, people with guns don't seem to be in short supply.' Her eyes rested on the muscly man, who was still stroking the rifle.

'He needs to get a room,' Bec said. She turned back to Amber. 'What took you so long? You missed them sorting out who was going in what vehicle.'

'Really? It didn't take them two hours to work that out?'

'Ren didn't give them a chance - he just bossed everyone up. He asked me to go in a car with hat man and hat woman. And she's going to drive - Ashleigh.' Bec pointed at one of the round-faced siblings.

'Hat man and woman have taken off their hats. You'll have to call them something else.'

Bec waved a hand. 'They'll always be hat man and woman to me.'

'What about me?'

'You're with Ren.' She gave Amber a sidelong glance. 'I don't think he trusts you.'

Amber's mouth twisted. 'I don't trust him.'

Bec pointed at the nervous man with the thinning hair, who was standing on the other side of the room, biting a nail again. He hadn't taken a rifle. 'He's your driver. I think his name is Mark.'

Amber looked down her nose at him. 'He looks like he'd run screaming if a Bonehead looked at him.'

'Apparently he races cars.'

'Really? Doesn't look like a race car driver.'

'Tev's driving Josie and Kim, and the others are all in the fourth car.'

Ren sent the Dubbo resistance members out in twos and threes, hiding their rifles under coats or jumpers.

He turned to Josie. 'Your turn.'

'About time,' she said, echoing the round-faced siblings.

Ren's eyes danced. 'Wreak havoc.'

'You too,' she grinned.

Amber, Ren and Mark were the last to leave. Ren sat in the middle of the ute. The humour had left his face after Josie left, and he looked grim and resolute. Mark was nervous. He fumbled with the gear stick, struggling to get the ute into gear, and then reversed too fast and almost hit a small pink car. Ren scowled, which increased Mark's nerves.

The streets were quiet, and very dark. Amber stared out the side

253

window, trying to work out why it was so dark, and realised that none of the streetlights were on. They must have been damaged in the bombing. There was a sick feeling in her stomach. Her mouth was dry. She clenched and unclenched her hand on the hilt of her sword.

Mark regained his confidence as they left the town centre behind them. He pulled over around the corner from the Downunder Technology compound, near where Tevita had parked earlier, to let them out. Ren tugged a metal box out from behind his seat, identical to the one that had held the explosives they'd used to blow up the tunnel in Newcastle. He nodded at Mark. Mark climbed back into the cab and drove away.

Dark figures melted out of the shadows. Amber clutched at her sword in fright, and then recognised Bec and hat man and woman. Ren and hat man each took one of the handles of the box and led the way down the road. Amber found herself next to hat woman.

'We didn't really meet earlier,' she whispered, 'I'm Jen.' She pointed at hat man. 'He's my husband - Ant. Anthony.'

'Amber.'

'Yes - I know.'

She fell silent. Their feet crunched on the gravel. Cicadas whistled, falling silent as they approached, and starting up again as they passed. A bird called - a long, mournful cry.

Ren took a roundabout route back to the white shed with the crenellated building that had offended Bec's sense of style. He and Ant lowered the box to the ground. Ant shook out his arm and rubbed his forearm, while Ren opened the box and removed some round, flat metal boxes. He slipped over to the fence, avoiding the cameras, and placed the boxes near the fence. He didn't ask for help, and seemed so grim and unapproachable that no-one offered. When he was finished, he rejoined them, checking his watch.

'Ten minutes.'

Amber pictured Josie doing the same thing with the explosives on the other side of the fence. The plan was that both groups would blow the fence and enter at the same time. Amber shivered and wrapped her arms around her.

Ten minutes. Ten minutes and then - maybe - she'd get Oliver back.

She stared up at the vast expanse of stars, flung across the sky. Out here, far from the ocean and the city lights, they seemed unending. She tried praying, but no words came. God knew what she meant, anyway. She shifted from foot to foot. It must have been ten minutes. Maybe Ren's watch was broken?

More time passed. Amber looked at Ren. He was staring at his watch. She was sure it had to be broken. It must have been more than ten minutes. She opened her mouth to speak, but he spoke first. 'It's time. Get down.'

They threw themselves down against the brick wall. Amber pressed her back into the wall and covered her ears and eyes with her arms, as Ren pressed a button on a hand-held detonator.

The quiet night was rent with a thunderous noise. Amber felt a wave of air press down on her. A split second later she heard a second explosion, from further away. She stayed where she was, covering her face, until she felt someone's hand on her shoulder. She looked up, blinking.

Ren jerked his head towards the fence. Amber unwound herself, stunned. Her eyes watered and tears ran down her face. She brushed them away and gaped at the fence.

A large section of the fence had been torn away and thrown hundreds of metres, where it had hit a corrugated iron shed and left a large dent in the wall. On either side of the hole, the metal was twisted and torn. The fence tilted inwards along its length. The security cameras were gone, or hung off the fence, looking as though they could fall at any moment.

'Wow,' Bec's mouth formed the word.

Ren's mouth was set in a smug smile, and his eyes danced. Lifting his rifle and keeping low, he jogged towards the hole. The others followed. Amber jumped as the silence was again broken, this time by the rhythmic pops of gunfire. Bullets smashed into the ground in front of them. They sprinted to the nearest building - a rectangular, white shed. Like the shed next door, there was a red brick building in front of it, so close that it touched the wall, but the designers of this one had resisted the urge to add crenellations. Ren flung himself against the corner and the others dived down next to him. He leant around the corner and fired a quick succession of bullets.

Amber slid around the building and tugged at a double glass door to the right. It was locked.

'You go,' Ant said to Ren, 'We'll keep them busy.'

Nodding, Ren slid back from the corner. Ant and Jen took his place, taking it in turns to fire.

Ren joined Amber at the door. 'Stand back.'

Amber leapt back as he fired a single bullet at the glass. Lines and concentric circles appeared on the glass, around a small bullet hole. He turned his gun around and hit the centre circle with the butt of the rifle. The glass shattered onto the ground.

He used the butt of his rifle to clear the remaining glass around the edges of the panel, and crouched down, his rifle pointed into the room, then climbed through the hole.

'Quickly.'

Bec and Amber slid after him, their ears ringing with the sounds of bullets.

They were in a front office. Two battered leather lounges took up one side. On the other was a long counter. Above the counter hung a framed business registration certificate and two framed licences. A piece of paper stuck underneath them had a picture of a motorcycle and the words 'Money can't buy happiness/But it can buy a motorcycle/And that's the same thing'.

Ren and Bec rifled through the cupboards under the counter. Feeling superfluous, Amber prowled around the room. She glanced behind one of the couches, and drew in a breath in surprise, her hand clutching at her sword.

A woman was sitting with her back against the wall, her body curled in a tight ball. Matted red curls, greying at the roots, covered her head. She was wearing jeans and a plain T-shirt that must have started out as white but now looked grey. She lifted her chin and glared at Amber.

'Who are you?' she demanded, her tone imperious, as though she wasn't the one hiding behind a couch.

Amber had received the same glare many times - from Alice.

'Elise?' she asked.

'How do you know who I am?'

'I know your daughters.'

Elise's gaze sharpened on Amber, and recognition dawned on her face. 'And I know you. Amber Yu. The person the Boneheads would most like to kill.' She stood up, her eyes taking in the other people in the room. Her gaze lingered on Bec. 'I see your sidekick is here, too.'

'I'm nobody's sidekick,' Bec said.

Elise narrowed her eyes at Ren. 'I've seen you on television before, too. Let me guess. You're here for the THONGs.'

Ren returned her suspicious look. 'Is that a problem?'

'No.' She waved at a door to the left of the counter. 'Go right through.'

Ren didn't move. 'Are there guards?'

'Usually. They disappeared when the explosions started. There's cameras, of course, but they already know you're here, don't they?'

With another suspicious look at Elise, Ren hefted his rifle, and flung open the door.

Light from large electric lights glinted off the grey metal walls and cream, vinyl flooring, giving the shed a bright, airy feel. Amber imagined it would be even brighter during the day, as there were long, thin skylights set at regular intervals along the roof of the shed.

A conveyor belt ran down the middle of the room, with red, hydraulic robot arms lining each side. Two men in their thirties stepped back from the conveyer belt and ran their eyes over Ren. They had identical blue jeans and black T-shirts with the letters 'DT' written in small, white font on the left side, short beards, dark hair and bags under their brown eyes, as though they hadn't slept well in a long time.

One of them looked past Ren to Elise. 'What's going on, Elise? We keep hearing gunfire.'

'Apparently the calvary is here. Or what do you call yourselves - the resistance?'

Ren ignored the question and strode through the doorway.

'Dom, Zach.' Elise waved a hand at the two men. 'I didn't catch your name.'

'Ren,' he said, his eyes scanning the shed.

'This was my husband, Nick's, dream.' Elise looked around the shed, her voice bitter. 'An electronic shield, that you could carry in your pocket, barely even notice it was there, which would automatically activate and stop bullets. He used to watch news reports of school massacres in the US and imagine all the school kids carrying them.'

Ren's eyes narrowed. 'Used to?'

'They killed him,' Elise spat. She didn't give any more details. Ren returned to his examination of the shed.

'Why THONGs?' Bec asked.

Elise's mouth twisted. 'It was a joke. Apart from when we went to the pub or somewhere where he had to wear shoes, Nick used to wear thongs all the time - summer, winter, whatever. He called his shields Total High-velocity Object Neutralising Gadgets, but he just came up with the name to fit the acronym.' She waved at Dom and Zach. 'We had a partnership with Downunder Technology, to make a small number at first, but Nick always dreamt of scaling up one day. He never imagined that the day would come so soon - or that his THONGs would be used to protect monsters, instead of innocent school kids.'

Amber hadn't heard a word of this discussion. Her gaze was locked on a third person in the room. He was seated on the only chair in the room, a desk chair in front of a computer terminal. He'd turned as they came in, and frozen, his eyes locked on hers, too.

'Amber?'

As though the word had broken a spell, Amber flung herself across the room and on top of him, almost pushing him off the desk chair and onto the floor. She wrapped both arms around him, buried her face in his shoulder, and sobbed. He hesitated, then wrapped his arms around her, too.

Ren, Elise, Dom and Zach stared.

'That's Adam,' Bec said, 'Her husband.'

A burst of gunfire, closer than before, reminded Amber of where she was. She scrambled off Adam's lap, tears still dribbling down her face.

'Have you seen Ollie?' The words tumbled from her mouth.

Adam wrinkled his brow in confusion. 'Ollie? Why would I have seen him?'

A sudden shock of cold ran through Amber's body, as though someone had flung a bucket of cold water over her. 'The soldiers took him. I - thought - they might have brought him here.'

'We wouldn't know,' Dom said, 'They haven't let us out of this building in days. We have to take it in turns to sleep on the couches out in the office.'

Adam was staring at Amber, his mouth open. 'You don't know where he is?' His tone was accusatory.

'That's what she said,' Bec snapped. Amber wished she wouldn't. Bec defending her would annoy Adam more.

Adam gave Bec a cool look. 'Rebecca.'

Ren had approached the conveyor belt and was watching the robot arms punching pieces of metal. 'Are these the THONGs?'

'They will be,' Dom joined him, 'They need programming first.'

'Do you have any that are working?'

'Not here. As soon as they're ready to go, the soldiers take them away. They don't want us using them to escape.' The bitterness in his tone matched Elise's.

'Where do they take them?'

Dom shrugged. He looked at Elise. 'Any ideas?'

Elise nodded. 'Your old shed. Other side of the compound.'

'Let's go,' Ren said.

They left the way they'd arrived, through the glass pane. Jen and Ant were still firing on the soldiers. 'How's it going?' Ren asked.

'Too many,' Ant gasped, 'We're never going to get back through that.'

'We want to go the other way, anyway,' Elise said.

Ant and Jen cast quick, curious glances at her, Adam, Dom and Zach. 'I don't think we have a choice,' Jen said.

Ant kept firing behind them as they ran along the edge of the shed, crouching low. They were close to the other corner when Ren froze, raising his rifle. Kim appeared around the corner, her hands clinging to two smaller figures - Alice and Lucy. Josie came up behind and flung herself down on the ground, firing back the way they'd come.

'It's getting pretty hot out there,' she gasped to Ren.

Elise let out a small squeak. A moment later, she was almost knocked off her feet as Alice and Lucy threw themselves at her.

'Mum!'

Bec laughed. She turned to look at Amber, expecting her to be delighted, but Amber had her arms wrapped around her stomach and there was fear in her eyes. Kim and Josie had found Alice and Lucy, but not Oliver.

A continuous pop of gunshots sounded on either side. Ren joined Josie at the corner of the building, firing.

Alice and Lucy had buried their heads in Elise's chest, one blonde, one red. Elise squeezed her arms around them both. Her eyes were full of fear, too.

'They've got us pinned down,' Josie yelled to Ren, 'Can we go the other way?'

'It's just as bad.'

The frequency and volume of the gunfire rose even more. Amber squeezed her arms tighter, but, to her surprise, Josie grinned. 'It's Christine's group!'

There was a moment's pause in the gunfire. 'Go, go!' Ren screamed. Josie dived across the road. Kim grabbed Alice's hand again, dragging her away from her mother, and ran across the road. Elise followed with Lucy. Amber went next, her feet pounding on the bitumen. She could hear more pops of gunfire, but didn't dare look anywhere but at her feet. With every step she expected a bullet to rip through her body. She reached the building and swung around, pressing her back against the wall and gasping for breath, as the others joined her, Ren bringing up the rear.

They had reached the cream shed in the photo that Dan had found on Lieutenant Colonel Nichols' laptop. Two large pots stood near the door, holding drooping cordylines. A pile of timber offcuts had been dumped next to the pots.

There was a keypad on the door.

'That's new,' Zach said.

Josie lifted her rifle to fire at the keypad.

'No need,' Elise said, 'I know the code.'

Josie frowned. 'They told you the code?' Her voice was full of suspicion.

'They trust me.' Bitterness filled Elise's voice again. 'They had my kids.'

Josie waved at the panel. 'Go ahead, then.'

Elise tapped the keypad. The door swung open.

The building was dark. Josie switched on a high-powered torch and shone it into the open door with one hand, following the beam with her rifle. Amber, peering over her shoulder, had the impression of a large, empty space. There was no movement. Josie pressed a light switch on the wall, but nothing happened. Ren moved forward next to Josie and scanned the room with his own torch.

All the lights came on. The room was ablaze with light. Ren and Josie stopped, blinded. A row of soldiers lined the walls, rifles pointed straight at them.

Lucy whimpered behind them. Amber swung around and saw a giant wombat, prowling towards Lucy like a cat hunting.

Alice grabbed a long, thin piece of timber from the pile of offcuts and ran forward next to Lucy, holding the piece of timber over her head. Amber had a moment's flashback to Dan trying to hold off the wombat with a star picket. Bec jumped forward next to them, lifted her rifle and fired at the wombat. Shots echoed around the compound, but the bullets hit an invisible barrier and fell to the ground.

'They're giving THONGs to their pets now?' Zach growled.

Someone called out in a foreign language. The giant wombat growled. It hunched down on the ground, its eyes focused on Bec, Alice and Lucy. Its backside quivered. Bec let the nose of the rifle fall towards the ground and clutched her injured shoulder, her face contorted in pain.

Several soldiers appeared out of the shadows, forming a semi-circle around the resistance fighters. Behind the soldiers, the unmistakable shape of three Boneheads reared up out of the darkness.

Sweat formed on Amber's skin, and her heart beat hard and fast.

'Amber,' Kim spoke in her ear. Amber looked at her. Kim had drawn her sword. She nodded towards the soldiers and Boneheads. 'Do the speed thing.'

'I can't,' Amber's whisper was a wail, 'I can't do it on command.'

Kim's look was pure impatience. 'I told you to figure out the difference between when you can move fast and when you can't.'

Amber's face reddened. 'I tried - there isn't anything.' Anger rose inside her. It was all very well for Kim to tell her to figure it out. Figure what out? She didn't even know where the power came from.

Then she hesitated. Could the difference be something to do with her, rather than the power? Every time she'd reached it she'd been so desperate she'd had no room for any other emotion, like anger.

'Amber,' Kim said, through gritted teeth.

Ignoring her, Amber closed her eyes, and took a deep breath. She exhaled, trying to let go of her anger - with Kim; and with Bec. The breath caught in her throat. It was easier to dismiss Kim - she barely knew her. But she didn't want to let go of the anger with Bec. It felt safe; comfortable. She frowned and took another breath.

Oliver. She had to stay alive to rescue him - wherever he was. Bec's mistakes didn't matter. Neither did her own. All that mattered was doing everything possible to keep Oliver safe. She exhaled again, letting the anger flow away. She took another deep breath and reached out to the power. This time it flooded her. She opened her eyes. A sense of peace and calm filled her.

She'd never experienced a feeling like it before.

She opened her eyes and looked at Kim.

'Ready?' Kim asked.

Amber nodded and drew her sword.

She felt a sudden, sharp pain in her neck. She wrenched back and swung around. Elise was standing behind her, holding a syringe.

Black spots swarmed over Amber's vision, and her legs felt disconnected, as though they didn't belong to her. She sank to the ground. Kim's face appeared above her, her eyes startled.

'What did you do?' Kim's voice was a growl.

'What I had to,' Elise's voice replied.

Amber tried to lift her head to see Elise, but her neck was reluctant to do what she wanted. She concentrated, and her head tilted back. Elise's face swum between the black spots. Her eyes were bleak. There was no sign of the laughing woman that Amber had seen in the wedding photos.

Amber felt her neck droop of its own accord. Elise had betrayed them.

Twenty One

Elise and Kim disappeared as the black spots covered her eyes. She could no longer feel her body, or the ground. She was floating in darkness. The power remained - a firm, glowing beacon. She concentrated on it. As she concentrated, it seemed to grow, in increments: sometimes slow, sometimes fast, according to its own rhythm. She had no idea how long she floated. As the beacon grew, it burned away the darkness. Feeling returned to her body. She could feel her heart beating. She could feel her chest rising and falling as she breathed. There was a smooth, hard surface under the left side of her body - she was lying on her side, on the floor. There were goosebumps on her skin. There was pain in her back, and head - she must have hit them when she collapsed.

She tried to move her body, but it didn't respond to her commands. Panic filled her mind. She was trapped in a frozen body. Her heart raced. As though in response to the panic, her eyes cracked open. She looked out onto the world through tiny slits, covered by her eyelashes.

She seemed to be lying on the floor inside the large room. A blonde soldier was standing above her. Amber thought she'd seen her before, but couldn't remember when.

The resistance fighters were in a rough group in front of her, surrounded by soldiers. Ren was at the front of the group, his chest thrust forward, exuding a commanding air. His attention - and that of the other resistance fighters - was on something behind Amber's back. She felt a shiver run down her spine. What was behind her? She couldn't turn to look. She took a breath and focused instead on the people in front of her. The resistance fighters' hands were empty - their rifles gone. Amber looked again at the enemy soldiers. They had two or three rifles each.

To her right, Amber could just see Kim. Her sword was gone. She was standing next to Elise, who was clutching Alice and Lucy's hands.

Alice gripped the timber plank in her other hand, her knuckles white. Lucy huddled next to her mother. She wasn't looking at whatever was behind Amber, but at the wombat, which was prowling behind her mother. A soldier stood behind the wombat - its handler, she presumed, but he wasn't watching the wombat. He was holding a sword, and running his finger up and down the blade, keeping a hair's breadth between his finger and the blade.

Amber checked her own waist. Her sword was gone, too, but

she couldn't see it anywhere. She concentrated on her body. Apart from her eyes, she didn't seem to have any control over it. She tried to clench her fingers or wriggle her toes in her shoes. Nothing.

She realised that she couldn't see the Boneheads. Were they behind her? More goosebumps ran down her back.

The blonde soldier spoke, in a gloating tone. 'Congratulations, Doctor Taylor. You played your part perfectly.'

Amber remembered where she'd seen her before: in the photo on Nichols' laptop. Major Mueller - the woman who Jerome had called 'the Mule' - the one he'd said had taken Oliver. If she was here, perhaps they'd been right - perhaps Oliver was here.

A black dress shoe nudged her.

'Don't worry,' the Mule said to the person wearing the shoe, 'Doctor Taylor just filled her with enough Quake to knock her out for half a day, and when she wakes up - assuming she does - she'll be dealing with hallucinations for another day or so.'

Amber wondered what Quake was - clearly nothing good. She took a slow breath. Let them think she'd be knocked out for half a day - she could use that to her advantage. If she could get her body to respond to her brain.

'Why?' Alice wrenched her hand out of her mother's grasp and stared at her, her face white. 'She was rescuing us.'

'Rescuing you?' Elise's face turned red, and her eyes bulged. 'You didn't need rescuing! I kept you safe! I did what I had to do - whatever I had to do, to make sure you and Lucy were safe. She kidnapped you from the university - her and her friend. I didn't sleep for eight nights, wondering where you were, if you were still alive! I've never been more relieved in my life than when you turned up here. And then these two turned up again. I knew what I had to do - protect you.'

'They didn't kidnap us, mum,' Lucy said, 'Alice made them take us.'

'You're children,' she snapped, 'You don't know what's best for you. And you,' she swung around to look at Bec, 'You - and her -' she waved a hand towards Amber, 'You didn't just put my daughters in danger, you put her six month old in danger. You have no idea what you're playing with. But I do. Nick refused to make THONGs for the Boneheads, and I watched them beat him with those horrible electric whips - the kindest, most caring man in the world - I watched them beat him into oblivion.'

The anger disappeared from Alice's eyes. Her shoulders slouched. 'Nick's dead?' Her voice quivered.

Her mother looked at her and Lucy, tears leaking from the sides of her eyes. 'Oh,' she said, 'Oh baby, I'm sorry, I didn't mean to tell you like this.'

Lucy closed her eyes. When she opened them again, she didn't look at her mother. 'No,' she said, 'No!'

She let go of her mother, snatched the piece of timber out of Alice's hand and leapt at the wombat. She beat it with the end of the plank, her movements so fast that the timber blurred in Amber's sight. Her eyes couldn't focus on it.

The wombat's handler sprang forward, but Lucy whirled the timber and he jumped back. Another two soldiers flanked him, and together they approached. Lucy sprung forward, leaving the wombat crumpled on the ground, and caught one of them in the stomach. The soldier doubled over on the ground, choking.

'She's like Amber.' Josie's voice was full of wonder.

Amber stared at Lucy through the slits. Now she understood what Jerome and Sam had meant when they called her inhumanely fast.

'Tev was right,' Kim said, 'Something possessed Amber, and now it's possessing her.'

Amber would have shaken her head, but it wouldn't move. Lucy wasn't possessed - she was just leaning on the power, like Amber had.

The two soldiers who were still standing circled Lucy, out of reach. A fourth soldier pulled Alice back and held her, as though concerned that she would turn into a whirling dervish like her sister, but Alice just stared at Lucy, her mouth open in a wide O.

A Bonehead stepped over Amber's body and drew its sword. It strode towards Lucy. Amber tried to lift her body, but it still wasn't doing what she told it to. She couldn't move.

'No!' Elise screamed. She swung around to the Mule. 'You promised not to hurt them!'

The Bonehead strode past the soldiers and swung its sword. Amber couldn't stop herself from gasping, but the sound was lost as an inhuman wail of anguish filled the room - Elise.

The Bonehead hit Lucy on the side of the head with the flat of its sword. She slumped to the ground.

Elise flung herself to the ground next to Lucy, still wailing. Jen broke away from their group and knelt next to Lucy. She leaned over and placed her cheek above Lucy's mouth.

'She's alive,' Jen told Elise, 'She's breathing.' With gentle hands, Jen rolled Lucy onto her side. Elise touched Lucy's cheek, tears running down her face.

Jen placed her hand on Elise's shoulder, comforting her. If she could have, Amber would have frowned. She couldn't believe that Jen had any sympathy for Elise, after what she did.

The Mule jerked her head at the soldiers. 'Take them away.'

One of the soldiers pushed Elise out of the way and scooped Lucy up. Her head fell backwards over his arm, and he didn't try to reposition her, treating her like a doll rather than a human. Elise scrambled to her feet.

Amber felt her heart racing. If she couldn't get her body to move, Alice and Lucy would be gone. She concentrated on the power again, feeling it grow inside her, burning the last effects of the Quake - whatever that was - out of her. She tensed her muscles, preparing to jump up, and leant harder on the power. She could feel it coursing through her.

She took a deep breath and used her arms to push herself up off the floor, springing to her feet. A look of shock appeared on the Mule's face. Amber jumped back - out of the Mule's reach - and swung around to see what was behind her. She froze, a matching expression of shock on her own face.

Lieutenant Colonel Nichols was standing behind her, wearing a mocking smile. The black dress shoe that had nudged her belonged to him. He stood with his feet wide, leaning his arms on the top of a sword, the point against the floor in front of him, the way a gentleman might balance on an umbrella in an old-fashioned movie. Two Boneheads stood behind him.

Next to him was Private Jerome - holding Oliver.

Amber's grip on the power wavered, and it started slipping away. She reached out with her mind and clutched at it.

'Ms Yu,' Nichols said, his mocking tone matching the smile on his face, 'I see that rumours of your incapacitation were exaggerated.'

He directed the smile towards the Mule. The Mule made a move as though to step backwards, then stopped. 'She should still be unconscious.'

Nichols looked at Amber. 'You do make a habit of surprising us, don't you, Ms Yu?' He quirked his lips. 'But this time, I recommend you don't do anything too surprising, or you'll never see your son again.' He looked at the soldier who was holding Lucy, and a look of impatience flashed on his face. 'What are you waiting for?'

The soldier's eyes widened, and he hurried towards the door. The soldier that was holding Alice tried to force her in the same direction, but she kicked him in the shin and pulled herself from his grasp. He seemed too surprised to stop her. She swung around.

'Amber,' she called, her voice full of urgency. She threw a small object straight at Amber's face. On instinct, Amber put her hands up and caught it. One hand closed around a round, ridged shape.

She opened her hand. A black ball, with smaller rotating balls, lay in her hand. Alice had given her a THONG.

The soldier's hands closed around Alice's arms, his grip firmer this time.

Elise's eyes widened. Her voice came out in a gasp. 'I gave you that to keep you safe!'

Alice met her mother's eyes with a look of defiance mixed with fear. The soldier dragged her out the door. Elise stood for a moment, her mouth opening and closing, then ran after her daughters.

'If we can get back to business.' Nichols sounded irritated. He gave Amber a cold smile. 'That THONG's not going to do you much good, Ms Yu. Let's not forget that we've got your son. I wouldn't make any hasty moves if I was you.'

The two Boneheads moved forward. Soldiers and resistance fighters alike kept their eyes on the towering figures. The smile continued to play on Nichols' face, but Jerome's eyes widened when one of the Boneheads stopped within an arm's length of him.

Amber pushed the THONG into a pocket on her pants, closed her eyes, and took a deep breath in. The power expanded, making her body tingle, and seeming to spill out of her body into the surrounding air.

Nichols seemed to sense that she was planning something. The smile disappeared. He passed the sword to Jerome, and raised his rifle, pointing it at Oliver's head. Jerome's eyes widened. He held the sword with an awkward grip in the hand that was supporting Oliver's bottom. Amber clenched her teeth, sure that it was her sword he was holding.

How fast could she move? The tingling in her body increased, as though the power was trying to give her a message.

I hope I'm understanding you. Amber spoke the words in her mind. She took the lack of a response as a yes, and flung herself forward, straight at Jerome.

Jerome took a step backwards, but time slowed more than it ever had before. Before he could move any further, Amber was on him. She tore the sword from his hands, reversed it and drove the hilt into his stomach. He doubled over, and she wrenched Oliver from his hands.

She jumped back next to Ren, the sword in her right hand and Oliver in her left, leaving Jerome curled up on the ground. Time sped up a little - still slow, but not as slow as it had been.

'Section, fire!' Nichols shrieked.

Shots rang out as the soldiers fired at her. The bullets hit the invisible shield and fell to the ground. The three Boneheads drew their swords.

Even in slow motion, the Boneheads were intimidating. Amber took another step backwards. Her eyes met the black, unblinking eyes of the largest Bonehead. She shivered. Her eyes flicked to the left and right. She caught sight of Kim. Kim could help, but not without a sword. She looked for the wombat's handler. He was kneeling next to the wombat, his hand on its furry head. The sword lay forgotten next to him.

Amber thrust Oliver into Ren's arms, so that he had no choice but to take him. He opened his mouth to speak, but she ignored him and ran straight at the wombat's handler. Focused on the wombat, he didn't see her until she was on top of him. She snatched up the sword with her left hand and narrowed her eyes. It would be so easy to run him through. They'd have one less enemy to worry about.

He lifted his head and met her gaze. His eyes were wet with tears.

What was she thinking? She thrust the sword into Kim's hands. Kim started in surprise, but her hands closed over the sword in an automatic movement.

'Section, fire!' Nichols shrieked again.

Amber let go of the sword, and swung around, lifting her own sword. The soldiers fired at her and Kim, but the bullets hit the shield and bounced away.

'Leave them to us,' the largest Bonehead growled, the light glinting off the rich, red mahogany plate on its head.

Nichols ordered the soldiers to stop firing. The Boneheads strode towards her and Kim. Soldiers and resistance fighters jumped out of their way. One of the Boneheads lunged forward to attack Kim, and the largest Bonehead rushed at Amber.

The Bonehead was so confident it held its sword over its head in both hands, not even bothering to protect itself. As it brought its sword down, Amber ducked under its arms and struck up with her sword under its jaw, into its exposed neck area. She pulled the sword sideways, ripping the Bonehead's throat open. The Bonehead fell forward, and she jumped back as it landed with a crunch on the floor.

She risked a quick glance at Kim. The Bonehead rained blows down onto her. Kim blocked each blow with her sword, her muscles straining, pivoting away, but it kept coming.

Amber turned as the third Bonehead, the one who had hit Lucy, attacked. This one had learnt from its comrade's experience, and held its sword low, protecting its body.

Amber hesitated as it got within range, unsure of what to do. The Bonehead lifted its sword, holding it horizontally in front of its neck as protection, and struck. She lifted her sword to block, feeling the strain on her arms as the Bonehead's weight pushed against her sword, then pivoted to the right, letting the Bonehead's sword slip off. The Bonehead pivoted with her and didn't hesitate before striking again. She knocked its sword sideways with the flat of her sword and struck out with her sword towards its face, stepping forward and breathing out to put her body weight behind the blow. It ducked sideways out of the way and, while she was still off balance, swung its sword towards her head. She ducked out of the way, but the blow clipped her left arm.

Pain exploded in her arm. She leant harder and the pain faded away. She jumped backwards out of the Bonehead's reach.

The Bonehead bared its teeth in a predatory smile.

She felt liquid on her arm, and realised that it was blood. The Bonehead charged again. She caught its sword on hers again, but it kept coming. She caught blow after blow, pivoting or moving backwards when she could, but it kept up with her. At least she didn't feel tired - another effect of leaning on the power. She tried to think about the moves Kim had taught her, but it was hard when the Bonehead kept raining down blows.

The Bonehead again lifted its sword horizontally and struck. Amber ducked under the blow and pushed her sword into its side with every ounce of power she had. She wrenched the sword upwards, ripping open the Bonehead's side. It fell, and she had to pull hard to get her sword free. She felt it scrape against bone, and shuddered.

She turned towards Kim. The Bonehead swiped low with its sword, slashing Kim across her right leg. Kim sank down onto her knees, somehow keeping her sword up to protect her body and face. The Bonehead lifted its sword above its head.

Amber ran towards the Bonehead, screaming. Before it could bring its sword down, she ran hers through its lower torso, just below the armour. As it fell backwards, she saw its eyes, deep within their sockets. They looked shocked. Blood sprayed over her and Kim as it landed on the ground.

Amber lowered her sword. An awareness of her surroundings

returned. Ren ordered the resistance fighters to move close to the soldiers, where their own THONGs stopped them firing at the resistance fighters. Soldiers and fighters drew knives or used their rifles as blunt objects to fight with. Ren flung Oliver into Adam's arms as the Mule rushed towards him with a knife.

Nichols melted backwards, to a back door that Amber hadn't noticed before. He cast a last glance around the room. He caught Amber watching him, and his face twisted with fury and hatred. Then he was gone.

Ren, fending off the Mule with his rifle, yelled something to Josie, and she stepped back from the soldiers, lifted her rifle to the ceiling and fired at the lights, plunging the room into darkness. Ren screamed at the resistance fighters to retreat to the vehicles.

Amber's hold on the power slipped away and a wave of nausea swept over her. She dropped to her knees and vomited onto the floor. A soldier tripped over her. She took a breath, gasping, and tried to stand, but another wave of nausea overtook her. She crawled away from the soldier, dragging the sword with her, and threw up again. Her head throbbed with pain, and the cut on her arm burned. She squeezed her eyes shut, then blinked them open. Lights from torches lit up the room in bursts, but most of the soldiers and fighters seemed to have disappeared. She could hear the loud pops of gunfire outside.

A beam from a torch hit a small blue object on the ground in front of her. Lucy had dropped her teddy.

Amber picked it up, smoothing its fur with her hand. Another beam of torchlight lit up the wombat, its eyes wide and glassy and its fur matted with blood. Its handler had disappeared. Bec hadn't been able to shoot the wombat, which meant it must have had a THONG. She wondered if it still did. She shoved the sword into her sword belt and crawled over to the body with the teddy in one hand.

'Amber?'

The torchlight hit Jen's face. She was still sitting on the floor where she'd been when the soldier picked Lucy up.

Amber dropped the teddy and ran her hands through the wombat's fur, feeling for its collar. Her hands found a round, hard ball. She tugged at the ball, then jerked back with a shriek. It felt like someone had shoved a needle into her hand. She pulled her hand away from the body. It brought up a small wombat, its canine-like teeth attached to the fleshy part of her palm.

'Ow, ow, ow!' Amber shook her hand, trying to dislodge it.

'Hold still!' Jen grasped either side of the baby wombat's jaws and pulled open its mouth so Amber could yank her hand out, the tiny needle-point teeth scratching the back and palm of her hand.

Jen held the wombat in both hands. Its canines crowded its mouth, as though they didn't belong. It had a large head, and a wrinkled, pink body with a light dusting of grey fur. The claws on its hands were enormous. Amber thought it the ugliest baby animal she'd ever seen.

'Give me your jacket,' Jen ordered, her voice so firm that Amber didn't think to argue. She took her jacket off. Jen bundled the baby wombat up inside it, with its nose poking out the top. She nursed the jacket against her chest.

Amber's hand was still seeping blood from where the wombat had bit her. She pushed both hands back into the dead wombat's fur, searching for the THONG. Her hands grasped it, and she tugged. 'Why are you saving that horrible thing?'

'How many deaths have you dealt today, with that sword of yours?' Jen's voice was light, but Amber stopped and gave her a wary look. 'If you just deal in death, and don't ever save a life - worthy or not - how do you know you're any better than the monsters?'

Amber lurched backwards, bringing the THONG with her. Jen's words were like a sword piercing her heart. Before she could respond, Ren was next to them, the beam from his torch lighting up the area. 'The room's clear, but it won't be long before they send reinforcements. We need to go.'

'Where's Oliver?' Amber demanded.

'With your husband - they've gone to the vehicles already.'

'Alice and Lucy?'

'No idea.'

'Come on!' Josie shouted. Ren's torch showed her and Bec holding Kim up, one on either side of her, near the door. Ant was standing just inside the doorway, firing into the darkness.

Jen stood up, holding the jacket and wombat in front of her with two hands.

'You're not taking that thing with you,' Ren said.

Amber held up the THONG she'd retrieved from the wombat. A genuine smile lit up Ren's face - one she'd only ever seen before when he blew something up. He tucked the THONG into his pocket and held out a hand. She picked up the teddy and let him pull her to her feet.

Once she was up, he let go of her hand, and started running. Amber and Jen followed. Ant glanced around and saw Jen. A silent look passed between them, and then he turned back and kept firing.

Amber heard the sound of squealing brakes. Tevita skidded to a halt in front of the building, followed by Mark.

Shots sounded nearby. Ren ducked down and ran out to Tevita's ute. He started firing from behind the tray.

Jen shoved Amber's jacket, with the wombat inside, into Amber's hands. She took up position on the other side of the doorway.

Ant turned to Josie and Bec. 'Go. We'll cover you.'

Josie and Bec ran with Kim to Tevita's ute. Through the windscreen, Amber could see Adam, white-faced, holding Oliver. She felt dizzy for a second. Adam and Oliver were safe - or as safe as any of them were. Josie and Bec thrust Kim into the cab next to him.

'Is everyone else out?' Josie shouted to Tevita.

'I think so,' he yelled back.

Gunshots sounded from behind them - inside the room. Amber swung around. A soldier appeared out of the darkness. He swung his rifle in a wide arc, firing. The bullets hit Amber's shield and fell to the ground. Ant jumped to Amber's side and fired back, and the soldier threw himself down on the floor, hiding behind another soldier's body. A flash of light hit his face, and Amber recognised him. Private Jerome.

Amber turned back, and saw Jen fall to the ground. She dived to Jen's side, dropped the bundle with the baby wombat on the floor, and rolled Jen over. There was a hole in her forehead, and her eyes held the same, glassy stare as the dead wombat's had.

Twenty Two

Ant threw himself down next to Jen. He seized her hands and squeezed them so tight that his forearms strained with the effort. Jerome started firing again. Amber's shield blocked all the bullets. She ignored Jerome, her eyes on Ant. His whole body was shaking, but he didn't make a sound.

Someone fired at Jerome from the doorway, and he flung himself backwards into the darkness. Amber looked up to see Ren. He slung his rifle over one shoulder and touched Ant on the shoulder. 'Let's get her into the ute.'

The words seemed to break through to Ant. He helped Ren lift Jen's body and race with it out to Tevita's ute. Josie and Bec sprayed the area with a cover of bullets. Ren and Ant dropped the body into the tray of the ute. Ant looked like he wanted to climb in after it, but Ren stopped him.

'Go in the cab,' he said, pushing Ant towards the cab of Mark's ute. Ant hesitated. Bec grabbed his arm and pulled him to the ute. Ren nodded at Josie, and she leapt into the tray with Jen's body.

Tevita pulled away at high speed.

Amber tucked Lucy's teddy under her arm and picked up the jacket. The baby wombat was still inside, but it had got one claw free. As she lifted it, it struck, leaving a wide scratch down her face. Cursing, she bundled a loose sleeve of the jacket around the claw and pulled it in tight.

Bec had gotten Ant into the cab next to Mark.

'You go in the cab, too,' Ren called to her, 'Amber and I will go in the tray - we've both got THONGs.'

Bec leapt into the cab. Amber couldn't climb with the bundle in her hands. Giving her an impatient look, Ren shoved her into the tray. She landed hard on the metal floor. Ren swung himself in after her. As soon as he was in, Mark accelerated away, slipping through the gears and taking the corners without slowing.

It was even more terrifying than the wild ride through Newcastle with Tevita. The blur of the darkened landscape rushing past made Amber feel ill. The wombat moved in its bundle, and she gripped it with one hand, holding the side of the tray with the other. The wind whistled over her. She started shivering. The tray felt cold and hard against her hips. She suspected she had collected some bruises from the rough way Ren had pushed her into the tray. She closed her eyes, trying to ignore the discomfort and the wombat scrambling to escape.

Light was seeping over the horizon and the sky had turned a light pink when Mark slowed at last. He had caught up with Tevita. Amber released her death grip on the side of the tray and smoothed the fur of Lucy's teddy. She'd never question Mark's driving again.

Tevita pulled off the highway and onto a quiet country road, and Mark followed. They drove past brown, dry paddocks, more dirt than grass. Small flocks of sheep or cows scratched for grass on the edges of the paddocks. At an invisible boundary the bitumen ended, and the road turned to hard clay. The utes raised waves of dust as they bumped over the road.

Shivers racked Amber's body. Her stomach was queasy with hunger. The baby wombat had stopped moving. She worried that it had died from lack of food, or exposure.

Mark pulled into the yard of a small, mudbrick farmhouse set within a backdrop of three forested hills, with a large shed in a nearby paddock. At the back of the paddock was a patch of scrub. Four children and two cattle dogs tumbled out of the house to greet them. The children had brown skin, tangled curls and well-worn clothes. The youngest looked about five. The oldest was around Alice's age, her eyes alight with interest. Amber's stomach clenched. She tried not to think about Alice.

An older Aboriginal woman followed the children out. She stood with her hands on her hips, watching as Josie and Ren climbed out of the ute. The dogs leapt around their ankles.

Josie gave the woman a hug. Ren shook her hand.

'Two carloads of shell-shocked people in desperate need of a shower turned up ten minutes ago, talking about explosions and gunfire. I figured they must be friends of yours,' she said.

'Where are they?' Ren looked around the yard.

'I sent them up to the shed. You'd better put your utes in there, too.' Her gaze held a warning. 'I've already had soldiers through here, wondering if I'm involved in the resistance. I managed to convince them I was an innocent victim of my husband, that I didn't know what he was up to, but they're still sniffing around.'

'We won't stay long,' Ren said.

'Good. If they catch you here, I'll be dead, and I've got the kids to consider.'

The woman narrowed her eyes in recognition as Amber jumped down from the ute, landing in the dirt and raising small clouds of dust. 'You've been busy,' she said to Ren.

'Amber, Deb.'

'Yeah, I know her name.' Deb looked at the bundle Amber was holding. 'What is that?'

Amber held it out. 'It's a baby. Its mum was killed. I think it needs food.'

Deb sniffed. 'Let it die. Wombats aren't meant to have canines - it's not natural.'

Amber pulled it into her body. She couldn't argue with Deb that the canines were unnatural. She had no real desire to keep the wombat - she had enough to do keeping Oliver alive - but she couldn't forget Jen's words to her. The last words Jen would ever speak. Was she turning into a monster? Two weeks ago, it would have been unthinkable for her to kill anyone. Today she'd killed three Boneheads and felt - nothing.

The eldest child came over and looked at it with interest. 'It looks about six to eight months. It'll need milk, but it should be able to eat grass. Or,' she looked at Deb, 'If it's carnivorous, does it eat meat instead of grass?'

Deb sniffed again. 'If you're determined to keep that - thing, Kirra can help you. She's raised orphaned wombats, and joeys, before.' She looked at Kirra. 'I have no idea what it will eat. It might be omnivorous. You'll have to try a few things.'

'I'll make up some marsupial milk.' Kirra ran into the house.

Deb looked at Amber. 'Wombats - even the grass-eating ones - don't make good pets. They poop everywhere, stay up all night, and destroy your house and garden.'

'The Boneheads have theirs well trained.'

'That makes them even more unnatural. Real wombats can't be trained.' Deb shook her head. 'Go up to the shed. Kirra'll bring the food up.' She looked at Ren. 'I'll bring human food up, too. You owe me.'

'Put it on the tab.'

'Oh, I will.'

Tevita and Mark started up their utes. Ren walked to the shed and slid open the long, corrugated iron door to allow them to drive in. Josie and Amber followed the utes inside. Ren slid the door closed, leaving a gap the size of the front door of a house.

The two sedans were parked to the left side of the shed, next to a small, green and yellow tractor. On the other side tools hung on hooks on the wall, and the floor held neat piles of bags of feed, fencing posts and chopped firewood. Swallows had built mud nests in the steel beams holding the roof up. They darted in and out, ignoring the people moving around below them.

The Dubbo resistance fighters were seated on the floor among the piles of feed and firewood. They looked exhausted. The muscly man was lying on his back, staring at the roof. Christine stared at them with red-rimmed eyes. Dom and Zach were seated a little apart from the others, casting wary glances at the fighters.

Amber ran her eyes over the group, mentally ticking people off. Bec joined her. 'Everyone made it,' she said in a low voice, 'Except Jen.'

'And Alice and Lucy,' Amber said.

Tevita helped Kim out of the ute. Adam slid to the ground with Oliver in his arms. Amber drank in the sight of them. Tears pricked her eyes.

It was over. They'd got the THONGs, and Adam and Oliver were back with her, alive and safe. She lifted her eyes towards the ceiling and said a silent prayer. 'Thank you.'

Ant staggered out of Mark's ute and stumbled to the tray where Jen's body lay. Josie, Ren and Mark helped him to lift her body down to the ground. He sat on the ground, cradling her body. Ben and Christine shot to their feet. The muscly man sat up.

'What happened?'

'A soldier shot her,' Ren said.

Private Jerome, Amber thought. She'd thought he was just a kid. In Brooklyn, she'd even asked him to come with them. He wasn't just a kid anymore.

Christine clapped her hand over her mouth. Ben knelt and put his arm around Ant. 'I'm so sorry, mate.'

The Dubbo resistance fighters gathered around, offering silent support.

'I've got some milk for your wombat.'

Amber turned around. Kirra proffered a bottle of milk. Amber unwrapped the bundle in her hands a little, and Kirra showed her how to feed the wombat.

'Thanks,' Amber said.

'I'll bring up some more milk after breakfast. They need a lot. And we should see if it'll eat grass, or meat.'

'Thank you,' Amber said, but her eyes were on Adam and Oliver. Kirra nodded, and danced out of the shed door.

'Can you hold it for a minute?' Amber asked Bec. Bec pulled a face, but she took the wombat and bottle.

Amber wiped the palms of her hands on her clothes and took halting steps towards Adam and Oliver. Adam met her eyes. He stood up. She felt almost shy. 'It's wonderful to see you,' she said, reaching towards him to give him a hug.

Adam pulled back, his arms clutching Oliver tighter. Amber dropped her arms and stepped back, her brow wrinkling. Adam looked around. Dom and Zach were watching them. 'Can we go outside?'

Amber nodded and followed him outside. She was more tired than she'd ever felt before. The sun had risen above the horizon, and the air was already heating up. It was going to be another sweltering day. But the cold seemed to have seeped into Amber's bones. She wondered if she'd ever be warm again.

Just outside the door, Adam turned to her. 'Those Boneheads - you killed them.'

Amber wrapped her arms around her stomach. 'If I hadn't, they would have killed us.'

Adam shook his head back and forth. 'You killed them with a

sword. Since when do you know how to use a sword?'

'Kim's been teaching me,' she said in a small voice. He was still shaking his head. She had to make him understand. 'You weren't there.' She heard the unintended accusation in her tone, and tried again. 'The soldiers took Ollie. They took him from me! I had to get him back.'

Adam's face had coloured. He said nothing for a moment, staring at Oliver. In a quick movement he thrust Oliver into her arms. 'I'm sorry. I just - I don't know what to think. I need some time.' He trotted back into the shed.

Amber buried her face in Oliver's hair. An arm wrapped around her shoulder. 'Men,' Bec said, 'So emotional. He'll get over it.'

The wombat made a hissing sound, and Bec removed her hand and continued to feed it.

'You heard all that?' Amber said, her voice muffled.

She huffed in answer. 'He should be congratulating you. You kicked ass! Who wouldn't want a superhero for a wife?'

Amber lifted her head. 'I'm not a superhero.'

'I'll make you a cape.'

Amber gave a snort of laughter, smiling despite herself.

Oliver started wailing. Amber sat down with her back against the shed and put Oliver against her breast. She felt the familiar tugging sensation and let out a sigh. She'd been worried that her milk would dry up after being separated from Oliver for so long.

Bec plonked the wombat down next to her, still wrapped up in her jacket. 'The blasted thing bit me!' She held out a finger that was dripping blood. 'You can keep that thing all to yourself.' She looked at Oliver. 'I don't know how you're going to manage. You don't have enough arms.'

Amber shrugged. She picked up the milk bottle and held it against the wombat's nose. The wombat started sucking again.

Bec put her arm around Amber's shoulders again, gave a quick squeeze, and returned inside the shed.

Amber closed her eyes, feeling the sun against her skin. Feeding Oliver usually made her feel hot, but she still felt icy cold inside.

Deb appeared, trailed by her children, carrying a crate filled with cereal packets, instant coffee, tea bags and milk. 'Breakfast,' she announced.

Amber watched through the doorway as Deb's two younger children darted around the shed, investigating the fighters and their belongings, particularly the weapons.

'Don't touch anything!' Deb called after them.

The children continued to press their hands against whatever they were looking at - unable to resist the temptation.

Kirra knelt next to Amber. She put a large cardboard box on the ground. 'Packets of marsupial milk powder,' she said, 'Just make them up with boiled water - there's directions on the packets. There's also bottles and some spare marsupial teats.' She passed Amber a cloth shopping bag with a worn blue baby blanket in the bottom of it. 'I use this for mine as a pouch. You can have it.'

'Thank you,' Amber said.

'Can I take it for a minute?'

'Be my guest.' Kirra scooped up the wombat and plonked it down on a large patch of green grass.

Oliver finished feeding. Amber held him against her shoulder and fixed her clothes, watching the wombat. It sniffed at the grass, and rolled on its back in it, but didn't try to eat any.

'Okay, let's try this.' Kirra took a small tub of cat food out of her pocket. 'Beef.'

She put it on the ground. The wombat sniffed at it, and then started gobbling it up.

'I guess that's what it eats.'

'Cat food?'

'At least it's easy to get. I'll bring you some more.'

Kirra helped Amber to settle the wombat into the cloth shopping bag. Amber slung it over her shoulder, making a makeshift pouch. With the wombat on one shoulder, and Oliver on the other, she felt weighed down. Kirra ran back to the house to get more cat food.

Amber's stomach clamoured for food. She walked back into the shed and poured a bowl of cereal with one hand. She felt like a juggler, spooning food into her mouth with Oliver asleep against her shoulder and the wombat scrambling in its pouch.

The rest of the group had almost finished breakfast. Christine was trying to coax Ant to eat some food. Amber's eyes sought Adam. He was sitting with Dom and Zach, and glanced away when she met his eyes.

Ren and Josie had set up a generator on the tray of Tevita's ute and plugged a laptop into it. Ren was typing. Kim and Bec watched over his shoulder. Someone had bandaged Kim's leg, and she was using a broom as a makeshift cane. Amber finished her cereal, washed out her bowl and poured a cup of coffee. The wombat seemed to have gone to sleep in the shopping bag. She walked over to stand next to Bec, holding Oliver in one hand and sipping her coffee in the other.

Ren stopped typing as she approached and spoke to Josie.

'Sam says the MG wants us to head straight to Base.'

'All of us?' Josie asked.

He nodded.

'When?'

'He's leaving that up to us, but I think we should leave as soon as possible. It's not going to get any safer in the next few days.'

'Deb won't want us to stay, anyway,' Josie said.

'What's Base?' Bec asked.

'Our base of operations,' Josie said.

'Wait,' Bec said, 'There is a resistance headquarters?' She looked at Amber, her eyes alight with laughter.

'It's just a camp in the bush.' Ren stood up. 'I'll go and talk to Christine.'

'Is Dan still with them?' Bec asked.

'I believe so.'

'Can I IM him?'

'As long as you let Josie check what you type.'

Bec sat down at the laptop as Kirra returned with the cat food. 'I think that's everything you need,' she said, 'Good luck.'

'Thank you,' Amber said, 'I really appreciate your help.'

Kirra gave her a brilliant smile and skipped away.

Bec looked up. 'Dan says he's broken into some folder on Nichols' laptop that's got some really interesting stuff in it. Want me to say anything from you?'

'No,' Amber said.

Bec shrugged and returned to the laptop.

Amber's eyes ached with tiredness. She found a quiet corner in the shed, curled up in a ball with Oliver on one side and the wombat on the other, and went to sleep.

Amber woke from a dream in which one of the Boneheads had cut off her hand. The pain remained. She shrieked. The resistance fighters leapt to their feet at her screams, rifles pointed towards her. Only Ant didn't move.

The wombat had somehow gotten out of its bag and wrapped its teeth around her wrist.

'For fucks' sake,' Josie said, swinging her rifle back across her shoulder and yanking the wombat away. 'I don't know why you want to keep this bloody thing.' The other fighters watched for a moment, then returned to what they had been doing.

Amber found the bottle of marsupial milk and pressed it against the wombat's mouth. Josie deposited the wombat into her hands and strode away. Oliver started wailing. Amber muttered swear words as she struggled to put him to her breast while keeping the bottle in the wombat's mouth.

Adam sank down next to her and took the wombat out of her hands.

'Thank you,' Amber said.

Adam looked down at the wombat. His blonde hair fell into his eyes. It had grown longer in the past couple of weeks.

'You really livened things up just then. I thought those resistance guys were going to shoot you.'

'That bloody wombat woke me up with its teeth.'

Adam was silent for a moment, watching the wombat suck.

'Ren wants to leave tonight,' he said, 'Go to this Base of theirs.'

'Gees,' Amber said, 'When Ren says he wants to leave as soon as possible, he really means it.'

'Are you going with them?'

Amber looked at him. 'I guess. Where else am I going to go?' She took a deep breath. 'Are you?'

He shrugged. 'I guess so, too. Ren assures me that it would be madness to go home.' He winced, and Amber wondered how Ren had made the point. He finally met her eyes. 'How on earth did you end up wanted by the Boneheads?'

It was Amber's turn to look away. She ran a finger over Oliver's tiny fingers. 'I was just trying to protect Ollie. It just - happened.'

Deb returned to the shed with more food. They watched her set it out.

Adam snorted. 'It's not like he cares about me - Ren, I mean. He just wants Dom, Zach and me to help them make THONGs.'

'Sounds like Ren,' Amber agreed.

'We told him we only know some of the steps involved. Elise was the only one who had the full picture.'

'And she's a traitor.' Amber gritted her teeth.

Adam looked at her through his hair. 'She's a mum. I would have thought you, of all people, would understand.'

'I would never betray anyone the way she did.'

'Okay,' Adam said, but he didn't sound like he believed her. The wombat seemed to have gone to sleep. He put it back into the shopping bag at Amber's side. 'I guess I should get some lunch.

You want any?'

'I'll get some in a moment. Ollie is almost finished.'

Adam nodded and walked away. Amber sighed, wishing for their easy relationship back. Wishing the past fortnight had never happened.

They didn't manage to leave that night. In the late afternoon, Ben approached Ren and Christine, flanked by Mark, who bit a nail, his gaze darting everywhere as though he wanted to escape.

'We're not ready to leave,' Ben said, his hands planted on his hips. 'We want to farewell Jen, and Ant isn't ready to choose somewhere to bury her yet. We need another day.'

Ren frowned. 'The longer we stay in one place, the bigger risk the enemy will find us.'

'One day won't make a difference,' Ben insisted, 'Deb isn't going to betray us - the Boneheads would kill her, too. And nobody else knows we're here.'

Christine's lips tightened, but she turned to Ren. 'He's probably right. One day won't matter.'

They slept on the floor of the shed, sharing what bedding they'd brought with them, and piles of blankets that Deb and Kirra delivered to the shed. In the morning, with Deb's help, Ant selected a spot in the patch of scrub behind the shed, underneath the fluffy green leaves of a large wattle bush. Deb told them that in late winter it would be covered in furry, vivid yellow balls.

Deb and the muscly man, whose name turned out to be Nathan, attached a backhoe to the small tractor and used it to dig a small grave. Ant and Deb wrapped Jen's body in a blanket, and Ben, Nathan and Ashleigh's brother Luke lowered it into the hole. They shovelled soil over the top, until the grave was marked by a low mound of dirt.

The sun was high in the sky and sweat dripped down their backs.

Christine read some bible verses from her phone - all verses that were popular at funerals. Amber suspected she had just googled good bible verses to read at a funeral.

Ben, who had gone to school with both Jen and Ant, spoke about Jen, painting a picture of a passionate woman with a talent for music. Ant started to say some words about Jen, but was racked with large, gulping sobs before he'd gotten two words out.

Ben put an arm around his shoulder. 'You don't have to say anything, mate. If she's out there somewhere, she knows how you feel about her.'

Most of the Dubbo resistance fighters were teary. Even Bec and Josie, who barely knew Jen, had moist eyes. Amber stared at the grave, dry eyed. The sun's rays had burned away the last of the cold that had seeped into her body after she killed the Boneheads, but she still felt numb.

Christine read one last bible passage. 'For I am convinced that neither death, nor life, nor angels, nor rulers, nor things present, nor things to come, nor powers, nor height, nor depth, nor anything else in all creation, will be able to separate us from the love of God in Christ Jesus our Lord.'

Amber clenched her fists. Neither death... but what if you were the one dealing the death? What if you were a killer? Jen's words mocked her. How do you know you're any better than the monsters?

Deb handed them each a small bouquet of flowers from her garden - bottlebrush, kangaroo paw and lavender. They took it in turns to throw their bouquets on top of the grave, so it was covered in colourful flowers. Amber was one of the last. She knelt and put her hand on the dirt.

'I kept the wombat,' she whispered to the grave, 'I don't know if it's enough, but - I'm saving a life.' She placed her bouquet on top of the others, and stood up, brushing the soil onto her clothes.

They had another quick lunch, standing in a circle around the food. Nobody spoke. The Dubbo resistance fighters shook hands with Ant, who had decided to stay on the farm with Deb for a while - not ready to leave Jen yet.

The drivers climbed into their respective cars and utes and moved them out of the shed. Amber settled the wombat into the shopping bag.

'Have you given that thing a name?' Bec asked.

Amber squinted up at her. 'Jaws.'

Bec let out a bark of laughter. Amber stood and slung the shopping bag over her left shoulder and her pack over her right.

'I need to talk to you,' Bec said.

'Okay.'

'I'm not coming with you to resistance headquarters.' She snorted. 'I can't believe there actually is a resistance headquarters.'

'You're not?' The blood drained from her face. She and Bec might have had their differences, but Bec had been the one constant in the last, unbelievable two weeks.

'I've got - unfinished business.'

'What kind of business?' Amber heard her voice rise to a squeak.

'You know I said I was IM-ing Dan? He reminded me that we still don't know what happened to Zhou. I owe it to him to find out - you said that yourself. And I might not be the last of my resistance group that's still alive. If others are - they might need help to stay that way. And there's Alice and Lucy.'

'Their mum is keeping them safe, remember?' She heard Elise's voice in her mind. You didn't need rescuing! I kept you safe!

Bec made a scoffing noise. 'Their mum couldn't stop that Bonehead whacking Lucy over the head with a sword. How safe do you think they'll be now the Boneheads know that Lucy can move super fast, like you?'

Amber blinked. She hadn't thought of that. 'You can't go on your own to do all that.'

'I won't be on my own. Nathan has some business in the city, too, and Ashleigh said she'll drive us. Luke is going to come too. And Dan said he'll meet me there.'

'Dan? But you called him a dickhead!'

Bec pulled a face. 'He is a dickhead. But I'm going to need help, and he offered. And he is good at hacking.'

'I could come with you,' Amber said.

'I'm not going to ask you to leave Adam - you only just got him back! And you've got Ollie to look after. Besides, someone needs to make sure the THONGs, and Adam, Zach and Dom, make it safely to resistance headquarters. If there's a war - and I can't see how else this is going to go - THONGs could be the difference between us winning and losing.'

'They don't need me for that.'

'Course they do. Kim's good with a sword, but she's injured. Ren and Josie are good at shooting and blowing things up, but you're the only one who's reliably killed Boneheads.'

Tears welled up in Amber's eyes. The others were sorting themselves among the vehicles. Ren gave them an impatient wave. Amber dumped her pack on the ground and dug around in it. She pulled out Lucy's teddy. 'For when you find Alice and Lucy.'

Bec took it, rubbing its blue fur with a solemn look on her face.

Amber threw an arm around her, squishing Jaws between them. 'Look after yourself, okay?'

'Of course.' Bec's voice was as cocky as ever. She punched Amber on the shoulder. 'You'll be fine - one less person to argue with.'

She glanced across at the utes. Ren was glaring at them. Adam was standing next to Tevita's ute, with Oliver in his arms, waiting for Amber.

'Do me a favour?' Bec said.

Amber raised her eyebrows. She wasn't fool enough to agree to do anything for Bec without knowing what it was.

'While you're saving the world and all that - find some time to give your husband a good bonking, until he gets over his issues.'

'Bec!'

Bec's peal of laughter filled Amber's ears as she hurried towards Adam, her cheeks burning.